D0341694

there's a word for that

word for

that

SLOANE TANEN

Little, Brown and Company

New York   Boston   London

Little, Brown and Company
Hachette Book Group
1290 Avenue of the Americas, New York, NY 10104
littlebrown.com

First Edition: April 2019

Little, Brown and Company is a division of Hachette Book Group, Inc. The Little, Brown name and logo are trademarks of Hachette Book Group, Inc.

The reference for AWARE on page 4 is from anxietycoach.com/overcoming-panic -attacks.html.

The publisher is not responsible for websites (or their content) that are not owned by the publisher.

The Hachette Speakers Bureau provides a wide range of authors for speaking events. To find out more, go to hachettespeakersbureau.com or call (866) 376-6591.

ISBN 978-0-316-43716-5
LCCN 2018949980

10 9 8 7 6 5 4 3 2 1

LSC-C

Printed in the United States of America

For Gary, Nick, and Harry

part one

Verschlimmbessern (verb): *To make matters worse in the process of trying to improve them*

Janine

New York

Janine was lost. The smell of bleach and sweat followed her through the empty halls. She could hear a woman arguing with someone somewhere on the floor above. Or was it below? What floor was she on, anyway? She pushed her weight against a door and found herself standing in an identical corridor.

That it all seemed familiar struck her as ironic, as she'd never gone to high school, let alone college. Maybe she was confusing the building with a hospital, with its similar organizational system based on numbers and letters that seemed foreign until they became so customary it was hard to believe they had ever held any mystery. The first time she'd been sent to McLean, she'd been a teenager. But this wasn't a hospital, she reminded herself, envying the sense of ownership the real students enrolled here must feel. She wondered if they were sad when it was time to leave it all behind. She hated endings almost as much as beginnings. Almost.

She found the classroom and took a deep breath. Her stomach cramped with anxiety. She was taking a cartooning class but could barely draw. How like her to pursue a dream for which she had only half the aptitude. Like being a blind bus driver, she thought. Having a good sense of direction probably wasn't enough.

Two men, sitting on opposite sides of a long table, were already inside the classroom with their portfolios in front of them. Neither of them acknowledged her when she entered.

The younger man had on a shirt with the name *Segun* embroidered on the pocket. The other man was middle-aged with a beard and a long, graying ponytail. He was wearing an oversize Batman shirt under an unbuttoned flannel. How could a man live in Manhattan and dress like that? she wondered, trying to imagine what kind of job he had. Subway maintenance? Toll collector? Only transportation would accept such sartorial negligence. She took a seat equidistant from the two men and quietly opened her portfolio.

The silence was broken when three twenty-somethings spilled into the room, looking like they'd fallen off an Abercrombie and Fitch billboard. Janine was undone by the unexpected presence of beautiful young people. Wasn't there a separate room for them? They positioned themselves on the table and chairs, reminiscing about some party or art event they'd been to the night before.

She felt the space around her expand as her heart began pounding. She tried to recall some of the tools she'd learned in therapy and on the internet. *AWARE,* she said to herself, grasping for the acronym like a drowning child for a floatie. *A: Acknowledge that I am afraid but not in real danger. W: Wait and watch. A: Actions to make myself more comfortable. R...* she forgot what *R* stood for. *E: End.* What the fuck did any of that mean? Maybe *R* stood for *Run?* She wasn't ready for this. Watching the performance of this coterie of hipsters was quickly exhausting her reserve of sanity.

She looked over at Big Foot, as she'd taken to thinking of the bearded guy with the ponytail. Did he feel as old and irrelevant as she did? He was sketching, seemingly oblivious to the noise around him.

The conversation stilled and she felt someone looking at her. She white-knuckled her pencil. If she had a full-blown panic attack now, she'd never come back. She stared at her portfolio and breathed in and out the way she'd been taught.

"Hi," a girl said.

Janine looked up, then glanced around to confirm the girl was actually talking to her.

"I'm Kayla," she said with genuine affability.

"Janine," Janine said, envious that simply being kind was enough to make a pretty girl like Kayla seem generous. She remembered how easy it had been for her to impress people when she was young and pretty. Being famous had helped too.

"This is Corey and Anya," Kayla started but she was interrupted by the hurried arrival of a little woman with spiky red hair and matching red glasses.

"I'm Joon Louie. I'll be teaching this course. Please open your portfolios and introduce yourselves." She put down her bag and picked up a clipboard. "And tell us a little about why you're here," she said, looking at Big Foot.

"I'm Mike Hemingway," he said. "No relation. I work as a production editor at First Second and I've always been into graphic novels. I love to draw. I want to publish a graphic novel before I croak."

There was courteous laughter as Mike pulled out a few sheets from his portfolio. It was no surprise that he was into graphic novels, Janine thought. She could picture his collection of action figures tidily lined up on a bookshelf. What *was* surprising was that his drawings were mind-blowingly good. There was a collective sound of appreciation from the class. "My problem is keeping the characters looking consistent from different angles," he continued. "That's what's been holding me up."

"That's a common problem and certainly one we will address here," Ms. Louie said with a brisk smile. "Thanks very much, Mike. Next."

"I'm Janine. I'm—"

"Last name, please," Ms. Louie said, looking at her clipboard.

Janine hesitated briefly. "Kessler."

"I *knew* you looked familiar!" the boy who'd come in with Kayla said, slamming both palms on the table. "You were, like, totally famous. You were mad-hot on that show."

5

Janine felt a rush of dread and looked down at her feet. Penny loafers? Was she kidding? In what possible universe did penny loafers represent the beginning of good things? They were meant to be ironic, of course. As if a forty-one-year-old woman taking an extension class should be expressing irony through her footwear.

"God, that show totally defined my childhood," the other girl said. She was staring at Janine like she wanted to lick her. What was it about fame that made people want to touch it, even after it had expired?

"Jenny Bailey," the boy said, then he made a whooping sound and pointed at Janine. His head was shaved and covered in tattoos. "I'm sitting next to Jenny frickin' Bailey from *Family Happens*! The crap we had growing up was so not as good as the old stuff on TV Land."

His friends nodded in silent agreement as Janine considered the words *old stuff*.

"My brother was way into you," he continued. "He had a poster of you on his closet door. You look different but it's so you. He's gonna freak." He examined her from head to toe. "You're like a hundred times smaller in person than you looked on TV."

The room was lit with the glow of glamour. People aged; fame never did.

"Class," Ms. Louie called.

"Whatever happened to you?" he asked, a faint look of distaste and curiosity on his face. "Why'd you cut your hair so short?"

"Um . . ." Janine started. She reached for the back of her neck, wondering again if the haircut had been a mistake. Being less recognizable was a bonus, but she'd begun to suspect resembling the latest Pokémon character might not be.

"God, Corey," Kayla said with a pout, jabbing him in the neck with the eraser end of her pencil. "Don't ask her that."

"Class," Ms. Louie said again.

"For real," Kayla whispered, turning to Janine. "I think he's starstruck. Your hair's savage."

Again with the goodness to spare, Janine thought. It was insufferable. Janine's looks had been enough to sell lunch boxes and posters back when dissecting celebrity faces wasn't a public sport. She was painfully aware of her current shortcomings and understood that people were troubled by her not being eternally fifteen. If she acknowledged what a disappointment it was that she'd had the gall to grow up, made a joke about it, maybe it would leave her audience without anything to say behind her back.

"Can we please continue?" Ms. Louie said. She looked at Janine with impatience. "Ms. Kessler, your portfolio, please."

Everyone was staring at Janine. This was not how the class was supposed to go. Every time she tried anything new, it was the same. She was the "Remember that girl" person, the "You'll never guess who I met today" woman. She was nothing but five minutes of conversation at whatever party or dinner everybody else was attending that night.

Her hands were trembling as she considered the options in her portfolio. She tried to shield the drawings from the others. Each page displayed some uncertain pencil lines with a joke written boldly underneath. They were jokes in search of an artist, the *New Yorker's* caption contest in reverse. She heard the click of a camera and saw Corey snapping a photo of her from the phone in his lap under the table.

"Seriously?" Janine asked him. She hoped she wouldn't look like she had a double chin from that angle.

"Don't be such a dick," Kayla said, grabbing the phone out of his hands.

He shrugged as a kind of apology.

Janine tried to focus on how best to show her work. Nobody said anything as she silently flipped through her papers, looking for something presentable, struggling to keep her hands steady. She pulled out what she thought was the best picture, a clumsily drawn couple sitting on a sofa with a basset hound between them and a child in front of them. The mother was speaking to the child: *Look, honey, it's not that your father and I love the dog more than you. It's just that we love the dog more than you.*

Everyone laughed and leaned in closer. Too close. Janine tried to arch back without being offensive.

"Have you had much experience with drawing?" Ms. Louie asked with a frown.

"No." She bit the inside of her lip until she tasted blood.

"Sometimes a life-drawing class is the best place to start. You see, once we are cartooning, we are exaggerating the familiar, so we need to be able to actually capture reality before we can successfully distort or exaggerate it. Do you understand?"

"Mm," Janine said, trying not to cry. "I thought if I could develop a style then I could work around my inexperience."

Ms. Louie's laugh was patronizing. "It's not that simple, Ms. Kessler. Maybe in the movies, having a style is enough, but in the world of cartooning, you must know how to draw."

Big Foot was nodding.

"You must have some instinct for the form," Ms. Louie went on.

Janine wanted to disappear. Being a somebody made everyone else a nobody. But being a nobody who used to be a somebody? The only thing more humiliating than that, she thought, was being a nobody who used to be somebody taking an extension class in cartooning at Hunter College. She could imagine more respectability in a drug overdose.

She felt the itching start around her ankles as she considered her options. She should probably pick up her things and leave the room before the rash kicked in. But she'd promised herself she would do this. Her new therapist had driven home the importance of Janine's finally sticking with something, had clarified just how many years she had lost doing nothing. She'd become so good at protecting her privacy that she'd failed to create a life. And the problem was that once she'd grown accustomed to hiding, it was hard to live any other way. Janine looked at Ms. Louie and blocked out the other students.

"I came here to learn. It's a level-one class. If drawing skills were a prerequisite, it should have said so in the course description."

"It was implied."

"It wasn't."

"Ms. Kessler—"

"Raw talent isn't everything, right? You can't teach someone to be funny, but you can teach someone to draw," she heard herself say, echoing her father.

"That's very true, Ms. Kessler. But you must be able to express your humor in visual terms if this is what you want to do, so some natural ability is an advantage and if it's not there, well..."

"But a unique worldview is most important," Segun said, coming to her rescue. "Look at John Callahan. He wasn't a trained artist but he was very successful."

"I'm not sure Ms. Kessler shares Callahan's colorful personal history but I do appreciate the point."

Absurdly, Janine raised her hand. "I'm an aging former child actress who's about three minutes away from being a complete shut-in. I've got two decades of therapy behind me, I subsist on a steady diet of pharmaceuticals, and I have a stint at a mental facility under my belt. My history is colorful."

There was nervous laughter; nobody knew if she was joking.

Janine thought of tossing in her mother's suicide too but she'd always disliked watching that shock register. The compulsion to voice the matter pragmatically, effectively punishing people for asking too many questions, wasn't worth the trouble of having to assure them afterward that she was "fine." Anyway, it was obvious she wasn't fine. She'd never been fine after the show. Her father had been right.

"Is there anyone other than Ms. Kessler interested in text comics?"

"I am," Kayla said, smiling at Janine.

"Let's see what you've got, then," Ms. Louie said.

Janine made herself look beyond Kayla's well-sketched drawing to the joke below. It was forced and unoriginal. "You can't teach funny," she heard her dad say again. Nobody was looking at her anymore. They had moved on to Corey, who was talking about his interest in storyboarding for short films. Her secrets were out. She was an unhinged former child star and an aspiring cartoonist who couldn't draw. What could be worse?

Calling her dad to ask for the money to pay for the class—that could be worse, Janine realized the next morning. She'd been up half the night worrying about the overdue credit card bill sitting on her kitchen counter since before Christmas. She'd put the six hundred dollars for the cartooning class on the card in November, figuring she'd deal with it later. Now it was later. She'd have to ask her father to send her the money. She could see no way around it.

Even with the monthly allowance her father sent her and her royalty payments, she had to live frugally. And there were times, like now, when cat-sitting for people in her building and teaching English as a second language didn't cover expenses. She'd initially thought about using her father's Visa to pay for the class, but it seemed that Gail, his girlfriend, was now combing through his credit card statements and highlighting anything she considered excessive. Gail had called Janine just last month wanting to know what *MTA* stood for after Janine had used his Visa to buy a *twenty-dollar* subway card. Janine had been mortified. Her father had always been happy to help in the past. His mantra had been "I'm your father. Tell me what you need." But Janine wasn't able to escape the shame that came with taking his money at her age. Whenever she called to apologize for having used his card, he'd stop her and say, "That's what it's there for. If I didn't want you to use it, I wouldn't have given it to you." With Gail, all that was changing.

"Fuck it," she said to herself. She grabbed the phone and dialed her dad.

Gail picked up. She'd taken to answering Marty's phone lately, making sure he was never available when Janine called. "He's sleeping, sweetie. You're up early."

"Busy day."

"Really?" Gail asked with an astute incredulity that made Janine hot with anger. "What's on the schedule?"

"Just stuff." She knew that swimming laps, going to therapy, and buying Col-Erase pencils for the cartooning class wouldn't constitute *busy* by most people's standards. Not that Gail was in any position to judge her. "Is it that hard to imagine I have things to do?" Janine laughed, failing to sound invulnerable.

"Of course not. I was just curious about what you were up to."

Janine knew exactly what Gail was curious about. She was curious about why her boyfriend's middle-aged daughter didn't have a job or at least a husband and maybe children who could justify her unemployment. It was a reasonable question but the answer was complicated and Janine wasn't about to get into it. However, she did need the six hundred dollars, and apparently she'd have to ask Gail.

"Mmm. Do you know how to type?" Gail asked once Janine had explained the situation.

"Type?" Janine laughed. "I'm gonna be a secretary?"

"You can be a personal assistant," she suggested. "There's always a demand for that kind of work."

"I'm forty-one years old and not exactly equipped to take care of someone else's business affairs." *You go be someone's secretary, you mercenary bitch*, she thought.

Janine had initially imagined that Gail might be good for her dad. She was a longtime family friend, *almost* age-appropriate, smarter than she was attractive, and comfortably well-off following the death of her second husband, Bob Engler, a few years earlier. Only once Gail and her father had become an item did Janine realize that Gail had married Bob Engler *after* his first round of chemotherapy and had, as she told anyone who'd listen, "taken care of him for years"

11

when "nobody else" (meaning his son) was available. "It's not like Bob had dementia," she would explain when forced to confront the raised eyebrows at her having inherited so much after a relatively short marriage.

"Cartooning just seems so . . . specific," Gail continued.

"I guess."

"What about nursing or teaching?"

The conversation was like the lowest points in therapy, a humiliating analysis of Janine's limitations that made her want to evaporate. It would take her eight years to get her teaching credentials or qualify for a nursing degree. She'd be in her fifties before anyone would even let her change a colostomy bag.

At least she wasn't like so many of her friends from the studio days. Seraphina was on *Celebrity Fit Club*. Both Tom and Noel had been on *Celebrity Rehab* and *Survivor*. The rest had overdosed or gotten multiple DUIs or become porn stars; a few had done all three. She'd rather be dead than humiliate her father like that. Once she'd tried to get a job selling makeup at Bergdorf Goodman but the flamboyant queen with the bad eyelift behind the counter had flipped out when he saw her name on the application. He'd made such a scene that Janine stayed home for five days afterward.

"There's always real estate," Gail suggested.

"I don't want to be a real estate agent," Janine snapped. She started crying, hating herself for letting Gail burrow under her skin.

"Janine," Gail said. "What did I say? I'm so sorry, honey. I didn't mean to upset you."

Janine didn't think anything Gail did was accidental. The woman scheduled her dinner parties based on the post-op recovery time from her sundry plastic surgeries.

"Let me talk to your father," Gail whispered in a conspiratorial tone. As if Janine needed Gail to ask her father for permission. As if Janine couldn't speak to her dad directly. As if Gail were the new sentry.

The next day Gail left a message on Janine's machine. "It's all taken care of, honey. The money was wired over this morning with a little bit extra. Go buy yourself something nice from us."

"Us?" Janine said out loud, even though she was alone. She deleted the message and looked out the window. Fuck, Gail *was* the new sentry.

Marty

Los Angeles

"I'll just go in," Marty said, smiling graciously at the receptionist as he walked past her and down the long hall of partners' offices. Marty Kessler was the only client who just walked into Ed Rothstein's office. Not even Tom Hanks did that. Ed Rothstein was a hotshot attorney now. His law firm represented everybody, but it was Marty who'd given Ed his legs. Ed had been green in 1975 but Marty had liked him immediately. Marty's career success was based almost exclusively on instinct and intuition, so why shouldn't he take a gamble on his attorney? It had been a smart bet. Ed was a good lawyer, an honest lawyer—something Marty had always thought was an oxymoron. And back in the day, when Marty was an executive on the rise and then, quickly thereafter, one of the most powerful producers in Hollywood, everybody wanted to use Marty Kessler's people. He couldn't entirely take credit for Ed's success, but a thank-you from him every now and then would have been nice.

Now Ed was in the power seat and Marty was a useless old fossil. But he'd be damned if he'd let Ed push him around. Ed had been trying for months to get Marty to come in for a discussion about the sad state of his finances and the importance of scaling back on expenses. Marty didn't want to talk about that. He'd had so much money once.

14

How was it even possible there was so little left? Marty walked into Ed's office and reluctantly took a seat.

Despite Ed's success, his office hadn't changed much over the decades. The room was humorless and stodgy, dark and lined with books. It still had the same Persian rug, the same leather tub chairs, and the same mahogany partners' desk. It even had the same executive paralegal who'd always worked there, Lynn. *She must be over eighty,* Marty thought. He knew the most expensive object in the office was the Tiffany Nautilus desk lamp he had given Ed on his fiftieth birthday. He admired the patinaed base, trying to remember how much he'd spent on it. Seven thousand dollars? Ten thousand?

Lynn walked in with a cup of coffee for him. She put it on the desk, and he stood to give her a hug and a compliment about her new hairstyle. She blushed and scurried out of the room.

"About your portfolio," Ed began.

Marty tried to reach for the coffee. His hands were too shaky. Why the hell had he skipped his morning bump, he wondered, looking at Ed and folding his hands in his lap. He'd try again in a few minutes. "I don't want to talk about my goddamn portfolio," he said, clenching his jaw.

"Will you just hear me out?" Ed asked. "You've got to promise me something. With all due respect, and I know you and Gail are getting serious, you cannot get married again." Ed tapped Marty's unopened file. "These divorces are cleaning you out. Not to mention the aftershocks." They both knew Ed was alluding to Marty's multiple stints in rehab following his most recent divorce, from Elise, seven years ago.

By the time Marty had realized that Elise was a serious drug addict, so was he. She'd been right about the efficacy of even a little heroin for his back pain when the Percocet stopped working, but how the hell had a man of his stature and supposed intelligence ever agreed to that first roll? What the fuck had he been thinking? Elise had been a complete catastrophe, the greatest blow being that he'd given her nearly twenty million dollars of his fortune when the marriage fell apart.

Elise was long gone. The cravings were not. Heroin was a mother-fucker.

"I'm *never* getting married again," Marty told Ed, hoping his hands were now steady enough for him to pick up the coffee. "So that takes care of that conversation." He successfully seized the cup and took a sip. It needed more sugar.

"I've heard that before, Marty. Three times," Ed said, holding up three fingers. "You've told me you're never getting married again three times."

"I was single for six years between Pamela and Karen. Nineteen years between Karen and Elise. That's a hell of a decent run."

"Single?" Ed laughed as he ticked off the names of the many women who had populated the years between Marty's official pairings. "Virginia, Ginger, Heather T., Whitney, Kelly, Heather B."

"I didn't marry them," Marty said, irritated. "They were friends."

"Expensive friends."

"Cheaper than inexpensive wives."

Ed smiled, ceding Marty's point.

Marty had been officially married four times, although most people didn't know about his first wife. Ed was one of the few people left in Marty's life who knew he'd been married before Pamela, way back when Bunny Small wasn't a household name and a perennial fixture on bestseller lists worldwide. That marriage hadn't lasted a year.

"Anyway," Marty continued, "since this isn't about my getting married—"

"I'm talking about girlfriends too," Ed interrupted. Marty knew Ed was referring to Gail—his latest and, hopefully, his last—and he didn't like it.

"You can't keep paying these women like they're on salary. You're still making Heather Bruckner's car payments and giving a monthly allowance to a woman I don't think you'd even recognize if she walked in here and gave you a hug."

"Of course I'd recognize her."

"What's her name?"

"Wendy."

"Whitney," Ed said. "Her name is Whitney."

"That's what I meant, for Christ's sake."

"I'm just saying, Marty. Please, no more payouts. No more wives, no more damsel-in-distress girlfriends. You cannot afford it."

"If Gail's a damsel in distress," Marty said, nodding his head, "Oprah's shy."

Ed sat quietly, leaving Marty to chuckle at his own bad joke. He knew Ed was right. Marty's reputation as a fearless negotiator had never applied to his personal life. Four marriages and he'd yet to utter the words *prenuptial agreement*. Not wanting to . . . what? *Offend?* As if the inevitability of divorce lacked romance. Who the hell was he kidding? Maybe he figured they'd earned it for putting up with him. Whatever his reasons, he understood that his foolish generosity had been catching up with him for years, and Gail had quickly made it her business to protect what remained. From whom and for whom she was protecting it was a little vague, even to Marty.

"Anyway, this isn't about Gail," Marty snapped.

Ed deflated. "So what is it you wanted to talk about, then? You sounded like it was something important. I'd hoped—"

"The will," Marty said.

Ed leaned forward, burying his long, lean face in his hands.

"It's *my* goddamn will, Ed."

"Marty."

"Don't Marty me. Just a few small changes. Nothing drastic."

"Like?"

"The charities."

Ed looked up and narrowed his eyes. "What about them?"

"Take 'em out. If the TreePeople are depending on my largesse to survive, they're in real fucking trouble. I'm clearly not solving the homeless crisis." Marty paused for a second. "Keep the elephant, though. Thirty-five thousand to that elephant in Georgia. But that's it."

Ed tapped his fingers on his desk a few times before speaking. He sighed and cleared his throat. "So this business about cutting the charities—it's Gail's idea?"

"No, it's not Gail's idea," Marty lied, furious. "I'm trying to make sure there's something left when I go."

"Exactly," Ed cried, hoping he was finally getting through.

Marty looked down at his lap. "Gail worries about money. I don't want her to have to worry."

Ed placed his palms together as if in prayer before speaking. "It's my job to protect you and your family. We've known each other a long time. Janine wasn't even born when we met."

"What's your point?"

"You've got to scale back. You've got to get smart about this. The charities are just the tip of a very large iceberg."

Ed wasn't wrong. Marty had even seriously considered cutting Sandro out of his will, but he couldn't do it. Sandro and Maria had worked for Marty's family for forty years, and they'd lived in his guesthouse for most of that time. Maria had practically raised his girls. Marty sat back, trying to tamp down the grief swelling in his gut. Her death last year still weighed heavily on him. Who the hell would have thought he'd outlive Maria? Now he was leaving *her* intended bequest to Sandro, whose salary Marty still paid and who lived on at the guesthouse rent-free but who was too depressed to do any gardening. Gail had been on him for months about firing Sandro. "The yard looks like shit," she'd said. True, he'd admitted. Jimmy Hoffa could be buried back there and nobody'd ever know. But Sandro didn't have anywhere else to go. So Sandro was staying. For now.

Ed looked at Marty, his fingers laced together tightly, as if he were clutching a rosary. "What about your girls, Marty? Think about your daughters."

There was a short silence before Marty spoke. Maybe it was the drugs—quite possibly it was the drugs—but he was feeling a little confused about his daughters lately. Gail had managed to make him see that it was okay not to leave them *too* much. Her parents hadn't left her a thing, she'd explained. Inheriting money was a crutch. "They'll never really grow up," Gail often said, "if they've got daddy cushions strapped to their asses."

"Amanda's okay," Marty said to Ed. "The divorce was tough, but she's teaching at Fairmont now."

"Fair Hills," Ed said, correcting him. "I know."

"She's getting job offers every other week since the *LA Times* reviewed her show last year. Sarah Lawrence in New York offered her a job. Did you know that?" Marty asked with satisfaction. "But she's happy at Fairmont. She likes being back in LA. She hated living in San Diego."

Amanda had done all right for herself. She'd gotten her act together after he'd pulled the plug on her acting career all those years ago. One teenage Hollywood casualty was enough. From what he understood, she'd become something of a star in the world of prep-school theater. Whatever the fuck that meant. No doubt the Kessler name had helped, Marty thought, quickly checking his lack of generosity toward his younger daughter. Why was it he could never allow himself to feel good about Amanda? He should be proud of her.

"And the twins—Hailey and Jaycee?" Ed asked. "Your grandchildren? What about college for them?"

"Amanda can take care of them," Marty said, not feeling convinced. "How long is her family my responsibility? It was her decision to divorce Kevin."

Ed sighed again, rubbing his closed eyes with his thumb and finger. "This is not a conversation I enjoy, Marty," he said, opening his eyes. "I am appealing to your better nature here. I am trying to have a real conversation with you. The *you* who I know wants to do the right thing."

Marty said nothing.

"If you'll pardon my saying so," Ed continued, "Amanda's ex-husband makes less than forty thousand dollars a year, which means it will be Amanda's financial responsibility to send *your* grandchildren to college. She doesn't make that much money and they're already sixteen. They'll be going in two years."

"It's not as if I haven't helped her along the way. I think we can agree I've been more than generous. I didn't tell her to marry a Jungian therapist."

"Your daughters still depend on you financially." Ed tilted his head, an invitation for Marty to disagree with him. "You can all continue to pretend that's not the reality but the fact is, you need to set up a trust. It won't cover college, but it's something. Obviously this should have been done years ago, as I've said many times, but it's not too late."

Marty took a deep breath, working hard not to explode with anger.

Ed briefly held his ace. Very briefly. "And what about Janine?" he asked.

Marty felt his stomach tighten. *What about Janine?* She still had his heart. Forty-one years old and living in that same one-bedroom Manhattan apartment with that same goddamn cat. She'd never married, never had a career after *Family Happens.* That her inertia might somehow be his fault felt like a shot to the head.

"I cover her living expenses," Marty said. "And she's got the residuals from the show."

Ed made a little wheezing sound. "The residuals from the show add up to about two thousand dollars a month. And that's good. If we hadn't worked out that sweetheart contract with NBC, she'd have gotten residuals only on the first rerun. But she can't live on that after you're gone. Twenty-four thousand a year, before taxes, in Manhattan?"

"Sweetheart contract, my ass."

Ed didn't say anything. He'd played his hand.

That stupid fucking show, Marty thought. Pamela's train wreck of an idea. It was still in syndication three times a day all over the country. He couldn't turn on the TV without seeing Janine at twelve or fourteen immersed in some hijinks with her television family. He should have at least insisted on a better deal for his daughter. He'd been in the position to get her whatever he wanted back then. Standard network protocol didn't apply to him. But he'd been too furious with Pamela for deceiving him, for encouraging the girls' acting careers when he'd wanted them to have normal childhoods. He'd convinced himself that taking a penny more of NBC's money would make him further complicit in what he thought of as prostituting his daughter.

That and he hadn't thought it would ever matter. He'd been very rich and he never thought that would change.

"You think I enabled them?" Marty asked Ed, circling back to the earlier topic, hoping Ed might absolve him of blame for the way things had turned out.

Absently, Ed took a silver letter opener out of the penholder on his desk and stroked its edges. "I think you did the best you could under the circumstances. You were a good father, Marty."

"Yes, Ed. I was a good father. I worked my ass off for my family. I never got a handout from anybody along the way. I started at the bottom. Not one fucking favor from anybody."

"I know that. Nobody is questioning the—"

"When do I get to enjoy myself? When do I get to relax?" Marty heard himself echoing Gail's sentiments.

"You were in Mexico with Gail over Christmas." Ed raised his eyebrows. "A thirty-thousand-dollar week."

"Should we have stayed at a Motel Six?" Marty said, his voice rising. "Is that the kind of thing you're advising me to do?"

"I'm just asking that you scale it back. The dinners, the gifts, the vacations. You're too generous," Ed said. "I'm sure Gail would sympathize with your situation. Who wouldn't understand a man's desire to leave something for his own children? His grandchildren?"

Both Marty and Ed knew that Gail would understand no such thing. There was a long silence. Marty's hand wandered to the base of the Nautilus lamp and ran over the cool bronze metal. Ed followed Marty's hand with his eyes before reaching across the desk and covering it with his own.

"So?" Ed asked. "What do you want to do?"

Something about the kindness of Ed's gesture, the spontaneity of the question, threw Marty. Ed was indeed appealing to Marty's better nature. But Marty didn't feel like being better! He felt like doing what he wanted. And doing what he wanted now meant spending the remainder of his money the way he chose to spend it. He resented Ed's intimacy, his simplification of things, as if following some moral compass led to happiness.

"Marty?" Ed said.

"Would you lay off?" Marty shouted, surprising both of them. Just then the moisture on his upper lip dissolved into a familiar metallic taste inside his mouth. He had a bloody nose again. "Fuck!" he said, wiping his lip with the back of his hand and seeing the evidence.

Ed pushed a box of tissues at him and looked away, embarrassed. "I can't do this anymore," Ed said. "We've known each other a long time. I love you. But I can't do this."

"That'll do me fine, Ed, because you're fired."

Ed looked at Marty and blinked slowly.

Marty shoved a wadded tissue up his nostril, stood, and walked out of Ed's office with as much poise as he could muster.

He stopped in Lynn's small office on the way out and leaned down to plant a dry kiss on her withered cheek. "Good luck to you."

"What happened, Mr. Kessler?" she asked, staring up at him with her bottom lip trembling. She looked back toward Ed's office, as though beseeching him to come after Marty. After all, they'd argued before, though never at such a decibel level.

"Lynn," Marty said. "You're a great dame."

She stood up. Two tears rolled down her cheeks and settled into the parched crevices of her lined face. Ed wasn't coming.

"Please have my portfolio sent to Jim Keating at Sullivan, Gifford, Doutré, and Keating," Marty said in a voice loud enough for Ed to hear.

A tiny gasp escaped before Lynn closed her mouth and nodded.

*   *   *

Every new lover meant the severing of old ties. Still, losing Ed Roth-stein was a big one. He trusted Ed. He loved Ed. Jim Keating was an asshole. You had to be half cracked, Marty thought, to entrust your fi-nances to an Irishman. But Gail would be delighted. Jim Keating was her lawyer, and the money manager at SGDK had done well for her. She'd been on Marty for months to switch.

He fished a handful of pills out of his pocket and dry-swallowed two of them on the escalator. He wasn't sure which was which, but he didn't see much difference between a Xanax, a Valium, and a Klonopin. They all helped take the edge off when what he really needed was a hit. Gail pulled up in his Mercedes the moment he walked outside. Did she have a goddamn tracking system on him? He got in and slammed the door.

"Why do you have a tissue hanging out of your nose?" she asked him.

"Bloody nose. I forgot," he said, gently pulling the Kleenex out and revisiting the past few moments with a bit less satisfaction. "It's noth-ing."

Gail gave him the look that said, *I'm concerned about your health, your drug problem, and your financial portfolio,* all in a single glance. "Well?" she asked, trying to raise a Botoxed eyebrow. "How'd it go?"

"Let's see what Jim can do for me."

"No! Really?"

Marty could see she was genuinely surprised. Nobody expected Marty to leave Ed. Leaving Ed meant Gail had made more progress in six months than all the other women put together had made in forty years.

He tapped the dashboard. "Let's go eat," he said. "I feel like pan-cakes."

"Pancakes it is." She wasn't going to argue for the virtues of a healthy lunch. Not today. "There's a new place on Santa Monica Boulevard that has a marvelous short stack with real maple syrup. Not the fake stuff."

Marty nodded, welcoming the feathery high that washed over him like a warm bath. The world softened. Gail was a Rolodex of important yet superfluous information. If he squinted, and the sun was at just the right angle, she looked almost beautiful to him.

"And," she said, obviously cheered by the events of the day, "I called our guy at the Barnes and Noble on Third and that new Alex Grecian novel you wanted is in. He's holding it for us so we can stop by and pick it up after lunch."

"Good," Marty said, surprised that he felt comforted rather than irritated by Gail's fastidious attentiveness. He closed his eyes and sighed, letting himself relax into the sunbaked warmth of the passenger seat. He could hear Gail chattering, but he wasn't listening. He was allowing himself the length of the ten-minute drive to mourn the loss of his dear old friend.

Bunny

London

"Pathetic," Bunny said. She was resting her forehead on the cold window of the black town car. "I'll be in adult nappies and Ian will be wheeling me around to publicity events with an oxygen tank."

Ian, sitting next to her in the backseat, cleared his throat.

"The reading is bad enough, but the Q and A," she said with a snort. "My God, how many bloody books do I have to write before I can stop smiling at their idiotic, juvenile questions? 'No, I don't have a writing ritual.' 'No, I don't have a favorite writer.' 'And no, I do not have any advice for you on how to become one.'"

"That's lovely, Bun," Ian said.

"'Do you sit in a special chair?'" Bunny continued, perfectly mimicking the speech pattern of a thirteen-year-old girl. "A special chair?" She laughed to herself. "Do they think the place I plant my bottom trips some auto-write button? Where do people get their ideas?"

Ian didn't say anything. He assumed, correctly, that the question was rhetorical.

"I'll have Ian's chub and balls in a nutcracker if anybody hugs me tonight," she muttered at the window.

"I am sitting right here," Ian said, shifting in the leather seat.

"I'm too old to pretend I'm still grateful," she went on, ignoring Ian and watching the London streets whizzing by. She ran a hand through her hair and adjusted the trousers that had cost her fifteen hundred pounds. "My God, I'm a fat old yak."

"Don't be absurd," Ian said. She knew she wasn't fat. She just liked to say so.

Bunny reached into the pocket of her wide-legged slacks and pulled out the slim antique silver hip flask her ex-husband Sam had given her years ago. "Before he realized quite how much I'd appreciate it," Bunny said with a snort.

"Bun?" Ian said. He took her free hand from her lap and loosened the fingers of her little fist. "You're talking to yourself again."

"Primrose Hill, Foyles, Pan, Dulwich," Bunny went on, spitting out the names of the most fashionable bookstores in London. "It's such a bore with the obsequious store owners and the shopgirls treating me like I'm made of glass. I'm not *that* old."

"It's really about the readers," Ian said. "Your fans."

"My *fans.*" Bunny laughed, choked on some gin, and used the back of her hand to wipe away the spittle. She finally looked at Ian, almost surprised to find him sitting there. "Why are my fans so unattractive, Ian?"

"What's that?"

"Why are those girls so dirty?" she asked. "Is filth a new fad? Even the boys resemble a grisly discovery one finds at the bottom of a bag of crisps. They're all so wet-looking. Greasy."

"Really, Bunny?" Ian folded his arms across his chest.

"Come, you must admit it. And they all want a hug, as if they think something other than Scotchgard might rub off on them." Bunny paused, waited for Ian to respond. "Ian," Bunny snapped. "Are you listening to me?"

"Am I listening to you complain about being adored, rich, and famous?" he asked. "Yes, I'm listening. And yes, everyone is filthy. Very, very filthy."

Bunny turned back to the window. "Someone's in a piss mood today." She took a deep drink.

"I'm not the one raging," he said. "Or going on a pub crawl right here in the car."

"Oh!" Bunny said, laughing. "Agent Ian is worried about my drinking again. Poor Ian. It's hard to wrangle the beasts. Prop up the pissed authors and make them appear human for an hour or so." Bunny loved Ian precisely because he wasn't afraid of her. Still, she thought he could be a touch more deferential sometimes.

"Bunny, darling, if you're not talking to yourself, then please stop referring to me in the third person. It upsets me. If you *are* talking to yourself, then please stop drinking because, yes, I am a little worried."

"About the reading?"

"About you."

"Piss off," she said and handed Ian the flask containing her latest passion: Nolet's Reserve Dry Gin.

Ian sniffed the bottle. He shuddered. "You know I don't like gin unless it's mingling with schnapps in an apple martini."

"This isn't Beefeater," she said. "It's very supple."

Bunny had recently switched over from Cabernet Sauvignon to the flagship Nolet's. The spirit was an indulgence at six hundred pounds a bottle but it made her very cheerful and left her clearheaded the next morning. Even Ian could see the flask's peculiar sex appeal. Still, *cheerful* wasn't the adjective he would have chosen to describe its effect on Bunny's moods, and while *she* might have felt clearheaded the next morning, anyone on the receiving end of her hostility felt decidedly hungover.

"Crap, it tastes like petrol." He winced.

"You get used to it," she said as the car pulled up in front of Primrose Hill. Hundreds of people were standing in line outside, and the bookshop itself was packed.

"Brilliant," Ian said, smiling. "They do love you. Now be nice." He took another small sip from the flask, gasped, and handed it back. "It must please you a little that after all these years, they still can't get enough of you."

"I'm chuffed to bits," Bunny said. She took another pull and slid the bottle back into her pocket. "Off we go, then."

"And please don't have a pop at anyone, right?" he called after her.

"Right," she said, pushing the door open and smiling at Mr. Toadenfroad or whatever the hell his name was.

Janine

In the 1980s, famous kids didn't go to summer camp. Janine had no idea what they did from June through August, but they didn't roast s'mores in the country with ordinary children. Most of the stage kids had parents who were dedicated to entertaining their breadwinners in the off-season. Janine had no such luck. Her father was at the height of his career. Her mother, empowered by alimony and her newfound sexual freedom, was busy distracting herself from the sour stench of time passing.

The first season of Janine's sitcom, *Family Happens*, had gotten so-so ratings, and the network was still debating whether to bring the show back. Janine's agent had tried to land her a small television role that summer, something for her to do until the fate of the show was decided, but all anyone could see was li'l Jenny Bailey. One unexceptional season and she was already an icon of teen spirit and banana clips. Not a director in town could get beyond it. Nobody ever would, but Janine didn't know that at the time.

Faced with the prospect of a summer involving actual parenting, Janine's mother, Pamela, decided that it was time Janine re-immersed herself in the world of regular kids. After years of making sure Janine was perceived as special, Pamela suddenly announced that her daughter needed a crash course in being ordinary. "You can't expect me to babysit a twelve-year-old girl loafing around all summer," Janine had heard her mom yell at her father over the phone. And so they agreed that Janine would go to Camp Shasta for four weeks, and she'd get there by taking the seven-hour bus ride to Mendocino with the other campers.

Janine was anxious about it, but going seemed like a better option than spending the summer listening to her little sister, Amanda, brag about landing "a *movie* role" as a psych-hospital patient in *A Nightmare on Elm Street 5* or, worse, staring at her mother's friends getting high and skinny-dipping at the Laurel Canyon house the three of them had moved into after the divorce three years earlier.

Janine said yes but only on the condition that she could go to camp incognito. This part was exciting and she was surprised that her parents had agreed to the idea.

"Are you going to wear a wig and dark glasses?" Amanda had asked as she stared at herself in the bathroom mirror and practiced panicky scream faces.

"No, you stupid idiot," Janine said, though the truth was she hadn't worked out the details yet.

The Saturday before Janine left, her father took her to Big 5 Sporting Goods and the Army Surplus in Santa Monica with the camp's list of recommended items. Marty would be damned if his daughter showed up without all seventy-six of them, including a neon poncho, a squat strap, and a couple of cans of Off with DEET.

"You think I should get a gas mask?" she asked, looking into the crowded shopping cart and hoping to make her dad laugh. "In case there's an air raid while we're kayaking?"

He wasn't laughing. "That hair," Marty said, shaking his head, agitated all over again that his ex-wife had allowed his daughter to dye her hair blond and get a perm. "You both went too far with this. You look like Sammy Hagar. And not in a good way."

"Dad."

"This whole charade is goddamn ridiculous. Your mother—"

"The hair was my idea. Please don't be mad at Mom. Please."

Janine knew that the charade he'd referred to was less about her hair and more about her career. Never mind that her dad was one of Hollywood's A-list producers. He'd always been adamant about keeping his own family a healthy distance from what he thought of as a fundamentally corrupt and immoral industry. The thought that his ex-wife could be so entirely indifferent to his feelings, to the point of sending his children on auditions behind his back, assuredly using *his* name to do it, never failed to enrage him.

He ground his teeth as he and Janine walked the musty aisles of sleeping bags and blankets. He was deep into some angry internal monologue involving his ex-wife and her scheming and childishness.

"Fuck that bottom-feeder Lou Webster!" he muttered, referring to the third-rate casting director Pam had been dating since they'd divorced. Lou had put Amanda in a commercial for a portable sandbox shaped like a turtle. Marty hadn't known a thing about it. The details of how Lou had encouraged Pam to start taking pretty Amanda on auditions had emerged slowly over time. And while Amanda did land a few parts, it was Janine (dragged along because her mom didn't know what else to do with her) who attracted attention with some off-color joke or waiting-room improv. Soon Janine, not Amanda, was cast in the Chuck E. Cheese commercial eating fake pizza at a fake birthday party. And it was Janine, not Amanda, who started getting callbacks for real shows.

Janine had hated the secrecy, suspecting all along that her father would be furious, but who could blame her for wanting to please her impossible mother while simultaneously outshining the stunningly pretty sister Pam so clearly preferred? Janine never knew if it was the reflected glamour that her mother liked or the act of deceiving her ex-husband, but by the time she was cast in *Family Happens,* she didn't care.

"I need a flashlight," Janine said, looking at her father. He didn't answer. She figured he was still busy chewing on the fact that his daughter felt she needed to wear a disguise to go to summer camp. "I need a flashlight, and stop worrying. I'm fine."

She knew he secretly hoped the show would get canceled, that he believed her immediate disappointment would fade and then she wouldn't have to spend her life feeling like a freak because she'd peaked young. "These things don't ever end well," he'd shouted (along with a lot of other things) when he finally found out about her being cast in the show.

He drove Janine home in his Jeep Cherokee, its trunk loaded with camp supplies. Usually their car rides were jokey and animated, but their moods were nicked by the awareness that they wouldn't see each other for a whole month. "I'm sorry I can't take you to the bus Monday." His chin was trembling the way it always did when he was trying not to get emotional. "I'm proud of you," he said, knocking on the dashboard. "It takes cojones to leave home for the first time. And the hair's not that bad, really."

Janine tried not to think about how much she'd miss him. She didn't say anything until she was sure the lump in her throat wouldn't give her away.

The next day, Maria, her dad's housekeeper, came by to help Janine pack everything into her camp trunk. Janine carefully wrote her "name" on the luggage tag: *Amy Tanner.* Screw anyone who insisted she was anyone else. Yes, she'd say when asked, she *did* bear an uncanny resemblance to that actress Janine Kessler. She heard it all the time. Chip McNamara, the camp director, had agreed to the terms. He'd also offered her the position of junior counselor in the drama department but she'd said no. She just wanted to be Amy. Amy Tanner, age twelve. A nobody.

Her mom took Janine to Nate 'n Al's in Beverly Hills, where they ordered an enormous to-go lunch for the long bus ride: macaroni salad, coleslaw, sandwiches, chips, pickles, three-bean salad, turkey, a cola, and cookies. Pamela was so enchanted with herself in the fleeting role of Good Mother that she didn't even flirt back with the cashier. It didn't take much for Pamela to impress Janine. Janine was so hungry for her mother's love that Pam buying her daughter a macaroni salad qualified as a satisfying substitute.

Pamela packed the lunch in a brown grocery bag and wrote *Amy Tanner!* on it. "You'll get a gorgeous tan, Amy," she said with a wink as she made room for the bag of food amid the bottles of Blue Nun, peach nectar, and canned tomato sauce in the fridge.

Two hours into the bus ride, Janine realized she'd left her lunch behind. She knew her mother would be furious. She tried not to think about Pamela as she watched Stacey Leary, her seatmate (and maybe new friend), unwrap a peanut butter sandwich from crumpled tinfoil.

"Are you sure you're not the girl from that TV show?" Stacey asked again. "You even sound like her."

Janine rolled her eyes. "Oh my God, Stacey! Stop." She tried to laugh it off the way she'd practiced, but she was feeling worn with hunger and anxiety.

"Is something the matter?" Stacey asked. She put her sandwich on her lap. Janine could feel herself begin to unravel.

"I forgot my lunch," Janine said, choking on a sob. "I mean, it's fine. I just, you know, my mom packed all this good stuff."

"Oh no," Stacey said. She rifled through her backpack and pulled out a Tiger's Milk bar and a bag of Funyuns. "Does anybody have any extra food?" she shouted to the entire bus. "Amy forgot her lunch!" Stacey had been attending Camp Shasta since she was seven. She was the tetherball champ. She knew everyone.

"Thanks," Janine said as she accepted the apples and unwanted sandwiches passed to her from all sides. She couldn't believe the kindness being rained on her in the form of snack foods from strangers.

"You look real familiar," a handsome older boy said as he handed a small bag of coveted Cheetos to her over the seat between them. Janine didn't think he'd be as easily distracted from this topic as Stacey had been. According to the HELLO, MY NAME IS sticker on his T-shirt, his name was Brandon, and he looked like her friend Todd Bridges from *Diff'rent Strokes*. Todd was older, but the resemblance was uncanny. Brandon had on a Van Halen baseball cap turned sideways.

"*I* look familiar? Whatchu talkin' 'bout, Willis?" Janine said, which made him blush and chuckle to himself before turning back in his seat. Janine dissolved with relief that she'd defused yet another *You look like Jenny Bailey* moment.

"I can't believe you said that!" Stacey pinched Janine on the arm and whispered in her ear, "He's so cute! Doesn't he look *exactly* like Todd Bridges?"

A few girls were helping to collect the handouts now. People had always liked Janine, but she'd assumed it was because of her powerful father or, more recently, because she was on TV. That she was already making friends as Amy Tanner was so thrilling, she could barely sit still. She couldn't remember ever having felt so free. And they were only hours into what she was now sure was going to be the best summer of her life.

And then, like a sailboat listing to the port side, the whole vehicle seemed to slope as a group of children ran over to stare at a spectacle out the windows. There, traveling parallel to them, was a vintage white Mercedes convertible with what could only be a famous actress honking the horn and waving at their driver, clearly determined to make him pull over. Her platinum hair whipped around her perfect heart-shaped face. Janine fixed her eyes on the seat in front of her and slumped down on the sticky vinyl.

"Oh God, please, no," she whispered.

"Do you know her?" Stacey asked.

"Kind of," Janine answered as the bus driver happily pulled onto the shoulder to see what benevolence was about to be bestowed upon him. Janine swallowed and held her breath. The doors creaking open, followed by the sound of Pamela walking up the steps, cued Janine for the impending horror.

Within seconds, her mother was scanning the sea of astonished faces, sunglasses dangling from her mouth, cradling the enormous lunch bag like a baby. She was wearing flip-flops, a camisole with no bra, and silky shorts that Janine knew were her sleeping pants. Pamela spotted Janine and began waving at her like they were in a noisy, crowded airport rather than on a silent bus.

"Janine!" she sang out, walking toward her, wafting the scent of Marlboro Reds as she passed the rows of slack-jawed faces. A gasp from the chorus of children as Janine tried to melt into the seat. "Your lunch!" Pamela smiled, breathless. "You forgot your lunch!" She obviously expected Janine to be thrilled to see her, to tell her that she'd saved the day, that she was a hero. Janine just stared as Pamela thrust the enormous bag onto her daughter's lap and stood before her, effectively naked. From the backseat came a snicker and then, to Janine's horror, a wolf whistle.

"Thanks," Janine said, torn between hot shame and disbelief that her mother had chased the bus for two hours to deliver her lunch. A silence ensued as the two looked at each other, both clearly disappointed.

"That's your mom?" Stacey whispered.

"Janine!" Pamela snapped. "I mean, um, Amy," she said, glancing at her daughter's name tag. "Oh, shit. Sorry."

Janine didn't say anything. There was nothing to say.

"Fuck it," Pamela said, and she turned abruptly and walked off.

Janine understood that her mother had been trying to be kind. She could envision Pamela opening the fridge door, seeing the lunch bag, swearing to herself, then grabbing her car keys and hopping into the car without thinking about getting dressed or considering her daughter's wish to be normal for a few weeks. Come hell or high water, Janine would have her special lunch because Pamela was feeling both generous and guilty. Janine understood all of this instinctively as she curled her body into a tight knot against the silence.

She'd stayed at Camp Shasta for three days. Once the other

campers knew that she was Janine Kessler and not Amy Tanner and that she clearly had not wanted to be recognized (to the extent that she'd lied about her identity and dyed her hair), half of them treated her like a freak and the other half were awkward and deferential. She went to see Chip and the matter was settled.

Her mother, feeling neither generous nor guilty after the heated phone call from Marty, picked Janine up in Mendocino and they drove home in a long, smoke-filled silence.

Family Happens was renewed six weeks later in large part due to the popularity of Janine's character. Her role would be expanded and the show would go on to be nominated for over sixteen awards, including two Emmys; Janine was nominated for three Youth in Film Awards. Her face would appear on magazines, lunch boxes, even a pink Swatch and a color-blending eye-shadow kit.

For many years, Janine thought about Amy Tanner and the life she might have had. She wondered what it would have been like to play tetherball with Stacey, make out with Brandon at the Sadie Hawkins dance, then return home after four weeks, filthy but happy, greeted by her smiling parents waiting eagerly at the bus station. She didn't feel regret, exactly, but a piercing curiosity about how different everything could have been.

Marty

Marty was what they called a "chipper." He never injected. Christ, no. He snorted only on Wednesdays and Saturdays and was strict about his schedule. No point getting addicted to heroin again. Not after all the money he'd spent in rehab. He carefully supplemented his habit with what he thought of as less addictive drugs—Ativan, Valium, Klonopin, and still the occasional Percocet. He considered his regimen a lifestyle choice. It worked well for him until something—or someone—ratcheted up his stress levels.

Since Amanda's big announcement about her job offer at Sarah Lawrence, he'd been chipping a little more. Last Thursday he'd taken a much-needed quarter bump. He'd gone off schedule again on Sunday, finding himself requiring the same therapeutic amount. Just a little, but still. Sure, he could yell at Amanda, but what could he say that didn't sound irrational? That he didn't want her to leave? That it would be thoughtless of her to accept a better job in New York after finally leaving her useless husband and moving back to LA? What was the point of having kids if they moved to fucking New York the minute you got old?

Gail, of course, thought it was a fabulous opportunity for Amanda and her family. The salary would be better, and the offer included campus housing and a free ride for Hailey and Jaycee at a top-notch prep school on the East Coast. All that, and apparently Sarah Lawrence was a good school now. The drama department was a big deal.

"Jill Clayburgh and Joanne Woodward went there," Gail had told him over dinner.

"Anybody since World War Two?" he'd asked.

She folded her hands on the table and narrowed her eyes. "Julianna Margulies, Emma Roberts, Lauren Holly."

Marty grunted.

"Larisa Oleynik, Gabrielle Carteris, Melora Hardin."

"Are you speaking English?"

"How 'bout Rahm Emanuel, Marty?" she asked. "Heard of him?"

"I doubt he spent a lot of time in the drama department," Marty said, mildly disturbed that a mayor of Chicago had gone to Sarah Lawrence. Marty suspected that Gail's convictions had less to do with his daughter's welfare and more to do with having him all to herself. She especially liked having his credit cards and car all to herself.

Certainly, changing financial advisers hadn't altered Marty's financial situation. The meeting with Jim Keating hadn't gone well. Keating, that glib Irish shit, had smiled condescendingly while informing Marty he'd be "broke as a joke" in six years. Six years! He'd gone so far as to insinuate that Marty's portfolio wasn't really SGDK material but that they'd take him on as a favor to Gail. A favor?

Marty kicked Keating's desk, accidentally knocking over a shitty orchid, making it clear that he wasn't looking for favors and that Jim wasn't to breathe a word of his financial standing to Gail. He'd sooner celebrate the Fourth of July in Afghanistan than have Gail, or anyone, know he'd blown through the bulk of his savings. He'd be eighty-one years old in six years. Old, broke, and single. How the fuck had that happened? He wasn't sure he even liked Gail but he didn't want to be alone. Now he'd have to make a show of being rich, for Christ's sake, just to prove a point.

He realized, as he stood to leave Keating's office, that he'd hurt his foot kicking the goddamn desk. He could barely walk. Jim winked and pressed a button. A man in a suit arrived at the office door pushing an empty wheelchair. Marty looked at Jim. "Do all your clients leave in that thing?"

Keating nodded but didn't laugh. Marty sat down in the chair and dry-swallowed three Percocets. Gail was idling in the parking lot when he was wheeled out. He limped over to the car and slid into the passenger seat without a word. Another humiliation.

Maybe a trip back to rehab was inevitable; it sure seemed like it a few days later. Marty had decided to take the car out on his own for some fresh air, and as he was backing out of his driveway, easing off the morning's bump with a kratom-and-Valium cocktail, he heard a loud crunching sound followed by the sickening sensation of something solid giving way under the car. Christ! It never ended. He sat fuming in the driver's seat, in no rush to get out and assess the damage. He let his head drop back on the headrest.

He was old and nobody gave a shit anymore. That's what it boiled down to. Nobody gave a shit how decent a man he'd once been, how dedicated a father he was, or how many Academy Awards he had in the garage. He'd be remembered only for the ways he'd fucked things up, the ways he'd let his family down. He got out of the car and slammed the door hard, then looked underneath it and moaned.

Gail pulled up to the house as he was in the process of trying to hide the remains of the neighbor's Fisher-Price Little Tikes basketball set that he'd backed over. She stood in the driveway with her hands on her hips and her mouth in an angry line, looking at him like he was a dog who'd taken a shit in the house. It wasn't as though he wasn't going to replace the goddamn thing. He just didn't want anyone to see what he'd done. He watched as Gail made a rapid-fire calculation. Clearly, he didn't just *prefer* that she drive when they went out, as he frequently said; he was actually often incapable of driving. It was also then, Marty knew, that she realized the extent of his habit.

"You've got to go back to rehab," she said. "I just can't take this insanity from you anymore."

"What insanity?" He sat down on the mangled plastic backboard of the basketball toy, feeling dizzy. He tried a sheepish grin. She narrowed her eyes.

"Good-bye, Marty," she said and turned to get into her car.

He couldn't have any more leaving. After Pamela, Janine, Ed, and, possibly, Amanda, he couldn't stomach it. "Fine," he called out to her. "I'll go back."

It didn't matter to him. He didn't plan on living another six years anyhow. What better way to prove his financial health than by flushing his money down the toilet at rehab? Let Gail think she was the reason he'd agreed to join yet another circus of Jesus-loving fuckups. It was a good idea to clean up a little. Not that he planned on abandoning the cloudy, blissful world of Valium and opiates. No fucking way. He'd taper, but he had no intention of stopping. His situation was preposterous, but so were a great many things.

That's how Marty suddenly found himself exiled from the comforts of his home and sent back for a sequel at Directions Rehabilitation Center in Malibu. Never mind that it hadn't worked before. Gail was certain it would work this time because (a) she was there for him emotionally; (b) she'd happily visit often (Marty was sure she would, since it was a fashionable facility and conveniently located close to her house); and (c) the staff kept patients as long as they felt necessary. This also meant that Gail could enjoy both his credit cards and his absence for what might be months.

After Gail and Amanda (his younger daughter had insisted on joining them on the trip to rehab) were sent off with their family-orientation packets, two nurses, a man and a woman, carefully sifted through Marty's suitcases. They took away his phone, his razor, his cologne, and the small stash of heroin he'd cleverly (or so he'd thought) taped between two book pages. They briskly confiscated the baggie. Then they took all his books, which he'd packed in a separate carry-on, and began loading the mountain of historical fiction into gray bins like contraband.

"What's wrong with those?" he yelled. "They're just books, I swear. Go ahead and look."

"Approved fiction and self-help only," the male nurse said as he sealed the bin and wrote something on the lid's label in black ink. Marty had planned on doing a lot of reading here. In fact, his entire recovery plan had been to stay alone in his room and read.

"And what the hell am I supposed to do all day?" Marty asked the female nurse. "Color in mandalas? I don't read self-help."

"That's okay, Mr. Kessler. We have plenty of other reading material." Her name tag said VANESSA. Generally, Marty liked women better than men. He wasn't so sure about Vanessa, though.

"Well, I can't wait to begin my new education in horseshit," he said, which failed to rattle her irritating calm. "I read my own books the last time."

"The rules change for returning guests."

"Along with the prices. Is that some kind of psychological deterrent? Charge more, give less? If I hear the name Deepak Chopra one fucking time," he said, raising his finger, "one time, I'm gone."

"I'm sure we can find something to your liking in our library." Vanessa smiled. "If not, I can speak to your therapist about making an exception for you. Okay?"

My God, Marty thought, feeling appropriately small and ridiculous in the wake of her kindness. *Why am I threatening this poor woman who is just trying to do her job?* It was one thing to treat the people close to you like shit, but Marty had always been respectful to the workers. That's where he'd come from. He thought of Maria with a stab of grief. What a goddamn mess.

"I'm sorry, Vanessa," he said. "I'm very tired. Please, call me Marty."

"No need to apologize, Marty." She took out his toiletry bag and began examining each item carefully. She paused at the discovery of a dirty, two-inch-long soft vinyl baby doll with matted hair, dressed in a worn yellow romper.

"A gift from my kids," he explained, embarrassed by the mawkishness. "A long time ago."

Baby Sweets was a vestige of the Sunshine Family, a coveted group of dolls he'd given to the girls one holiday. Marty had liked that twisted-looking baby and always chose him when the girls asked him to get down on the floor and play. Janine and Amanda had wrapped up Baby Sweets and regifted him the following year, renaming him Little Marty in his honor. Marty had kept that crazy baby next to his sink ever since, a sort of rabbit's foot, standing at attention alongside his razor and colognes. He never left town without Little Marty inside his toiletry bag. He'd dragged him halfway around the world and back, from New York to Paris, Singapore to Spain.

Vanessa nodded, reassured that Little Marty wasn't a drug mule, and put him back in the toiletry kit. Then she pulled the pillbox out of his messenger bag and emptied the contents into a large Ziploc.

"Wait. Those are prescription. I can't sleep without those."

"No benzos or opiates, Marty," she said. She sealed the bag and handed it off.

"Seroquel?" he asked, embarrassed at his fluency in drugs. "That's not an opiate."

Vanessa shook her head. Marty shifted his weight from one foot to the other. He hadn't fallen asleep without a pill in over twenty years. He had a small stash hidden in the lining of his Lakers cap (and another one in the waistband of his sweatpants) but it was going to get dicey.

"You'll be okay," Vanessa said. "I have a good feeling about you." She smiled, looking at him with the sort of compassion he could tolerate only from a complete stranger. He nodded, blinked hard, and stuffed his hands into the pockets of his khakis to hide the trembling.

Bunny

Bunny sat at her burled walnut desk, fingering the advance copy of her new book. She looked out on the cold, rainy morning. At least, she thought it was morning. Who could ever tell in London? Her head hurt. She'd had too much to drink last night. How else to get through dinner with an ex-husband and his earnest second wife? She was still friendly with Sam—he was Henry's father, after all— but why must he always bring that pedantic bore of a wife along? After dinner, Sam had called Bunny a mean drunk. A drunk. The word scraped at the bottom of her stomach. It was shocking, really. She scanned her memory for anything awful she might have said but nothing stood out. It couldn't have been *that* bad.

So what if she liked a drink? It wasn't as if it affected her work, and she knew she could stop if there was a compelling reason to. And she did fine at social events. Hadn't she made it through that dreadful literary benefit with all those writers a few years back? Something to do with Eckhart Tolle's *The Power of Now Get Me a Bloody Drink*—or so she'd jokingly called the book as she chatted with her then friend Martin Amis.

She couldn't remember why they didn't speak anymore.

Bunny's office was connected to her bedroom by a long hallway that had the advantage of allowing her to travel from her bed to her desk without ever having to get dressed. It also meant she didn't have to see anyone until hunger or restlessness drove her out of her cozy den and into the stark main rooms. She'd been spending an increasing amount of time in her pajamas the past few weeks, wearing an imperceptible path in the runner that led from the bedroom to the bathroom to her office. For the first time in her career, she couldn't write. Or she didn't want to write. The whole thing was ludicrous, of course. Bunny didn't believe in writer's block any more than she believed that obesity and fibromyalgia were real diseases. These were just euphemisms for the gluttonous and the lazy, respectively.

Bettina, her maid, came and went, as evidenced by the fact that the bed was always made when Bunny returned to it, the mail was neatly arranged on her desk each day, and the dirty cups and ashtrays were miraculously cleared away when Bunny wasn't looking.

Where *was* Bettina? Bunny wondered, pressing the intercom. Probably she was in the laundry room, the one place Bunny hadn't thought to install a speaker. Bunny wanted a plate of cold pasta Bolognese and a Diet Coke. The thought of traipsing across those chilly limestone floors to the kitchen made her shudder. Her decorator was a fascist. Bunny had said *modern*, not *barren*. There was an echo in the living room and a stone pillar in the kitchen. Who wouldn't be driven to drink living inside a de Chirico painting?

Bunny decided against hunger, lit a cigarette, and turned her attention to the pages on her desk.

"'*Henry Holter and the Heathcoff Family,* by Bunny Small,'" she read aloud. *Henry Holter and the Winwick Family* was considered her best to date, but this new one, *Heathcoff,* was damn good. She had named the character after her own son, who'd been barely two when the first book was published, and Bunny took pride in the fact that the fictional Henry Holter had evolved into a complex young adult and that his flaws were giving the latest books a dimensionality even the critics appreciated. Her spin-off series had all been wildly successful, of course, but the beauty of Henry's immortality, not to mention the time-traveling bit, meant she always had her favorite character exactly when and where she wanted him.

Ian had messengered over the advance copy of the book first thing this morning. The cover art was questionable, as always, but Bunny had given up on that quarrel long ago. "Let the art department do their job," Ian had argued after the ghastly first cover came round for her approval. "They know what they're doing." So she'd allowed Henry Holter to be portrayed as a faggy-looking little thing. What did she care as long as the books sold? And they did sell. Only J. K. Rowling's book sales had surpassed hers. Bunny had been there first! The world was always comparing the two, and Bunny resented easy analogies as much as the press liked gobbling them up.

She had been as surprised as anyone by her initial success but, like most successful people, had grown accustomed to its privileges—primarily the right to be a shit if and when she felt like it.

"Wrong, wrong, wrong," Bunny said aloud, looking at the swarthy family illustrated on the book jacket and wondering if anybody in the art department ever bothered reading her books. Her newest character, Lucy Heathcoff, was supposed to have red hair! Bunny reached for her reading glasses and lit another cigarette as she read the attached note.

The first copy for my First Lady. And not a peep about the cover. Apparently gingers don't sell, but I still love Lucy!

Cheers,
I.

Bunny let out a snort. She adored Ian. They'd been together from the start. He was the only taker Bunny didn't resent. Unlike the others, Ian earned his share, and so what if his devotion to her was as much about his 15 percent as it was about the pleasure he got from her company? Bunny had become a very difficult woman, but at least she'd made Ian a very rich man. Hadn't he been the only one who even bothered to read her five-hundred-page typewritten manuscript all those years ago? In her twenties and divorced, she'd just returned to England from Los Angeles. That first book (an Orwellian fable of sorts) hadn't been very good, but Ian had seen her potential. As inspiration, he'd given her an obscure novel called *The Shades,* by Betty Brock, and encouraged her to dip her pen into the then-pristine waters of young-adult fantasy. Her first Henry Holter novel was published shortly thereafter. So many decades later and there was still nobody else she really trusted.

The phone rang. She was sure it was Ian, calling to see if she'd received the book but also to talk about her birthday party. She didn't pick up. Bunny usually arranged a small party at Mirabelle, but this year she hadn't. Seventy wasn't an easy age. Sixty had been a kind of milestone, but seventy was just old. Nothing good happened after seventy. She'd far exceeded her own career aspirations, been married and divorced twice, and had a son who didn't seem to like her. What was there left to experience other than cancer or maybe a paralyzing stroke?

She flipped to the last page of the book and stared at her face above the author bio. After all these years, her author photo never failed to perk up her spirits, especially on days like today, when she knew she bore little resemblance to that cheerful, tidy woman. The picture was over twenty years old but she didn't see the point in updating it.

Her son had taken it. Had she looked so happy then because she'd been with Henry? That was just before he'd decided to throw a decades-long hissy fit because she'd named the little hero in her novels after him, and the books had had the great misfortune of becoming successful. Literary immortality was apparently a great burden.

Certainly she'd aged since, but she was nevertheless quite good-looking even now, especially for a woman of her years. Her eyes still sparkled, and her face, though slackened by gravity, hadn't wrinkled.

It was a face untouched by the sun or a surgeon. If anything, Bunny thought, the years had given her a more commanding appearance, which properly undercut the absolute absurdity of her name. She was much too squeamish for needles and knives, and, my God, didn't those women all look awful anyway? It was one thing to be vain but quite another to walk around wearing your panic on your face. Bunny had been so disappointed when her best friend, Elaine, took the plunge. At first, Bunny had to admit that Elaine looked better. But four years and God knew how many procedures later, Elaine was beginning to look like something cooked up in Michael Jackson's uterus. Who did she think she was kidding? Bunny understood the foolishness of trying to look young and she had therefore succeeded in not looking old. That was important.

She put out her cigarette and stabbed Bettina's call buzzer with an impatient index finger. Where the hell had Bettina gone? The phone rang again. Bunny let out an exasperated sigh. How on earth was she expected to get anything done?

"Hello, Ian."

"Did you get the book?"

"Yes, thank you, darling. Got to dash. I'm busy."

"Working?" he asked with far too much enthusiasm.

"No, actually. Not working."

He wheezed. "Oh. I see. Anyway, I wanted to tell you something."

Bunny sighed, impatient. "I'm listening."

Ian was silent, obviously concerned about Bunny not working and trying to determine what needed to be done to remedy the situation. He'd lost his ease.

"Right," he mumbled. "I just . . . I had . . . I had some good news is all."

"Out with it, then. I've things to do."

"Oh. Yes. I wanted to let you know the initial print run. Epic, really."

"What was *hers?*" Bunny asked, not missing a beat.

"She Who Shall Not Be Named?" Ian asked lightly, hoping to

reestablish their usual intimacy by using their nickname for Bunny's biggest competitor.

"Mm."

"W-well," he stammered. "A bit higher."

"So what's your good news?"

"Don't be impossible," he said, amused. "It's a hell of a first printing. Our biggest ever."

"I suppose."

"And there's always your next book," Ian said, more as a question than a statement.

"We'll see."

"It's just a matter of sitting down and getting to it. You know—"

"Good-bye, Ian." Bunny could hear him talking as she hung up. Poor Ian. He was a wreck. Tony Elliot, his other cash cow, had pancreatic cancer, and now Bunny was doing God knows what when she should be at her desk typing up his next paycheck. Still, she was irritated. One thing was for sure—she wasn't about to sit down and get to it. Bunny marched to her closet with an air of defiance. She was going out. Maybe she'd clear the air with Sam. "Mean drunk, indeed!"

Bunny's mood lifted as she walked down Peel Street, passing one person after the next without being recognized. She relaxed, allowing herself to feel a joyous camaraderie with the hoi polloi. The rain had stopped. It was a gorgeous day now. Sunny. How many days like this had she missed? Bunny wondered with uncharacteristic regret. Was she depressed or just exhausted by the recent unproductiveness of her working hours? It was hard to say. This restlessness was new to her. She'd spent so many years happily enveloped in her own imagination. Her fictional world was all-encompassing. She never gave a thought to the goings-on outside her flat between the hours of seven a.m. and five p.m.

But lately she cared. The sounds of delivery trucks, people shouting, even cars honking would all draw her to the office window. She'd begun to feel suffocated in her flat. So she started venturing out. She'd gone to Hyde Park last Monday and even bought her own fags at the local grocery on Saturday. Nobody had noticed her! If she wore a hat that hid her hair, she found she could get away with these outings. Her hair, as smooth and white as a sheet of paper and cut sharply at her chin, was the giveaway. She'd had the same haircut for thirty years. The other essential thing was to go out in the morning, when young people were in school or taking pictures of themselves at home.

In a rather brave stab at emancipation, she'd even gone to the Tate Modern alone last Thursday. She'd been excited to discuss her impressions of Mark Rothko with Henry, assuming it would give them something to talk about. But that had been a mistake. It was unbearably overheated in the museum so she'd taken off her hat without thinking. She wished that Ian had not e-mailed her the picture of herself that had appeared in the pages of *Hello!* She looked like a cow at a slaughterhouse staring dumbly into some idiot's iPhone. *Ms. Small in Turbine Hall!!!* the caption read. Ridiculous that anybody should care. And the magazine's overuse of exclamation points was maddening. The copyeditor ought to be incarcerated.

At least she wouldn't have to worry about Henry seeing *Hello!* He didn't pay any more attention to his mother's press than he did to their strained phone conversations. He was far too busy analyzing trees and clouds in mediocre American landscape paintings to worry about her.

"Sam?" Bunny called out as she pushed open the heavy iron door of his shop, greeted by the chemical bouquet of old varnish and mildew. The walk had softened her mood. She decided to be gracious toward Sam, perhaps even give him the chance to apologize.

"Ah. If it isn't Sherlock Holmes," he said, looking sideways at her outfit and rising to give her a kiss.

"Not a word." She pulled off her deerstalker cap and loosened her scarf. "I'm already cross with you."

"You?" He laughed. "Cross with me?"

"You called me a mean drunk, in case you've forgotten."

"Yes, well..."

"Well what?" She looked at him, always struck by how well he'd aged, his thick white hair contrasting with his still-youthful features. Bunny had never understood why Sam enjoyed rotting in a shop all day fussing with antiquities, no matter how precious and rare they might be. He was tall and industrious-looking, the kind of man you'd expect to see fly-fishing or building something useful outdoors. But decade after decade, there he'd sat, legs crossed, looking like the actor Sam Elliott dropped into a Dickens novel.

"You don't need to say everything that comes to mind," he said. "That's all."

"I couldn't have been that bad." She was rubbing her hand along a lovely blue and gold cloisonné vase she'd picked up.

"You were condescending and patronizing, but I forgive you, if only for the comic relief you've provided with today's..." He paused, searching for the right word. "Ensemble."

Bunny shrugged. Sam was too sensitive. Always had been.

When they'd first met, Bunny had adored Sam's rugged good looks and relaxed, easy company. He worked in art restoration but seemed to dislike his job. He'd go on for hours about how overzealous restorers were destroying the entire corpus of Western art. He'd eventually managed to get himself fired from the Victoria and Albert Museum.

Bunny admired his integrity for all of ten minutes.

Soon enough, his lack of ambition and copious sentimentality drove her mad. The man couldn't throw anything away, be it a playbill from a favorite West End show or a brass horse bit he'd found in the garbage bin. "This was in the rubbish!" he'd cry, presenting his latest find to her as if it were a newborn baby. But they'd gotten married, and after she sold her third book (the advance was enormous), she set Sam up in an antiques shop on Portobello Road, where, to everyone's surprise, he'd done quite well. He accepted her generosity without guilt or excessive gratitude. The shop gave Sam a sense of purpose. Once he began traveling to stock the shop, Bunny thought their marriage might make it. It was just those few months when he was in town that presented a problem. Sam felt couples should talk, and Bunny couldn't think of anything to say. Her work was the only thing that really interested her and she didn't care to discuss her ideas with anyone. When Henry was old enough to be more interested in his mates than his parents, Bunny decided she wanted a divorce. Sam was disappointed but agreeable, as always. Much as he loved Bunny, he wanted a wife who looked up from her typewriter when he came home.

Whatever issues they'd had as a couple disappeared after the divorce. They were fond of each other and connected by Henry. Bunny still enjoyed Sam's company, and now that his shop was so fashionable, they could meet as equals. Well, they were hardly equals, but what harm did it do to indulge him a bit?

"Spoken to Henry?" Bunny asked, feeling suddenly weepy. She hadn't talked to him in weeks. She was an irrational sort of mother and envied Sam's ease with their son. Fatherhood came as naturally to him as writing came to her. Or used to come, anyway.

Sam clapped his hands together, obviously eager to snap Bunny out of her reverie. "Shall I pick him up at Heathrow or just send a car round?" The moment the words left his mouth, his handsome face went the color of beets.

"Henry's coming to London?" she asked excitedly as she carefully replaced the vase she'd been holding. "When?"

"Shit." Sam leaned forward and pressed his thumb and index finger against his eyelids. "Ian's going to crunch my balls in a nutcracker. Please, please don't tell him I've ruined the surprise party. Really, Bun. Please."

"Surprise party?" Bunny giggled. "Oh my!"

"Bloody hell." Sam moaned and mussed his hair with both hands. "Fuck. Fuck."

Sam never swore. Bunny was delighted. "I'll pretend I didn't know a thing. I'm a good actress."

"You're a terrible actress."

"This will give me time to work on it, then."

"Must you look quite so triumphant and fiendish? I'm cooked if Ian finds out."

"Forget Ian, would you? It seems to me you should show a bit more concern about ruining my fun. Man up, Sam! Ian won't ever know."

"Just promise you won't tell him I said anything?" he pressed.

Bunny laughed. "Of course I'll play along. The important thing is that Henry is coming. Oh, and be sure to send a town car for him. Better yet, call one of my secretaries and arrange to send the Bentley, would you? Maybe you can find a girl with a cap to drive it? He'd like that, no? Make it nice for him and he'll come more often. Put him up at the Lanesborough."

Sam made a face. "You don't need to buy his affection with whores and limos, for God's sake. He wouldn't like any of that. I will get Henry at the airport. He'll be quite comfortable staying with Daphne and me."

Bunny shuddered. "If you say so. When is he coming?"

"I'm not saying another word."

"Don't be so hard on yourself, darling. Please."

He smiled apologetically, happy enough to allow Bunny to forgive his indiscretion.

"I'm off, then," Bunny said.

"What about tea?" Sam asked, turning over the cloisonné vase Bunny had been holding.

"Next time, darling. I should pop into Browns for a new dress...for the party. Now that you've exercised your usual lack of discretion, you can't blame me for wanting to look my best, can you?" She gave him a quick kiss on the cheek.

"Mm. I suppose not," he said, obviously still worrying over Ian.

"Care to come?" she asked, stopping and smiling enormously so that Sam would understand that it was a good thing that he'd told her. She hadn't felt so pleased in months. "It would be so much less tedious if you came. You know how much I hate to shop and you'll be honest about what suits. Can't trust the sycophantic salesgirls, and once I take off my ensemble, there'll be a crowd," she said, realizing that she actually needed Sam to come with her. "You can chase away snoopers."

"I can't imagine a more fulfilling afternoon."

"Lovely." She tucked her hair back into her hat and tied up her scarf again.

He grabbed his keys and called out to his assistant that he was leaving for the day.

"That's what I admire about you, Sam. Your work ethic."

"And that's what I admire about you, Bun," he said. "Your ability to insult a man and persuade him to be your companion in the same sentence."

Janine

Janine had to press the intercom button three times before somebody answered.

"Hi, Janine."

"David?"

"It's Frank."

"Hi, Frank. Um, is David there?"

"He's at lunch. Something wrong?"

"Lunch? It's five o'clock."

"He's on the night shift."

"I think there's a black widow in the closet."

Frank laughed. "There's no black widows in Manhattan."

"I just saw a black spider the size of Iowa with a red hourglass on its stomach."

"The red is on their backs," Frank said like he was a fucking arachnologist rather than a doorman.

"Frank?"

"Yep?"

"You need to get up here. Or send Manny. I'm freaking out."

"I'm the only one in the lobby, honey. I can't leave. I'm sorry. You know I would."

"Okay," she said, trying to calm down.

"You all right?"

"No."

Janine had known Frank since she was twenty years old. The whole staff of the building had been there forever. She was famous back then. They treated her like a daughter of their own who needed protection. They were like a family.

In many ways, they felt like a much better family than the one Janine had in LA. Not today, though. Today they were failing her. Today she regretted tipping Frank so generously at Christmas. Didn't he understand this was an emergency?

"Janine?" Frank asked. "You there?"

"Yeah."

"What you want me to do?"

"Can you call Mrs. Nguyen?"

"In eight G?" he asked. "What's she gonna do?"

"She's not scared. She took a mouse out of three A once."

"She cooked it and ate it," he said, laughing.

The doormen didn't like Mrs. Nguyen. She ordered everyone around and never tipped. Still, she came in handy.

"I'm totally not amused, Frank. I'm upset."

"Let me see if Freddie's around. Hang tight."

Janine heard the line switch off. She dropped the phone and ran back to the closet. *Hang tight?* The spider was in her shoe, just waiting. When the doorbell rang, she didn't move. She wasn't taking her eyes off the monster. "Come in!" she shouted. "It's open."

She was expecting Freddie. He was one of the newer hires. He was short and didn't speak English very well. Whenever nobody else was available, Freddie was dispatched to the scene.

She heard a woman's voice. "Hello? Hello?"

"Hi, Mrs. Nguyen," Janine said, still not moving. She couldn't believe Frank had actually called Mrs. Nguyen. Or that she had come! "I'm in the bedroom."

"You got spider?" Mrs. Nguyen was in her bathrobe and slippers. She had pink foam curlers in her hair, the kind Janine hadn't seen in years. "Move over," she said, giving Janine a little push. "Let's see."

"Thanks for coming," Janine said, so grateful she wanted to wrap her arms around the old lady and cry.

"Where's big boyfriend?" Mrs. Nguyen asked. "This his job."

"Jürgen?" Janine asked, always astounded by the way gossip got around the building. "He's not my boyfriend anymore. He's married."

"Mm. Too bad for you." Mrs. Nguyen raised her eyebrows. "I saw him in elevator yesterday?"

Janine wondered where Freddie was. She didn't feel like explaining her relationship with Jürgen to Mrs. Nguyen. "He was here fixing my ceiling fan. He's a contractor."

Mrs. Nguyen narrowed her eyes, looking as if she weren't convinced.

Jürgen and Janine were still close, despite the breakup, despite his marrying someone else. He never talked about his wife, Birgit, and Janine never asked any questions. She hadn't even realized that she still needed him until she'd seen him holding hands with his pretty wife at Zabar's a couple of months ago. Their happiness had filled her with an inexplicable urgency to *do* something, anything, with her life. She'd enrolled in the cartooning class that night.

"How long he been married?" Mrs. Nguyen asked, clearly more interested in Jürgen than the spider, which was now crawling out of the shoe.

"It's moving!" Janine screamed, pointing at the spider.

Mrs. Nguyen looked. Her eyes grew wide and her mouth turned into a circle. "That's black widow."

"It is?" Janine asked, even though she'd been certain already. Stupid Frank. What did he know? Janine gave Mrs. Nguyen a boot.

"What's that for?"

"Can you kill it?" Janine asked. "I'm scared."

"No way. It's bad luck."

"I'll give you a hundred dollars."

Mrs. Nguyen laughed. "What good a hundred dollars if I got lifetime of bad luck?" She looked at Janine and then turned away.

"Where are you going?" Janine asked. "You can't just leave!"

"I go get a cup."

"And then what?" she shrieked. "Carry it down the elevator and release it on Madison Avenue?"

Mrs. Nguyen shrugged.

"You watch the spider," Janine said, talking slowly. "I'll get the cup. Don't move."

Mrs. Nguyen pursed her lips. "Yeah, okay."

Janine hurried off in search of an encyclopedia or an art book big enough to kill it. There'd be no cup. She was having dinner with a friend in an hour and she didn't believe in luck.

When she came back, Mrs. Nguyen wasn't there. What the fuck? Maybe she was onto Janine's execution plan. "Hello?" she called, clutching Taschen's colossal *Cabinet of Natural Curiosities*. "Mrs. Nguyen?"

She was gone. Janine ran over to the closet. The spider was gone too! Gone! Janine knew she'd have to move out now. Twenty years was a good run, but she'd never fall asleep in this room again. She sat on her bed and kept her eyes fixed on the closet. Kitty Fisher came over to see what the matter was.

"You're useless," she said, pulling the cat onto her lap. She could hear reggae music next door.

Janine had always had an irrational fear of insects. One night when she was seven or eight, she'd gone to ask her mother to kill the daddy longlegs she'd seen on her bed. She knocked lightly on Pam's door, whispering her name, being careful not to interrupt whatever might be going on in there. She knew it wasn't kid stuff. But if someone didn't kill the giant bug on her bed, she thought she'd die. Janine still wasn't used to the new house her father had bought them in Laurel Canyon. She wasn't used to her new mom either. This mom suddenly wanted to be called Pamela instead of Mom and had taken up smoking and had parties and boyfriends. This mom announced she was a feminist and had a mirror over her bed. Janine knew there was something embarrassing about it all but she wasn't going to argue because this Pamela person seemed, at first, to be a lot nicer than her old mom.

Pamela had even let her and Amanda choose what color carpeting they wanted in their new bedrooms. Amanda picked a salmon pink. Janine picked powder blue. The master bedroom and hallway were a deep forest green. Janine couldn't believe her mother would allow such a brazen lack of cohesion. "Fuck the rules," Pamela had said, too loudly, as they giggled over swatches in Banner Carpets. "Choose whatever makes you happy." It didn't matter that the colors clashed, Janine later realized, because their doors would always be shut. Each bedroom was a habitat unto itself, a holding cell of female expectations and dissatisfactions.

Janine had sat that night on the green carpet outside her mother's door whispering "Pamela" like a prayer, listening to the music coming from inside mingled with the hushed tones of a man's voice. The man was probably Ken, her mom's new favorite, an actor with big white teeth who enjoyed juicing, moon boots, and being naked. (Thinking about it now, adult Janine felt a stab of sympathy for her younger self. It wasn't like Pamela had been a paragon of motherhood when she and Janine's father were married, but her mom's leap into the pool of sexual liberation presented a new roster of issues. Would it have been so hard for her mother to ask her boyfriend to wear a robe or at least some underwear?)

That night, the sound of the front door closing woke Janine. Pamela came over and knelt beside her in the hallway, a silk negligee grazing her thighs. "What are you doing out here?" she asked. A dam of reckless tears broke as Janine tried to explain about the spider.

"Why didn't you come in?" Pamela asked. She looked at Janine as if she had been completely irrational in her hesitation to walk right into her mother's bedroom. And even though this was years before her mother's depression began to manifest itself, before Pam started to smell funny and spend her days dressed in that worn, stained terrycloth bathrobe she used to put on only when she dyed her hair, Janine had never felt like she could just go into her mom's room uninvited. "Oh, baby," Pamela said, pulling Janine up to her feet for a hug. "Let's go kill that motherfucker."

Janine squeezed her mom hard. She was always surprised at how her mother's sympathy undid her. She was defenseless against her kindness. But when they went into Janine's room, the spider was gone. "Now I don't know where it is," she cried, inconsolable. "It could be *anywhere!*"

Her mom tried to calm her down; she took the sheets off the bed, shook them out, remade the bed, then shook out the quilt for good measure. It was no good.

"So come and sleep with me in my room." Pamela yawned. Janine looked at her. She'd never been invited into her mother's bed before. Janine began to dry her eyes, imagining herself next to her mother, warm and safe under that quilted white satin comforter. "Ken left," Pamela explained, sensing Janine's hesitation and extending her hand.

Janine grabbed her mom's hand and dragged her to her bedroom. She flew into the disheveled bed. "Good night, little burrito," Pamela said, wrapping Janine up in the blanket like she was swaddling a newborn. Janine looked at herself in the mirror overhead and smiled. This was how she had liked to sleep when she was very small. She was surprised that her mom remembered.

It was funny, Janine thought now, staring into her closet, the way spiders and mothers just disappeared. You couldn't look away, even for a minute.

Janine canceled dinner with her friend. Manny and Freddie helped her move things out of her bedroom and into the hall. At first it was just the shoes and clothes. When the black widow failed to reappear, they called Frank and David. It was almost nine o'clock and every piece of Janine's furniture was in the hallway. Manny was vacuuming. Janine had never felt so loved or so panicked.

"What's happening up here?" Mrs. Nguyen asked, poking her head out of the elevator. "It's too loud. Very annoying." She was dressed elegantly in a red quilted jacket with matching slacks and red flats. Her black hair was pulled into a tight bun.

"We're trying to find that black widow," Janine said, narrowing her eyes at Mrs. Nguyen, who had obviously been out enjoying her evening.

"You're crazy, Janine. All of you, crazy," she said, pointing to the exhausted staff. "I killed that spider before. You took too long to get cup. I got things to do. Can't wait all day for a cup."

Now everyone was staring at Janine.

"I thought you said it was bad luck?" she asked, barely audible.

"Nah. I had good night. Lobster was delicious and taxi smelled okay. You stop making noise now? I'm tired. Go to bed."

Hailey

They were visiting Grandpa Marty in rehab again. As far as Hailey could tell, not much had changed since the last time, a few years ago. At least the drive was a lot shorter now that they'd moved from San Diego to LA. The best part of Directions was seeing famous people. The place was crawling with them. Celebrity spotting was the only thing that was better in LA than in San Diego. Everything else in this city blew.

Hailey and her sister were trailing their mom to the therapy rooms. Jaycee gestured to the back of a promisingly tall woman in a T-shirt and jeans. They were both disappointed to see it was just another model. And she looked at least thirty-eight. Hailey figured being an old model couldn't be easy.

When they reached the therapy rooms, the twins took seats on the long white sofa next to their mom. The new mediator, some fledgling douche named Dan, leaned forward on a metal chair and prepped them for Marty's arrival. He talked slowly, instructing them on what they should and shouldn't say to "help move the session along in a constructive way."

"We know," Hailey said. "It's not like this is our first time visiting him here."

"Hailey!" her mother snapped, annoyed that Hailey had made Marty look like a serial rehabber, which he was.

"It's okay, Amanda." Dan smiled at Hailey like he understood something about her. He looked at Jaycee and winked. Hailey wanted to punch him in the face. Then Marty was at the door and they all stood up to greet him.

"Sit," Marty said after giving them all perfunctory kisses, as if they were meeting for a casual meal or something. He took a seat on the chair opposite the sofa. "Why isn't Gail here?"

"The first session is immediate family only," Dan answered. "Okay by you?"

"Why the hell not?" Marty said and he proceeded to blow his nose into a tissue he pulled out of his baggy sweatpants. He poured himself a glass of iced tea from a pitcher on a tray. Hailey noticed how tired and thin he looked. But more than that, he looked old.

"So," he said, leaning back, "tell me the good news."

The twins looked at each other. Marty was quiet, chewing on an ice cube as he considered his granddaughters.

"Why don't you tell Grandpa about the school play, Jay?" their mom suggested after too long a silence. Hailey looked at Jaycee and smiled naughtily.

This was the first year since nursery school that Hailey wasn't in the school play. Her mother hadn't even let her audition because of her "poor academic performance." *So yes,* Jay, Hailey thought with hostility. *Why don't you tell Grandpa all about the stupid play?*

"Um," Jaycee started reluctantly, "well, it's *Hairspray.*"

"He knows *that.*" Amanda laughed, even though nobody had said anything remotely funny. Their mom was idiotically invested in this show, not only because it was her first big production at Fair Hills but because, once it closed, she might get to workshop it at some theater in San Francisco. Her mom thought that was a big deal.

They were all looking at Jaycee now. In fact, Hailey noticed mediator Dan looking at her sister with more interest than seemed appropriate. Her stomach tightened into a familiar fist. It was always the same. Jaycee was the prettier twin. Their general packaging was the same, both of them petite with long blond hair, but Jaycee was softer looking, more feminine. Hailey had made a lifelong study out of her sister's features, carefully logging them and noting where her own came up short. Not only was Jaycee's nose smaller, but her face and lips were significantly fuller, like their mom's. Hailey's chin was too long, and her nose, which tipped downward at the end, also had a higher bridge. Jaycee wasn't as beautiful as their mom—neither one of them had inherited those wide cheekbones or slanted green eyes— but Jaycee had gotten the lion's share of their mom's looks, leaving their dad's genes to fill in the blanks on Hailey's face. She glared at Dan and slumped in her chair, racking her brain for something good to tell her grandfather when it was her turn.

Was it good news that her mom had told her she'd done a nice job washing the egg pan that morning? It was the first compliment her mom had given Hailey in she couldn't even remember how long. Should she tell her grandpa she was homing in on her vocation as a career dishwasher? Would he like that? Would not having a pimple that week qualify as good news? Jaycee had gotten an A on her English paper. Probably she'd talk about that. Mrs. Fallows had called Hailey's much more ambitious paper on John Green and Tolstoy "a reach." No, she really couldn't think of anything at all good to say.

Dan leaned forward. He was all lit up. "Marty, can I ask why it is you want to hear only the good news from your family?"

Hailey was really glad Dan had asked that question. It headed off her turn to talk.

"What you're really asking for when you ask for the good news," Dan continued, "is for your family to entertain you. I would imagine that feels like a lot of pressure on them to perform?"

Hailey's mom nodded and exhaled. Hailey narrowed her eyes. Why was *she* so relieved?

"That's what we call a negative behavior pattern," Dan went on.

"It can be very destructive. What if there was something difficult your family wanted to discuss with you? Something that wasn't good? What if your daughter Amanda had some bad news? Would that be okay, Marty?"

"Of course it would be okay. You think they represent the fucking Lollipop Guild? All I hear about is their problems. Is it so much to ask for a little good news once in a while?"

"That's not fair—" her mom started, but Dan held a finger to his lips.

"Marty," Dan said, "when you say, 'Tell me the good news,' it might give your family the impression that it's not okay to have an authentic conversation."

"Maybe I'm trying to focus on me right now. How's that for authentic...Dan? Is that an eighty-nine-thousand-dollar-a-month feeling I'm allowed to have, Dan?"

"All of your feelings are valid. They're real. They're your feelings. Guilt is the gift that keeps giving, Marty."

"Guilt?" Marty asked. "What do I have to be guilty about?" He rested his head on the back of the chair so that he was staring up at the ceiling. "Sweet, sweet Jesus. I give this one fifty K a year. I give my other daughter God knows how much money. What else can I do?"

Hailey made her eyes into slits. All her mom ever talked about was what a parasite her sister, Janine, was, but apparently she had been taking money from Grandpa all along too. What a complete and total hypocrite! Hailey glared at her mom, who made herself busy pretending not to notice.

"We're not talking about money," Dan said.

"We're always talking about money, Dan. Trust me."

"Okay. Can I make a suggestion?"

"Knock yourself out, Dan."

Hailey knew that when her grandpa used a person's name over and over, he was mad.

"Rather than it being about your feelings or their feelings or who's

failing whom, might we work on how you all interact together? In the
end, it's really about the dynamic of your family."

"Ahh," Grandpa Marty said, rolling his eyes. "The family dynamic."

"So," Dan continued, "if, for example, your daughter was having a
tough time, it would be okay for her to share that with you? Is that a
fair assumption?"

"Allow me a moment to meditate on the profundity of that question, Dan," Marty said, ramming the palms of his hands against his
eyelids. "Oooooohmmm..."

Hailey and Jaycee laughed nervously. Dan smiled at them but Hailey noted his beady eyes still lingered on Jaycee. Why did people ask
if they were identical when they were obviously anything but? Hailey
wondered. The slip of a difference between them made a mockery of
her life. She was the less-than twin. If Jaycee weren't always around
making her look bad, *she'd* be considered pretty. *She'd* have a choice
part in the school play. *She'd* be the one going out with Devon Pierce.
He had said "Hi" to her first, when they started at Fair Hills Academy
in September, before he'd gravitated, like everyone, toward Jaycee.

Jaycee smiled at Dan. *That* was totally inappropriate, seeing as she
was going out with Devon. And Dan had to be at least twenty-five.
Maybe even thirty. Hailey scowled at her sister.

"Hailey," her mother said, looking at Hailey like she'd kicked a
baby or something. "Are you with us?"

"Yes. God."

"And Amanda," Dan said, standing up theatrically, like he was
about to perform a magic trick. "You seem very eager to please your
father. I almost get the sense you are terrified of disappointing him?"

Her mom's face was blotchy. Hailey clenched her fists and prayed
her mother wasn't going to start talking about sacrificing the job at
Sarah Lawrence again. She hadn't shut up about her selflessness since
Grandpa had checked into rehab and she'd "finally" decided she had
to "be in LA for him." As if her mother had *ever* had any intention
of moving to Yonkers! As if she'd survive one winter having to wear

a parka! As if it weren't totally obvious she'd just used the job offer as leverage to get a promotion at Fair Hills. Now she was head of the whole drama department! Only her mother could spin *not* taking a job she didn't even want to her advantage.

Dan cleared his throat. "I guess what I'm getting at is that I'm noticing some codependency issues between you all." Then to Marty: "I have to wonder if that tension creates a stress that causes you to either avoid your family or self-medicate."

"Boy, Dan, you're really getting at something weighty here," Marty said, winking at Hailey. She smiled. One thing she liked about her grandfather was that he seemed to prefer her to Jaycee. Dan was out of his depth with Marty. He'd failed to get him to "have a dialogue" with the family. And the more Dan eyeballed Jaycee, the harder it was for Hailey to take any of this rehab bullshit seriously. Why should her grandfather listen to what a pedophile had to say? Besides, her grandfather was much smarter than Dan. It was hard to cheer on the dumb guy.

"Jaycee, why don't you sing your audition song," her mother suggested out of nowhere, like a crazy person. "I'm sure everyone would love that."

"Are you kidding?" Jaycee asked. "Nobody would love that."

Hailey knew Jaycee didn't actually like being the center of attention. She was more of a quiet compliment collector, the kind of person who gradually stole the show and then acted all surprised that it had happened. Or maybe she really was surprised. But Hailey knew that putting Jaycee on the spot like she was a show pony was probably the worst thing her mom could do.

And anyway, hadn't they just spent the past five minutes talking about how unhealthy it was that they all felt compelled to entertain Marty? *Poor, frantic Mom,* Hailey thought with delight. All you had to do was look at Grandpa's expression to see that there was nothing he wanted less than to endure a Broadway serenade from his granddaughter, whose middle name Hailey would bet ten bucks he didn't even know.

"Please, Mom," Jaycee said. Hailey *almost* felt bad for her sister. Her mom's desperation to be in good standing with Grandpa Marty was just sickening.

"Amanda." Dan wiped his sweaty face with the back of his hand. "This really isn't—"

But Amanda had already begun clapping her hands to an invisible beat. Nobody was getting off this train. Jaycee squirmed as she made a tentative move to stand, buckling under the weight of their mom's outrageous request.

Hailey looked at the slight twitch working the corners of her grandpa's mouth. He was looking at Dan, triumphant.

"Sing!" Amanda cried.

Jaycee stood, cleared her throat, and launched into "The Legend of Miss Baltimore Crabs." Right there in the room!

Is there anything more uncomfortable than being trapped in a small space while somebody is singing? Maybe if it were Barbra Streisand or Beyoncé, it would feel like an honor, but this proximity to Jaycee's kind of talent was a punishment. Jaycee sounded crap without instrumental backing, while Hailey could sing a cappella in her sleep! Hadn't *she* led their Varsity Vocals team to victory in middle school? Hadn't *she* won the sixth-grade talent show with her mind-blowing rendition of "Hallelujah"? Jaycee was *okay*, but Hailey was better.

And as if the whole show-tunes-in-rehab situation weren't bad enough, Jaycee started really getting into it, gesturing, swaying her hips, throwing an invisible baton in the air, and, for some unknown reason, singing in an over-the-top faux British accent. Her mom was smiling and bobbing her head. And then she raised her hands and started *conducting* the unfolding travesty! Dan looked on in fixed horror. At least that infatuation was over.

Hailey glanced at her grandfather. His knuckles were white from clutching the chair, and his head was down. His body was quaking, but he was very, very quiet. She thought maybe he was having a seizure but then realized he was laughing. Jaycee croaked out the last, endless note with her eyes bulging from the effort and *finally* sat down. Her mom and Dan gave her a polite round of applause.

"Bet you could use a big fucking bag of heroin about now, huh?" Hailey asked. Marty unleashed a bark of laughter that shook his body so violently he looked inhuman.

"Hailey Loehman!" her mother shrieked ferociously.

"I'm sorry," she cried. "I didn't even mean to say it out loud. It just came out!"

"That's okay," Dan said. He'd dropped his sanctimonious act now that he was also laughing. He tried to collect himself. "Humor is a terrific way to deal with feelings of discomfort and addiction."

"You shut up!" Amanda snapped at him.

"I'm really sorry, Mom," Hailey said. She glanced at Jaycee, who looked exhausted, like that singing frog from the Bugs Bunny cartoons. "That was just, like, so awkward."

"C'mon, Amanda," Marty said. "Give her a break. 'Bet you could use a big fucking bag of heroin about now.'" He chortled to himself. "Christ Almighty," he said, smiling at Hailey. "That was a great line."

Amanda glowered at her father, an expression packed with thirty-five-plus years of similar humiliations.

After ten minutes, Dan finished his tedious wrap-up, and they stood to go. On the way out of the room, Grandpa Marty gave Hailey a real hug, pulling her in hard.

"Don't let your mother give you any shit, Jaycee," he whispered, mussing up her hair affectionately.

"It's Hailey," she said.

"That's what I said." He smiled and gave her another hug.

Janine

—Original Message—
From: Amanda Kessler <Akessler@akessler1000.com>
To: Booth.Temple@SarahLawrenceCollege.com
Bcc: JKessler@yahoo.net
Subject: With sincere apologies...

Dear Dr. Temple:

It is with great regret that I write to inform you that I will be unable to accept your offer of employment at Sarah Lawrence. Due to family circumstances beyond my control, I cannot leave California at this time.

I will, no doubt, look back at this decision with mixed feelings. I had so looked forward to shaping the Performing Arts program into a world-class institution for the dramatic arts. At the same time, the unparalleled opportunities available to my daughters at Bronxville Prep would have changed the course of their lives forever.

It is painful to close the door on such an opportunity. And

yet, with nobody else to care for my father, I feel I cannot abandon him during his time of need.

With heartfelt gratitude for your faith in me and sincere apologies for any inconvenience I may have caused the administration,

Sincerely,
Amanda Kessler

Janine groaned as she stared at the computer screen. Her sister was such a bad writer, florid and overbearing. She was embarrassed. Had Amanda actually sent that letter to the head of Sarah Lawrence? *I had so looked forward to shaping the Performing Arts program into a world-class institution for the dramatic arts.* Seriously? You're a fucking high-school drama teacher; Sarah Lawrence was doing just fine without you! Humility was never Amanda's strong suit. She might as well have signed off *Your brilliant martyr . . .*

This was how Amanda communicated with Janine these days: She blind-copied her on e-mails. They weren't directed *to* her but *at* her. At first Janine had thought Amanda was being economical with her time but she quickly realized her sister just wanted a virtual podium from which she could accuse Janine of failing to hold up her end of the familial responsibilities without giving her the opportunity to respond.

Still a brat, Janine thought, wondering that their relationship had always been so strained. Janine knew Amanda blamed her for some ambiguous offense that had occurred after their mom had died. But it wasn't like they'd gotten along *before* that. It wasn't like Janine could magically forget how *mean* her mom and Amanda had always been to her about her acting. Their obvious bewilderment at Janine's unlikely success when Amanda was so clearly the pretty one had always chafed. Pamela and Amanda's exclusive twosome had left Janine feeling like an outsider, even though her father had tried hard to compensate. After all these years, Janine continued to harbor an irrational resentment toward her mom and sister. It certainly didn't help that Amanda was *still* angry with her, as if, when Janine had finally lost it back then and left the show and then LA, she had done it just to annoy Amanda. Her sister's self-absorption was almost funny.

Janine had sewn this narrative together, but she always got caught on the same loose stitch. Amanda had been only twelve at the time of their mom's suicide. Could Janine really blame her for anything? At twelve, Amanda was just old enough to understand that the parent who loved her most was gone but still too young to process all the creepy stuff that Janine chewed on to blunt her feelings about her mom's death—her boyfriends walking around naked, their bare bodies oiled up with Bain de Soleil, joints dangling from their mouths; the token copy of *The Feminine Mystique* buried under dog-eared issues of *Cosmopolitan* and *Hustler* on her mother's night table; their mom sleeping for days on end or not sleeping at all. Janine was pretty sure Amanda didn't remember any of that stuff. Or if she did, she'd whitewashed it, summoning Carol Brady to clean up Betty Draper's mess.

Janine thought Amanda was the lucky one. Amanda could pretend the way they'd grown up was normal. She could grieve in a way Janine never could. Yes, Janine should have emotionally supported her little sister more than she had, but how? They'd always been adversaries, not friends, and Janine herself had been only fifteen when Pam died.

She considered not responding to the e-mail at all or just sending a quick reply saying *Thanks for keeping me in the loop*. Of course that would infuriate Amanda. Janine had promised herself that she wasn't going to call her this time. Ever since they were kids, Janine had been the one who apologized, regardless of who was at fault. If this was how her sister wanted to communicate, so be it.

From: JKessler@yahoo.net
To: Akessler@akessler1000.com
Subject: RE: With sincere apologies . . .

Hi, Amanda:

Wow. Sorry to hear you aren't taking the job. It sounded like a great opportunity, and based on the contract you e-mailed me from SLC last month, the salary was certainly generous.

Am I to assume that your copying me on this latest letter was meant as some sort of attack on my character? It feels that way. Copying me on e-mails as if I'm an attorney rather than your sister is getting kind of weird. So let's try and be honest with each other, okay?

I'm not planning on coming back to Los Angeles. I know Dad is in rehab at Directions again. I got the receipt you obviously (and inexplicably) asked Gail to e-mail me. He called me too. He sounded good.

I came out the first two times he went to rehab (in Oregon and in Arizona), and, as you know, it didn't make a difference. All he really wanted was a vacation from his family. He wasn't interested in getting clean then and I don't think much has changed. If anything, I think he checked himself in now so that you wouldn't leave. Amanda, if there is one thing I've learned in therapy, it is this: If you don't draw boundaries, people will bleed all over you.

You know I love Dad. I think the best thing you could do is take the job. He has Gail, and either he's going to get his act together or he's not. Your presence is irrelevant. I don't mean to sound harsh but Dad will continue to "need" you as long as you make yourself available. You are a crutch and I think removing yourself would be good for him.

I am confident that, in his more lucid moments, he would want you to fulfill your dreams. If your dream is teaching at

Sarah Lawrence, I really think you should take the job. If your dream is keeping an eye on Dad's finances while proving your loyalty to I don't know whom, then do that. Either way, Dad will be fine. He always is. It's you I'm beginning to worry about.

With love,
J.

From: Akessler@akessler1000.com
To: JKessler@yahoo.net
Subject: RE: With sincere apologies...

FUCK YOU

From: JKessler@yahoo.net
To: Akessler@akessler1000.com
Subject: RE: With sincere apologies...

It's nice to hear from you directly. How are things?

Janine knew Amanda wouldn't respond again. She seemed incapable of real communication. Janine took out a pencil and paper and pushed Kitty Fisher off her lap. She was due at Kayla's apartment in two hours and wanted to finish her drawings.

Janine was feeling almost confident about the cartooning class. It seemed like everyone wanted to partner with her for the ad assignment. Over the past few weeks she'd come to understand that while most of the students had drawing skills, she had something else. She was a good satirist and had a natural way of turning a phrase. Even Ms. Louie had taken a shine to the bite in Janine's deceptively innocent cartoons. "Your self-doubt speaks to the collective," Ms. Louie had said, and Janine had had to excuse herself before she cried in front of everyone. If other people could relate to her insecurity, she wasn't alone. For the first time in ages, Janine didn't need to apologize or feel ashamed. She could be proud of her emotional scars. Maybe learning cartooning was a dumb idea, but her attraction to it made sense now. Making the dark stuff funny helped defuse it.

And Janine was making friends without having to lie about who she was. Though it wasn't likely she was going to be a career cartoonist (her drawings still looked like something the mother of a six-year-old would display on the fridge), her curtained world was opening onto something larger.

Janine was surprised at how nice Kayla's apartment was. It was not only big but stylish, in an all-I-need-is-a-tapestry-and-this-six-hundred-dollar-teapot sort of way.

Janine walked into the crisp, clean loft. *Minimal* was an understatement. The wood floors had been painted white, and a Pendleton blanket was tossed over a very low, deep sofa. A biergarten table was the only other piece of furniture. She wondered where Kayla kept things like lamps and books. "Great place," she said. "I wasn't expecting it to be so nice."

"Uh, thanks," Kayla said with a smile. She closed the door behind Janine and walked toward the open kitchen. Janine followed her, carrying her portfolio bag, and didn't fail to notice how Kayla managed to make sweatpants and a tank top look so carelessly chic.

"I didn't mean it like that," Janine said, assuming Kayla was likely on a parental payroll too. "You're just so young, and it's fancy."

"I rented it when I was modeling. I'm not sure how I'm going to keep it now that I'm old and washed up."

"Shut up," Janine said. "You're a baby."

Kayla looked agitated as she started searching for something, opening and closing the tidy kitchen drawers quickly. Her face relaxed once she found her cigarettes in a small basket on top of the fridge. She tapped the box against her hand and offered one to Janine, but she declined. "I'm twenty-six," Kayla said, "but seriously, I might as well be forty. Not that forty is old," she added quickly. "It's just, you know, it's old for modeling. A lot of the new girls are twelve and thirteen."

"I get it. No explanation required." Kayla was always talking about her age around Janine and then apologizing. Janine wondered what Kayla would do instead of modeling but didn't want to ask. She was more concerned with her feet hurting after the long walk from the subway and wondered if minimalism had eliminated chairs along with bookshelves and appliances.

Leaning against the fridge, Kayla slipped a cigarette between her lips. "I gotta figure out rent. Corey is living here now, but, you know," she said, tilting her head and lighting the cigarette, "I like him but not…forever kind of like."

Janine was relieved that Corey, whom she hadn't grown any fonder of since their first class, wasn't Kayla's idea of Mr. Right.

Kayla slowly exhaled three perfect smoke rings. "He kind of sucks, huh?"

Janine smiled, put her bag on the floor, and happily took a seat on one of the narrow benches Kayla magically pulled out from under the dining table. Janine was surprised at how much she liked Kayla. Young, beautiful people generally intimidated her, but Kayla was eccentric and loopy in a way Janine found irresistibly charming. Like when she'd stood up in class and done an unabashed demonstration of the Smurf dance for Ms. Louie. Who could possibly resist a gorgeous girl willing to make a fool of herself? Not that she'd really made a fool of herself. She was a good dancer.

"What about you? You have a boyfriend?" Kayla asked. She took a seat on the opposite bench. "Married?"

"No," Janine said, thinking of Jürgen, no longer her boyfriend but still pathetically on her speed-dial. They'd been together almost ten years, until Jürgen decided he wanted to get married and have kids, at which point Janine decided it was time to break up. Thinking about the actuality of marriage, of being a mother, had made her inexplicably sad.

She loved Jürgen but not enough to abandon her nostalgic longing for something else, something she couldn't even put her finger on.

"There's a word for that," he'd said lightly, because he didn't want her to feel guilty about breaking things off and because he knew how much Janine had come to love his German tutorials—how succinctly one word in that language could contain so much meaning. It had started years before, when they'd been reading the *Daily News* on the subway and he'd casually noted that Ted Cruz had a *Backpfeifen-gesicht*—a face that needed a fist. Janine had been so amused and delighted that such a term really existed that she'd made him spend the entire train ride teaching her to pronounce it correctly. The word he'd used the day they broke up was *Sehnsucht,* and although Janine couldn't remember exactly what it meant, she understood it to imply she'd probably never be happy.

"Anyway," Janine said to Kayla. "I don't want to get married. I prefer being alone, and I can barely take care of my cat."

"Right on," Kayla said, holding up her hand for a high five. "Marriage is archaic."

Janine was confident Kayla would be married with three kids and a Maltipoo by the time she was thirty-two. "Can I get you a glass of wine?" Kayla asked. She stood and walked back to the kitchen.

"Sure."

"Red or white?" Kayla asked, beaming. "Or Scotch?"

"Scotch?"

"Yeah, Corey turned me on to it. It's yum on ice. You should totally come to our next tasting party."

Janine nodded, touched that Kayla wanted to be friends. She started unzipping her portfolio. "Did you want to go with cat food, underwear, or the dating service?" Those were the choices for the ad-campaign assignment.

"I was thinking cat food?" Kayla said, putting down two gold-rimmed tumblers with ice that had appeared magically from the kitchen. She held an amber bottle. "I already had some ideas."

"Great," Janine said, pushing her work for Soulmates.com back into the stack of pages as Kayla finished pouring their drinks and then disappeared to get her own pages. Janine had had some ideas, too, but she was willing to yield to Kayla if hers were better. She walked over to the window and wondered what it would feel like to be Kayla. She wasn't sure she'd want to be that young again. All that pressure to conquer the world when just getting through the day without drawing attention to herself had seemed overwhelming. She'd wasted so much time, but she didn't really want even an hour of it back.

Kayla returned a few minutes later with what appeared to be a year's worth of drawings. The cat-food-ad assignment had been straightforward: They were to create three mock-ups for an illustrated print campaign for Fancy Feast cat food. "Wow," Janine said as Kayla excitedly unrolled sheets of fully executed colored art proofs.

"I hope you like them," Kayla said. "That you think they're funny or whatever."

Janine realized that Kayla was seeking her approval. Kayla had been working hard to impress her. It was a feeling she hadn't experienced in a long time. Janine felt the warmth of the Scotch. She took another sip and relaxed.

Kayla finished spreading out her pages and weighted the corners with four more tumblers she'd grabbed from a cabinet. The first page showed an expertly drawn cat with its paw immersed in a fishbowl. Instead of a fish, it was trying to catch a can of Fancy Feast cat food. "Clever," Janine said, smiling. The next page showed another cat, equally well drawn, standing outside a Tom and Jerry–like mouse hole and staring at the just visible can of Fancy Feast. *Huh?* Janine thought, but she said nothing. The last one, which Kayla had just started to sketch, showed a cat staring at a birdcage from outside a window. No bird in it, just a can of... Fancy Feast cat food.

"You're a wonderful artist," Janine said and swallowed the contents of her glass in a hurried gulp. Her throat burned. She poured herself another without asking for permission, unsure how to explain the problem to Kayla without sounding harsh.

"You hate it," Kayla said. She pulled her hair off her face and gathered it into a tight ponytail with the rubber band she'd had around her wrist. Her face was screwed up.

"No! It's just...maybe we should go with all cat-and-water themes?" Janine suggested. "Like a cat fishing for Fancy Feast on a boat, and a cat..." She ran out of scenarios. She gazed fixedly at her Scotch, waiting for Kayla to understand.

"You don't like these two?" Kayla stared down at her work.

"I do," Janine started. "It's just, well, unless I've been shopping in the wrong aisles, no one sells mouse- or parakeet-flavored cat food. Canned house bird? I think maybe it's confusing."

Janine could practically hear the spinning wheels in Kayla's brain before the last cog snapped into place and she covered her face with her hands. *"Oh my God!"* Kayla screamed. "I'm the biggest idiot ever!"

"No," Janine said, relieved and feeling slightly buzzed.

"Okay," Kayla said, crumpling up the beautiful drawings as if they were newspaper. "What have you got? And do not tell anyone about this."

"Don't do *that*," Janine said, trying to grab the drawings away from Kayla, who laughed outrageously when Janine accidentally ripped one of them in half. "Shit. Seriously, I like the first one a lot. We could use it."

"Let's just move on," Kayla said, swiping her remaining drawings onto the floor before topping off both their glasses. She drank it quickly, like a shot, then nodded at Janine to do the same. "But first," she went on, pulling out a small drawer from the underside of the table, "we need to get high. Or I do, anyway."

"To forget?" Janine laughed and emptied her glass.

"To bury," Kayla said.

Janine didn't smoke pot but she was having too much fun to say no.

"You're up," Kayla said, handing Janine the joint, exhaling a long stream of smoke into the bare living room, and pointing at Janine's portfolio. Janine took a hit, coughed, and felt her head swimming almost immediately.

Hesitantly, Janine slipped out her drawings. She'd gone with the dating-service option. It struck her as odd that anybody would choose to do cat-food or underwear ads over dating-website ads.

"Do not make fun of my drawing," she said, wondering how she could possibly be this messed up from a hit of pot and a little Scotch.

"Promise." Kayla lit another cigarette. As Janine had expected, it took Kayla a few long minutes to grasp the ideas. The words were there, but the drawings were rough. Janine waited, sipping her drink nervously now, as she watched Kayla process.

The first picture showed what was supposed to be a bar where a gussied-up lady squirrel was staring at a man squirrel with six heads. The tagline said, *Barry wasn't exactly what Mindy was hoping for, but he was Jewish.* In bold print it read, *Soulmates.com—because nobody wants a funky nut.* The second drawing showed a princess squirrel wearing a tiara and kissing a frog. The tagline read, *Anastasia was through making out with Ethan. He was never going to change.* Then: *Soulmates.com— Because you can't change a bad nut.* The last one showed the bow of the *Titanic* with a lady squirrel and the ship's captain looking down into the water. The tagline read, *I don't know, the last thing he said was something about being king of the world, and then I may have accidentally pushed him.* Followed by *Soulmates.com—because sometimes you just need a new nut.*

"You're like a fucking genius," Kayla said, looking up at Janine, who was busily tearing the cuticle away from the nail on her index finger.

"For real? You like it?"

"I *love* it. I mean, this could, like, totally be a real campaign."

"You think?"

"I *know.* Why don't you use some of your, you know, connections?"

"I don't have any connections."

"Well, I'm gonna draw these up and send them to Match or JDate."

"You are so high," Janine said, smiling so hard her face hurt. Kayla didn't seem dumb at all. Suddenly Kayla seemed like the best thing that had ever happened to her.

"Do you want to smoke some more before I get started?" Kayla asked. "I'm psyched about this!" She did a little jig and ran into the kitchen.

"Yes, ma'am," Janine said, marveling at Kayla's generosity.

"I'm getting the bong now!" Kayla giggled.

"Can you draw when you're high?"

"I draw better high!"

Corey got home hours later; Kayla was passed out on the living-room couch, and Janine was lying on the floor next to her. He whistled but got no response from either of them. "Hey," he whispered in Kayla's ear.

"Go away," Janine heard Kayla say. "Sleeping. Need to sleep."

Janine was too exhausted to move, although she knew she probably looked ridiculous, splayed out on the rug with her skirt twisted around her thighs, an ashtray full of cigarette butts on her left, the empty bottle of Scotch on the coffee table, and dirty water from a spilled bong pooling near her hair.

"Jesus, ladies," Corey said. Janine opened one eye for a moment; he was admiring the artwork but assuredly not getting the jokes. Janine had a vague sense of him pulling his phone out of his pocket and getting as close to her face as he could. For some reason, he moved the Scotch bottle onto the floor near her hand. She fell asleep again before she could ask him why.

Bunny

"You didn't!" Bunny cried, placing her hand on her chest theatrically as she pushed open her front door and took in the crowd gathered inside. She immediately saw Sam and Elaine along with a blur of twenty other familiar figures.

"I did, darling," Ian deadpanned, eyes searching the room. He was standing next to Bunny in the doorway. "Happy birthday, sunshine."

"Look at this place!" She beamed, squeezing Ian's hand.

It was a good thing Bunny almost didn't recognize her flat; it allowed her to feign surprise. The rooms had been transformed for the event. Something deeply exotic had been done with the lights, and the entire living area was tented in dark blue velvet. Gold rope drew back curtains on the back wall revealing hand-painted chinoiserie panels where the Alex Katz portrait of her usually hung. The doors to the wraparound deck were all open, and the railing had been delicately and generously dressed with thousands of tiny blue lights. Two long tables were covered in elaborate Garnier-Thiebaut cloths and set with pink dahlias bursting out of mismatched Murano glass vases. Lilac tufted-leather sofas joined the tables. Her large Gerhard Richter painting had been moved and replaced with a mirrored pagoda bar.

Bunny was spellbound by the voluptuous excess. The room was so tacky, it was magical.

"It looks like a Chinese jewelry box. Or like the Artesian Bar!" Bunny practically squealed. "How on earth did you pull this together?"

Ian smiled stiffly. They had been gone for only two and a half hours. Amazing what lots of money could buy.

* * *

Bunny knew that Ian had needed to get her out of the house so the staff could set up and the guests could arrive. Bunny played along, not wanting Ian to suspect that she knew anything was afoot. She'd made it clear months ago that she didn't want a party this year and Ian had assured her that oysters and champagne in the private room at Bentley's would be the extent of the celebration. But when Bunny removed her coat at Bentley's and revealed a brand-new *sexy* Armani dress, Ian's knickers vaulted into a twist.

"And what's all this?" he'd asked, looking wary. His round face colored.

"You don't like it?" she asked. The waiter poured champagne as they settled into a banquette. She took a sip and looked at Ian.

"You look ravishing but . . ."

"But nothing. I wanted to buy something special. I'm seventy years old, for Christ's sake. These arms maybe—maybe—have two more years of airtime."

"I don't believe I've ever seen them." He was staring at Bunny's white limbs with disbelief, no doubt thinking, *How dare she be so thin at seventy?*

"Well, you know I don't like scaring the natives." She giggled, then signaled for a refill.

"What else have you got under there?" he asked, fiddling with his cuff links.

"Absolutely nothing of interest to you, certainly."

"I'd say you're the one who isn't interested," Ian said, a reference to a setup Bunny had agreed to a couple of weeks ago only because Ian had sworn the man was simply irresistible.

"He smelled like chips, and his pants made this awful noise when he walked," Bunny said in her defense. "Christ, Ian," she whispered, "he must have been ninety-nine years old. It might have been a colostomy bag making that racket."

"He is seventy-five, which, dare I remind you, is age-appropriate."

"If seventy-five is age-appropriate, I'd rather die alone. Quite honestly, I can't think of anything more appealing than dying all alone in bed. And I'm happy. Don't I look happy?"

"At the moment," Ian granted, most likely wondering why Bunny was so uncharacteristically cheerful. "So, a younger man?" he asked.

"Stop it, Ian! No man." A waiter refilled her empty glass. "A younger man would only be after my money."

"But you're fabulous—"

"Not *that* fabulous," she said, cutting him off.

There was a short pause while he silently agreed, and then Bunny fell into a fit of giggles.

"What is all this?" Ian finally asked, gesturing to Bunny's dress and never-before-seen arms and décolletage. "Just admit it! He told you," he cried. "Your linty ex-husband told you about the party and ruined everything I've been slaving over for weeks. Have you any idea what's gone into this?" he asked. "What in the name of Jesus H. Christ is wrong with him?"

"Party?" Bunny asked. She was a terrible liar.

"Oh, cut the shit. The new dress, the chippie smile, the willingness to go and celebrate. *He* told you," Ian whined, his voice cracking with disappointment.

"It was an accident, Ian," Bunny admitted. No point in carrying on with an undignified charade. "Sam feels terrible. And he will simply evaporate if you confront him. Just let it go. I don't like surprises anyway."

"I should never have told him," Ian snapped.

"True, but what good is hindsight?" Bunny asked lightly. "Look at Chernobyl, the *Exxon Valdez,* and the rejection of Hitler's application to art school."

"Very funny," he said, sulking. He ran both hands through his hair and massaged his scalp as if struck by a terrible headache.

"What difference does it make, darling? I'm deeply grateful to you." She grabbed his hand. "Nobody will know that I found out. I'll clutch my chest, fake surprise, and Bob's your uncle, yes?"

"Yes," he said, smiling because he had no choice.

"Now fix your hair and tell me exactly who you've invited." She beamed, thrilled she could cut the pretending.

"I will tell you nothing." Ian smoothed his hair and zipped his mouth with his index finger and thumb. If he divulged any details before the party, Bunny's mood might change and he couldn't afford that. Now that her prick son wasn't coming, Ian was feeling very nervous. He could only pray that Sam hadn't told her that Henry had promised to be there. Anyway, as long as she stuck to champagne, Ian felt the evening would be a success.

Bunny did not stick to champagne, and the evening was not a success. Nothing trails fanfare as brutally as disgrace. Once Bunny realized Henry was not there, the party sank like the HMS *Victoria,* nose buried in the silt, any recovery effort impossible. The guests would have had more fun in prison watching *Requiem for a Dream* on a loop.

What set her off? The Frankels brought a bottle of Nolet's Reserve Dry Gin. Bunny had promised herself she wouldn't buy gin anymore, but if someone gave it to her? Well, that was a different story. Besides, it was her birthday. Such an extravagant gift from the Frankels— whom Bunny hadn't even liked until then. She drank her gin as she greeted her guests graciously. She knew she looked wonderful and was in great spirits.

"Where's Henry?" she finally whispered to Ian, who was the picture of empathy as he sat on a sofa listening to Gene Sparrow complain about his current representation. Ian knew Gene was unlikely to leave Conville and Walsh but these were the moments he lived for.

"Henry?" Ian murmured distractedly. He was being ripped away from his prey too soon.

"Yes, Ian," she said in such glacial tones that his nose frosted. "Henry...my son."

Ian stared at her blankly.

"Sam said he would be here," Bunny went on. "When he told me about the surprise party a few days ago."

Ian turned to locate Sam, who was making an urgent dash toward the loo.

"Forget Sam!" Bunny grabbed Ian's forearm. "Where is Henry?"

"He had to cancel at the last minute, Bun." Ian whimpered. "He had some kind of emergency. I'm sorry."

"What kind of emergency?" Bunny asked, registering Gene's presence and releasing Ian's arm with a dim smile. "He's an art historian, for fuck's sake!"

"Maybe one of his students died of boredom?" Ian said, possibly hoping a stab at levity might be welcome. He laughed and looked at Gene, who raised his eyebrows and smiled. He was enjoying this.

"Fuck both of you." She pointed at them, grimaced, then trotted off after Sam, who had double locked the bathroom door.

"Open the bloody door, Sam!" she shouted as she pounded the door and twisted the knob. He finally did.

The party continued uncertainly as Bunny disappeared into the bathroom with Sam. When the door reopened at last, everyone turned away, pretending not to notice Sam standing there, looking like he'd been bled by leeches.

"It's all piss and wind anyway," Bunny announced loudly, reentering the anxious room with an empty glass. "Let's eat."

When the twenty-odd guests finally sat down to dinner, Ian made a toast. Bunny half listened, using the time to evaluate everyone who had come to celebrate her entrée into dotage. Bunny behaved herself through the starters. But by the second course, she decided that the dinner was a forum for her to disabuse her guests of their ideas that they were important in her life or in the world at large.

"I like this one so much better than the other," Bunny said to Gordon Kretcher, one of Thatcher's former chief whips, as she reached over to straighten his marginally lopsided wig. His eyes grew wide but he remained silent. "Alopecia?" she asked, struggling to remember the particulars of his condition.

"Bladder cancer," he answered. "But I'm fine now."

"Of course you're fine. And let's not pretend you weren't bald as an egg before." She laughed, giving Gordon a friendly jab in the shoulder.

Bunny snapped her fingers in the direction of one of the caterers, gesturing for a refill. She noticed Elaine and her face-lift trying to make eye contact with the girl, shaking her head as if to tell her that Bunny's request should be denied. Bunny narrowed her eyes.

"Doesn't everyone think Elaine looks fabulous?" Bunny asked loudly, waiting for the group to look at Elaine and nod in silent agreement. "The sides are a bit swelly," Bunny continued, blowing out her cheeks and holding the air. She exhaled, grinning. "But I'm sure things will settle down. Hard to get the timing just right, I'd imagine?"

"My God, Bunny," Elaine said.

Someone at the far end of the table gasped.

Gene Sparrow laughed and whispered something in Daphne's ear.

"Oooh, Sam, careful now. Keep an eye on Gene with your little wife there." In a stage whisper, Bunny added, "Rumor has it Gene was shagging his son's girlfriend. Quite a mess that was."

Gene playfully raised his glass, eager to let Bunny know he was in on the fun, encouraging her to continue. Gene was a lightning rod for mischief and discord. Bunny winked at him and took another sip, peering over the rim, searching for a more susceptible target. She put her glass down and settled on Daphne, who looked as if she'd spent all of ten minutes dressing for the party. Of course, the subtext of her plainness was that she was much too practical a person to be bothered with the frivolities of fashion and hair dye. Well, Bunny thought, Daphne might be younger than her, but she was not so young that she could get away with making quite so little effort. Not by a long shot.

"Bunny," Sam said in a warning tone, reaching across Gordon and pushing Bunny's glass away from her. She seized the glass with her right hand and placed her left gently on his hand. Gordon scooted his chair back.

"I'm just trying to be helpful, Sam. Gene doesn't mind. Do you, Gene?"

"Not in the least," he said, still smiling.

Sam cleared his throat. "All well and good, but I think—"

"Darling," she interrupted, "remember when we went to Scotland all those years ago?"

"Yes," he said, shifting uncomfortably in his chair.

"What was the name of that town? It was so picturesque. Not that we saw much of it." She laughed and nodded agreeably at Daphne. "If you know what I mean."

Sam stood up, knocking over his wineglass. "That's enough, Bunny."

"Oh, sit down, Sam. Don't be so dramatic." Bunny snapped for someone to clean up the wine. She took another drink as the guests at the table struggled to regain their conversational composure.

"Does he still have a big cock?" she asked Daphne a few seconds later. Daphne gasped and stared into her own lap. The table went quiet. "I suppose he must. We women, unfortunately, just shrivel up," she said, looking at Camilla Frankel, who had, like Bunny, made the choice to age naturally. "Camilla, darling," Bunny whispered loudly, "you should ask Elaine for her doctor's number. A little nip and tuck might help you get through this difficult time with Randolph not working. Well, perhaps not Elaine's doctor, but there must be someone..."

"I think that's sufficient," Randolph said meekly.

"Ah," she said, pointing her finger playfully at Camilla's pocket-size husband. "Do you now, Ran? It's really no wonder Camilla looks so exhausted, supporting the lot of you."

By the time the salmon arrived, she'd called Ian "a gouty parasite with a taste for rugby cock"; her friend Ayala, a famed journalist and aspiring novelist, "a bit long in the tooth to attempt to be a *real* writer"; and Sam "a dusty old junk collector with the prudence of Truman Capote."

"You're just awful," Daphne said, finally standing up to defend her husband. *About time,* Bunny thought, and then she laid into her about the inadvisability of wearing an ombré dress past the age of fifty.

She was merciless, but the quote that made the *Daily Mail* was Bunny's asking the editor in chief at British *Vogue*, "What will you be wearing to the Duchess of Cornwall's birthday party?"—a party to which the editor had, quite publicly, received no invitation. It was at this point that most of the guests excused themselves, some to lick their wounds, some to escape before being humiliated, and most, Bunny suspected, to talk about how sad it was that Bunny Small had come undone. Even Ian left. Bunny was alone with an empty bottle of six-hundred-pound gin, twenty-five servings of banoffee pie, and warm brandy snaps. Even Chef Keller must have slipped out; he was gone before she could tell him the rillettes were too salty.

Hailey

In retrospect, everything had happened pretty quickly after that nauseating "We will always be your mom and dad but we aren't going to be husband and wife anymore" conversation last year. Hailey knew everybody's parents eventually got divorced, but seeing her dad only every other weekend sucked, commuting back and forth from San Diego sucked, and the For Sale sign on the front lawn of her childhood home sucked. That sign made the house look so average, as if anybody other than Hailey could have slipped and broken her arm in the pink shower belting out "Reflection" from *Mulan*. Or anybody other than Jaycee could have been dumb enough to eat the gel air freshener in the laundry room on a dare. They'd spent fifteen joint birthday parties in that yard, sitting at the picnic table eating fondant cake from SallyWally's Bakery decorated with pictures of Elmo one year and Cinderella another year and, last year, a winking emoji. Why hadn't her parents told her that their house was *already* for sale? Nobody told her anything.

"Did *you* know?" Hailey asked Jaycee, staring at the sign as they pulled up the driveway.

Jaycee nodded. Hailey glared at her. She was still reeling from having found birth control pills in her sister's backpack last week while she was rooting around for her math homework to copy. Birth control pills! Jaycee was having sex with Devon Pierce and hadn't even told her. So of course Jaycee knew the house was for sale before she did. Her mom probably told her all the details while they swapped sex tips en route to the gynecologist.

Unlike Hailey, Jaycee didn't appear to be struggling with their parents' divorce, the move, or starting a new school junior year. Jaycee was acing her classes, had seduced the hottest guy in school, was a starting forward on the field hockey team, and had landed a choice role in *Hairspray*. So what if Hailey was having a hard time? Did her mom really think banning Hailey from the play would help her get her grades up? Did she really think Hailey was going to go home and study for three hours a day while *everyone* who mattered was in rehearsals?

Fuck Fair Hills Academy with its Olympic diving coach, its state-of-the-art theater, its stupid cafeteria with its stupid taco bar and sushi sampler. Fuck her sister and her perfect life with her perfect boyfriend and her perfect grades. Fuck her dad for not missing them and for staying in San Diego. But most of all, fuck her mom and her bullshit play and her big plans for San Francisco.

The family rule had always been that their mom never cast them in leading roles so it wouldn't look like she was playing favorites. Never mind that they were both better than almost all the kids at whatever school they happened to be attending. Never mind that performing was the one thing Hailey was actually better at than Jaycee and that her mom knew it. *Good luck without me, Mom*, Hailey thought after Jaycee's hideous preview at their grandfather's therapy session. *Good fucking luck.*

"We're going to really clean house, girls," their father had said, hustling them through the front door before Hailey could ask any questions. He was wearing his cycling gear. She hated seeing him in Lycra.

"The house goes on the market next week. And we, my girls, are having a yard sale!"

"Ugh," Jaycee groaned, making a beeline for their bedroom. Inside they found empty boxes their father had prepared and labeled SELL, KEEP, and TRASH in black Sharpie.

"It's bad enough we're being forced out of our home," Hailey said, flopping facedown on her bed. "Now we have to sell off bits of our childhood for three dollars and under?"

"Just do it," Jaycee said. She was sitting cross-legged in front of their bureau digging through old clothes.

Hailey flipped onto her back and stared up at all her old stuffed animals on the bookshelf. Was she supposed to just throw them in the TRASH box? She watched Jaycee carelessly fling her clothing and then her childhood toys into the boxes marked SELL, dumping her once beloved Calico Critters in there with as much sentimentality as if she were pouring bad milk down the drain. *She's a fucking alien,* Hailey thought.

"Aren't you saving *anything?*" Hailey asked.

"My good stuff is at Mom's. This is all junk." She turned over the tin phone they'd made in fourth grade. Hailey smarted as she watched Jaycee toss it into the trash.

"Done," Jaycee said after forty minutes. She put her one KEEP box on top of her bed and sent a text message to someone. The only things she'd saved were some playbills from school shows they'd done over the years, a few pictures, and an old diary. She wiped her hands on her jeans.

Hailey laughed, disbelieving. "You're done?"

"I'm going to get something to eat with Carrie at Del Taco. Want to come?"

"I can't, obviously," Hailey said, thigh-deep in memories she was having a harder time sorting out. She wanted to crawl inside the KEEP box and take a nap.

"See you later," Jaycee said, closing the door behind her.

Hailey walked out to the front yard holding Peanut, her stuffed koala bear. Her father was arranging boxes on their picnic table.

"You're getting rid of our picnic table?"

"It's a small apartment, hon. No yard and it's not going to fit in your bedroom. Unless you want to sleep on it!" Then, seeing her face: "You okay?"

"I know we've talked about this, but I really don't want to stay in LA."

He sat down and motioned for her to take a seat next to him.

"Can't I live with you? I promise I won't be a bother."

He slid closer and slung an arm around her shoulder. "If you feel like you want to keep some more of your things, I think there's some storage downstairs in the apartment complex. I get that this isn't easy for you."

"It's not about that. LA is so stupid. All anybody cares about is the way you look. I can't connect with anyone there, and Mom and Jaycee barely even talk to me. It's like I'm invisible."

"You belong with your mother and your sister."

"Please, Dad."

He shook his head. "I would love to have you here with me. And in a year or so, we can revisit the subject. It's just not the right time."

"Do you have a girlfriend?" she asked, because it was suddenly so obvious.

"I don't have a girlfriend."

"Then why can't I stay here?"

He closed his eyes for a moment and let out a long whistle. When he finally turned to Hailey, his eyes were glassy. He cupped his hands over his nose and mouth so that when he spoke, his voice was a bit muffled. "I have a boyfriend."

Hailey laughed, mostly because she couldn't think of how else to respond. Maybe he was joking.

"I'm just coming to terms with this myself. His name is Gil and—"

"Oh my God, please stop!"

"I'm very happy."

"Well, I'm so glad *you're* happy! What about me? I'm not happy."

"Please don't personalize this, Hai. It has nothing to do with you. I mean, it does in that I want you to know Gil but...this doesn't change anything."

"Oh my God. You're so dense."

"Hailey."

"Does Mom know?"

"Yes."

"Is that why you got divorced?"

"Well, it's obviously an enormous factor, but our marriage hadn't been working for quite some time. She wasn't happy here, with me, even before. This is better for everyone."

"Are you fucking kidding?"

"Don't speak to me like that."

They sat in silence for a long time.

"You want to come on a ride with me?" he finally asked, pointing to her old bike. They used to ride together every weekend. "It might clear our heads. Then we can talk more."

"No."

"We need to talk about this, Hailey. You need to process."

Hailey shook her head. "Please. Just go."

"We'll talk later." He stood up and kissed her forehead. "I'm here for you," he said, already snapping his shoe into the pedal. "I hope you know that. I'm right here."

You're right here? Hailey thought as she watched him ride down the street. *You don't want me to live with you, you're spending our last weekend in our house on your bike, and you ditched us for a freaking* man? *In what universe are you here for anyone but yourself? No wonder you don't have any patients!*

How was she supposed to "process" that the dad she'd always counted on had been replaced by a gay man in a unitard who was more intent on wasting away in Margaritaville with Gil than he was on ensuring the stability of his sixteen-year-old daughter? And that her mom was so profoundly self-involved that she'd failed to notice that the husband she'd devoted the past fifteen years to emasculating was gay? Or that her sister wasn't even thoughtful enough to hide the fact that she'd thrown the collage Hailey had made her in third grade in the TRASH box?

Alone in the suburban silence of her childhood home, Hailey walked quietly from room to room. The furniture looked naked. She glanced at the detritus of her youth, scattered among the twenty-odd taped-up boxes of things her father had decided were worth keeping. She went into the kitchen and sat down at the wooden table where they'd eaten God knows how many meals together. She traced her finger around a white ring Jaycee had accidentally left from a glass of orange juice when they were kids. Their mom had really laid into Jaycee about that. She'd made her cry over a water ring. Hailey had felt so bad for her sister then. That's when they were still connected, when an injustice toward one of them was felt equally by both.

Hailey stood up to get a glass of water. She ran her fingers across the handles of the knives in the cutlery block and pulled out a pair of kitchen scissors. Then she went into the bathroom.

Hailey started cutting at the crown of her head so she couldn't chicken out, and she kept going until the bathroom floor was carpeted with long blond hair. Looking in the mirror, she tried to steady herself against the swell of nausea, but it was no good. Not only did she throw up, she nearly missed the bowl, sending splashes of vomit all around the toilet. Then she sat down on the floor and laughed and cried and couldn't stop crying until Jaycee opened the door.

"Holy shit, Hailey."

Hailey started laughing again because Jaycee's expression was straight out of a horror movie. She watched as the emotions played across her sister's face, panic melting into anxiety and finally, awfully, settling into sadness. Hailey stopped laughing.

"God," Jaycee said, kneeling down next to Hailey and reaching for her. "Come here."

Jaycee's tenderness struck Hailey in the center of her grief. Jaycee held her sister for a long time while Hailey cried freely, her face soaked with tears and snot. She stared absently at the pink-tiled wall over her shoulder. Jaycee was crying too.

"Oh God," Hailey finally said, disentangling herself from her sister. She looked around at the mess of her beautiful long hair.

"Don't worry," Jaycee said. She tried to catch Hailey's hand before she got up. "It'll be okay."

Hailey walked over to the mirror and inhaled sharply. She'd hock her virginity for a rewind button. She resembled a psychiatric patient or someone from a cult. It so wasn't okay. Looking back over her shoulder, she saw that Jaycee had pulled herself into a ball, knees drawn to her chest, arms wrapped tightly around them. Her head was down, moving slightly side to side. She knew Jaycee was thinking about their mom too. Amanda cared a lot about the way things looked to other people. Never mind that Hailey was troubled—the fact that she *looked* troubled would be completely unacceptable.

"What if I tell her I freaked out about Dad being gay?" Hailey said after a minute. "I mean, that's reasonable, right? That's not nothing. They should have told us. It's kind of their fault for not telling us." Hailey instantly realized Jaycee couldn't know about their dad yet and was sorry she'd just blurted it out without thinking. "Shit—" She started to explain, but Jaycee interrupted her.

"When did you find out Dad was gay?" Jaycee asked nonchalantly. "Today?"

"You already knew?" Hailey screamed, dissolving into tears again. "What the hell?"

"It's not a big deal. It was kind of obvious."

"That's right. Everything's so obvious to everyone but me." She snorted and wiped her snot on the back of her arm. She looked in the mirror again. "Fuck, Mom's going to kill me." Hailey pulled at the clusters of hair springing out of her head like clumped, undercooked macaroni. She sank back against the wall and slid to the floor, supine. Jaycee lay down next to her. They stayed like that for a bit, silent, looking up at the old light fixture in the ceiling. "What am I going to do?" Hailey finally asked. "I can't even run away and support myself as a prostitute looking the way I do. Who would pay for this?" She paused, thinking. "Maybe somebody in, like, China?"

Jaycee shook her head.

"Lebanon?"

Jaycee laughed and sat up. "I have an idea."

"Romania?" Hailey asked as she absently watched Jaycee stand and clear a path to the sink. Jaycee closed her eyes and braided her long hair. She opened her eyes, looked in the mirror at Hailey, and took the scissors off the basin. She positioned them at the nape of her neck.

"Oh my God, Jaycee! Don't!" Hailey screamed, sitting up as she watched her sister's ropy braid unwind and fall like a dead bird onto the bathroom floor. Once the braid was gone, Jaycee went at the rest of her hair without vanity or care. She looked at her reflection and started to laugh. Hailey recognized the particular pitch of her sister's laughter; it had sounded like that when they were kids. She smiled.

"Well?" Jaycee asked, turning to face her, proud. For the first time Hailey could remember, Jaycee looked really, really bad.

"God."

"Now we go to Supercuts and have whatever crap-ass stylist there try to make *this*," Jaycee said, pointing to her head and then her sister's, "look somewhat acceptable. It's not like Mom won't be pissed, but at least she won't know you had a freaking psychotic break."

Before they left, Jaycee carefully cleaned up the bathroom. She didn't even complain about the smell. Then she grabbed two old ski hats from a SELL box, and they ran, laughing and holding hands, to Supercuts in the strip mall on Solano Avenue. There was something totally freeing about the moment, mostly because it was chased so quickly by regret. It was important to stay ahead of it, Hailey thought, even though you knew that wasn't possible. Hailey's heart throbbed with affection for her sister.

Hwan, the stunned stylist at Supercuts, chopped Hailey's hair into a badass punk style. Hailey liked it at first because it made her appear tough rather than insane. He gave Jaycee a pixie cut, which made her look—everyone at the salon said so—"like a young Mia Farrow." Was it that obvious to a middle-aged Korean *man* that Jaycee deserved the Audrey Hepburn treatment while Hailey warranted the Siouxsie Sioux? Was it that obvious to everyone? Hailey tried not to fixate on this. She tried to stay focused on how much easier it was going to be to face her mom now that Jaycee was on her side again.

Hailey would never forget how Jaycee took the blame for everything later that night. Their dad took one look at them, ordered them into the car, and drove them right back to LA. He dropped them off in front of their mom's apartment without a word. He didn't even ask for an explanation.

Unlike their dad, who was too petrified of his ex-wife to venture upstairs, Jaycee was a hero in the face of their mother's wrath. She maintained that the haircuts had been *her* idea. And no matter how many times Amanda demanded the truth and insisted they were both little liars, Jaycee stuck to her story. As a result, Hailey didn't even get upset when their mom texted her (but not Jaycee) the name of the school therapist with the instructions to make an appointment "yesterday." None of it mattered. Jaycee had taken the fall for her.

Over the next few days, Hailey found herself stealing glances at her twin, obsessing about how good Jaycee looked with that pixie. She might even look prettier now than she had with long hair. Would Jaycee mind if she got the same haircut? She didn't think she would. They'd always had the same haircuts when they were kids. And because her sister had always been her best friend—and because she was feeling close to her again—Hailey told her the next morning before school that she was thinking of getting a pixie too. That was a mistake.

Jaycee listened but didn't say anything. She shoved her jacket into her backpack and put on her sneakers.

"What's wrong?" Hailey asked.

"You can't be me, Hailey. Don't you get that? You need serious help."

"I'm not trying to be you. Forget it. I was just thinking about it."

"How about you *stop* thinking about it? How about you *stop* thinking about me? You're like Single White Sister or something. Do you think I don't know that you go through my shit all the time? That you steal my homework to copy? And do you really think I don't know about that selfie you sent to Devon last month from *my* phone? Don't you think he knows what *my* tits look like? Don't you think he knows *I* would never do that?"

Hailey pinched her thigh hard so she wouldn't cry. She'd totally forgotten she'd done that. She couldn't even remember why she had. "That was before—" Hailey started, and then she stopped, realizing there was no excuse. "I don't know. Maybe I thought it would be funny or something. Why didn't you say anything?"

Jaycee rolled her eyes. "Because Devon asked me not to. He felt sorry for you. *Everybody* feels sorry for you. That was fucked up. You're fucked up. Therapy won't help you."

Hailey narrowed her eyes. "Did you tell Mom I needed therapy?"

"She figured it out, Hailey. Everyone in the state of California has figured it out. You don't make it that hard."

"Why'd you even bother lying to Mom about what happened at Dad's?"

Jaycee zipped her backpack and stood up. "I don't know. Maybe I thought I could protect you. I was freaked. What you did was fucking straitjacket-crazy." Jaycee slipped her backpack over one shoulder and walked toward her sister. She stopped a few inches from Hailey's face, so close Hailey could smell the toothpaste on her sister's breath.

Hailey stepped back. "Get away from me."

"Think about it, genius," Jaycee said, tapping her index finger on Hailey's forehead. "I was trying to *help* you."

Hailey waved Jaycee's hand away violently. "I don't need your help, you fucking traitor."

"Good timing, because I'm so fucking done." With that Jaycee turned around and walked out, slamming the front door, never even bothering to look back to see if Hailey was okay.

Hailey stood there, numb.

Janine

Janine chased two Advil with her morning coffee and reread the e-mail Amanda had forwarded from her ex-husband, Kevin. Some long rant about how he and Amanda had both failed as parents and how he couldn't be held responsible for the girls' hair. On what basis did Amanda think Janine had even the faintest interest in her nieces' hair? She barely knew them. Her head was pounding. Days later and she still hadn't fully recovered from the night with Kayla.

She had woken up at four in the morning and slipped out, taking some consolation in the fact that Kayla—draped over the sofa like a wet towel—didn't look much better than she did. Janine felt old. Maybe she was getting the flu. She sipped her coffee, waiting for the Advil to kick in, and opened the next e-mail from Amanda. She clicked on the link.

ANOTHER ONE BITES THE DUST: WHATEVER HAPPENED TO LI'L JENNY FROM *FAMILY HAPPENS?*

When Janine saw the headline, her heart began to beat like a rabbit's. As she scrolled down, she felt the saliva in her mouth evaporate.

She swallowed hard, coughed to keep the sides of her throat from sticking together. There it was. A photo of her, taken from a foot away, passed out on the floor at Kayla's apartment. She had an empty bottle of Scotch next to her hand, an ashtray full of cigarettes by her side, and a spilled bong leaking dirty water inches from her gaping mouth. Her eye makeup had bled halfway down her face. The caption under the photo read *Yikes! Yep, it's Janine Kessler, all grown up, but looks like li'l Jenny still needs a chaperone.*

Janine clicked on the picture. It took her to the TMZ site. The photo appeared again, larger this time, with a little narrative under the caption.

This is priceless. The Greta Garbo of child stars reappears twenty years later looking, well, like your typical washed-up former child star. A source says Kessler is known as a "party girl" who likes to hang out with a pretty crowd half her age. Not that we can blame her. This photo was snapped after a lovelorn Kessler was reportedly rejected by a twenty-six-year-old—wait for it—*woman!*

Janine scrolled back up to the photo. She could make out Kayla's hand touching the floor behind her head. She scrolled back down, reread the paragraph, and saw that there were 211 comments. She knew she should stop, that she shouldn't read them, that she should turn off the computer and throw herself out the window. But she couldn't help herself.

The first comment was from someone who called himself Exlax:

WHO THE FUCK IS THIS UGLY CRACK WHORE?

From Wakawakawaka:

I remember her. She was v. cute. So sad. Drugs and liquor. I hope she finds God before it's too late.

From Toilethead:

Throw this old dyke in with the other washed-up child stars and lock them in a house together. Now that's a reality show I'd like to see. Better yet, throw them in a garbage can and lock the lid.

From Jackster:

You've never had one too many? Never tried a drug here or there? Give her a break. You feast on this because you have no life of your own...lol

From Toilethead:

And what are you doing today, Jackster? Taking a break from the heart surgery your preforming at the hospital? Prepping for your P.H.D. on astraphysics? Your obviously reading this shit to so who the hell do you think you are to judge me?

From Jackster:

I make no apologies. YOU are the loser who can't reconcile the fact that you have to judge people because you have no life. You also can't spell.

From Exlax:

Why are we still talking about this old hag? Get a life. Both of you.

The comments continued.

Janine pushed her chair away from her desk and ran into the bathroom in search of her inhaler. She didn't use it a lot because she didn't really have panic attacks anymore, but there had to be an expired one around. "Where is it?" she screamed, wasting precious air working herself up. An old bottle of her most expensive perfume, a gift from Jürgen, fell on the floor and shattered.

"*Fuck!*" she cried, sitting on the toilet to catch her breath. She tried to slow her breathing through conscious meditation the way she'd been taught. The tightness in her chest increased. The air was filling her lungs too slowly. She stood up and stepped on a piece of glass so large, she could feel the edge slicing into her heel like a dull knife into a Christmas ham. Dizzy from the sight of all the blood, she sank to the floor and crawled into the kitchen for her phone. She dialed Jürgen.

"Hiya," he said in his thick German accent.

"I need you," she cried.

"Janine, you know I can't just—"

"Please. I did something bad. It's an emergency. I'm bleeding."

"Okay, I'm coming," he said. "Don't hang up." He said something in German, and then she heard the voice of his wife, Birgit.

"I'm going to stay on the phone, okay, Janine?"

Janine didn't say anything. Through the pain, she tried to unravel why she was on the phone with her ex-boyfriend's wife, how pathetic it was that she had nobody else to call.

"Janine?" Birgit said. "Are you there?"

"Yeah," she said, surprised that Birgit seemed so completely fine talking to the woman who'd been her husband's girlfriend for ten years. And she sounded so young.

"Janine," Birgit said again. "Just relax. I'm on the line."

"Okay," Janine said. "Thank you, thank you." She panted, feeling the air leaving her body for good. Kitty Fisher sauntered over, examined the scene, sniffed disdainfully, and left the room. Janine was going to die of a panic attack, but she knew everyone would think it was an overdose. She hoped her father would know the truth—that she'd never do that to herself, that she'd never do that to him.

*   *   *

"Just turn it off," Jürgen said, watching Janine from the kitchen she'd hired him to renovate so many years ago. A decade later and he was still her best friend, the person she called when she needed a favor or had good news to share, her occasional cat-sitter. Now her leg was propped up on a tower of pillows he'd made as she stared blankly at her computer.

Janine had been in bed for two days, since Jürgen had brought her to the hospital and then back home. She'd been given stitches and crutches, but moving around was painful, even with the Vicodin. Worse than her foot was the certainty that she could never, ever go back to class now. No amount of Vicodin could numb that humiliation.

Jürgen had come over every day, bringing groceries and cooking her meals. She was grateful to him but she just wanted to bathe in self-pity. His German upbringing was intolerant of such self-indulgence.

"I don't understand your relationship with your sister," he said now, pouring the ravioli he'd made into a colander. "She's a *Rotzlöffel,*" he went on, trying to cheer Janine up.

She looked at him. "What's a *Rotzlöffel?*"

"A snot spoon. A brat."

Janine nodded, the hint of a smile breaking through despite her commitment to being miserable.

"What kind of human being is she, with these stupid e-mails about you getting drunk and some asshole taking your picture? Who cares?" he asked, indignant. "Why is this news?"

"She just wants me to know that the pictures are getting picked up by all the tabloids. That it's not going away."

He carried a plate over on a tray. Jürgen had never understood about the world of fallen celebrity, didn't get that this was just the sort of incident Janine had been so careful to avoid. Maybe there was a small part of her that liked proving something to him, as if her public shame spiral was evidence of her worth. Paparazzi had been stationed outside her apartment since the first picture was posted. Obviously it was a slow news week in the land of celebrity screwups, but still.

Three other pictures had come out in the days since, obviously taken by that asshole Corey, all equally unflattering. In one, he had hiked up her skirt so that the viewer could make out a small patch of her underwear. A big cartoon star had been placed over her crotch as if to suggest she hadn't been wearing underwear at all. Janine read all the articles silently. She was beyond crying.

"Has your father seen it?" Jürgen finally asked. He knew this was the question she couldn't bring herself to ask her sister. Janine didn't think her dad knew. She assumed Amanda's sending her every single feed was her way of letting Janine know how very hard she was having to work to keep it from him. Janine consoled herself with the thought that her dad was in rehab; his access to the outside world would be minimal and it wasn't likely anyone would come bearing bad news. Not even Amanda. She had nothing to gain from upsetting their father. Upsetting Janine, however, Amanda was clearly enjoying.

"It will kill him if he finds out," she said to Jürgen.

"He's doing a good job of that himself," he said, illuminating the absurdity of her family. "He's in a drug-rehabilitation center and *you* are worried about embarrassing *him?*" Then he smiled sympathetically. "Try not to let it swallow you up."

Jürgen had always taken a tone of amused disapproval in regard to Janine's family, as if they were Scientologists or part of some weird Hollywood cult. But even cults had their rules of conduct, and Janine had violated one of the unspoken laws: She'd made a spectacle of herself. She felt the burning shame of tripping on a runway while wearing a bikini and being stepped over by a cooler model.

Jürgen sat down on the edge of the bed and kindly put his hand around her good foot. She closed her computer and smiled at him. Janine wondered about Birgit. She'd been so calm and reassuring on the phone. Had Jürgen told her what had happened? Did she know where her husband was now? Janine wanted to make sure she wasn't causing any more trouble than her phone call might have already started.

"She doesn't mind," Jürgen had said yesterday when Janine asked if it was okay that he was there. "She understands." Janine had nodded. She didn't ask what exactly it was Birgit understood. That her husband's ex-girlfriend was a loser? It nagged Janine that their long history together, tepid as it might have been, hadn't inspired even a spark of jealousy in Birgit.

Now Jürgen instructed her to stay off the computer and promised to be back the next day with provisions for her and the cat. He told her to call him (or Birgit!) if she needed anything.

The moment he left, she reopened her computer and clicked on another e-mail from Amanda. Along with a screenshot of what appeared to be her sister's finalized divorce papers, there was Kevin's rental application for an apartment in San Diego with someone named Gilbert Monk as a cosigner. A roommate? Highlighted in yellow was Amanda's signature on the application. Amanda was her ex-husband's guarantor? Janine felt a little thaw in her heart for her sister. Amanda really was having a hard time—there was everything going on with their dad, the divorce and the move to LA, the girls acting out. And who the hell was Gilbert Monk?

Although Janine had promised herself that she would not call Amanda first, she picked up the phone and dialed. Amanda's cell phone rang and rang. She called her sister's landline and left a voice mail there.

A few hours later, her cell rang. "Aunt Janine?" It was a young girl's voice, packed with sorrow.

"Yes. Who's this?"

"Aunt Janine?" the girl said again. "It's Hailey. I heard your message. Can you talk?"

"Of course," Janine said, undone at how young and sad Hailey sounded. She sat up straight, assuming the role of a necessary person, an adult.

"Can you come here?" Hailey said, as if she were asking Janine to hold the door or bring her a glass of water.

Janine was caught off guard by the directness of the question. Did Hailey really expect her to just hop on a flight to Los Angeles when she was in the midst of a scandal, with stitches in her foot and a cat to feed? "Yes," Janine said without any hesitation. Why hadn't she thought of going to LA? Why not ditch the local paparazzi and never, ever set foot in that cartoon class again? Jürgen would take Kitty Fisher, and she really should see her dad. He probably missed her, needed her. He hadn't been to New York in almost a year. She was being really selfish. And Hailey! How many years had it been since she'd seen her? Eight, maybe nine? The girl obviously needed her too, Janine thought, quickly reflecting on some of Amanda's weirder e-mails. Undoubtedly Amanda could use some support as well.

"Yes, Hailey," Janine said again. "Of course I can come."

Hailey

Hailey didn't tell her mom she'd spoken to Janine. She definitely didn't tell her that Janine was coming to LA. She relished being the one to finally have a real secret, and the upside of not being in the school play was all the free time she had after school. Since her conversation with her aunt, she'd been spending hours watching old episodes of *Family Happens* on TV Land.

"Why do you have any interest in *that*?" her mom asked when Hailey brought up the show in an attempt to broach the ever-touchy subject of her aunt.

"I don't know. I'd never seen it. Aunt Janine was really good."

"Mm."

"I didn't realize she'd been nominated for an Emmy," Hailey said, excited. "Twice. I feel like maybe I could do that."

"Do what? Get an Emmy nomination?" Amanda snorted. "Don't start spinning some yarn around Janine. She's nothing but a cautionary tale."

"But—"

"Don't start with me, now. The show's opening in a few days. Do you have any idea how important this is for me? The San Fran production is just weeks away. How long have you heard me talk about being a part of the theater initiative? So focus on school. Focus on therapy. I get that it's new and uncomfortable but that's the whole point." Then Amanda sighed, as if this mothering thing was just too exhausting. "And after that stunt with your hair, I think we can all agree that you're too emotionally fragile to even think about acting right now. Just let it go, Hailey."

With considerable effort, Hailey swallowed a smart-ass comeback.

"Do you want to end up in a nuthouse and then splashed all over the internet?" her mom went on, unable to let *anything* go. "Living like a hermit with no family, no career?"

"No," Hailey answered, skulking back to her room. She did, however, want to know what had happened to Janine all those years ago. Janine had been a comic genius. She deserved those Emmy nominations. She should have won! All that watching and thinking and Googling got Hailey thinking that if Janine had made it despite being the "uglier" sister, why couldn't she? People thought she was funny too. Maybe she was even Emmy-funny.

Hailey couldn't wait to see her aunt. She'd sounded so nice on the phone, normal. Hailey didn't really remember her well. They'd met only a few times when she was a kid. Maybe Janine would answer some of her questions when she came to town. She'd told Hailey she'd be there soon. "As soon as I'm off the crutches," she'd said on the phone. "I promise."

So Hailey set about the business of being good. She stayed out of her mom's way, got a B+ on her math test that week, even took the recycling outside. When Janine did show up, Hailey didn't want her mother to have a single reason to prohibit her from seeing her aunt. Hailey vowed to be a better daughter, a better student, and, most of all, a better sister. She even apologized to Devon about that stupid selfie she'd sent.

Brimming with good intentions, Hailey headed off to opening night of the show with roses for both her mom and her sister. She felt generous as she settled into the front-row seat. She waved to her mother when she peeked out from behind the curtain and smiled nervously.

The packed audience went nuts after Jaycee did her showstopping number, the same song that had seemed so completely stupid in front of their grandpa in rehab. Exactly when had she learned to sing, dance, and twirl a baton like that? Hailey sat paralyzed. That was the thing about theater—when it all came together, it was magic. Jaycee was magical. It wasn't that Hailey wasn't happy for her sister, or her mom, for that matter, but the applause made her feel that she wasn't worth being noticed, that her place, even in her own family, was in the audience. Frozen in the dark, surrounded by the cheering crowd, Hailey was blinded by how lonely she felt. And this loneliness was laced with the terrible shame that she'd become a nuisance, that she'd burdened everybody with her unhappiness. She didn't know why she felt so bad all the time. She didn't know why she did stupid things occasionally. She just wanted to be appreciated for who she was. When had the accomplishments of her sister and her mom become the yardstick by which she was judged? It wasn't fair. She wasn't like them.

As Jaycee's ovation swelled with a renewed round of clapping, all Hailey's benevolence and goodwill evaporated. Her magnanimity was extinguished by Jaycee's spotlit face, by the idea of their mother grinning backstage, maybe even crying with pride. Hailey ground the roses under her shoe. She stood up and stormed out of the theater before the cheering had died down. It was only the middle of the first act, but she knew her sister and her mother wouldn't notice that she'd left. And if they did, so what? Why should she care about hurting their feelings? Had they ever given her that much consideration?

* * *

The cardinal rule of field hockey is not to hit the ball hard with a forehand edge stroke; it's too difficult to control its height and direction from that angle. But Hailey had grown tired of rules. So on Monday, without the least reservation, she angled her stick and struck as hard as she could in an attempt to strategically wallop Jaycee in the face with the ball.

She missed.

She got a penalty.

And while nobody else might have known the intention behind her foul, Jaycee did. All Hailey could remember next was Jaycee's mouth, tight like a baby's fist, and the sight of Jaycee's hockey stick coming down hard on Hailey's not-as-pretty face.

At first Hailey thought she was dead. Or if she wasn't dead, she would be soon. There was so much blood. No pain. Not yet.

"What the hell, Loehman?" she heard Coach Lindstrom yell as a sea of screaming girls bent over Hailey's body. It took Hailey a minute to realize Coach was yelling at Jaycee and not her. Hailey saw nothing but cleated feet and snatches of horrified faces and blue sky. Callista Cunningham fainted. Jaycee went down on a knee and then Hailey couldn't see anything else. She was blind. Her mouth tasted like ink.

"Oh my God, oh my God, oh my God," Jaycee cried while being pulled away by one of the seniors. "Is she dead?" she screamed. "Is she?"

Hailey heard sirens and the hysterical pitch of the assistant coach's voice as she told the girls to make room. "Step away, miss," the paramedic ordered someone as he strapped Hailey onto the gurney and then rolled her into the back of the ambulance. "You're in the way."

"I'm so sorry. She's my sister," Jaycee said, sobbing over Hailey. "Oh my God, look what I did. *Look at her!* Oh God. Hailey? Hailey?"

Hailey reached up and felt a lumpy mess of sticky, wet cartilage where her nose used to be. She tried to open her eyes but couldn't. What had happened to her face? She was deformed. Not just ugly but deformed. When she tried to touch her cheeks she felt a strong arm pull both her hands away and strap them down.

"What's going on?" She moaned, her panic rising. Her words were being drowned in blood. "What happened?"

"Stay calm," she heard Coach Lindstrom say while someone wiped at her face with a wet towel and a gloved hand scooped something out of her mouth. "Just breathe, Hailey. Breathe."

She tried to protest but she couldn't talk. Her mouth felt like a hot sponge. She pushed her tongue against her teeth and felt nothing but mush. Hailey wanted whoever was in charge to just let her die. She didn't want to live without teeth and a nose. She tried to tell them to just let her die but she couldn't talk and it's not like anybody ever listened to her anyway.

Bunny

"Bunny? Are you there? It's Sam. Pick up the phone. Enough with the self-flagellation routine. The press are hunting me down; you're not returning my calls. Everyone is worried. Henry is worried. Please, Bun. Call me."

"Self-flagellation routine?" Bunny snorted. "To hell with you, Sam. You think I'm *sorry?* You think I'm feeling apologetic? That I give a crap what everyone is saying?" she asked the empty air around her, lighting a cigarette. Still, she had to resist picking up the phone. Was Henry really worried or was Sam manipulating her?

Bunny hadn't left the back rooms of her flat in the days since the party. She hadn't spoken to anyone but Bettina. She hadn't read a newspaper, turned on the computer, or answered the phone.

Ian was the only person that Bunny was feeling a bit sorry about upsetting. He must be furious with her. Well, he should have known better than to tell Sam anything. He should have known better than to count on Henry. He should have known better than to throw her a surprise party and invite Gene fucking Sparrow. He'd get over it. He could patch up his ego with the percentage on her next book, which, she'd just decided, was going to be her last. She was done with Henry Holter. Her hero would go back and shag Violet Winwick, and she'd give him that new H041 strain of gonorrhea and both of them would die from septic shock within days, Bunny thought with a wicked laugh. *Henry Holter Gets the Clap.* "Oh yes," Bunny said. She emptied the last of the gin into her coffee mug, drew on her cigarette, and reached for a legal pad and pencil.

"Pardon?" Bunny heard someone say.

"Dear God." Bunny gasped and dropped her cigarette. She rolled out of the down comforter she'd been coiled up in to fetch it off the floor. "I didn't hear you come in," she told Bettina.

She appreciated Bettina's mute meanderings, but her sudden appearances could be a little startling. Bunny threw the bedcovers aside and stumbled to the closet. She pulled out a bag and an envelope and held them out to Bettina. Inside the bag were three empty bottles to be thrown away at least four blocks from the flat. The envelope contained two thousand pounds for a few days' worth of groceries and gin. She instructed Bettina not to speak to anyone outside the flat and to purchase the gin from different shops, one bottle at a time.

Bettina nodded, taking the empties from Bunny without a hint of reproof. "What about the press, ma'am?" she asked, referring to the lingering paparazzi who'd been camping outside the flat hoping to catch a shot of... what exactly? Bunny flinging herself from the window?

"Ignore them. Pretend you don't speak English. And remember, one bottle at a time. Inconvenient, I know, but I don't need anything fanning those flames," Bunny said, more to herself than Bettina.

"Yes, ma'am." Bettina turned to leave.

"Can you get me some fags too?" Bunny called after her. "Please. Make it a carton." She watched Bettina's uptight little figure walk away.

Bunny made her way into the kitchen and grabbed a bag of crisps and an apple. As she headed back to her office, she took a bite of the apple and noticed a pile of gifts on the round table in the foyer. The party décor, mercifully, had been cleared out at some point. She considered the packages. So there had been a reason to leave her back rooms after all! With a mixture of shame and delight, she set about opening the presents. She rifled through them like a spoiled child on Christmas morning.

There was a lovely little Milton Avery painting from Elaine, a first edition of *To Kill a Mockingbird* from Ian, a bottle of Nolet's from Gene (perhaps he wasn't so bad), and a few books on gardening and some picture frames from those who clearly had no business being at her party in the first place. The last gift was a sloppily wrapped but carefully taped-up box very clearly from Sam. He never had the patience for wrapping things. Bunny had to go to the kitchen to get some scissors. She was so furious by the time she'd finally made it through the bubble wrap and Scotch tape that she almost dropped the gift: the beautiful cloisonné vase she'd admired in Sam's shop. Inside it was a tiny sealed envelope. Bunny opened it.

To My Dearest Bun,

Like all precious things, you've only grown finer with time.

With all my love,
Sam

Bunny burst into tears. "Oh, Sam, you fucking fucker," she cried aloud.

But where was Henry's present? she suddenly wondered, rummaging through the detritus of ribbons and cards, paper and bubble wrap. "Nothing for you this year, Mummy," Bunny said, then she opened the gin and pulled on it like it was a baby bottle. She made a little pillow out of the bubble wrap and lay down on the soft rug next to the foyer table. Gin in hand, Bunny began to relax in her home for what might have been the very first time. She took in the view of the living room from the unusual vantage point of the floor. The midmorning light made the starkness of the place nearly soothing. She wriggled her toes deep into the fibers of the rug and looked at the portrait Alex Katz had painted of her years earlier. It was ridiculous to have a portrait of oneself, she thought, nonetheless admiring how that flat-as-a-pancake face staring back at her was so clearly her own. "You make it look easy, Alex," she said, holding the bottle up for a toast to the absent painter. "I suppose all we artists do."

She was alone with nothing but a bottle of gin and seventy years of feeling sorry for herself to catch up on. She was on her way. She felt deliriously grateful.

A loud scream was followed by the sound of shopping bags and glass crashing to the floor. Bunny flinched but found she couldn't move. Somebody started shaking her. "Wake up, Mrs. Bunny! Please. Wake up!"

Bunny could feel her eyes roll back in her head.

"Oh God, Mrs. Bunny. Get up!"

Bunny was so tired. Why couldn't everyone just let her be? A cold hand slapped her face. It was a pathetic slap, really. It didn't merit a reaction. "Oh God, she's dead!" Bettina cried, and Bunny heard her small heels clapping frantically on the polished concrete floor toward the kitchen.

Bunny wasn't dead but she wouldn't have minded if she had been. She imagined herself in a cozy satin casket being lowered into the ground. The image was oddly comforting. She replayed it several times in her head. Bettina started crying again. What was she carrying on about? Bunny could just make out the sound of a phone ringing on speaker as drawers in the kitchen were yanked open and slammed closed.

"Ian Merrick's office," an officious voice said.

"*Hello?*" Bettina shouted into the phone. "Tell Mr. Merrick it's Mrs. Bunny's housekeeper calling. It's an emergency! She's dead!"

Bunny wanted to tell Bettina she wasn't dead but her mouth wouldn't move.

"Please hold," the receptionist said without emotion.

"Bettina?" Bunny heard Ian say almost immediately. What was Ian doing in her kitchen? That was so odd. "Bettina," Ian repeated. "Tell me what's happening."

"I went out to buy some groceries and I just got home and she's in the foyer, dead!" She paused, sobbing. "I found her collapsed in the entry hall, sir. All her presents from the party have been unwrapped. I think maybe there was some liquor in there because there's a bottle and it's empty."

"The whole bottle?"

"Yes, sir."

"How do you know she's dead?" Ian said urgently.

"She's kind of blue, sir."

"Bettina," Ian said. "Listen to me very carefully. I want you to walk over to Mrs. Bunny and see if she's breathing. Take me with you. Is she breathing?"

Bettina was hovering close now. Bunny could smell her finger under her nose and feel the panting of her warm breath.

"Does she have a pulse?" Ian asked. "Pick up her wrist and feel for a pulse."

"I can't feel anything!" Bettina shrieked. "I'm calling an ambulance now."

"Dr. Slattery is already on his way, Bettina. Do not call an ambulance. Do you understand? There will be even more press crowding around and the doctor will not be able to get in and help her."

"Please, sir, hurry."

"Listen to me, Bettina. Is she on her back?"

"Yes."

"I want you to roll Bunny onto her side. Can you do that?"

"I'll try." Bettina whimpered, set the phone down, and took a deep breath. Then she exhaled loudly and pushed Bunny's body with such force that she flipped right onto her stomach.

"Faack owff!" Bunny groaned, scaring Bettina so terribly she fell backward.

"Thank God!" Ian's voice announced over the speaker as Bettina scrambled for the phone.

Bettina cried, relieved and terrified. "She's alive!"

"Good girl. Now keep her awake until we get there. Just a few minutes."

"Everything is going to be fine, Mrs. Bunny," Bettina said loudly into Bunny's ear, as if she were deaf. Had Bunny been able to move, she would have socked her in the face. "Stay right there. I'm going to get some nice cold water to help bring you back around." Bunny rolled over onto her back again.

A blissfully long silence was followed by the sound of running water coming from the kitchen. Bunny drifted off like a child. She didn't want to wake up.

"What the—" Bunny shrieked as she was drenched in ice-cold water. Her eyes popped open and the room stopped spinning long enough for her to see Bettina standing over her with an empty bucket. *Like a scene out of that terrifying Stephen King film,* Bunny thought, staring up at her housekeeper in her crisp uniform.

"Oh, thank God, ma'am!" Bettina wailed like a child. The elevator bell rang. "Thank God, thank God, thank God."

"You're fwired!" Bunny shouted, but Bettina's heels were already clip-clopping toward the front door and out into the hallway. Bunny looked around at the pool of soaked wrapping paper, the indestructible bubble wrap, the drenched Milton Avery, and the ruined first edition of *To Kill a Mockingbird*. "You're fwired, you're fwired, you're fired!" she yelled after Bettina, who seemed to have lost her mind.

Bunny tried to get up but found that she couldn't. Her skull felt as if it had been hollowed out and filled with sand. She saw the empty bottle of Nolet's. Had she finished it by herself? She kicked the bottle as hard as her leg would allow. It slid quickly down the hall behind the umbrella stand. She felt herself fighting off sleep despite her irritation with Bettina's odd behavior. And where had Ian gone? Hadn't he just been here?

She forced herself to sit up and promptly vomited (to her horror) onto her own lap. Bunny never vomited. The sheer force of the act shocked her so much that she began to cry. "This must be what war is like," she said aloud, resigning herself to the indignity of the situation. She heard a man's voice in the hallway outside the apartment and Bettina whispering hysterically to him as they neared the front door. Bunny forced herself to stand, slipped, and landed face-first in a pool of water and vomit. Then everything was quiet again.

"I can't breathe!" Bunny said, coming quickly out of a deep sleep, relieved to find herself in the comfort of her bed. She closed her eyes and kept them tightly shut against the light pouring in from outside. Why were the blinds open? "Bettina," she moaned. "Bettina!" She felt as if a moose were sitting on her face.

"You've broken your nose, Bunny," a man's voice said as Bunny reached to her face to feel the bandages. "I took care of it as best I could"—he paused— "considering I'm not a plastic surgeon."

Bunny forced herself to open her eyes again. She squinted. Max Slattery, barely recognizable without his white lab coat, was sitting on the edge of her bed. Why was he there? He had on a shockingly inappropriate suede shirt that had obviously been ordered by his American wife from that dreadful Robert Redford catalog that sold clothes to octogenarian cowboys.

"You also vomited all over Harper Lee," a more familiar voice said. Bunny used all her strength to turn her head in the direction of Ian.

"Oh," she said. She tried to summon an apology, but the hammering in her head forced her to close her eyes again.

"How are you feeling, Bun?" Sam said. He was in yet another corner in the room.

"Sam? What the hell is going on here?" she asked, surprised by the pain in her throat and the cragginess of her voice. "Am I dead? Is this hell?"

"Dr. Slattery, Sam, Bettina, Ian, and I have come here today to help you," an unfamiliar voice said from the far side of the bed, as she heard the blinds being raised a bit more. "You're not dead, Bunny, but it was close. You have Bettina to thank."

"Whoever the fuck you are, can you please close the blinds?" Bunny snapped. She sensed the room darken enough that she could bear to open her eyes again. She saw a skinny, unsavory-seeming bald man standing by the window. She looked desperately at the others but they said nothing. They just gazed down at her as though she were a car-struck deer they were debating whether to shoot or call wildlife rescue for.

"My name is Charles Dana. I'm a professional interventionist."

"A professional interloper?" Bunny asked. "I didn't realize that was a paying job."

"A professional interventionist." He smiled as if he'd heard that jab before. "I work with families and friends to help loved ones get the help they need."

"Oh, piss off, all of you," she said, sitting up in bed, wondering why on earth she was wearing a long nightshirt. Did she even own a nightshirt? Who had dressed her? "I don't need your help. I don't need help from any of you self-satisfied leeches." Bunny paused. "I thought I fired you," she said, glaring at Bettina, who looked disturbingly unrecognizable in some kind of matching casual trouser-and-jacket set.

"Bettina saved your life," Ian said, pursing his lips angrily. He was the only one who seemed at all agitated. Sam, Bettina, and Dr. Slattery were calm.

The interventionist moved close enough that Bunny was able to confirm she didn't like his face one bit. He had very thin lips and a ropy neck, like an iguana's.

"People with addiction issues often don't see the negative effect their behavior has on them and others. It's important for us," he said, indicating those gathered in the room, "to help you stop your behavior before you really hurt yourself. Try and think of an intervention as giving your friends and family a clear opportunity to support you in making changes before things get really bad."

"They're already bad," Ian said.

"Okay, then," the iguana said. "Before things get worse."

"How dare you let this happen, Ian."

"Bunny," the interloper continued. "I've asked each member of the intervention team to detail specific incidents where your addiction has resulted in problems. They've been asked to keep it very brief—"

"Well, thank God for that," Bunny interrupted.

"And they've been asked to write down their feelings and read them to you. Remember, this is not an attack. These are the people who love you and are concerned for your welfare."

"These are my loved ones?" Bunny asked, registering Henry's absence. "My maid, my agent, and my gynecologist?"

"I'm an internist," Dr. Slattery said.

"Dr. Slattery is here as a medical professional. He won't be participating."

"Well, I can't wait. Let's start with my best friend Bettina."

"Please, no," Bettina said.

"Ian?" the stranger asked. "Why don't you begin."

Ian stood up from the table, walked to the center of the room like a schoolboy, reached into his pocket, and pulled out a sheet of folded, lined paper.

"You don't need to stand up, Ian. If you prefer to sit and read, that's just fine."

Ian stood where he was, unfolded the paper, and began to read. "'Bunny, you are my best friend. There is nothing in this world I wouldn't do for you other than stand by and watch you destroy yourself like this. When you drink, you take every act of human kindness for granted. You don't think twice about humiliating, demeaning, and demoralizing people. You go after perfect strangers and close friends with the ferocity of a lion. You put me in the terrible position of having to protect others from the person I love most in this world. Do you know what that's like? The consequences of your drinking have taken a toll on our friendship, on your writing, and on the trust your public places in your hands.'"

"Ha!" Bunny barked loudly. Charles Dana silenced her and gestured for Ian to continue.

"'I know that you can beat this,'" he continued, his voice growing shaky. "'You are the most powerful woman I've ever known. But even the lion needed the mouse to gnaw through the netting. I beg you to go into rehab and let real doctors help you fix what you cannot fix yourself.'"

"Rehab?" she squawked.

"I miss my best friend, Bunny," Ian said. He took a deep breath and looked at her. "If you don't stop drinking, we can't work together anymore. I can't stand by and watch you destroy the woman and the career you spent so long cultivating."

"*You're* threatening to cut *me* loose, Ian?" She laughed. "I'd like to see that!"

"Yes," Ian said with no trace of his usual irony or queenly sarcasm.

"Well, let's see who will have a harder time replacing whom, shall we?"

"Please, Bunny," the iguana said, lacing his fingers together and pointing his hands at her. "Your job is to just listen."

Ian folded up the paper, sat down, and wiped away a tear with the back of his hand. Bunny noticed it with a bit of suspicion. Ian wasn't a crier.

Bettina took Ian's place, took out her letter, and drew in a sharp breath before she began. "'I've been proud to work for you all these years, ma'am,'" she started, holding her letter so taut that Bunny thought it might rip. "'I never have a gossip about you to anyone. I'm not one to buzz about, you know. Just ask anyone you like. All I say is that you are a good and fair lady. But lately, you are not good and you are not fair. You have me throwing away your bottles in the alley like a criminal. You send me sneaking around London buying alcohol for you. You have *me* sacking people who work for you! The maid firing the secretary!'" she wailed, fishing for a hankie in her pocket. "'You scold me like I'm a child when you run out of drink or cigarettes. I've done my best, ma'am, but I can't keep it up much longer. Truth be told, I can't imagine working for anyone else, but I can't imagine coming home and finding you the way I did again either. I thought you were dead, ma'am. I've never been so frightened in my life.'" Bettina started sobbing. "Please, Mrs. Bunny, you—"

The iguana cleared his throat as a way of gently interrupting her. "That's wonderful. You can have a seat now, Bettina."

Sam casually waved a piece of paper to indicate that he was ready. He didn't bother opening the folded sheet. He began talking from where he was seated.

"Bun, you need help. The world knows all the wonderful things you are but those of us here also know the hideous things alcoholism has done to you. Your personality changes when you drink. Not for the better. You are a spoiled child who has gotten everything she's wanted for too long. You have hurt me, you have hurt my wife, and, most important, you have hurt our son. You need to go away from here, take a break and get the help you need. You need to reconcile with Henry, who, despite everything, loves and needs his mother. This is something you cannot do on your own. I know how it pains you to be labeled something as pedestrian as an alcoholic, but that is what you are."

"If Henry were so bloody concerned, why isn't he here?" Bunny shouted before the last words were out of Sam's mouth.

"He's angry, Bunny," Sam said. "I'm not saying he's not angry."

"I'm angry too," she said, dissolving into tears. "Stop staring at me!"

"We've arranged a place for you at Directions in Malibu," the mediator said. "Ian feels the British press is too salacious for you to attend a facility in England. It's the very best rehabilitation center of its kind in America and they're well aware of the difficulties of celebrity patients. They understand privacy. And it's a very posh spot. You won't have to do anything other than not drink. There is a car waiting downstairs."

"Now?" Bunny asked, feeling a sudden alarm.

"Right now." He arched his barely there eyebrows as if challenging her. "Your bags have been packed and there is a private plane ready to go. All you have to do is go downstairs and get in the car. The rest has been taken care of."

"It's in Los Angeles?" Bunny asked. "Will I see Henry?"

"That's up to your son."

Bunny looked at Sam. He lifted his shoulders a little as if to say he didn't know.

"What about my nose?" Bunny asked Dr. Slattery.

"It'll be okay to fly," he said. "The cabin pressure may make things a little uncomfortable."

There was a long silence as Bunny got out of bed and walked slowly to the bathroom. She let out a shriek upon seeing her reflection.

"Holy fuck," she said, taking in her matted cluster of unwashed hair, her black eyes, the crusty patches of what she prayed wasn't vomit stuck to her collarbone and along her neck. "Okay," she said, holding on to the sink for balance. "Okay."

"Okay what?" the man called from the bedroom. "Okay you're ready to go?"

"Yes, you motherfucking professional fucking fucker. I'm ready to go."

part two

Zugzwang (noun): *The obligation to make a critical move when one would prefer to do nothing at all*

Henry

"I am the son of the illustrious Bunny Small," Henry Holter said in a loud voice, ripe with mock self-importance. All alone at his kitchen table, ignoring the stack of student papers he had to grade, he was talking to himself again, a habit he seemed to have just recently acquired. "I *am* a lucky, ducky boy," he said with derision, raising his water glass in the air. "She is a *great* woman. Even the queen loves me mum." He grunted, recalling Bunny's being awarded the Order of the Companions of Honour a few years back. "A little late in coming," she'd explained to him on the phone afterward, "but I suppose one can't argue about *when* one becomes a national treasure." Henry raked his hair off his forehead, pulled off his glasses, and buried his head in his hands.

He was having a very bad week. It had started on Monday when his teaching assistant intimated that the woman Henry was dating had been carrying on with another professor. Henry had suspected the affair, but exactly when did his teaching assistant find out? Who else knew? Not that he should have been surprised about Risa. Between the fitted blouses and the recent TED Talk she'd given wearing a suede miniskirt without stockings (two million views for a lecture on Alexander Pope!), it seemed that every male academic in America, and maybe a few of the females, wanted to sleep with Risa. That she'd chosen Henry in the first place was, he had to admit, the thing he liked best about her. It might be the only thing left that he liked.

Since discovering the news about Risa, Henry had taken to reflecting on the greater history of his failed romantic life. His unusual childhood as Bunny Small's son had prepared him for feeling quite comfortable alone. Maybe that's why he wasn't preoccupied with human companionship. He never chased women. The women he dated pursued him. It might also explain why every relationship he'd had followed an eerily similar trajectory—a few months of pleasant excitement that inevitably deteriorated into disappointment and bewilderment when he realized that he simply preferred being single to whatever romantic alternative had presented itself.

He'd been flattered by Risa's attention, so he'd allowed his vanity to blind him to the fact that she was not only something of an exhibitionist but also possibly far more interested in Henry's mother than in him. Risa was, in truth, the apotheosis of every misdirected romantic decision he'd ever made.

He still hadn't been able to confront her about the affair, dreading a scene and, absurdly, not wanting to embarrass her. They had precious little in common other than that they were both single, still relatively young, and faculty members at the same university. Aside from the deception, which rankled, he wasn't even angry with her. They hadn't promised each other anything, and whatever it was they were doing had surely run its course. He was secretly relieved to have an out. Clearly she felt the same, since she'd been shagging August Tennenbaum, the knob who chaired the anthropology department and walked around campus in alligator wing tips. Henry had been assuming (hoping) Risa would initiate the breakup conversation. But she'd yet to say a word.

Ian's phone call from London announcing that Bunny would be drying out at a rehabilitation center in Malibu had further soured his mood. Dear God, why couldn't his mother sober up in the English countryside? He was horrified at how close she'd sounded in her phone message yesterday, happily announcing her arrival in Malibu and her wish to see him "first thing."

Henry stood up and fetched a bottle of Pinot, a corkscrew, and a large burgundy glass, all of which he carefully carried back to the table. He poured himself a glass and reflected bitterly on his father's insinuation that Henry's failure to attend the great Bunny's bloody birthday bash had contributed to whatever epic tantrum had apparently occurred. So it was *his* fault she'd landed herself in rehab? Henry had to laugh at that. He couldn't be held responsible. He had a job! Not that his father or Ian or his mother, for that matter, seemed to care.

No matter how far he fled, he failed to escape the long shadow of Bunny Small. Just that morning at the ENT's office, the new nurse had called out his name from the door and he'd had to endure the looks and laughter that ensued. Why had his mother named that ridiculous character after him? If only his father hadn't been so hurt at the prospect of Henry changing his last name on his twenty-first birthday. He'd had tears in his eyes, for God's sake!

The nurse had appraised Henry en route to the exam room. "Really? Henry Holter?" she'd asked with an arched brow, as if he'd made it up to be clever. Then Dr. Zimmerman had informed Henry, in no uncertain terms, that his hearing aid was no longer a viable alternative to the ear surgery he'd been putting off—a procedure necessitated by too many untreated ear infections as a child. He was terrified of the prospect and agitated at Dr. Zimmerman's suggestion that he stay out of the pool until after the operation. How on earth would he manage his mother without the catharsis of his evening swims?

How well Henry remembered the innumerable nights he'd stood outside his mother's study when his father was traveling, off hunting for antique treasures around the world and, no doubt, enjoying a reprieve from his exhausting spouse. Henry had been petrified of disturbing his mother's "creative process" but unable to endure the relentless throbbing in his right ear. He recalled her put-upon sighs as she shooed him off to bed with half a Valium, two baby aspirin, and a perfunctory kiss so she could get back to work.

Henry was staring at his papers in a stupor, wondering at the injustice of it all, when he heard the sound of a key turning in the front door. Risa. Had she told him she was coming over tonight? He clenched his teeth and pretended to be engrossed in his work.

Now that she was here, he'd have to do the thing. He couldn't wait. Not with his mother in town. *Don't get drawn in,* he told himself. *Just do it.* He couldn't stomach two unhappy women, two failed relationships. He took a breath, bracing himself.

"Henry?" Risa called. "Hello?" Her dark curly hair was loose, spilling down the back of her snug, silky blue blouse. Her skirt was typically short. "My day was crazy," she said, smiling at the unexpected bottle of wine. She pursed her full lips, always painted the color of ripe tomatoes, as she poured herself a glass. After slipping off her heels, she sat down on the chair beside him and began to massage one perfectly manicured foot. Henry stared, turned on despite himself. How he loathed his baser instincts, his superficial side. He cleared his throat. "We should talk," he said.

"You know that Quentin Mayer kid?" she asked, ignoring his comment. "The PhD candidate I told you about?"

Henry knew exactly where this was going.

"He tried to kiss me," she said. "At least, I think that's what that was." Risa went on to describe the play-by-play of Quentin Mayer's declaration of desire. Henry was only half listening. Men were constantly hitting on Risa and she was constantly dashing home to report the events to Henry and complain about the general burden of being so attractive. Did she hope he'd be impressed? Jealous? She really should have the grace to be the one to end things between them. Why make him do the work?

"What do you think?" she asked, peering at him seductively over her wineglass.

"About?"

"Quentin Mayer."

"I think maybe you should button up and let your hem down if you don't want your students or your therapist or the valet outside of Whole Foods to get the wrong idea."

"I sure as hell hope you're not implying that it's my own fault that I'm harassed."

"Of course not," he said, flustered. But he *was* suddenly angry about August, too angry to let it go. Despite everything, Henry was a monogamous man, and although he realized he was getting sidetracked, he went on, unable to resist. "You know, if you're so put out by the onslaught of male attention, you might turn off your light."

She moved her chair closer to him and began, maddeningly, stroking his hair. He felt tense with irritation. As if the bestowal of her focused attention would neutralize her crimes. As if all would be forgiven. "My light is *not* on," she said.

"Okay," he said. "It's not on." He glanced at her silk shirt, stretched tight across her breasts, and imagined her rolling around in bed with August Tennenbaum. "A nice cardigan might function as a dimmer, though."

She slid her chair back and narrowed her eyes.

"I'm sorry," he said, knowing his approach was all wrong, stepping back from the edge. "My mother's arrived. It's been a bad day."

Henry chose not to mention the trip to the ear doctor. Risa would not be sympathetic about his needing surgery or the fact that he couldn't swim his daily laps at the pool. But anything involving his famous mother fascinated her.

"Your mom is here? In LA?" Her face was alight as she leaned forward, her elbows on the table.

Henry picked up a pen and started spreading the student papers out as if he were making a paper barrier between himself and her barrage of questions. He'd always wondered if Risa's interest in him had more to do with his last name than with anything else. Her appetite for prestige, for celebrity, would be hard to satisfy in academia. But if she was tied to Bunny Small, however frayed the string, that might be just the ticket.

"Are you going to see her?" Risa asked.

"Tomorrow."

"I'll go with you. I'll cancel my classes."

"No."

"Let me support you in this, Henry. I want to. What can I do? Should we have her for dinner? I can make the walnut chicken with the cherry sauce."

"She's in a rehabilitation facility, Risa. I don't think they let her out for dinner parties."

"Well, I want to do something."

"Why are you always so interested in my mother?" he asked, putting down his pen. "I understand the global obsession with celebrity, but why are *you* so interested in her?"

She paused for a moment before answering. "She's fascinating, of course. But this is about you. Whatever I can do for you."

"Bollocks," he said, his anger triggered by her blatant hypocrisy. Risa had as much interest in extending herself to help him as she did in stopping the onslaught of male attention brought on by her sartorial choices. Dread washed over him immediately. There was no turning back.

"I think it's time we went our separate ways," he said. He hadn't intended to sound so curt, but he felt a welcome relief now that he'd finally said it.

"What?" She looked at him and laughed. "Is this about our conversation the other night?" She'd decided they should discuss her moving in, since she spent two or three nights a week at his place anyway. Henry had been mystified, considering the August Tennenbaum information, and he'd quickly changed the subject. "It wasn't a marriage proposal, Henry. You really are the most commitment-phobic man. Forget I mentioned it."

"It's not about that. Look, I know you like the *idea* of me, but I'm fairly certain the real me doesn't quite come up to scratch. I'm too"— he paused, searching for the right word—"*introverted*. This isn't going anywhere. You need more. You deserve more."

"No. I love you, Henry."

"Love me?" He raised his eyebrows, stunned. "We don't get on, Risa. I don't think you even particularly like me."

"Don't tell me how I feel. I fucking love you."

"You see, the thing is," he went on, finding the courage to finish the conversation now that he'd started it, "I know about August."

"Nothing happened," she said too quickly. She stood up and started pacing. Her eyes filled with tears. She swallowed. "Please, Henry."

"I understand. You don't have to explain anything to me."

"But I want to." Her face was flushed.

"It's not necessary. Let's not do this."

"It was just the once."

"You just said nothing happened!" he said loudly. What rubbish! Risa didn't love him.

"It just sort of happened. It didn't mean anything."

"The thing is, it means something to me. I only brought it up because you wouldn't have done it if you liked me, let alone loved me. We're simply not suited. It's all right."

She was still for a moment, as if collecting her thoughts, preparing her case. Then, pouting her lips, almost pleading: "I never know where you are, Henry. It's like everything I say gets on your nerves. You just sort of lock yourself away and there's no access. I need to know I'm appreciated."

"Appreciated?" he asked, grasping for his outrage amid the threat of her emotional manipulation. "Appreciated how, exactly?"

"I don't want to be with Gus. I want to be with you. Long term," she said, as if he might be flattered.

Gus? Was she serious? He shook his head. "It won't work, Risa. We're a mismatch."

She looked at him in disbelief. Then she laughed. "So *you're* break-ing up with *me?*"

He didn't say anything. It was an awkwardness that had to sit. She marched into the bathroom. He could hear her gathering some of her things. "You're like Meursault," she said, returning. She pointed her toothbrush at him like a handgun. "You think indifference will pro-tect you from suffering."

Now it was Henry's turn to laugh. Risa couldn't discuss their rela-tionship without bringing up Camus. The woman taught eighteenth-century literature, for God's sake; she clearly had no business dipping into the twentieth-century canon.

"You can't escape emotional pain, Henry. You can't go around act-ing like you exist outside the rules of civility and thinking it's okay."

"You're the one who screwed August Tennenbaum," he said, hating himself for saying something so trite. "And *I* exist outside the rules of civility? It's something, the way you've managed to make me the ass-hole here."

"You are the asshole here."

She threw her toothbrush, a compact, Vaseline, and some medica-tion into her purse. "You can't choose to block people out because you're afraid of getting hurt. You're like a hedgehog. Afraid of inti-macy."

Her barrage of bad similes was rankling. "Why don't you stick with Pope and Swift," he snapped. He felt guilty for upsetting her, but it wasn't as though anybody gave lessons on how to end a bad relation-ship with grace.

"Fuck you, Henry. This is about your fucked-up relationship with your mother. You're going to regret this. I'm a catch, Henry. Take a good look." She flung open the front door and turned to him. She had black mascara ringing both eyes. "Good luck finding someone willing to put up with your shit."

Henry kept his mouth shut.

"Fuck you," she said again and slammed the front door behind her.

He was still sitting at the table, contemplating the silence, when the door opened again.

"I forgot my bag," Risa said. She stopped to look at him, perhaps allowing him a moment to change his mind. He made no move to get up.

"Fuck you!" she said a third time, picking up her purse. On her way out she snatched a lovely little pre-Columbian figure from the bookshelf and threw it across the room. It shattered into a thousand pieces. Henry gasped. Risa knew he loved that statue. He'd bought it at auction with his father, a museum-quality ceramic Mesoamerican corn goddess. She'd survived five hundred years only to be destroyed by a hysterical assistant professor of English.

After Risa left, Henry cleaned up the shattered remnants of the statue and dumped them into the garbage. That seemed wrong, so he dug out the larger shards and put them in an old cookie tin. At some point he'd bury them or scatter the remains somewhere fitting. It was the least he could do. Henry went to the bookshelf and moved some books over the area where the figure had been. Tomorrow he would drive to Malibu and visit his mother.

Janine

Janine had gotten in last night and opened the front door of her father's house to the familiar smell of firewood and floor polish. For a brief moment she was reminded of how things used to be when she came home: the barking dogs greeting her, their house-keeper, Maria, running across the yard to give Janine a hug, and her dad...she would see him through the window. He'd be standing in the kitchen, trying to act casual, when she knew he was always too excited about her homecoming to do anything other than pace the floor waiting for her.

But yesterday wasn't like that. The house had been so dark and lifeless. She'd felt like a ghost, or at least like she was surrounded by ghosts, standing alone in the cold hallway with her suitcase. No dogs, no Dad, no Maria. She'd crawled right into her old bed, not even bothering to shower or unpack.

The relentlessly bright California sun woke her early the next day, illuminating the familiar contours of the bedroom she'd moved into full-time after her mom died. She lay in bed, mentally preparing her-self to visit her dad in rehab. When she finally got up, she opened the blinds en route to the bathroom, and the sight of the backyard hit her hard. The scene was almost supernatural. The once lush and colorful landscape was a dry and withered tangle. Stepping out through the glass door, Janine tried to absorb the level of decay. Why hadn't anybody told her how bad it was, how sad it was? Or maybe someone had tried to tell her and she hadn't been listening.

Working in the yard had long been her father's therapy, an escape from poor box-office numbers, nagging ex-wives, calls from the office. Sandro did the heavy lifting—the mowing, raking, irrigating, and fertilizing—but Marty was the beating heart. The glory of his garden was a reflection of how demanding his job was at that moment; the higher his stress levels, the more fully his weekends were occupied by the immediacy of weeding, pruning, and planting. The giant eucalyptus trees that shaded a sea of yellow barberry, the clivia brightening the understory of three giant palms, the potted cacti that framed the pool, and the fuchsia bougainvillea crawling up the barn doors—all these were his pride. Janine had spent countless hours watching him tool around outside, trailing after him as he watered, clipped, and planted. Sometimes he explained about the plants; more often he just happily listened to her chatter.

When had her father stopped taking care of things? He hadn't been at Directions *that* long. And she couldn't help but be irritated by Sandro's neglect, despite how bad she felt for him in the wake of Maria's death. A few months back, her father had told her (once it became clear that Sandro was too depressed to work) that Gail had hired a Japanese gardener to take over. Sandro didn't want to work, but he certainly didn't want anybody else doing his job either. He'd chased that Japanese gardener around with a BB gun until the man had driven off, never to be heard from again. Marty found the story wildly amusing; Gail found it less so. She had thrown up her hands and ceded the yard to Marty's "misplaced sense of loyalty."

Janine was relieved her father was still faithful to Sandro. Marty had always been susceptible to the women in his life, but Gail's emotional manipulation was so complex that he actually believed he was lucky to have her. Janine didn't like to think about how much her father had changed since he'd started seeing Gail, how easily he'd set aside his moral compass when his girlfriend didn't like the direction it was pointing. That he hadn't fired Sandro, despite everything, was a good sign.

Janine scanned the garden now for any evidence of Sandro. All she saw was a plate of half-eaten cat food on the outdoor dining table. At least he seemed to be feeding Roger, her father's cat. Stepping back inside, Janine considered her options for the day. Visiting with her nieces was off the table. She had finally called Amanda from the airport in New York yesterday, but Amanda hadn't picked up. Janine left a message, but when her plane landed in LA, she'd received an e-mail from her sister making it clear that she wouldn't be seeing Jaycee and Hailey anytime soon. The girls had watched her little cameo on TMZ, Amanda had written. *Hailey seems to have spun some fantasy world around you, and while I'm hoping her hallucinations are a side effect of the pain medication, I obviously have to take every precaution to protect her.* With that—and without any explanation of why Hailey was on pain medication—Amanda had signed off, saying that she'd see Janine "without the girls" at their father's birthday dinner, a week from Saturday.

Janine was annoyed and disappointed. Not only would she have liked to see the twins, but she thought Amanda might have some insight into the state of the yard—what it meant, how long it had looked that way. Janine had never been able to deal with the hopelessness of things falling apart. Maybe that's why she'd stayed in New York. In Manhattan, at least, the evidence of the passage of time felt natural, not criminal. The city never deteriorated in an obvious way, and the old people seemed oddly content. Janine liked seeing them on the bus, braving the elements to go to concerts at Lincoln Center, enjoying dinner at the local diner. Like the models and the businessmen, the homeless and the handicapped, the elderly were essential to the city's landscape. LA was different. The closest thing to elder respect in LA was when an actor received an Academy Award for

lifetime achievement at the Oscars. And even then, the producers invariably had the old-timer wheeled offstage midspeech, knowing the
audience needed to see Jennifer Lawrence again before their anxiety
over their own mortality ruined the evening.

So it really was no surprise that as soon as her father retired, as
soon as the spotlight shifted, Los Angeles had no use for him. Once
the phones stopped ringing and the meetings ceased, once the maître
d' no longer had a table for him, Marty was left with nothing to do
but convince himself that he didn't care, that he didn't mind the long
empty hours.

Janine lay back down on her bed, curled herself into a ball, and
reluctantly considered the silence. Perhaps her favorite thing about
Manhattan was the general chaos. It kept her from getting trapped
in her head and revisiting the phantoms of her childhood. But the
smell of eucalyptus paired with the muted purr of LA—a Pavlovian
trigger—invariably pitched her back to those days. Most of her memories were painted in broad strokes now, but the details of the
afternoon her mother died were so finely etched, Janine could trace
every line.

It came back to her now: The sound of her flip-flops slapping the
floor as she ran into her mom's house, late after her swim lesson, hoping Pamela wouldn't be angry. She'd been so desperate not to drain
Pam's limited maternal generosity with a stupid mistake like being
late. Her silver Emmy dress with the crystal sweetheart neckline was
carefully laid out on the dining-room table. But nobody was home.
There was no note. No blinking light on the answering machine. Janine had walked through every room, calling her mom, wondering if
there had been some mix-up. Was she supposed to meet her mother
at the tailor's? But the dress was here, so that couldn't be right. Pam's
Mercedes wasn't in the garage. Janine had quickly showered and put
on a lace blouse she hated but that her mom had given her the year
before. She walked through the rooms again, breathing in the stale
smell of cigarettes and popcorn, as if maybe she could have over-

looked her mother the first time. She'd finally called Maria to pick her up and take her to the tailor's before they closed.

Pamela didn't show up at the fitting. Janine figured her mom had simply forgotten and gone to an aerobics class or to see a double feature, or maybe she was with Randy, the latest loser in her diminishing pool of suitors. Or possibly she was in one of her creepy moods, in which case Janine preferred to be with Maria anyway. Those moods had been more frequent of late, signaled by the peculiar flatness in her mother's voice as she talked about her crackpot business ideas or went on long rants about the injustices of aging. Pam would say *Logan's Run* was her all-time-favorite movie. She was taken by the idea of dying before she got "old and ugly."

Janine had been joking around in the car with Maria when she found out. The phone rang. It was a novelty to have a phone in the car back then, and the contraption was giant, the size of a man's shoe. Her dad had had it installed because Maria was usually the one conveying Janine to the set, to the pool, or back and forth between her parents' houses. "Hi, Dad!" she said, always happy to hear from him, to talk about nothing. But his voice was somber and he'd immediately asked to speak with Maria. Without even hearing the conversation, Janine knew that her mother was dead. She made herself rigid. Maria pulled the car over and wept.

At the time, Janine had conceived of the suicide as her mother's way of ensuring that Janine didn't get to go to the awards ceremony. It was the kind of thinking only a fifteen-year-old girl could come up with, but it felt true just the same. When she thought back to that afternoon, she always remembered how still the house had been and how uncomfortable the blouse had felt buttoned high around her neck. She recalled staring at the dashboard of Maria's car, feeling not grief or sadness but guilt and relief.

She still wondered what kind of person felt that way, what sort of daughter. Her therapist at McLean had tried to explain that experiencing relief at the death of a difficult parent was normal, but Janine didn't believe him. She should have been devastated; in fact, she felt she should have kept it from happening in the first place. It wasn't as if she didn't know her mother was depressed. Even though Janine was only fifteen, that much was clear. Her mom had taken to spending entire days watching TV and smoking cigarettes. She ate nothing but Jiffy Pop.

Now here she was, twenty-five years later, feeling every bit as useless as she watched her father spiraling down through his own slower, more insidious self-destruction. She looked out the window again at the overgrown backyard. She stood and got dressed for the day.

The kitchen was spotless, and there was ground coffee. She brewed a cup and poured it into one of the Italian mugs she had bought with her father on a trip to Rome years ago. Then she scalded her tongue. There'd been no milk or cream in the fridge, and the freezer held only pints and pints of half-eaten Ciao Bella pistachio gelato.

She'd go to the market right away. God knew, she was in no rush to get to Directions. There was nothing like visiting her dad in rehab to illuminate how far he'd fallen in the world. Every stint at rehab, Janine knew, confirmed Marty's fear that he was no longer essential, that in getting old, he'd become useless. She had to brace herself for the way he'd look at her almost confusedly for a minute, disappointed that she was no longer twelve—not because he loved her less for growing up, but because he'd liked *himself* so much more when she was young.

Henry

Henry woke to a series of chillingly hostile texts from Risa. He stopped reading after she accused him of never being the man his mother was. He couldn't argue with her there.

He was expected at the rehab facility at eleven o'clock. Had it not been for the evening with Risa, he couldn't have imagined a less agreeable activity. Certainly he wouldn't be engaging in whatever New Age therapy they were spooning out. He'd say his hellos and make a dash for the exit. If he'd learned one thing in his youth, it was that nothing good ever came from trying to have a real conversation with his mother. Keeping a detached air and a few thousand miles between them was the key.

He found his Subaru transformed in the carport. The windshield wipers had been broken off and the word *A-hole* was scrawled (in Risa's handwriting, with her Sensodyne toothpaste) across the glass. Risa wasn't one for brevity, so she must have been running out of toothpaste and figured abridgement was required. Nice to think that, if nothing else, her teeth were sensitive.

Henry set his coffee cup on the roof of the Subaru and went to get paper towels and Windex. Of course he wished he'd handled things better but he didn't regret the split, especially when he returned and discovered the difficulty of removing toothpaste (and what appeared to be a thick underlayer of petroleum jelly) from window glass. He did the best he could.

As he was finally backing out of the driveway, he realized he'd forgotten the coffee, which toppled off the Subaru's roof and spilled down the windshield. How astonishing that the day could be off to such a shit start and he hadn't even seen his mother yet.

The drive to Malibu was interminable. Over an hour later, his GPS seemed to be directing him curiously close to the Getty Villa. Not that he wouldn't prefer to spend the afternoon ambling through that glorious Roman estate, admiring the art of Greece, Rome, and Etruria. *Dear God!* he thought, panicked. What if the Getty had been turned into a rehab center for the rich and famous? That seemed just the sort of thing someone would do these days. Very few people went to museums in LA, but everybody went to rehab. Etruscan antiquities didn't stand a chance.

The GPS directed him past the Getty, and, relieved, he kept going. After a series of hairpin turns, he landed in front of an imposing iron gate with the words SOBRIETY IS FREEDOM emblazoned across the upper half. An odd choice, he thought, one that couldn't help but remind him of ARBEIT MACHT FREI on the gates of Auschwitz. He wondered briefly if this was all some sort of a joke when the gates opened and he saw an architectural atrocity that made Gaudí look like a minimalist. The smattering of fountains and waterfalls was offset by an assortment of grassy knolls and a large circular driveway. The building itself was enormous. A Mediterranean Revival style with a nod to the Chinese apparent in its hip-and-gable roof. A valet in white shorts was helping a woman with cropped brown hair get out of a red Honda Civic. Henry took a deep breath.

"Are you visiting or checking in?" another valet asked Henry. His name tag read TODD.

"Visiting," Henry said in a loud voice.

Todd looked askance at the sludge on Henry's windshield before directing him to the main lobby.

People in bathrobes and leisurewear populated the sunny main atrium. The staff wore uniforms like Todd's, white shorts and polo shirts with name tags. Henry's gaze was drawn to an old man in a wheelchair having coffee. Was he an addict? A barefoot girl in a sundress came running through the lobby holding a tennis racket. She looked all of fifteen.

The woman he'd seen get out of the Honda was standing in line at a reception desk. He took his place behind her while a jumpy young man, dressed in a tank top and shorts, hopped into the line after him. The woman was wearing baggy blue jeans and a man's shirt, loose around the collar, so Henry could see her long necklace disappearing down her back.

The man behind Henry reached over him and tapped the woman on the shoulder. "Hey, do I know you?"

She turned to him, surprised. "I doubt it."

"You're Jenny Bailey."

She turned back around and stared at the floor. "No."

"Yes, you are," he said, maneuvering forward so that he was standing in front of her. He waved his finger playfully. "I remember you. You were on TV." He grinned idiotically.

Henry pretended to be reading a text on his phone. He turned it off, slipped it into his pocket, and began cleaning his already pristine glasses with his shirt.

A woman whose name tag read CORNELIA approached them at a fast clip. "What are you doing here, Doug? We've had this conversation. So many times."

"I'm just fuckin' around," he said and laughed. "Remember her, Cornelia? It's Jenny Bailey. What's your real name, Jenny Bailey?"

The short-haired woman looked at Cornelia, accidentally catching Henry's eye. He yawned, feigning a lack of interest.

"I'm very sorry," Cornelia said to her with an apologetic grin. "Are you checking in?"

"No, I'm here to see my father."

Henry nodded and raised his hand as if to indicate that he and Jenny Bailey had something in common.

They all looked at him.

"Well, no, I'm not here to see her father," he said. "I'm here to see my mother."

"And I thought you were just eavesdropping," she said. Doug laughed at that.

Mortified, Henry began fiddling with his glasses again.

"Sorry about the confusion," Cornelia said. "The visitors' check-in desk is to the left, just around the corner. Do you have appointments?"

"At eleven o'clock," Henry said, flushing.

Jenny Bailey shook her head.

"I'm afraid appointments are required. You can make one over there."

"But he's expecting me today."

"I'm sure they can fit you in later."

"Okay," she said, visibly irritated. "Thank you."

"Of course. And sorry I don't recognize you. I know I should."

"No," she said. "I'm not... I'm nobody."

"I'm sure that's not true," Cornelia said with a friendly wave, ushering Doug out of the room.

"Perhaps a good thing," Henry said, trailing Jenny Bailey to the appropriate area.

"What's that?" she asked, stopping just short of the check-in desk. She looked at Henry as if surprised to find he was still there.

"Being nobody."

"Oh, yeah," she said with a half smile. "I think it might be."

"Henry," he said, extending his hand. "Henry Holter."

"Bond," she said after a brief pause, not taking his hand. "James Bond."

"Sorry?"

"I gather we're keeping it anonymous?"

Henry stared at her blankly, momentarily distracted by how pretty and unassuming she was.

"Henry Holter?" she asked. "Really?"

"Oh," he said. "Right. That's actually my name."

"Well," she said, turning away from him and walking toward the person behind the counter, "say hi to the Winwicks for me."

"Right." He pushed his hands into his pockets and tried to smile.

Why was it that every failure, every loss, every humiliation could be traced so directly back to his mother? Some men would assuredly say he should get over it, grow up, and move on. Well, he'd like to see one of these men walk up to an attractive woman, offer his hand, and say, "Hello, I'm Christopher Robin, care to dance?"

Bunny

Who needed to drink when the circus was in town? Bunny was having the time of her life at Directions. She loved walking about, staring at people, listening to strangers divulge their most personal details to any available set of ears. And the anonymity! Amazing what two black eyes, a bandage, and a hair clip could do. Nobody seemed to recognize her, or if people did, they were doing a superb job of pretending not to care. Being a writer in Malibu was like being an anchovy at an aquarium—nobody stopped to look at you.

She hadn't attended a group meeting yet, but she'd had a pedicure and a hot-stone massage in the spa. She'd even had a private yoga class on the lawn. The only fly in the ointment was that Bettina had packed for her, so there wasn't a bit of linen or cotton to be found in her suitcase. Bettina clearly had no idea where Malibu was. Judging from the contents of Bunny's suitcase, she must have thought it was somewhere in Antarctica.

"If only they hadn't rushed me out of my flat like some sort of fugitive," Bunny said to Mitchell, the founder of Directions, pulling at the turtleneck of her oversize cashmere sweater en route to the meeting room. "I can't go in there like this. I'm so bloody hot."

Mitchell stopped short and looked at Bunny meaningfully. "I know you're nervous. It's going to be fine. You've got to trust me. Can you do that, Bunny? Trust me to be your guide on the path to healing?"

"Mm," she said, because what response was there to such drippingly Californian parlance? She was anxious about seeing Henry. He was the only reason she'd agreed to come to Los Angeles. She could never understand why their conversations over the phone always quickly devolved into arguments. He was very hard to read with all those miles between them. What they needed was face-to-face time.

Mitchell began walking again. Bunny trotted alongside him. She suddenly felt weak with misgivings. Her bitterness toward Henry had been reduced to a simpering desire for his affection. Whatever grudges she held toward her son never lasted. She always sensed that somehow he had a right to be angry with her, that she'd done something terrible to him. But what? What had she ever done but love that boy?

"It's nice to see you, Mum," Henry said, standing up to give his mother two mechanical kisses on the cheeks. She touched her face self-consciously, waiting for him to make a comment about the injuries, but he didn't. He smiled tightly and sat down. Then he looked at Mitchell, who had taken a seat, and asked, "Are you staying?"

Mitchell nodded. "I'll be mediating."

"I see." Henry looked confused. "I thought this was just a family visit."

"It is," Mitchell said. "A mediated family visit. We recommend a week of family therapy before our guests attend their first group session."

"Mm."

"You look wonderful, Henry. Doesn't he look wonderful, Mitchell?" Her eyes were wet as she settled into the chair across from her son. Bunny felt a surge of pride and affection. She couldn't wait to set things right. "Have you lost weight?"

He nodded. "I've been on antibiotics for my ear for a few—"

"Oh." Bunny laughed and turned to Mitchell. "Henry and his silly ears. He's always on antibiotics for something or other. God knows where he gets his fragile constitution. Not from me, I can assure you."

"It does help to have your organs pickled in gin," Henry said, stiffening. "Inhospitable for bacteria and such."

She shrank away from him. The phone wasn't the problem. Henry was the problem. He was so self-righteous, so quick to accuse her, to attack her. All she'd done was say he looked thin. "Maybe a drink's just what the doctor ordered, then." Bunny narrowed her eyes. "God knows I always thought you could use one."

"Well, it's nice to know you thought of my needing *something*. I was under the impression you felt children were like sea turtles, self-sufficient from birth."

"These must be the sorts of intellectual nuggets one can pick up only in Los Angeles." Bunny looked at Mitchell, waiting for him to step in. "Sea turtles indeed."

"Fantastic," Mitchell said, clapping his hands.

Henry inhaled dramatically as he began massaging a little Buddha head placed in a bowl of potpourri on the table next to him. He exhaled very slowly before speaking. "I'm not doing this with you. I promised myself I wasn't going to get manipulated into a scene, and I'm not going to."

Bunny was outraged. "Do you see now, Mitchell? Do you see the way he just attacked me? He calls me manipulative and then behaves as if *I've* done something wrong. Why, Henry? I was so looking forward to today."

"Oh, me too, Mother. There's nothing a son fancies quite so much as visiting his mother at a sanatorium."

"It's not a sanatorium! I'm trying to get help."

"Ian and Dad are trying to get you help," Henry said in a controlled whisper. "You simply spin this way and that, knocking everyone down in the process. Though from the look of things, you've managed to knock yourself about a bit this time."

Bunny reached for her nose. "You're insufferable."

Henry rolled his eyes. "Please don't weep. You must remember I've seen this all before. What did you think was going to happen? That I would be flattered that you chose my town to desoil yourself in before taking your sparkling personality back to London?"

"I didn't choose any of this, you smug little ass. I just wanted to see you. I never can get it right with you, can I?"

"Poor, talented, capable, helpless Mum."

"Why do you hate me so much?" wailed Bunny. She was desperate for Mitchell to intervene, but he just sat there listening.

Henry squared himself in his chair, ready to face off. "I don't hate you. I'm tired of you. I'm tired of your drama. I'm done falling for your helpless routines. It's not that I don't care, it's that I'm exhausted. You are an exhausting person. I just want a quiet, peaceful life."

"Can't you see I'm trying to get better? I'm here."

"Being an alcoholic is the very least of your problems. You can't treat narcissism. Certainly not in Los Angeles."

"Mitchell," Bunny said, grabbing his arm.

"This is very good," Mitchell said, nodding. "Excellent work. Both of you. I'd really like to thank Henry for being so honest about his feelings."

"And I'd like to—"

"Bunny," Mitchell said, holding up his hand. "Henry is telling you how he feels. Clearly there's a lot of anger, but he's very brave to share. He's helping you, he's helping himself. He's helping us heal here today and I must say I'm impressed."

Bunny sprang out of her seat. "Impressed? You're impressed? I thought you were *my* spiritual tour guide! The only thing he's helping me do is clarify all the reasons we don't get on. It's not me. It's him. It's you, Henry. You are the reason our relationship is so strained."

"Strained?" He laughed. "It's pulp, Mother."

"Yes, well, I see that now." She sat down and began arranging her sweater. "No reason to keep trying. You've made your feelings very clear."

Henry leaned forward, trying to get her attention. "Now you can cut me off, cut me out. Won't that feel good? You can punish me like the bad, boring, uninspiring boy I turned out to be. But here's the catch, Mother. I don't need your support. I don't need anything from you. You taught me not to rely on anyone and I don't. So good job there."

"You're a terrible son."

He was shaking like a wet dog now. "And you were a terrible mother!"

Bunny gasped, feeling as if Henry had slapped her across the face. She'd always suspected he felt that way, but that he'd said it aloud, in front of Mitchell, was shocking. He did look a little guilty.

"Aha!" Mitchell said, obviously delighted. "*Were*. You *were* a terrible mother. I emphasize the past tense here because—"

"Because you think I should forgive her?" Henry asked, putting his hand to his ear as if he were in pain. "We've been doing this a long time, Mitch."

"It's Mitchell," he said with an affable wink. "I think you're very angry. But I'm not entirely sure your mother can be blamed for everything you're mad about."

"I appreciate your five-minute armchair analysis, but I'll stick with my narrative, if you don't mind."

"Why's that?"

"Because it's the truth. You try following a fictional character through adolescence like a crippled shadow."

Bunny moaned. "God. Not that again."

"Suppose it is the truth," Mitchell said. "But why hold on to a narrative that makes you so angry?"

"We can't rewrite history," Henry said, rubbing the decapitated Buddha again. "Or do we do that here?"

Mitchell smiled. "Ever heard of forgiveness?"

A tear belied Henry's hostile position. "It's funny that I keep being asked to forgive her," he said, looking at the Buddha. "I can't remember ever hearing an apology."

"An apology for what? What did I do to you?" Bunny asked.

"Case in point," Henry said.

"Henry," Mitchell began again, "I think you did a good thing coming here today. I know Bunny appreciates your coming, don't you, Bunny?"

Bunny had her face turned to the window. She was straight as a board.

"Bunny?"

"I'm sorry, Henry. I'm sorry if I worked too hard, if I didn't give you what you needed. I'm sorry."

"Heartfelt," said Henry.

"It's a start," Mitchell said. "Can we agree on that?"

"I need a cigarette," Bunny mumbled.

"I'd like to point out how very right Henry is about something," Mitchell continued. "Henry's dead-on about your drinking not really being the problem. The drinking is your balm. *This*," he said, drawing an invisible circle around Bunny and Henry, "*this* is the problem. *This* is where the works starts."

"Oh no," Henry said. "There won't be work. I'm not working on anything. My work is done."

"May I suggest that we cut things short today?" Mitchell asked.

"You read my mind," Henry said.

"Let's digest all this and reconvene once everyone has had a chance to calm down. Can you come back tomorrow?" Mitchell asked Henry.

"God, no," Henry said. "I've got classes all day. No, absolutely not."

"Tuesday?"

"No."

"Wednesday?" Mitchell smiled. "We can keep going. I'm a very patient man."

"Fine," Henry said, standing up. "Wednesday. But this won't be a regular thing. I'm busy. Too busy, too old, and too tired for this. And for what it's worth," he said, glowering at Mitchell and pointing at the Buddha in potpourri, "using the severed head of Buddha as décor is an insulting cultural misappropriation. Can you imagine decapitated Jesus ornaments scattered about? You people should have some respect."

Janine

Janine scheduled an appointment at Directions for later that day, left, and returned two hours later having accomplished nothing. She'd stupidly thought she could go to Carneys and be back in time for her appointment, that her dad would get a kick out of her showing up with a bag of Carneys chili fries and hot dogs. She hadn't been there since she and Amanda were kids. She knew the funny yellow train car perched on the Sunset Strip was a tourist trap these days (maybe it had always been), but she had laughed to herself en route, excited at the prospect of surprising Marty, knowing he'd appreciate having something so benign to talk about. She wondered about that signed headshot of her hanging on the wall between Leif Garrett and Michael Landon. Would it still be there? She realized the old pictures would probably have been taken out of their frames and replaced with images of newer, more relevant celebrities. There wasn't room for everyone. Still, she hoped Michael Landon remained there, grinning, like a relic from an era when thick flannel and smiling were still cool.

As it turned out, her memories of Carneys were as out of date as her memories of driving in Los Angeles. That she'd been clueless enough to think she could get from Malibu to West Hollywood and back again in two hours clarified just how out of touch she was. The traffic was a joke. She'd had to turn around in Westwood, and she still had barely gotten back in time. Now she was starving and even more irritated than she'd been when they'd sent her away. At least she'd made it. She was given a visitor's badge at the reception desk and handed off to a friendly woman named Sheila, a short, round blonde with a thick Southern accent.

"Your dad talks about you a lot," Sheila said as she led Janine down a long tiled corridor. Directions seemed more like a spa than a rehab facility. It was certainly nicer than the other rehabs she'd visited.

Janine couldn't help looking around for that English guy from the morning. He was cute, with that shaggy hair and glasses. She liked his accent and the way he held eye contact with her. But what a jerk with the Henry Holter routine. Was that supposed to be funny?

"Your dad is just so excited you're here," Sheila continued as she opened a door to an all-white room. A sliding glass door looked out onto a portico with a fountain and a statue of a peaceful-looking Buddha. Janine felt herself relax a little as she took a seat. Maybe she'd get one of the little heads in the gift shop. Directions probably had a gift shop.

"He'll be right in," Sheila said.

"What's with all the Buddhas?" Janine asked, not wanting to be alone.

"Oh. Buddha symbolizes self-perfection and the four truths," Sheila said. Her Southern accent was at odds with the academic rhetoric she'd clearly committed to memory. "Life is full of suffering. Suffering is caused by craving. Suffering will cease only when craving dies . . ." Sheila sighed. "I forget the fourth truth." She looked distraught at not having successfully delivered Buddha's message.

"Sounds hard," Janine said.

Sheila shrugged. "It's good to aspire, I guess. I try and apply the truths to my fitness routine and diet, and I always fail. I just love carbohydrates. French fries, pies, chips."

"Who could possibly live without desire?"

"Buddha," Sheila said. "I bet he didn't crave his grandma's cheese grits."

"No." Janine laughed. "Probably not."

Sheila waved and turned to go.

"Wait." Janine realized she was absolutely terrified to see her dad. Visiting him in rehab wasn't a new experience for her, but they'd both been younger the last time, more optimistic, at the very least more willing to pretend things might improve. She also hadn't been running away from an internet scandal back then. Did he know that was why she'd suddenly put the airline ticket on his credit card and shown up? Was he mad at her? Now that she was here, any convictions she'd had about him felt so much less certain.

"It'll be okay," Sheila said, opening the door to leave. "Everyone's nervous."

"Sheila!" Janine heard her father say just outside the door. "How's the diet?" His voice was jovial.

"Well, you know. It's not easy, sir."

"You look damn good to me," Marty said, sounding like a big Texan oil mogul. "Leave yourself alone."

"You're sweet," Sheila said. "But nobody wants a fat girl in Los Angeles."

"Fuck 'em," Marty said. "Fuck 'em. You're a Southern belle. To hell with 'em."

Janine's heart swelled. Her father always started talking with a Southern accent when he spoke with anybody from the South. It wasn't entirely an affectation. He'd grown up in Fresno, the son of Polish immigrants, and thought of himself as a man of the people. And Marty always loved an underdog. It made sense that he'd sympathize with Sheila and her private battle with cheese grits, just as he'd always sympathized with Janine as the less pretty sister, the damaged former child actress, the daughter his wife didn't love. God, he was impossible to dislike. He always found the interesting part of someone's generally uninteresting personality, and he made people feel they were very special. Probably that's why his movies were so good. He'd made the geeks the heroes long before that idea had occurred to anyone else.

"Hi," she said, standing in the middle of the room. He was in the doorway. She willed herself not to cry. The booming voice she'd heard in the hall was wholly disconnected from the old man in front of her. He was shriveled up. Janine felt an adolescent urge to cut herself, to release the pain before it swallowed her whole.

"You're too thin," he said as he walked into the room, wobbling a little. He opened his arms and held on to her tightly when she stepped into them.

"*I* am?" she asked, strangling her emotion with forced laughter. He gazed at her with adoration. Nobody looked at her that way. How long had it been since she'd seen him? Maria's funeral had been over a year ago. Several times he'd made plans to visit her in New York, but each time Gail had called Janine up and explained in hushed tones that it might be best to put it off because "as much as he wants to see you, he doesn't want you to know he isn't feeling well."

"Nice hair," he said now, not sounding entirely convinced but clearly needing a neutral topic so he could catch his breath. He looked at her a moment too long, as if trying to make sense of something, maybe marking the passage of time on her face too. Then he blinked away his tears, never one to wallow in emotions. "Have you seen Gail?"

"I just flew in yesterday." She wiped away her own tears and decided not to mention that Gail had already left half a dozen messages on her phone, no doubt in a panic that Janine would be seeing Marty alone.

"Call her. Call her today," he ordered as he carefully sat down on the sofa. Janine didn't want to call her. This trip wasn't about Gail and she could live without her unsolicited advice on how Janine should behave with her own father. "She can't wait to see you," he went on. "How about your sister?"

"I just got here, Dad. We e-mailed."

He wrinkled his forehead. "Is something going on between you two?"

"No. We're good." Janine had no intention of getting into it. Her dad didn't want to hear the details any more than she wanted to explain them. "How are you, Dad?"

"Me?" he asked, as if it were a strange question. "Good. I'm good."

Really? He was good? He was in rehab . . . again. And even now, sitting with him in the meeting room, Janine didn't feel she could come right out and ask him how the detox was going. She'd sooner ask him about his sex life. In the same way, if her dad did know about TMZ, he'd pretend not to. That was the way they did things in their family. You didn't talk about anything meaningful. There was no point in picking at the scabs.

"Sheila seems nice," Janine finally said because she couldn't think of anything else to say.

Marty looked confused for a minute. Then: "Sheila!" he shouted. "Sheila's terrific. She's from Atlanta. Her parents can't understand what she's doing in LA. Frankly, neither can I. I keep telling her to go home."

"So what's it like here?" she asked, because she didn't really want to talk about Sheila. She wanted to know how her father was doing.

Marty launched into a biting, albeit funny, recitation of daily life at Directions: The vegan breakfast buffet, the benefits of canoe catharsis versus equine therapy, and the director's fireside chats, which Marty had never actually attended. He hadn't tried the canoes or the horses either, only the gluten-free oatmeal.

She couldn't help feeling disappointed that he actually believed his jokes and obfuscations would convince her, of all people, that he was fine, that nothing had really changed. Or maybe he was putting on the show not for her but for himself. Whatever the case, it was becoming clear that her dad wasn't committed to any sort of rehabilitation. Janine knew that last time he was here, he'd smuggled in drugs. Is that what was going on now?

"Gail's great. She's been terrific," he said in response to a question Janine hadn't asked. "She really looks out for me."

"That's good," Janine said, shifting uncomfortably. They were stepping into a hazardous zone now, and she had to proceed carefully. Her dad was asking her to sing Gail's praises, but Janine wasn't about to comply. Maybe her apprehension was a cliché, but a lifetime of experience with her father's ex-wives and girlfriends had taught her to be suspicious of Gail's motives. She'd bet a finger Gail wouldn't have been looking out for him quite so well if she weren't anticipating some long-term financial gain.

It's not that Janine wasn't grateful to Gail. In some ways, she'd been good for her dad; she'd gotten him to rehab, however futile this stint turned out to be. Like a one-woman concierge service, she got the seemingly impossible done. The problem was that her father was so dazzled at the prospect of somebody else taking care of things for a change that he'd completely abandoned himself to Gail's competence. Janine resented the way Gail enfeebled him, made him doubt his ability to think for himself and distrust the people he loved most. And Janine found his exhausting insistence on selling Gail to her—and maybe, more depressingly, to himself—hard to stomach.

"You and your charming sister could be a little warmer to her," Marty said with a frown. His voice was brisk now, disapproving. "She's trying with you two and I think it's about time we stopped playing the 'I don't like Daddy's girlfriend' card. You two aren't exactly little kids anymore."

"I'm plenty nice," Janine said, humiliated and a little furious. What the hell had she done? She was glad she hadn't brought him chili fries, much as she could have used some herself.

"Maybe you can have dinner or something with her?" he asked, his tone softening. "You like her, right?"

"Sure. I like her fine."

"Good." He wiped the perspiration off his forehead. "Good. How long can you stay in town?"

She did her best to shrug off her annoyance about Gail. Gail didn't matter. "I'll stay as long as you want."

She saw his jaw start to tremble, the way it always did when he felt emotional.

Now she wanted to change the subject. "What do you want for your birthday? We celebrate a week from Saturday, right?"

"How about a ride home?" he said with a choked laugh. Then he looked at her and said, his voice cracking, "Thanks for coming out to see your fuckup of an old man."

She bit back her tears before saying anything. "I missed you too, Dad." She wanted more than anything to get out of the room. "Can we go for a walk or something?"

He nodded and stood, shakily. "Call Gail today," he said again. "Don't forget."

Hailey

"Do you mind getting the door?" Jaycee yelled from inside the bathroom.

"God," Hailey said. She put down her book and threw the blanket she was under off the couch. "I thought you were supposed to be taking care of me." She stomped to the front door and swung it open. A messenger was holding a long gold box and staring down at a handheld device. He looked all of twenty, with oily skin and a raging case of acne.

"Just a sec," he said, not looking up as he entered some numbers. "You Amanda Kessler?"

"No," she said. "But I can sign for her."

"Great." He looked up. "Oh. Hi."

"Hi," Hailey said. He handed her the machine and showed her where to sign. She could feel his eyes on her. She was self-conscious about not having on a bra, just a tank top and sweats. They made eye contact as she handed him the machine. He wasn't staring at her tits. Or maybe he was. But he was looking at her face too.

"Are you gonna give me those?" she asked, gesturing to the box of what she knew was more flowers. Her mother had been receiving flowers from school donors and delighted parents every other day since the show closed. Despite the fallout the production caused in their family, *Hairspray* had been a success, and Fair Hills, for the first time ever, had been officially invited by YPTI (Young People's Theater Initiative) to take the show to San Francisco. The best drama teachers from high schools and colleges all over the country attended YPTI. School grants were given out there.

"Can't imagine these are meant for anyone but you," the messenger said. He was practically gawking at her as he put the machine in his satchel. Then Hailey remembered her bruised face.

"So you'd think," Hailey said. "But they're not."

Since the accident, she'd been out of the house only once, to have the bandages and stitches removed. Her face was still swollen and bruised. She probably looked like she needed flowers.

Jaycee walked over to the door. The messenger briefly noticed her before his eyes darted back to Hailey. His gaze rested there and he smiled. Hailey's thrill grew in intensity with each passing second. It was a small moment, but both girls felt it.

"Thanks, then," Hailey said with a grin. She began to shut the door.

"Bye." He stood there too long with his hands in his pockets. She closed the door in his face and tossed the flowers onto the counter. "Weirdo."

"Are you gonna put those in water?" Jaycee asked, annoyed by the stream of deliveries. Every new floral arrangement was a reminder that Jaycee wasn't allowed to go to San Francisco with the cast, that the school had put her on probation for what she'd done to Hailey, that she'd nearly been expelled.

Hailey plopped back down on the sofa, pulled the blanket up, and picked up her book. She was in the middle of *The Buccaneers* and she didn't like being interrupted when she read.

Jaycee opened the fridge. "Should I make lunch?"

"I'm not hungry."

"You have to eat. You're getting way too skinny."

Hailey didn't think she was getting too skinny. She liked the way her collarbones popped out and how her stomach was concave when she lay down. She didn't know what to make of her face. None of them did. She was still bruised and puffy. Her features had a moist, almost newborn quality. She thought she might look good in that flat-faced, Icelandic-model sort of way. Hailey thought of Dr. Mintz smiling to himself as he removed the last of the bandages. He'd asked a nurse to take more pictures. He'd even called in a couple of other doctors to discuss the way he'd shortened Hailey's philtrum, or the groove between her upper lip and nose. The doctors all nodded in appreciation.

She didn't know how to interpret the way her mom and sister seemed to be stealing glances at her when they thought she couldn't see. It wasn't just that she looked different; it was that she didn't really resemble her sister anymore. It was as though Jaycee had smashed the twinness out of her. Now that her old face was gone, Hailey kind of missed the familiarity of it. Her reflection was a constant surprise, like someone significantly better-looking was standing in her way. She'd wake up in the morning and run to the bathroom, needing to confirm that she was the person staring back at her. After what had happened on the hockey field, she was grateful that she had a face at all.

"You want me to get you some Pop-Tarts?" Jaycee asked. She sat down on the edge of the coffee table opposite Hailey.

"The Vicodin kills my appetite. Can you get me another pill?"

"Do you *need* another pill, Grandpa Marty?"

"Very funny. I'm in pain. And in case you forgot, this is all your fault."

Jaycee shifted her weight and cleared her throat. Hailey could feel her staring.

"What?" Hailey snapped.

"I still feel guilty about what happened," she whispered in that weird, hangdog voice she'd adopted since "the accident," as she called it. "You just seem so, like, calm."

"I am calm." Hailey shot Jaycee a look. "Maybe it's the antidepressants, which, by the way, I'm not staying on. I don't care how many kids take them or that the person who smashed my face in and her psycho mom seem to think *I* need them. They cause weight gain. Like getting fat wouldn't be totally depressing?"

"You're really skinny right now."

"Eventually. Eventually those pills cause weight gain."

Jaycee was quiet.

"I'm just taking them to get everyone off my back."

Jaycee scrunched up her face. "I just feel so bad."

"About the antidepressants or about smashing up my face?"

"Both."

"Don't," Hailey said. She was thinking about all the things Jaycee had to feel bad about. "I'm stoked to miss school."

"I wish being suspended were as much fun as sick leave. It's like everyone on the whole faculty thinks I'm a monster. Mom and Dad can't even look at me. And you know I'm not allowed to go to San Fran with Mom now, right? She gave Nelly Blythe my part! Nelly!"

Hailey went back to her book. She wasn't mad at Jaycee but she didn't feel sorry for her either. She had to know there would be consequences. "Can I get that Vicodin, please?"

Jaycee watched Hailey reading for another good minute or two. She finally stood up and walked to the door. "Maybe you should take a Tylenol?"

"Vicodin," Hailey said, reaching for a bowl of crackers on the coffee table as a demonstration of her appetite. Jaycee disappeared into the bathroom and came out again with the white pill. She put it down with a cup of water next to the cracker bowl.

"Maybe some tea too?" Hailey asked. She winced a little as she sat up so that Jaycee would understand that there was suffering going on.

Jaycee narrowed her eyes, clearly running out of patience. "Lemon or chamomile?"

"Lemon. Thanks."

"Okay," she said, turning to go.

"Hey, do you know if Mom's talked to Aunt Janine yet?" Hailey asked. She tried to sound casual. Their mom mentioned that Janine had arrived in LA but Hailey was pretty sure Amanda didn't know that she'd had anything to do with her coming. Hailey loved that she'd pulled that one off. But why hadn't she seen her aunt yet? She was getting frustrated and impatient. When she asked, her mom just sighed and reiterated that Hailey needed to recover in peace.

Hailey suspected that her mom was keeping Janine away on purpose. It was probably because Hailey had forgotten to clear her search history last week. That was so stupid. Hailey was still following the TMZ story. She really couldn't get enough of Janine. She wanted to know everything. And so, after totally invading her cyber-privacy, her mom had yelled at her about "lionizing" her aunt, finally toning it down only because her poor daughter found it too painful to cry with two nasal tampons stuffed up her nose.

"How should I know if they've talked?" Jaycee asked. "Why are you so obsessed with her anyway?"

"I'm not obsessed. Jesus. Forget it." She swallowed the pill and put down the water. She looked up at Jaycee, who was glaring at her as if she'd suddenly had enough of being nice. Hailey immediately regretted that she'd maybe pushed Jaycee too far, that her sister was annoyed with her again.

"Well, I don't know anything about her," Jaycee said. Her eyes were slits.

"I heard you. Okay."

"Okay. And why don't you get your own damn tea," Jaycee said, stomping into the bedroom. "It's not like I broke your fucking legs." She slammed the door behind her.

Henry

"Christ Almighty," Bunny said as Henry got out of his filthy car. She was standing outside alone, smoking a cigarette. The valet wasn't there.

"I haven't had time to wash it."

"Wash it? You need to burn it."

Since the toothpaste debacle, Henry had been so busy with teaching and driving to and from Malibu that he hadn't had time to deal with his car. In the interim, the Santa Ana winds had come and deposited a film of dirt and insects on the sticky paste smeared across the windshield.

"It's quite something, Henry." Bunny lifted her sunglasses and stepped forward to examine the mess at closer range. A discussion of the sad state of his vehicle was going to be the prologue to today's meeting. That was okay by him. In the past few days, they'd been getting along surprisingly well. There was almost a jocularity between them. She'd managed to call him and apologize, albeit grudgingly, and he'd come back, reluctantly. Their second session wasn't much better but Henry could tell she was making an effort. He'd been coming every other day since, and this new tone was a meeting place from which they were both able to air their grievances without the whole thing collapsing into an argument.

"Why not just buy a new car? Cleaning it isn't going to change the fact that it's lumpy and old." She held up her finger before he could interrupt and took a drag on her cigarette. "You have a trust fund," she said, exhaling cigarette smoke. "I understand that you're making some puerile point by not spending the money but—"

He laughed. "I can afford a new car on my own."

"Well, then?"

"The car doesn't usually look this bad."

"What is that stuff anyway?" she asked, gesturing at the windshield.

"Toothpaste and petroleum jelly, among other things. Risa's a very angry woman."

"So that's over now?"

"Quite. We split up recently. She also broke my Mesoamerican corn goddess."

"Well, I've no idea what that means, but she sounds dreadful. Can I buy you another one?"

"Thank you, but no. It was one of a kind. I bought it at auction."

"Well, talk to your father. I'm sure he can dig one up."

"That's about what he'd have to do." Henry looked around for a valet. "Why are you outside?"

"I was waiting for you. I wanted a few minutes alone. To talk."

"Ah," he said. He still didn't want to be alone with his mother. For all the progress they seemed to have made, he knew how quickly things could turn sour, and Mitchell (for whatever it was worth) was an astute moderator.

Finally Todd, the valet, returned, pink-faced and running. "Sorry, man. I'm having a little stomach trouble."

Henry reluctantly handed him the keys. As Todd wrote out his valet ticket, Henry whispered to his mother, "There was a horrific outbreak of norovirus at the university last year. I didn't have office hours for two weeks."

"Oh, Henry," she said. "I'm sure he just ate a bad tofu sandwich."

Bunny and Henry laughed at that as they watched Todd drive the car away. Bunny saw it before Henry and gave a little gasp. There, neatly written on the bumper in gummy white letters, was the word *creep*.

"It's quite something what she can do with a tube of toothpaste," Bunny said after a short, stunned silence.

How long had that been there? Henry wondered, horrified. Had Risa come back with a fresh tube of toothpaste or had he simply not noticed it for a week? He shuddered to think how many people had seen it and not said anything. He was certain everyone on the faculty was having a good chuckle at his expense.

"You must have hurt her very badly, Henry."

"She cheated on me! I simply told her it was over. We weren't compatible."

"Well," she said with a sigh, "that's clear. She's beneath you. Shall we?" She wrapped her scarf around her shoulders to insulate herself against the ocean breeze. "Mitchell will be waiting."

"What is it you wanted to talk about, then?" Henry asked, trying to shake off the sight of Risa's handiwork and bracing himself as they walked inside. His bad ear was throbbing now, as it often did when his blood pressure went up.

"We've been getting on well, haven't we?"

"Mm," Henry muttered as he walked alongside her.

"I had an epiphany," she continued. "I'm certain it's the distance that's created this fracture between us. I think you should move back to London. I'm not getting any younger, you know. Neither is your father. We won't be here forever."

Henry stopped and looked at his mother with a gentle smile. "Don't write yourself off just yet. I'm flattered that you miss me. Truly. But I have a job, you know. I happen to be the leading expert in my field. And USC is the leading university in my area."

Bunny frowned and crushed out her cigarette with her shoe. "I don't buy it. You chose that university precisely because it was in Los Angeles, as far away from London as you could get in a city that you know I don't care for. Nobody goes to Los Angeles to quench an intellectual inquisitiveness."

"Mum—"

She shook her head, not finished. "I'd have understood if you'd come here to become a movie star or to open a doughnut franchise. But I think you moved here to escape me. Am I right? And yes, Henry," she said, not waiting for an answer, deep into her monologue, "that hurts me. But you know what? I say we put it all behind us now. Come back to London. We'll get you a nice job. I can help."

Henry laughed. "Nobody teaches American landscape painting in England."

"Exactly!" she said. "We can carve out a whole department for you. Oxford. Cambridge. Whatever you want."

"I'm happy here."

"You don't mean that."

"Stop telling me what I mean," Henry said, losing his cool as they walked into the main atrium. "You don't even know who I am. You've never bothered to figure it out."

Bunny glared and the fading bruises on her face turned an angry red. "Maybe if you hadn't moved six thousand miles away, it would have been easier."

"Maybe if you'd tried a bit harder in the twenty-two years leading up to my departure, I might have stayed."

"So it's all my fault?"

People were starting to stare.

"Hey, hey, hey," Mitchell said, running up to them. "Is everything okay here? I'm not sure you two meeting alone is a good idea at this point."

"And what point is that?" she asked.

"A critical one."

Bunny looked furious as they all walked toward the counseling room in silence. Henry sensed it was going to take more than the therapeutic properties of cigarettes and nature today. He was right. She couldn't seem to get off the subject of his "leaving" her and he refused to feel guilty for having a life of his own. She asked what exactly this life of his own consisted of. Where was his wife? Where were his children? Where, she'd even asked, were his friends?

By the end of the session, he was feeling depressed. And not just depressed in the way spending time with her generally made him feel. This was a more global tug-down.

After a brisk good-bye, Henry nearly jogged to the valet and collected his Subaru. Grateful to be alone, he sank into the hot seat, comforted by the womblike warmth of his car. He started to drive off the grounds, but he had to pull over to compose himself before facing the long ride home. His head felt like it had been sent through a food processor. He rifled through the glove compartment for aspirin, but all he found was a sheaf of inscrutable DMV papers and an old stick of gum. The view of the majestic ocean out the window made him want to cry. He thought about the sad, small boy he had been. He thought maybe his mother was right. Other than his career, what kind of life had he made for himself?

He watched the sun play over the water. How strange to live so close to the sea and never glimpse it. Los Angeles was quite a good city in many ways. He wondered what it would be like to swim in the Pacific. He felt light-headed at the prospect. Did he have his trunks in the back? Then he remembered the upcoming ear surgery and Dr. Z.'s directive not to swim before then.

"Fuck it all!" He slammed his fists on the steering wheel three times. "Fuck it, fuck it, and fuck it!"

"You okay?" someone said. Henry startled, so shocked he forgot where he was. He looked up. A woman in sunglasses was standing next to his car, gesturing for him to lower the window.

Henry thought about hitting the accelerator but, thankfully, noticed the closed gate in front of him. He hadn't even left Directions yet. He was parked just in front of the exit with the motor running. Looking back up, he saw the short-haired woman from the other day, the one he'd met at reception. She looked smaller than he'd remembered, standing there with her hand shading her sunglasses. Jenny something or other?

"Oh, hullo," Henry said, rolling down his window, trying to sound casual.

"Henry Holter, right?"

"That's right," he said, remembering now how annoyed she'd seemed after he'd introduced himself. "It really is my name. She's my mother," he said, feeling, God knows why, that he owed this woman an explanation. "Bunny Small."

"Okay." She sounded more amused than impressed. "That's who you're visiting?"

"Mm."

"That can't be easy," she said.

Henry gave her a listless shrug. It was bad enough to be dragged through therapy without having strangers commenting on his emotional state afterward.

"Okay," she said apologetically. "Sorry to have bothered you but you're kind of blocking the exit." She pointed at the gate. "And you seemed, I don't know... I'll be on my way. I can go around you."

"No, no, please." He opened the door and got out of the car. "I'm sorry. I'm a bit muddled after today. Stay." He laughed self-consciously and pushed his hair off his brow. He needed a haircut. "I just hate all this emotional claptrap. Digging up the past, airing grievances. What's the point?" he said. Then he stopped himself. "Forgive me. I'm prattling on."

She removed her sunglasses. Her eyes were round and dark, the color of Cadbury's chocolate.

"The thinking behind family therapy eludes me too," she said. "Like anything good could come out of a process that's so fundamentally uncomfortable."

They smiled at each other and stood there for a few awkward seconds.

"New car?" He looked at her posh black Range Rover and wondered where the Honda Civic had gone. He'd registered it only because normal utilitarian cars (like his) were so rare in Los Angeles, especially at places like Directions.

She regarded him curiously. "My dad's leaser. He didn't like me driving a rental car."

Henry nodded and tried to think of something witty to say, but he had nothing. Why had he mentioned her car, for God's sake? He must sound like a stalker.

"Okay, then," she said. She put her sunglasses on and waved lightly before heading back to her SUV. He waved back, abashed, and got into his Subaru.

He pressed the button for the gate and began the slow descent down the mountain to the highway. Damn. He'd forgotten to ask her name. He watched her in the rearview mirror as she followed closely behind him. It wasn't until he was halfway down the hill that he remembered the *creep*.

Marty

At least Janine would be at his birthday dinner Saturday. That was some good news, Marty thought. Seeing her a few times had taken the edge off his moods a little. They'd gotten their old rhythm back after a couple of visits. Janine had always known how to make him laugh. Not that she (or anyone) had called to wish him a happy birthday today. And not that spending his birthday in rehab sounded like a good time. Seventy-five years old. Christ!

He remembered last week's Kinfolk Dinner with Gail and Amanda and wondered again why Janine hadn't come and why the more high-profile guests, the actors and politicians he'd seen around, weren't there either. Did they have a *separate* dinner? A better dinner? Was he flying economy class now?

As it turned out, Janine hadn't been invited because Amanda "wasn't ready" to see her sister. Whatever the hell that was about, he didn't want to know. And Gail was trying to use Janine to manipulate him. He was still chewing on Gail's barbed insinuations that Janine would be disappointed to learn the extent of his apathy at Directions, to find out how little her father had been participating in the program, how little he seemed to care about getting healthy. Gail had even suggested that she herself might not be around when he got out if he didn't stop ridiculing the staff and start *sharing* in Group. Was she getting daily progress reports on him? How very fucking infantilizing. He wondered at what precise moment his life had turned into a Molière farce.

He'd been carefully rationing the tiny bags of white powder he'd slid into the lining of his Lakers cap. He knew he had to make the supply last but the dope he'd packed had shorter legs than Tom Cruise—either that or his tolerance was higher than he'd thought. The rush hadn't even carried him through the appetizers of that Kinfolk Dinner. He shut his eyes and tried to block out the memory of Gail arriving with newly plumped lips and a three-thousand-dollar handbag he'd never seen but had assuredly paid for. He tried to block out the memory of Mitchell, the charlatan founder of Directions, delivering his inspirational liturgy under that forty-foot-high fiberglass Buddha in the center of the dining room. Mostly, though, he tried to block out how badly he wanted another bump.

Now that he'd spent some time with Janine, he felt a little better. She didn't seem disappointed in him. She seemed happy to see him. He took a deep breath. He just had to get through today's Group.

Alice, the moderator, was standing in the center of a circle of eight chairs. "Would you like to begin?" she asked Marty, not without sarcasm. He'd been going to Group as required, but he'd yet to really participate. He shook his head. He wasn't quite ready.

"C'mon, guys," she said, looking past Marty for a more forthcoming contributor. "Who can tell us why it's important to *participate* in group therapy?"

"Because it helps us feel like we're not alone," Tommy said.

"In part, yes," Alice said. "And?"

"And to help us feel less shame through sharing," he added.

Tommy was an overweight CEO who had gotten drunk and driven over his caddie at the golf club. The kid was in a wheelchair now. It was a sad story but Tommy's gnawingly earnest regret irritated Marty. And what self-respecting adult went by the name Tommy?

"Shiva?" Alice asked. They all turned to Shiva, the exceedingly fuckable housewife with the Persian accent and the bored, wanton stare. Shiva sighed and examined her nails as if she had a spa appointment and this meeting wouldn't hold her interest much longer.

"We do the group to feel like it's okay, you know," she said without looking away from her hands. "The crazy shit we do. Or have done."

"And to know we're not alone," Lauren, the friendly crack addict, added, checked out and oblivious to the fact that she was repeating what Tommy had just said.

As far as Marty was concerned, the only discernible benefit of Group was that he felt better about himself by virtue of not having run over a kid (Tommy), locked his children in the car while getting a coke fix (Shiva), or shot at (but missed) his ex's new girlfriend "because she deserved it" (Lauren). Group made Marty feel like a goddamn Boy Scout.

"Talking in a group," Alice began again, "allows us to alleviate some of the shame, sorrow, and *guilt* we feel about our addiction. Addiction causes us to do things we regret and feel guilty about. But"—dramatic pause—"the things we have done in the past don't define who we are today. You with me?"

Everyone nodded. Marty thought that was bullshit. If the choices you made didn't define who you were, what did? Good intentions?

Alice passed out paper and pencils to everyone in the circle. Marty dropped his pencil. Alice picked it up and looked suspiciously at his shaking hands. His fingers had been tingling and numb the last few days. The sensation disappeared within a few minutes of taking a Xanax, but he had to be conservative with those too. He'd packed a two-month supply but the fascists at intake had found and confiscated most of them. He had twenty-eight pills left, all crammed into the waistband of his sweatpants. Not enough to sail through rehab without experiencing some discomfort, but better than nothing.

"In today's exercise," Alice began, "I'd like you to imagine that this is your last day on earth. Write down what you would do. Who would you spend the day with? Would you be happy with the way you've lived your life?" She grinned as they groaned in collective protest. "What do you think people would say about you at your funeral?"

A few moments of blessed silence as people wrote down their responses. Marty stared at the floor, not wanting to make eye contact with Alice, hoping to avoid participating. He hated these exercises, the pretense of a catharsis that always ended in an embarrassing admission of self-loathing. That's what Alice wanted, for them to admit they hated themselves so that she could force them into phase two of the charade: assuring one another that they weren't so bad after all. They were like a support group for the goddamn Legion of Doom. What a joke!

Alice allowed them five minutes to write. She called on Tommy first. As expected, he started to cry, blubbering about how he wouldn't deserve a funeral. Alice promptly suggested an exercise in forgiveness while Shiva and Noelle began bickering. Then, as if on cue, Cathy, an heiress to the Clorox bleach fortune and Marty's favorite fellow fuckup, stood and walked over to Tommy.

"You didn't put the kid in the wheelchair, Tommy," Cathy said in her mannish voice, so gravelly it sounded paved in asphalt. "The alcohol did. Not you." Cathy was a big woman, easily as tall as Tommy. She put his big red face between her big red hands. "You are not your addiction."

Tommy nodded. He was clinging awkwardly to Cathy's ample back.

"Thank you, Cathy," Alice said. "That was very well said."

Cathy was a good dame but this was her sixth stint at Directions. Her veteran status and gin blossoms were testament to the fact that the program didn't work.

Marty raised his hand. He figured if he comforted Tommy, Alice might spare him from the sharing bit today. Alice nodded encouragingly, delighted to call on him.

Marty leaned forward in his seat. "You gotta give it a rest already. Beating the shit out of yourself every day isn't helping anybody."

Tommy feverishly nodded in choked, emotional silence. "Thanks so much, man," he finally said. He stood up, opened his arms, and started walking toward Marty as though he wanted to give him a Cathy-style hug. Marty leaned back and shook his head but Tommy was approaching fast. He threw his arms around Marty, who remained seated, so his face was crushed into the soft fold of Tommy's generous belly. Alice looked like she was going to have an orgasm as Tommy returned to his chair. Marty thought about making a run for the door.

"Very, very well put, Marty," Alice said, beaming at him. "What about you, Tobey?" Alice gestured to his sheet of paper. "What would you do on your last day on earth? What do you think people might say about you at your funeral?"

Tobey was the newest addition to the group. He was just a kid. He hadn't shared yet but Marty had overheard his roommate telling Lauren that he'd taken a loan out on his parents' house to finance a marijuana dispensary in Harvard Square. Tobey didn't smoke pot; he just sold it. He was into the junk.

"I'd get smacked on hayron with my lady and feel pretty fuckin' good till departure time. Don't care about my funeral, as I won't be there."

"Touché." Marty clapped, laughing. "Touché."

"You think you're cool?" Noelle asked Tobey. "You think going to Harvard makes you above us, you arrogant piece of crap? That this is all some kind of joke?"

"No," Tobey said. "I think this place is a joke."

"Why is Directions a joke, Tobey?" Alice asked, but she didn't give him a chance to answer. "If you keep reminding people how little you care about yourself," she said, addressing the whole room now, "eventually people will give up on you. And that's a shitty, lonely day. Trust me. I've been there."

Marty's heart quickened, almost painfully. He felt like he'd disappear if Janine gave up on him. He'd written her name, shakily, on the paper. He'd spend his last day with his older daughter. He loved Amanda, but their relationship had never been easy. Not that they didn't love each other, but they didn't seem to like each other all that much. Janine understood him. In his heart, where such things mattered, he had never put anyone before her. She'd even say so at his funeral. He was sure of it.

Just then the door opened and an attractive older woman walked tentatively into the room. She had a Band-Aid across her nose and two black eyes, though the bruising was fading to a greenish yellow. Marty squinted, sensing something familiar about her. Her white hair was sleek and pulled back at her neck. She had on silk pajamas. An actress?

"Is this Alice's group?" she said in a British accent.

"Yes," Alice said. "Come on in, Bunny. Please. Have a seat."

"Sorry I'm late," she said. "I was—"

"Oh no," Marty said with a feverish shake of his head. "No, no, no, no."

Bunny looked at Marty and squinted. She obviously didn't recognize him. That pissed him off. She looked around at the other attendees, wondering what she was missing.

Marty dropped his head between his knees. He looked up at her after a few seconds, red-faced. "No, no, no!"

"Martin Kessler?" she asked with a glimmer of recognition. She leaned in, as if a closer look might erase the past fifty years from his face. "Martin! You've gotten so old!"

"Perfect," he said, throwing up his hands. "Just fucking perfect."

"I guess I should be flattered you still recognize me even though I'm looking a bit worse for wear!" Bunny touched her bruised face and then waved her hand like she couldn't care less. "My God, Martin, what on earth are you doing in my group therapy?"

"No way, folks. Not happening."

"You know each other?" Alice asked.

"This, ladies and gentlemen," Marty said, standing up to offer her the seat he'd planned to vacate momentarily anyway, "is my ex-wife Bunny Small."

"Bunny Small!" they all said together, as if Elvis himself had just walked in.

"No last names!" Alice shrieked. "What is the matter with you, Marty?"

Noelle gasped. Shiva had her hands over her mouth. Even Tobey looked impressed. Everybody made room for Bunny. Everybody wanted to sit next to her.

"Did you not hear me?" Marty said, straining to be heard over the commotion. "She's my ex-wife. I don't care if she wrote the fucking Constitution. This ain't gonna work. I am not exorcising my demons with my ex-wife and a Greek chorus."

Alice took a deep breath. "I'll talk to Mitchell, but we're not your audience, Marty. We're all just working together."

"Not on my dime, sister."

"I think you're overreacting," Bunny said with a smile that was more crooked and gloating than he remembered. "We barely knew each other. It's water under the bridge and all that sort of thing." Her tone conveyed both astonishment at his presence and complete indifference to it. "It's too strange that you're here but it couldn't possibly really *bother* you after all this time, Martin."

How dare she? Marty thought. How dare she pretend she'd evolved so goddamn much that sitting around swapping rock-bottom confessions with her ex-husband was just fine by her. "Don't call me that!" he barked.

"What?"

"Martin. Don't call me Martin."

"Okay. Well," Bunny said, "for the record, I don't have a problem with this arrangement . . . Marty."

"Is that so?"

She nodded, looking a little too pleased with herself.

"What do you say, Marty?" Alice asked him. "Bunny's fine with the arrangement."

"Ah," Marty said. "Is this another opportunity to see why Marty can't let go of his anger? To see why Marty thinks being trapped in this shit shack is pretty bad but why being trapped in this shit shack with an ex-wife might be just a wee bit too much to ask? I'm feeling a little tested here and I'm not sure I like it."

"There are no coincidences in AA," Alice said.

"But this isn't AA," Marty said, seething.

"It's still a good slogan," Alice said with a wink. "I'll talk to Mitchell about all this, but for now, I need everyone to just calm down. Let's just all sit together and do some deep breathing, okay?"

Bunny took the empty seat next to Tommy. He stared at her as though she were a rib-eye steak.

"Tommy," Alice snapped. "Eyes closed, please."

A few minutes passed. Bunny looked up and met Marty's eyes.

Happy birthday, Martin, she mouthed.

Despite himself, he felt his throat tighten. After all these years . . . his heart swelled with gratitude and sadness. Bunny Small, whom he hadn't really thought about in over forty years, had remembered that today was his birthday.

Henry

Henry finally told his mother about his upcoming ear surgery after their therapy session. He'd explained that he wouldn't be able to visit her for a week or so afterward, that he'd miss some of their meetings. She seemed touchingly concerned, pulled out her jadeite lighter, and lit a cigarette. They both looked wordlessly out at the water.

He was anxious about the surgery (the surgeon would be going through his skull, for God's sake), but he'd done his best to hide his apprehension from Bunny. No point rousing her dormant maternal concern this late in the game. As expected, once he'd reassured her he wouldn't be absent for longer than a week, she was more than happy to change the subject.

"You'll never guess who's here, Henry."

He waited.

"Martin Kessler." She was beaming.

"Who is Martin Kessler?"

"My first husband!" She swatted his shoulder and looked at him as if he were mad for not recognizing his name.

"I thought he died."

"My God, Henry. Why would you say such a thing?"

"Because that's what you told me the last time you mentioned him, which would have been about thirty years ago."

"I never said any such thing."

"You did, actually. You told me he'd died and that you felt lost, so you decided to move back to London and that's when you met Dad."

"Don't be absurd. We got divorced and I moved back to London."

Henry was irritated but not surprised. His mother's personal narratives had always been unreliable. Historical events were nothing but bits of fiction to be told however she saw most fitting at the moment. He had to take a few deep breaths to keep himself from "emotionally attacking her," as Mitchell so delicately put it. "If you say so."

"Of course I say so." She laughed. "What an imagination you have." Henry noticed a curious smile tugging at the corners of her mouth. "He was in my group-therapy meeting," Bunny said. "Can you imagine that? It's just, it was so strange to see him there. He looks so old! Why did I marry him? We had nothing in common at all."

"I'm sure you've changed quite a bit too." Henry knew very well she didn't like to be reminded that she aged just like other people.

"You couldn't possibly understand at your age. It's just that it all goes so damn quickly and at some point you realize it's completely meaningless. It feels like yesterday I was married to this brilliant, handsome young man and now he's a little old chap in a drug-rehab center. He must be seventy-five!"

"And you are seventy, Mother. A resident of the same drug-rehab center. Perhaps you had more in common than you thought."

"I just thought you'd be interested about Martin," she said. "Forget I said anything."

"I'll do my best. I've got other things to worry about at the moment."

"Oh yes, the surgery," she said. Her face went stiff with gravitas.

He bit his lip in an attempt not to laugh at her go at sincerity. "You're no good at empathy."

"I'm good at everything I do. Even sobriety. I don't even miss booze. This is all an exercise in futility. I'm not an alcoholic. I'm just good at drinking."

"You'll be here, though?" he asked, realizing that he actually wanted his mother in town for the operation. Even if she was locked up in a gilded cage in Malibu, her proximity, for the first time in as long as he could remember, was a comfort.

"Of course I'll be here," she said. "I'm having a fabulous time." She reached for Henry's arm with a conspiratorial grin. "I'm going to ask Martin to have dinner with me tonight, if I can find him. It's his birthday. I remembered that!" She tapped her forehead. "I still have an excellent memory. You should have seen his face, Henry."

"I'm glad you're making the most of your time here, Mum."

"Thank you, darling. I am."

Henry went to the YMCA in Santa Monica after his visit with Bunny. He'd gone after their last couple of visits, needing to burn off energy. Dr. Zimmerman had strongly advised him against swimming, but Dr. Zimmerman wasn't spending every other day in family therapy with his mother. The Y was on his way home from Malibu, and the pool was clean and nearly empty in the evenings.

He dived into the heavily chlorinated water and tried to keep up with the other swimmers, a few elderly people, all doing laps at an impressive pace. How he loved the silence and weightlessness underwater. He'd stopped for a rest when he noticed a woman in a navy swimsuit and a red swim cap standing at the edge of the pool. He decided to get out, not wanting to share his lane. He swam to the stairs.

"Don't get out on my account," she said.

"I was finished anyway," he said, pulling himself up on the railing and removing his goggles. He didn't welcome the cold air any more than the unwanted conversation.

"Henry Holter?" she asked, looking him up and down. He pushed his chest out a bit. Henry had been told he had a young man's body.

He took a childish pride in that fact, if for no other reason than that he did so little to maintain it.

"Yes?" He took off his cap and removed his earplugs. He didn't recognize the woman without his glasses on but there was something pleasing about the blurred view of her. That she didn't remove her cap was a testament to her lack of vanity.

"I'm Janine," she said, lowering her body into the pool. "We met at Directions."

"Ah!" Henry said, genuinely surprised. "I don't think I ever caught your name. Didn't recognize you without my glasses and with you wearing that cap."

"You look as if you're feeling better."

"Ah, well. Perhaps I've been empowered by the Q-TIP technique." Janine appeared confused.

"'Quit taking it personally,'" he clarified, wondering that Janine wasn't familiar with the Directions vernacular. In a typical display of sanctimonious theatrics, Mitchell had introduced the concept after handing both Henry and his mother their very own Q-tips. Henry laughed at the memory. "I find there's nothing like a catchy acronym and a symbolic cotton swab to set forty years of familial dysfunction right."

She grinned and Henry felt his stomach tighten as if he suddenly had something at stake. "So, you swim here?" he asked idiotically. He was distracted by her eyes, which were expressive and, like her smile, a little hard to read.

"I used to swim here when I was a girl. And then I stopped."

"Why's that?"

"My mom died."

"I'm sorry."

"Don't be. It's not your fault."

"No," he said. "Hard to know what to say is all."

She put on her goggles, adjusted them, then disappeared into the pool. He felt a sense of urgency. His heart was racing. He stood at the edge of the water, staring in like an ass. She broke the surface with a beatific expression, any sorrow seemingly washed away. She laughed when she saw him, maybe finding it funny that he was still standing there.

He sat down where he'd been standing and let his feet dangle in the pool. "It's really a coincidence seeing you here, you know, after Directions. Do you mind if I join you?" he asked, noticing that four of the five swimmers had cleared off. "I don't want to interrupt."

"Not at all," she said. "But I thought you were done."

"I was."

She smiled and pushed off to the center of the pool. He reinserted his earplugs. He couldn't see her but he knew she was down there, somewhere under the water, like a lost pearl.

Janine

"Would you like to have dinner?" Henry asked. They'd gotten out of the pool. He was leaning against a railing on the broad deck space as he dried off his feet. His movements were youthful and self-assured. The halogen lights cast a warm glow over his surprisingly slender body. Janine thought he looked better half naked than he did clothed. That wasn't true of most grown men, she thought, remembering her old boyfriend Jürgen and his slight potbelly. When she'd first seen Henry at Directions, his wrinkled khakis and button-down shirt had given him a dated, Indiana Jones look. She would never have guessed that Han Solo was underneath all that fabric.

"Dinner?" Janine asked. She looked from her pruned fingers to the clock. "It's late. We've been swimming for almost an hour."

"A snack, then?" He threw her a towel.

"With you?"

"I suppose you could have it alone but that would have made my question rhetorical and I loathe rhetorical questions."

"Mm."

"That's all right," Henry said, looking a little embarrassed. "Why don't we get changed and let me at least walk you to your car."

"Oh," Janine said. She wished she hadn't dismissed the invitation

186

so quickly. She was starving and she liked the way they had been swimming together without talking. Moving quietly side by side in the water, fully aware of each other's presence but careful not to disrupt the other's solitude, had been an oddly intimate experience.

"I am hungry," she said. "But I don't—"

"—want to have some inane first-date conversation at nine o'clock at night?"

"Something like that."

A few teenagers came out of the locker room and dived recklessly into the pool.

"That's my exit cue," Henry said. "Youth in swim attire."

"You don't like young people?" she asked.

"No." His answer was so blunt and unapologetic, it was funny. "I do not like them here or there, I do not like them anywhere."

Janine laughed. Was he serious?

"Anyway, maybe think about dinner while you change?" He began toweling off his hair. He had great hair. It was thick and a little too long without looking intentionally forgotten. "How about we don't even discuss our parents? We can talk about swimming, music, art, whatever you like."

"Sounds very good," she said. "Can we talk about that Leshan Buddha reproduction at Directions? There's something about a massive naked man in a dining room I find unappetizing."

"Ha!" He jerked his head three or four times to the left to release water from his ear. "Agreed."

"Hai Tong must be spinning in his grave," she said, all too aware of her pathetic attempt to impress him. Maybe it was just the accent, but Henry seemed really smart. It was show-offy, but what was the point of her self-education if she couldn't use her knowledge while flirting? And God, how long had it been since she'd flirted with anyone anyway?

"Have you been to China?" he asked.

"No. I just like big things." She smiled, pleased with herself. "And I like art. Since I can't buy art, I buy big art books."

"I'm an art historian!" Henry said, smiling too broadly. "I *write* big art books."

"You're a professor?" She felt a cramp in her pelvis. Janine had an irrational adulation for academics. It was something she probably would have outgrown had she gone to college, but she hadn't, and the very idea made her giddy with desire. "Seems like an odd vocation for someone who hates young people."

"I don't hate them," he said. "I just don't like being around them."

"Oh. Okay, then."

"Liking my students isn't a prerequisite for the job. Office hours are a bloody circus. The personal problems, the whinging that goes on. I honestly don't understand how the lines got so dreadfully blurry. You should hear the nonsense I'm forced to endure."

"Well, don't get touchy."

"I'm not getting touchy," he said, though he clearly was. "Last month I had a PhD candidate—*PhD*—wanting to discuss various aspects of his father's extramarital affairs! I have a first-year graduate student, Kate something or other, who came to me last week with the idea of writing a paper on the homosexual undertones in the Hudson River School paintings. She was serious too. Thought she was being quite clever."

"That's not a personal problem," Janine said, defending Kate. "It's valid."

"Valid? They're landscapes!" he almost yelled. "I'm not saying some of the painters weren't homosexual, but what difference does that make?" He looked at Janine. "Those paintings were intended as a celebration of nature, of God in nature. It's not *contemporary* art," he said with a trace of disdain. "How the artists got their jollies is entirely irrelevant. To suggest that a tree is anything but a tree is like saying..."

"That Georgia O'Keeffe's flowers are vaginas?"

"That's different. And if I tell Kate how ludicrously specious her argument is, I'll have Harriet Hooper and the Gender Studies Department on my ass. And if there is one department to avoid at all costs, it's Gender Studies."

Somewhere, not so deep down, Janine knew Henry's rant was a titanic red flag. Still, there was something about his lack of conformity to the rules of political correctness that she found refreshing. She was sure Harriet Hooper hated him.

"Do you collect?" Janine asked, hoping to change the subject. "Art?"

"A bit." He relaxed his shoulders, looking self-conscious about his outburst. "If you like Chinese, I have a nice collection of ceramics and bronzes from the Han and Wei dynasties. Would you like to have a look?"

"That's quite a line."

"You rejected my dinner offer. Can't blame a chap for trying."

"So you're showing off?" she asked, flattered.

"I don't get many opportunities. My last girlfriend thought *contrapposto* was an Italian wine."

Janine laughed at that, feeling herself blush. She liked that he was peacocking for her, liked that she was being singled out for being smart, that she was being singled out for anything, really, other than having been Jenny Bailey.

"Not that she's unintelligent by any stretch," he went on. "But she is an English teacher. Academics aren't polymaths. They tend to specialize fanatically."

"What's your area?"

"American art of the nineteenth century. Not very sexy, I know."

"Unless all those boulders really are giant testicles or breasts."

"There is that," he said.

"Oh, wait! I know you. H. Holter? I have your book!" Janine said with an excited familiarity. "There was a show at the Met."

"The National Gallery."

She could see his face redden despite the poor lighting. It was like watching a glass of wine being filled. "But of course," she said in a mock British accent. "Very foolish of me."

"And what about you?" he asked, embarrassed. "What do you do? You're some kind of an actress, right?"

Janine looked at him, surprised. How did he know that?

"That fellow from Directions the other day," he explained. "He seemed to have been quite a fan of yours."

"Oh." Janine cringed at the memory. "No. Well, I was, but that was a long time ago. When I was a kid. I don't really do anything right now," she said, hating how lame she sounded. "I live in New York. I'm just visiting. I'm just here to help my dad."

"Well, I hope you won't be going back too soon?"

"I'm not sure. I'm not in a rush. I'm trying to be useful."

He didn't say anything for a minute. "And is that what you want?" he asked with unexpected seriousness. "To be useful?"

Janine nodded, afraid to speak. She was humiliated by her emotion. Was that all she wanted? A useful life? Her eyes started to sting.

Henry looked stricken. His mouth was a little open, forehead wrinkled as if he were in agony. "Oh God. Did I say something wrong?"

Janine shook her head. Then she buried her face in her towel and wiped her eyes, pretending to dry her hair.

"I don't believe you," he said. "I'm afraid you'll have to prove it by coming over. No funny business," he added, crossing his heart. "I can make *panini con palle di nonno* and *barba di frate*. Which translates to 'sandwiches with grandpa's balls and friar's beard,' but I promise it's just salami and greens."

Janine laughed again, impressed that he seemed to speak Italian and relieved he wasn't taking her emotional fragility too seriously. And his dopey humor kept surprising her. "Where do you live?" she asked.

"Laurel Canyon."

She stopped laughing. "That's a long way to go for a snack."

"I'm a very good cook."

"You can't be that good."

"I'll drive you and bring you back."

"In little pieces?" she asked, remembering how funny Ted Bundy was supposed to have been and still wondering about the word on his car bumper. "You have the word *creep* written on the back bumper of your car. I assume you didn't put it there?" Janine didn't want to bring it up but it did sort of require an explanation. Certainly before she went to his house.

"I promise you I'm not a serial killer," he said as if reading her thoughts.

"Who said serial? It only takes one."

"Drive your own car," he suggested. "But come. Despite all my clumsiness, I'm feeling unusually chipper."

Janine opened her mouth to say something witty when Henry Holter put his finger to her lips. She was struck by the confidence of the gesture, by the smell of his chlorinated hand.

"I was just going to ask if there would be wine," she said, trying to breathe evenly.

"I've got a Chenin Blanc and an Umbrian red from Torgiano."

It was as unlike her to be impulsive as it was for her to go into a locker room—she had a horror of being recognized while naked. She'd planned to just put her clothes on over her suit. The last time she'd trusted a stranger, she'd wound up with her pictures splattered all over TMZ. She knew she was going to sleep with Henry. The certainty was liberating. She didn't feel embarrassed or apologetic.

"I'll see you in ten?" Henry said as he held the door of the women's locker room open for her. "I can promise it will be the best meal you had since yesterday."

"You're funny," she said, turning to go inside and shower off.

"Nobody else thinks so."

"Maybe they just don't get your jokes."

"That's what I've always thought."

Bunny

After an exhaustive search, Bunny finally located Martin, chuckling to himself as he read *Pride and Prejudice* on the lawn. "They took away my books," he offered by way of explanation, "but it's damn good." He shook the Austen. "Damn good. I'd forgotten." She pressed him to join her for dinner that night. She was very curious about what he'd been doing (other than drugs) for the past four decades. He seemed spectacularly uninterested in having dinner with her, no doubt still shocked by her unexpected appearance, but once she'd pointed out that it *was* his birthday and that he obviously had nothing better to do (Directions didn't allow family meals Monday through Thursday), he reluctantly agreed.

Now that they were entering the dining room, Bunny was excited. She thought Martin looked happy, or at least amused.

"This is lovely," Bunny said, waiting for Martin to pull out her chair at the dinner table. When he did, she sat down. The dining room was nearly empty. They had agreed to eat late, after the addicts had gone to bed, all of them too bored to face another evening without drugs or alcohol. "Who would have thought we'd be dining together after all these years?"

"In our pajamas, no less," Martin said.

"These are not pajamas," Bunny said, pulling at her oversize, over-priced silk pants.

"Do they have an elastic waist?" he asked.

"That is none of your business."

"Relax." Martin laughed. He pushed out his chair to show her his white sneakers. "I didn't exactly pack for dinners *à deux* either."

"My maid packed for a cruise around Spitsbergen." Bunny's lips stiffened as she thought of Bettina.

"The help these days." Martin's voice dripped with sarcasm. He shook his head and rapped his knuckles on the table twice in a gesture that took Bunny back almost half a century.

"Don't be a bore, Martin," she said. She raised her glass of water. "Happy birthday. To getting old."

"Beats being dead," he said, clinking her glass as the waiter delivered the menus. "I think."

"It's shocking, isn't it?" she asked. "How quickly it goes?"

"Only because we're always the same age inside."

"Yes!" she said. "That's exactly it. Well put."

"You can thank Gertrude Stein. She said it."

Bunny was annoyed, even after all these years, at Martin's erudition. It had always taken her by surprise when they were married, though she'd hated to admit it. She felt she should have been the better educated one.

"That's my problem, anyway," he went on. "It's like I wake up every morning thinking, *Today I'll be the person I used to be,* but I never am. I'm just an angry old guy pissed off that nobody gives a shit anymore."

"Mm. I don't have that problem."

"No," he muttered. "I wouldn't think so." He broke a bread stick in two. "You always did think you were smarter than everyone else in the room. Turned out you were right."

Bunny smiled, not sure if Martin was giving her a compliment or a jab. She decided not to dwell on it. She didn't care either way. "So tell me what you've been doing. I followed your career for a while—it was hard not to—but then you just sort of vanished."

"I probably retired too early," he said. "I wanted to exit gracefully before I was pushed offstage. I don't know why that was so damn important to me. But it was."

"Well, having been married to you was *almost* something to brag about. Six Academy Award nominations," she said, smiling. "Well done."

"Nine. Not that I'm counting. Anyway," he said, as if shrugging off an unpleasant memory, "I've got a couple of great daughters." He pulled out his phone, which Directions had wiped clean of everything other than the approved contacts and photographs. He showed Bunny a few pictures.

"Pretty!" Bunny said, taking the phone and scrolling past a mousy brunette before zooming in on a good-looking blonde. "Is she married?"

"Divorced."

"What a shame," she lied. She thought the woman looked just the thing for Henry. "What does she do?"

"Amanda? She's a drama teacher," Martin said. "Well known, actually. She's got two terrific daughters in high school. Twins."

"Lovely," Bunny said, nodding with approval.

"I guess so," he said, as if he were surprised. He looked melancholy. "My older girl has had a harder go of things. Depression, social anxiety. I'm sure I'm to blame. They just sort of tear your heart out."

"Oh, I know," Bunny said. "My son's half the reason I'm here. He thinks I drink too much. You? What are you in for, Martin? Alcohol, marijuana, cocaine?"

"Heroin."

Bunny rolled her eyes. "Such a wit, Martin."

"I'm not kidding. I wish I were."

"Christ."

"It's not as bad as it sounds. Back pain that led to pills that led to needing something stronger. It's not really an issue. I manage it, you know. But Gail thinks it's a problem, so—"

"Gail?"

"My girlfriend."

"Ah."

"And you? You still married?"

"God, no. Relationships," she said, waving the word away like a gnat. "I'm off them. Especially now that I'm so goddamn old. You know, I can admit it now—I never went in for that sort of thing."

"What sort of thing?"

"Sex."

He laughed. "You never went in for sex? With anyone?"

"It certainly wasn't ever my idea of a good time. I never initiated it." She paused for a moment, looking for the right way to put it. "It's a bit like washing the floors. I never wanted to do it beforehand, sort of enjoyed it while it was happening, and was quite pleased when it was all over."

"You never washed a floor in your life," he said.

"That's not true. Don't you remember Beatrice?"

"Your mother," he said, as pleased as if he'd answered correctly on a quiz show. "Hard to imagine you were a street urchin," he said. "I forgot."

"I wouldn't go that far." She looked around to make sure nobody was listening. "But God knows I've done enough...floor-washing, both real and metaphorical, to last a lifetime."

"Well," Martin said. "That's good. I thought it was just me that you didn't want to be with." He paused. "In that way."

"No." She began folding the edges of her napkin in her lap. "Never fancied it. It wasn't my cup of tea."

"What about your second husband?" he asked, taking a sip of water.

"I didn't like that tea either."

He laughed hard, nearly spitting out his water.

"Most women don't like it, you know," she said in a whisper.

"That's ridiculous."

"Well, maybe when they're young. When they're puffed up with hormones, foolish enough to confuse objectification with passion. When a compliment about your ass seems a solid foundation to build a life on."

"You can't be serious."

"Oh, I'm serious. Past a certain age, women would rather do almost anything else. It's a real bore. Trust me. Especially with the same man, week after week, year after year."

"I got it, I got it," he said. "How do you weave all these romantic notions into your teenage claptrap?"

"I have a stellar imagination."

"You might want to sprinkle some of that imagination over your relationships. They might work out better."

"Like yours?" she asked.

"Touché," he said, raising his glass again.

Bunny wished she had a gin to toast all these revelations. Had she ever told anyone the way she felt about sex? Of course she liked being desired—who didn't?—but she'd always wished the men in her life could take care of their business elsewhere and come back around when it was time for dinner and a show. She hadn't minded at all when Sam had his little dalliances, so long as he was discreet (which he was).

"Anyway, what do I know?" she asked. "It's just what I think. But if sleeping with a man is essential to staying married, no, thank you."

"Yes, I've really missed you," he said. "It's all coming back to me now how much of a laugh you were."

Bunny smiled. It was too much fun teasing Martin. He was so easily ruffled and then smoothed.

They ordered dinner and settled into an easy silence.

"You're probably right about women and sex," he said, relaxing. "Every one of my relationships—all those women were just in it for the money."

"Well, don't get to feeling sorry for yourself. You're good company."

"Yes," he said. "Call Marty for a good time and a prepaid mortgage too."

"Have you got a mortgage on your house?" she asked, appalled. The idea of being in debt, of being a borrower, horrified Bunny.

"No." He hissed into his water glass. "Not on mine. But I have about three on various ex-wives' and girlfriends' homes."

"But why?"

"If you pay their bills monthly, they remember they're on the payroll. They're waiting on your goodwill. Otherwise they forget."

"What's the point in being remembered that way?"

"I guess it makes me feel more alive."

"You mean more important?"

"Who knows?" His face colored again.

"What happens when you die?" she asked.

"Is that a philosophical question?"

"With the mortgages?"

He clapped his hands together and grimaced. "This is very cheerful. This is a nice conversation."

"I'm desperately curious, Martin. It's all so, so . . ."

"Operational?"

"Yes!"

"The houses get paid off."

"In full?"

He nodded, broke another bread stick in half.

"So you do have the money?" Bunny asked with relief.

"I have it, but I'd rather keep it in the bank. I live off the interest."

"But when you die?"

"Whatever I owe comes out of whatever's left."

"It comes from your estate?" Bunny said, aghast. "But that's for your girls."

Martin leaned forward and took a noisy sip from his almost empty water glass through a straw, like a boy. "All of them, unfortunately."

"How could you be so stupid, Martin? Do you even care about these women? Surely they're capable of looking after themselves. They managed to convince you to give them a lifetime of free rent. They sound like absolute geniuses to me."

"They all have problems," he said, trying to end the conversation.

"I think you're underestimating their ability to survive without your largesse."

"I think you're underestimating how difficult it is to be a middle-aged woman in Los Angeles."

"Ah! Middle-aged women are a charity now? And you're their benefactor?"

"Let's just say it gives me something to be angry about when a more pressing issue isn't waiting for me to fix it."

"But why is their well-being your responsibility?"

"Well, I'm beholden to the ex-wife by law, one of the ex-girlfriends would probably be homeless if I didn't help, and the other one had me sign a contract."

"A contract? What sort of contract?"

"I don't want to get into it."

Bunny was staring at Martin.

"She was looking out for her family. You can't fault her for that."

"Quite the contrary. I applaud her ingenuity. Why would anybody get a job when they have you? Explain to me how it works, Martin."

"How what works?"

"The contract."

"Her lawyer sends it over to my lawyer, my lawyer tells me I'm an asshole, and we sign."

"That's brilliant. I'm sure your daughters were delighted."

"They don't know anything about it. It's got nothing to do with them."

"It's got everything to do with them. And your girlfriend?"

"Gail's got her own money," Martin said quickly. He obviously didn't want Bunny to think his only allure was his pathetic bank account. "Can we please change the subject? Rehashing my mortality and romantic prospects isn't exactly what I had in mind when I agreed to have dinner. Let's get back to you."

"There's nothing to say. I like a drink. But I'm certainly not an alcoholic. Everyone's just concerned that I haven't been as productive as usual. They're worried the old cash cow's gone out to pasture."

"Or to the bar."

"I don't go to bars, for God's sake."

The waiter came and placed a naked chicken breast with a wedge of lemon and a side of broccoli in front of Bunny. Martin had tomato soup and a grilled cheese with chips. Sometimes Bunny hated being a woman. It wasn't that she was on a diet, but she'd committed herself to getting into better shape at Directions so at least she'd have something to show for all the money she was spending.

"You go to a lot of cocktail parties and dinners?" Martin asked, raising his eyebrows before taking a small bite of his sandwich.

"Some," she lied. Bunny hated parties. She hated dinners out. Everybody knew that. "I have a drink at home now and again," she admitted. "Is that a crime? I wasn't aware I was breaking any laws. I am of age, you know."

"'The other day I got invited to a party,'" Martin sang, drumming on the table. He crooned the entire song, obviously tickled that he'd remembered all the words to the national anthem of drinking alone. Bunny busied herself cutting her chicken into tiny cubes as he came to the end.

"Charming. Are you quite finished?"

"I've always said there's nothing so unattractive as a drunk woman," he said.

"Yes, I remember your sentiments on the subject. An octogenarian with a heroin habit, however? That's a very sexy article."

"I'm not an octogenarian."

"Yet." She smiled, then popped a bite of chicken into her mouth.

"Tell me, Martin," she said, putting down her fork. "Is drugging something you do at parties or alone?"

"It's not a social habit. A bump here and there gets me through the days. I might have overdone it a few times. But all this," he said, pointing to the Buddha and the oval dining room, "all this isn't going to change anything. Sometimes my life needs more color. So I give it some."

"I couldn't agree more," she said. She was irritated by Martin's insinuation that she had a problem while he merely had a habit. "I'm taking this California getaway as an opportunity to shape up, drop a few kilos, maybe. I've no intention of giving up drinking for good." She eyed Martin's chips. "That would be preposterous and a bore. But if a show of abstinence is required to appease these people, so be it. It's not hard for me to abstain. Not in the least. Alcohol is just a luxury. And I've lived without luxuries."

"A long time ago," Martin reminded her. "I don't get the sense you take kindly to the word *no* these days."

"My son loves telling me no," she said.

"That's parenting," Martin said. "You give, they take, gratitude not included."

"The funny thing is," she went on, "he doesn't even want anything from me. I'm richer than Croesus, and what's it all for?"

"I'm not familiar with that particular problem."

"No." She nodded. "It doesn't sound as if you are."

"Get married again," he suggested. "That'll get his attention. Or give it all to a charity. They pretend not to care about your money until they think you're giving it to someone else."

"I could never do that," she said. "Can I have a chip?" she asked, reaching for his plate. Martin blocked her hand.

"I thought you were on a diet."

"I am, but just one. I just want to try them."

"No." Martin shook his head. "Eat your broccoli."

"Oh, for God's sake, give me a chip. You haven't touched them."

"No, Bunny. I don't want to enable you. I'd like to support you. I could be your french fry sponsor."

"Piss off."

She stood up and reached for his chips. Martin pushed them farther away. She made a dive for them, but he got up and blocked her. As he lunged for the plate, his bad ankle gave way, and he fell onto the table; Bunny lost her balance and collapsed on top of him, which made the table wobble, sending Martin, Bunny, the food, and the water glasses all toppling to the floor with a loud crash.

In the moment before Bunny started guffawing, before the frantic Directions waitstaff made their way to the table, before Martin could overcome the shock of ice-cold water soaking through his briefs, they both knew that neither of them had had that many laughs in a very long time.

After dinner, Martin walked her back to her room. "That was great fun," Bunny said as she stood in the doorway. "Thank you." She put her hand on Martin's arm.

He flinched and Bunny moved her hand away. Did he think she was making a pass at him? She wasn't! She was just having fun. Or was she? Had she? Either way, his response felt like a reprimand.

"Do relax, Martin. I didn't mean anything by it. Obviously!" She went into her room and slammed the door in his face.

Henry

Directions was big on the cathartic effects of "activity-based family bonding." Mitchell suggested they give hiking a try. His mother had gotten hold of what Henry thought were ridiculously large trekking poles, the kind you'd use to scale Mount Fuji, not walk a horse trail.

"How was your dinner?" Henry asked, wondering why his mother was being so uncharacteristically quiet. He had plenty of papers to grade but he was there, for her sake, and if he was spending his time at Directions rather than at work, he expected at least a little conversation. Bunny stopped and looked up at him, confused. She was gasping for air, leaning heavily on one of her poles. "With the not-dead ex-husband?" he clarified.

"Fine. We had a nice time." Then, narrowing her eyes: "Why do you look so cheerful?"

"Do I?" he asked. "I don't know." He started walking again.

Henry's evening with Janine had been spectacular. She was so smart and well educated, which was shocking, considering she'd primarily had only tutors as a child. He found her curiosity about everything exciting. He was thrown by how easily they had fallen into bed, but one can hardly complain about such happy accidents.

Her face was almost childlike: soft pale skin stretched over rounded cheekbones, big, curious brown eyes, and a small mouth that surprised him with its generosity when she smiled. And her hair! The clean sweep of bangs across her forehead. The impish points at her ears. He'd never been to bed with a woman with short hair. The nakedness of her smooth throat and the small bones rising up the back of her neck fascinated him.

"Well, I've got something else to cheer you up," Bunny said with satisfaction. She stopped short and launched into a sales pitch for some woman called Amanda, her ex-husband's very pretty, very single daughter. She was a high-school drama teacher, she explained, with twin girls well out of nappies. Martin's other daughter was plain, but Amanda, Bunny assured him, was just the ticket. There were more details, but Henry stopped listening. He'd have to tread carefully. His mother didn't like any form of refusal.

"I'm going to pass, Mother. Being set up with your confined ex-husband's newly divorced daughter sounds like a bad idea all around."

"But why?"

"I can find my own dates, thank you."

"You're doing such a good job of it too." She laughed.

"The truth is, I met someone."

"Met someone? When? Ten minutes ago?"

"We met here, actually. And then I ran into her at the YMCA pool. Quite a coincidence."

"I'll say!" Bunny shouted, waving her pole close enough to Henry's face to make him worry about losing an eye.

"Hey, be careful with that thing!" He stepped back to avoid injury. "She's kind, even offered to pick me up from the hospital after my surgery next week."

"I'll bet."

"What is your problem?"

"She obviously sniffed you out. Don't be daft, Henry!"

"Yes, Mother. She's stalking me because I'm such a catch." A short pause. "Oooh, I see," he said, finally getting it. "I'm a prize because of you. Is that what you think? That she's mercenary and wants a crack at your fortune, so she's floating around in public pools hoping I might show up on a whim?"

Bunny picked up her pace. Why on earth was his mother being such a capital twat about this?

"I know it's impossible to believe that somebody might like me for me," Henry continued, following her. "But some women, quite a few, actually, seem to like me very much and have no interest whatsoever in your bank account."

"I just wish you'd listen to me every once in a while. You met her, what, three days ago? And now you're splashing around together and she's getting in by taking you to hospital?"

"Getting in?" Henry asked, incredulous. "You've no idea what you're talking about. She's lovely. You'd like her. And she offered."

"Why didn't you ask me to take you?"

"You're in rehab!"

"It's not my fault if you haven't a friend to help you out. It's mystifying what you've been doing out here all these years. Obviously not socializing."

"I do have friends I could ask," he said, knowing that wasn't entirely true. "But she suggested it, and why not? It's an easy outpatient procedure, after all."

"So now it's easy? Last time we discussed it, you made it sound as if you were having a triple bypass."

"What is this about? Really?" Henry asked. His mother's face was pink and her eyes were glassy. She turned quickly and began walking back down the hill. "Where are you going?" he called after her. "We haven't reached the top yet. Hey!"

She was moving at a brisk clip now, almost running. "Slow down!" he shouted. He was afraid she'd fall, despite the ridiculous trekking poles, which she manipulated with surprising grace. But she was fast and nimble, more so than Henry, as it turned out.

"Wait!" By the time he spotted her again, she was at the bottom of the hill, just at the point of crossing the street that led back to Directions. There was a FedEx truck idling. His heart stopped when he saw her lose her balance, twist awkwardly, and fall down, hard. She lay flat, not moving.

The truck started beeping and backing up and Henry knew the driver didn't see her there. He was going over the poles. Was he on the phone? Listening to music? Henry could hear the crunching of metal. It was a horrifying sound, all the more so because he kept imagining it was his mother's head. Bunny let loose a harrowing scream. Then the beeping stopped and all was silent.

He was too stunned to move when he saw her stand up, straighten her shirt, collect the poles, and limp over to the front of the vehicle. She held the bent poles midshaft and began repeatedly driving them into the hood, as if she were stabbing someone to death. Henry could hear her screaming as she adjusted her grip and continued thrashing. Then she started on the headlights, aiming at them sideways, like a baseball player swinging at a ball. It might have been comic had the madwoman not been his mother.

"You stupid bloody pillock! Why don't you look where you're going, you fucking wanker!"

Then she walked to the side of the vehicle, where Henry knew the driver sat exposed. As she stood with her feet shoulder-width apart and lifted the poles, Henry started sprinting down the hill screaming for her to stop. She'd kill the driver, he was sure. Just when the poles were about to make contact, the truck jerked forward and drove away, fast. Henry could see the terrified expression of the young driver as he peeled off. He left Bunny standing there, holding her poles aloft.

"Are you all right? What the hell are you doing?" he asked, running up behind her. She was red with rage, covered in dust, and her nose was bleeding. One of her sandals was three feet away. She looked disoriented.

"He didn't even stop!"

"He was scared for his life!" Henry shouted. "You were terrifying!"

"He could have killed me. Did you see that? He drove over me. He just drove off!"

"He didn't drive over you. He drove over the poles. He didn't even see you until you started smashing up his truck."

"You're defending him?"

"We're lucky he didn't plow you down trying to escape!"

She dropped the poles, sat on the ground, and began to weep. Henry had never been so uncomfortable. He hadn't a clue what to do. She was sitting cross-legged, her tears mixing with the dirt on her face.

"Mum?" He gathered her shoe and the poles and sat down next to her.

"He doesn't find me attractive, Henry."

"You tried to kill him. Of course he doesn't find you attractive."

"No, no," she cried. "Martin. Martin doesn't find me attractive anymore. Getting old is an attack on the soul, Henry. It's a long, boring, fruitless war."

"I'm sure he finds you attractive. You're a beautiful woman." It was true, odd as it was for Henry to consider the fact.

"But I'm not sexy anymore," she said, sobbing. "Nobody wants to have a go with a seventy-year-old woman. Not even a seventy-five-year-old man."

"I'm not sure what to say." Henry shifted awkwardly, deliberating whether to give his mother a hug.

His conversation about Janine must have been what set her off. She wasn't jealous. She was simply mourning her own lost youth. Still, her violence had terrified him. Perhaps she was detoxing and this was simply what alcohol withdrawal looked like.

"I think I made a pass at him," she confessed, burying her face in her hands. "I made a pass at my ridiculous, ancient, drug-addled ex-husband, and he rejected me."

"I'm sure that's not true," Henry said, trying not to imagine what "making a pass" might entail.

"I'm so mortified I could die. I can't go back there. You'll see," she said, pointing a finger at him, accusing. "You'll get old too. One day there won't be any more water nymphs. Not that it's the same for men if they have money. You'll have plenty of it," she said, slightly cheered. "Buckets."

"I don't want your money, Mother. But thank you for thinking of me."

"Of course you say that now," she said, smearing dirty tears on her forearm. She started putting on her sandal. "Being poor is the most terrible thing in the world. You've no idea."

"Have you?"

"Some," she said. She closed her eyes and shivered.

Henry found it hard not to laugh. "You don't really fancy Martin, do you?"

"No, I don't. It was just a moment. It wasn't really a pass, just a gesture. But it was embarrassing. I so rarely put myself in a position of vulnerability and now I remember why. I'm such an ass."

"Let's get back," he said, helping her stand. She looked a mess. "We'll have to tell Mitchell what's happened. If he hasn't heard already."

"I need a drink," she said, hobbling. She was holding his arm and her voice was pleading, like a child's.

"Well, yes," he said. She was admitting that she needed something from him, though it was something he couldn't give her.

"Please."

"No, Mother."

"Piss off, Henry."

"Well, yes," he said.

Marty

"Knock, knock." Marty was standing in front of Bunny's door with his gym bag slung over his shoulder. It was after dinner. No answer. "Open the door, Bunny."

Nothing.

"I'm coming in," he said, turning the handle. None of the doors at Directions locked. He was certain Bunny was in there. He hadn't seen her since their dinner. Was she hiding from him? He was bored without her. She was a pain in the ass but she livened the place up. He liked giving her a hard time. He opened the door and found her on the bed, supine, with an eye pillow placed sloppily across her face.

"Go away," she said. "I'm sleeping."

"I brought you something."

She sat up slowly, grimacing. Her wrist was wrapped in an Ace bandage, and the right side of her face looked like a skinned knee.

"Jesus. What the hell happened to you?"

"I got run over by a FedEx truck." She arranged her features into a frown. "I fell."

"I fall too now," he said, reassured. He sat down on the edge of the bed. "It's like the ground just gives way and I'm down. I never understood about all the broken hips until recently. Who thought that would happen to us?"

"I don't know what you're talking about. My footing is excellent. I was running away from Henry and I tripped over a branch and fell."

"And then got run over by a FedEx truck?"

"I'm glad you find it funny."

"Why were you running away from Henry?"

"Because he's getting his willie wet and thinks he's falling in love again. He never listens to me. He just moves from one slag to the next and always seems surprised that things don't work out. I want grand-children! I've a right, haven't I?"

"You can't decide who your son dates."

"When was the last time you fell in love?"

"I fall in love all the time."

"I really don't know whether to envy you or pity you."

"Me neither."

"About the other night..." she started.

"Forget it," he said, not wanting to revisit that awkward moment. It wasn't that he didn't find Bunny appealing—he did. But he didn't believe in cheating, and he was too old and too tired to start over again. Besides, he knew Bunny wasn't really attracted to him. They'd spent half the dinner discussing her lack of interest in sex. She was just bored, enjoying a nostalgic ride on the tracks they'd laid down long ago. Being with Bunny was like touching hands with his younger self. Assuredly she felt the same way.

Bunny stood up. She limped across the room and pulled a sweater over her head.

"You could sue FedEx."

"I don't think so. There would be publicity." She paused. "And I beat the truck into a state of disrepair."

"Ha! Good for you."

"Rehab is much less relaxing than I'd hoped. I find the emotional turmoil exhausting. I'd like a drink when this is all done. Or, at the very least, I'd like to get away."

Martin smiled conspiratorially as he unzipped his gym bag. "Where would you go?" he asked. "I assume you've been everywhere, spreading your goodwill around."

"Italy," she said, perking up. "I do like Rome."

"Let's have a toast, then. To Bunny in Rome." He reached into his bag and pulled out a bottle of vodka. Bunny looked at the bottle, then at him. Her mouth was open. For a moment he thought she might be angry. It was a stupid thing to do, really. The woman had a drinking problem. They were in rehab. He might have some issues, but never with booze. He'd somehow failed to see the difference between Bunny's addiction and his little habit when he'd slipped Erika from the Directions spa five hundred dollars to get him a bottle.

"Genius," Bunny said. "Get the glasses."

"Who needs glasses?" he asked, relieved. He unscrewed the top and handed the bottle over. "Up your ass, Mitch!"

Bunny took a whiff and made a face.

"Best I could do under the circumstances," he said.

Bunny took a very long, very deep drink. She took another few sips before handing it over. Marty took a series of gulps and hissed as the liquid seared his throat and swelled like a wave in the river Styx at the bottom of his stomach.

"I always could drink you under the table," he said, remembering a night when they were doing shots at a pre-Oscars party. She'd vomited into Terrence Malick's lap. Faye Dunaway helped clean her up in the ladies'. Bunny didn't drink much after that. At least not while they were married.

"Maybe in the old days." She took the bottle back. "Not anymore. Let's say I've built up a tolerance. Shots?"

Marty hobbled into the bathroom and took the two glasses off the vanity. He noticed, not without irritation, that her bathroom was larger than his and equipped with an eight-headed shower and a private steam room. He walked back to the bed, put the glasses down on a brochure, and began filling them both to the top. "How much do you pay here a month?" he asked.

"No idea," she said. She looked transfixed by his presentation, as if he were performing a magic trick. He handed her one of the glasses.

"Ready, set, go!" he said and they both downed their cups. They screamed at the sheer pain of it, then laughed as Marty refilled the glasses.

"Ready, set, go!"

Marty felt a little queasy but they kept going until the bottle was empty. The whole thing took about ten minutes.

part three

Schnapsidee (noun): *A plan so stupid, it must have come from a drunken mind; literally "a schnapps idea"*

Janine

Janine was sitting next to her dad in the Directions dining room, trying to joke him out of a bad mood while they waited for Gail, Amanda, and, with luck, the twins. She'd arrived early, nervous about seeing everyone, had even put on her best black jeans and a cropped blazer. Her dad was red-faced and grouchy, entirely uninterested in her routine about eating next to Buddha's giant fiberglass toes. If she hadn't known better, she'd have sworn her dad was hung over. She knew he could think of nothing less appealing than celebrating his birthday at Directions.

Gail arrived in what Janine thought was an outrageous outfit for dinner in rehab (an emerald-green Gucci cocktail dress and heels). She embraced Janine while cheerfully reprimanding her for not returning any of her calls. By the time Amanda showed up, twenty-five minutes late and without the twins, their father was in a silent rage.

"You're late," he said before asking where the kids were. Janine noticed right away how pretty her sister still was. Despite Amanda's sloppily pinned-up hair and her blah beige pantsuit, all the eyes in the room had followed her across the dining hall.

"They're grounded," Amanda said. She looked at Gail, who nodded her head almost imperceptibly.

"Just teenage nonsense," Gail added, preempting any further explanation from Amanda. Janine wasn't sure what was going on but she was coming to understand that one of Gail's self-appointed jobs was insulating their father from his own family.

Amanda sat down and squinted at Janine, as if trying to draw some conclusions about her state of mind from her physical appearance—her short hair, her thinness, her outfit. Nobody but Amanda could make Janine feel so instantly insecure.

"Hello," Janine said. She leaned over to plant a loud, wet kiss on Amanda's cheek. Then she smiled. The only way she'd ever been able to penetrate her sister's frostiness was to disarm her, make her either laugh or squirm.

Amanda made a face and wiped the saliva off her cheek.

"Will you two please get over it?" Marty said, distracted. His eyelids were heavy but his expression was tight, as if he were halfway between a nap and a panic attack. His thumbs were pushed into his temples now. "Let's call it a birthday wish. I've neither the patience nor the inclination to endure whatever bullshit is going on between you. You're sisters."

"What's the matter with you today?" Gail asked him. "You look exhausted."

He took a sip of water and nervously glanced around the room. Then he put the glass down and started speaking quickly. "Listen, I've got to talk to you all about something. Right now."

"Marty?" Gail asked. "What is it?"

"I would have waited, but since you're all here, and the twins aren't..." He took a deep breath and looked toward the entrance again. "My ex-wife is here."

"Elise?" Janine asked, horrified.

Marty shook his head. Gail was frozen.

Amanda looked over her shoulder. "Karen?" she asked in a low voice.

"My first wife," he said, irritated.

"Don't be gruesome, Dad," Amanda said. "Mom's dead."

"My very first wife. It was ages ago. Before your mother."

Janine pushed her glass out of the way and leaned forward. Then, almost in unison, she and Amanda said, "You were married before Mom?"

"For a minute," he said. "I told you that."

"No, you didn't," Janine and Amanda said together.

"There's *another* wife?" Gail asked, incredulous.

"You never told us you were married before Mom," Janine said.

"Of course I did," he snapped. His face was getting redder. "Anyway, it lasted five minutes. It's ancient history."

"Our history," Janine said.

"No, mine, actually." His voice was loud now, on the cusp of anger. "You think I orchestrated this? That I'm happy my ex-wife is here?"

"You don't sound *unhappy*." Gail was looking at Marty like she'd never seen him before. "How long has she been here?"

"Fuck," he muttered as he clumsily pushed out his chair and stood. An older woman in silk pajamas was heading purposefully toward their table. Janine could see that the woman was good-looking, elegant, despite appearing as if she'd been in a street fight. Her face was scabbed and she had an Ace bandage wrapped around her wrist. She also had a limp she was clearly trying to hide.

"Speak of the devil," he said, holding on to the back of his chair for support as he feigned a casual air. Janine had never seen her father look so completely flustered. "We were just talking about you."

"This must be your family." She looked around the table at the circle of pinched faces.

Gail stood up slowly, mustering whatever dignity she could in what even Janine recognized was a very awkward situation. "I'm Gail Engler," she announced grandly. She extended her hand with gravitas.

"Bunny Small," the woman said, shaking Gail's hand.

Janine's stomach dropped.

"*The* Bunny Small?" Amanda squeaked.

Janine smiled without warmth. Was this a joke?

"Well, I don't want to interrupt. Just wanted to say hello. You've got a lovely family here, Martin. Congratulations."

"Marty," he said and took a seat.

"Sorry?" Bunny asked.

"Marty, not Martin."

"Yes, right. Well, see you, Marty."

"Bye," Amanda said, waving, glassy-eyed. Gail remained standing, watching Bunny leave.

Marty pulled on the hem of Gail's dress. "Would you sit down, for Christ's sake."

"Please do not tell me *she* is the ex-wife," Janine said. "Please." She slumped over the table, fingers laced together over the back of her head.

"We were married three hundred years ago, before I met your mother."

Janine didn't lift up her head. "You were married to Bunny fucking Small and never bothered mentioning it?"

"She wasn't Bunny Small when we were married. She was a script reader. Why are you behaving like you didn't know?"

"Because you never told me!" she shouted, straightening up. Then, looking at Amanda: "Never told us!"

"I thought I did," he said with a dismissive chuckle. His mood seemed to have improved now that his secret was out. "And what was there to say? It's dust in the wind." His eyes lit up as he apparently decided he should share another juicy piece of information, seeing as he had everyone's attention. "I'll tell you this, though. We got a little loaded last night. She was so far gone, she was quoting passages from her own books."

Gail made a little gasping sound. "I'm sorry. You got drunk with your ex-wife in *rehab?*"

He nodded as though Gail would appreciate the irony. "I slipped the masseuse five hundred bucks for a bottle of nineteen-dollar vodka," he said with pride. "Bunny can't hold her liquor any better than she used to." He laughed again.

Janine snapped to attention as she thought of something. Exactly what did her dad mean by "three hundred years ago" precisely? Could her father be Henry's father too? Had she had sex with her half brother? She started perspiring as she considered the possibility that she'd unwittingly committed incest. And then, focusing on her spoon to stop the spinning, she pushed away those thoughts. She would deal with the immediate issue instead.

"Getting drunk with Bunny Small," Amanda said excitedly. "That's crazy."

"What did I tell you?" Janine asked Amanda. "What did I tell you? He doesn't want to get better. It's all a big joke to him. Isn't it, Dad?"

Her father tried to look offended, but he just seemed embarrassed, as if maybe sharing his little story hadn't been the best idea.

"You drag us all out here and for what, Dad? Attention? You think that's a funny story? What the hell are you doing here? And as far as your secret marriage," Janine hissed, not about to let him get away with his lies, with not protecting her from committing incest, "what the fuck, Dad?"

"Hey! What's the matter with you?" he asked, stunned. His forehead was bunched up. His eyes flashed with concern.

"What's the matter with *me*? Are you kidding?"

He held up his hands in mock surrender. "Okay, maybe you're right. Maybe the booze was a bad idea. But it's not like I killed someone. And so what if I didn't tell you that I was married before you were even born? Big deal."

"This is a big deal!" she nearly shouted. She looked at Amanda for support. "Hello?"

Amanda, recovering from the shock of Janine's outburst, looked at her sister, then at their dad. "I agree you should have told us."

"That's it?" Janine asked her. "That's all you have to say about this?"

"Christ," he moaned, rubbing his head. "Can I get an aspirin in this place?"

"I see no reason why not," Gail said. "Apparently you can get just about anything you want in here."

"I have to go to the bathroom," Janine said, standing up.

"Janine," Marty called as she walked away. "Hey!"

"Let her go," she heard Gail say. "She needs to process it. We all do, Marty."

The text from Gail appeared as Janine sat on the toilet. What had it been, three minutes?

> Hi, honey. I'm waiting outside the bathroom. I didn't want to follow you in. So, I'll be outside the bathroom. Waiting for you.

"He's something else, isn't he?" Gail asked as Janine exited the ladies' room. She crinkled up her blue eyes, pulled Janine over to a nearby seat, and handed her a tissue before taking one herself. "Drinking in rehab! Who ever heard of such a thing? Only your father," Gail continued, trying not to cry. "So thoughtless."

Janine suddenly found herself painfully aware of the charm of Gail's company. She was dependable and sympathetic, an irresistible combination for the needy. "I'm sorry," Janine said. She had her own reasons for being angry but all this couldn't have been easy for Gail either.

"Bunny Small," Gail said, wiping a glob of mascara off her face. "I understand he's not obligated to tell me every last person he ever married, but that he was married to *her,* was *drinking* with her," she whispered. "In *here!*"

"Maybe we should tell Mitchell?"

"Not yet," Gail answered, fishing through her cosmetics bag. She cleaned up her face using a mirror in a small gold compact and then snapped it shut. "No, I think I'll handle it. Besides, what would they do to him? Make him stay here longer, with *her?* Force him to paddle around in a canoe? He's got to understand that his actions have *real* consequences, wouldn't you agree?"

Janine nodded, unsure exactly what she was agreeing to.

Gail's voice was full of resolve when she spoke again. "I've invested a lot of time and energy in your father, you know. And he just...he obviously just doesn't understand the way things work." Then a shade of panic clouded her tenacity. "You don't think something's going on between them? Bunny Small and your father?"

"No," Janine said, happy enough to reassure Gail on that front. "He's not a cheater. He just likes to flirt."

Gail nodded, comforted. "Mm. And they have no chemistry together. Anyone can see that." She took a deep breath, satisfied. "I'll have a talk with him later. Help clarify things. Anyway, I'm more concerned about you now," she said with seemingly genuine affection. "You were very angry in there."

"I'm fine," Janine said. Her voice cracked.

"Oh, honey. You are not fine." Gail swallowed Janine in a hug and a cloud of cloyingly sweet perfume. Janine had to work to hold back the tears. Nothing undid her like maternal affection. It was her kryptonite.

Gail sat back and took Janine's hand. "C'mon, sweetie. Tell me."

"He just invents these narratives, like, *Oh, yeah, I told you that I used to be married to her,* blah-blah-blah. It's insane. He just wants to sweep all the problems or whatever under the rug, pretend it's normal, that everything is okay. Meanwhile he's a fucking drug addict, clearly *not* fine, but we're not supposed to talk about *that* because— what? It makes him uncomfortable?" Janine let out a mocking laugh. "Just like my falling apart after my mom died made him uncomfortable so he encouraged me to slither away to New York rather than telling me to go back to acting or to high school, to college. How about making me do something with myself? How about being a parent? I was fifteen!"

"I think you're conflating a lot of issues," Gail said, obviously confused at the conversational turn. "You can't blame him. It was a very difficult period. He did the best he could."

"I do blame him. And he didn't do the best he could! He did what was easiest. He just paved over the cracks with an allowance and an apartment and the delusion that everything was fine. He had to know it wasn't. I know he means well, but he lies to himself until he believes the bullshit he's saying. Which brings me back to this secret first wife. And don't tell me it's the drugs. It's not the drugs. It's his personality. I always forgive him and this is just unforgivable."

"Now, that was a shock." Gail paused, clearly more interested in Marty's first marriage than in Janine's issues with her father. "But hardly unforgivable. I'm not making excuses for him, but I can certainly imagine it would have been difficult for him to tell you girls so many years later. He wants you to idolize him. He doesn't want to do anything that might mar your perception of him."

"Seriously? He's getting loaded in drug rehab with an ex-wife I never knew he had. It's a little late to pretend he's Ward Cleaver." Then, thinking of Henry, Janine stood up quickly and started pacing in tight circles. "Fuck!" she said loudly. "Fuck!"

"You've got to calm down," Gail said, looking around the room, then at Janine, confused by her uncharacteristic dramatics. "I can't excuse his drinking with her. But I think you've simply got to think of his not mentioning his marriage as a calculated omission."

"Yeah? Well, I just had sex with the son of his calculated omission," she blurted out. "With Bunny's son."

"Is *that* what this is really about?" Gail suddenly smiled, blue eyes sparkling. "Well, good for you! He must be very wealthy."

Gail was certifiable. Janine had no words.

"What's his name?" Gail asked. "Bunny Small's son?"

"Henry," Janine said. She was wondering if she should talk to Henry or just casually disappear from his life. She wasn't quite ready to discuss her bigger concern, that Marty Kessler could be his father. Not with Gail anyway.

"Henry," Gail repeated, almost wistfully. "Like the character, of course! That's wonderful." She looked at her watch and immediately stood up, smoothing the green dress over her girlish hips. Janine could feel Gail's urge to get back to her dad now, to show him how forgiving she was, to tell him how she'd saved the day by talking his fragile daughter back to the shores of sanity. "Look, honey, tell him how you feel, clear the air, but not today. It's his birthday dinner. Let's try and get through this, all right? And one more thing..."

Janine looked up at Gail.

"Patch things up with Amanda? It's important to your father that you two get along. She's had a hard run lately, with the divorce and the kids. She needs you."

Janine exhaled, resigned. Gail reached into her bag for a small perfume bottle. She spritzed her wrists and rubbed them together. "Let's go back in now," Gail said, and she teetered off in the direction of the dining room. Then, from a few steps ahead, without looking back, she said, "And smile, Janine. You're practically as pretty as Amanda when you smile."

Marty

Marty spent the morning making calls. Once Gail had been assured he wasn't getting it on with his ex-wife in the detox ward, he had to admit she'd been pretty decent about the whole thing. Of course, Gail had made it clear that his transgression would cost him. But that wasn't news. If he didn't want to spend the rest of his life alone, it was looking more and more like he'd have to marry Gail. Lately he'd come to think of himself as the Sisyphus of matrimony. He just wished the boulder would stop pulverizing him on the way back down. Anyway, at least she was helpful. She'd even managed to talk some sense into Janine, help her understand that she'd overreacted.

Perhaps it hadn't been his finest moment, but he was nonetheless mystified over his daughter's uncharacteristic rage. Hurting Janine was the very last thing he wanted to do. The simple truth was that he was embarrassed about his exceedingly brief first marriage. The whole thing was clearly a mistake, a youthful transgression he'd hoped to bury, just like that ducktail pompadour he'd gotten on his seventeenth birthday. He'd never seen any reason to tell his daughters (or anyone) about that first marriage. What possible good could have come of their knowing?

He wanted to apologize, but he also wanted to talk to Janine about his financial situation—about *her* financial situation. His dinner with Bunny had floodlit just how poorly he'd managed the money he'd earned, how easily he'd given it away. He'd misled his girls into thinking they didn't have to worry. They *did* have to worry. They wouldn't be left with nothing, but if he wanted to keep Gail happy—and he knew what Gail expected for her services, for her companionship—they wouldn't get much. He owed his daughters the truth or, at the very least, a version of it.

"So we're good?" he asked Janine on the phone after a clumsy plea for forgiveness. "You gotta know I feel like a real asshole. The booze was a stupid move and maybe I never told you about Bunny because I figured it would just complicate what was already your fairly complicated childhood." He laughed. "The marriage was a blip." He paused. "And I'm sure I told you at some point?" He took in the silence on her side of the phone. "I guess I never did. Sorry."

"Okay," she said, gracefully accepting his apology.

"Good. Anyway, I need to talk to you about something else now," he started, trying to come up with a way to tell her about the grim reality of her financial future.

Janine, as Marty had expected, wasn't interested in hearing it. He could practically see her digging her fingers into her thighs, holding her breath, once he got to his will. He couldn't help but be touched that his daughters always found these conversations so distasteful, especially compared to Gail's response; for her, the topic seemed to function as an aphrodisiac.

Over the years he'd tried to talk to his girls about what they could expect, but they always received the information as clumsily as he delivered it. They had a childlike faith that it would all work out and that he would never actually die. All three of them behaved as if his will were akin to that earthquake-preparedness kit he kept in the trunk of his car. Good idea to have it, but best not to dwell on an unpleasant and unlikely scenario.

"It's just that I always thought there would be enough," he tried to explain to Janine. "There was so much for so long and...I'm just sorry is all."

"Stop, Dad. Everything's good."

A short pause, as he didn't know what else to say. "Maybe you could go buy yourself something?" he said, his voice catching on a sob. "You should do that. Treat yourself to something nice. Put it on my credit card."

"I've got to go, Dad. Amanda's texting me."

"What about?"

He was happy enough to change the subject and he was pleased his daughters were communicating.

"I don't know. Something about Hailey. It's fine," she said, anticipating his next question. "Talk later. Love you." And she hung up.

Marty stared at the phone. He wasn't sure that he'd accomplished what he'd set out to do, but at least he'd tried. That was better than nothing.

Janine

Janine hung up with her father and reread Amanda's text.

Can you come over? I need a favor for the kids. It's an emergency.

Janine didn't want to deal with Amanda's problems. She was obsessing about that conversation with her dad and wondering what possible job opportunities there could be for middle-aged former child actresses with no work experience or skill sets. She took a deep breath and swallowed a Xanax to calm the wave of panic. She messaged back.

What kind of emergency?

Kevin's an asshole.

What does that have to do with me?

Now he says he can't stay with the girls next week while I'm away. One of his dipshit patients is "in crisis" and Kevin claims he can't abandon him. 🙄

Again, why do I care?

I'm not comfortable going to San Francisco with the cast if I don't have anyone staying with the girls. I HAVE to go to SF!!!!

Was Amanda kidding? Janine typed quickly.

To clarify, you want ME to take care of your precious daughters? As of yesterday you weren't even letting me see them. Now you want me to be their baby-sitter? That's funny.

Please don't be a pain in my ass right now.

No way. I don't know anything about kids. Just send them to San Diego for the week.

Jaycee is on probation and she can't miss school. Hailey just had surgery. I can't send them anywhere. They're not cats.

Can't they just take care of themselves?

What about their behavior suggests they can be left alone together? I have nobody else to ask, Janine. Unless you want me to go to Gail. Have I ever asked you for a favor? Ever?

She didn't have the emotional wherewithal to deal with Amanda today, not after that conversation with her dad. Not after the horrifying story Gail had relayed about Jaycee whacking her sister in the face with a stick. Fuck. Her phone chimed again.

Sorry. I'm stressed. Just come over so we can talk about it. You can hang out with Hailey. She'll be thrilled. Like Make-a-Wish Foundation thrilled.

Janine went to the bathroom before responding.

Fine. I'm leaving in ten minutes.

Can you leave right now? I have an imp meeting. Thanks. ☺

Fifteen minutes later, Janine parked in front of an ugly stucco apartment building in Brentwood. She checked the address again. Janine always thought of Amanda as having nice taste. She remembered the house Amanda and Kevin had owned in San Diego as being modest but charming.

"Welcome to mediocrity," Amanda said after she opened the door and gave Janine her perfunctory version of a hug. She was dressed in a powder-blue pencil skirt, heels, and a matching blazer so tight it doubled as a Wonderbra. "Jay's back at school. Hailey's asleep."

"Okay," Janine said, stepping inside, taking in the space. She had been wondering if maybe she could move in with Amanda if things got really bad financially. No way. The apartment had the sterile, anonymous look of a bachelor pad. It was like a hotel-brochure photo without the benefit of a long lens. How could her sister live without art on the walls, without rugs on the floor or books on the shelves? In LA, living in an apartment past the age of thirty suggested something had gone wrong.

"The apartment was supposed to be temporary," Amanda said, registering Janine's unspoken assessment. She led the way to the kitchen. "But I can't afford anything better in the area. Totally depressing, right?" She pointed to the windows. "Fucking venetian blinds."

"It's not so bad. You could make it cute if you decorated a little."
Janine tried to say something about curtains but the words came out
wonky, unintelligible. She held on to the kitchen island for support,
wondering why her sister was dressed like a porno Pan Am stewardess.

"Are you on drugs?" Amanda snapped her fingers in front of Janine's face. "Why are you staring at my tits and talking so slowly?"

"I took a Xanax," Janine confessed. "After talking to Dad."

Was she talking slowly? She was trying to act alert but the Xanax
had made her loopy. She had noticed it in the car on the drive over.
She hadn't had a panic attack since the TMZ thing and she never, ever
drove in New York. Did driving a car count as operating heavy ma-
chinery?

"What did Dad say?"

"He apologized about Bunny Small."

"And?" Amanda asked, impatient.

"He launched into 'the Will' talk."

Amanda visibly shrank in on herself. "Ugh."

"I know. But he's got a new twist," Janine said. "I'm not totally sure
what he was getting at...something about his being really worried
because there wouldn't be as much left as he'd thought. Then he said I
should buy myself something. Like we're going to be so poor I should
buy something while there's still a little cash left."

"*Buy* yourself something?" Amanda said, squinting. "Like a sweater?"

"Maybe a really nice sweater." Janine laughed. "Cashmere from
Saks? Or possibly he meant a car? I don't know. I had a panic attack."

"I'm going to die in this shit-box rental apartment." Amanda said,
her voice shaky. Then, after exhaling slowly: "Okay, I cannot even begin to think about that on top of my kids and having to whip Jaycee's
middling understudy into shape by next week." She paused, looking
at Janine. "Assuming I can even go next week?"

"I'll watch them," Janine said. She'd help Amanda but she wouldn't
stay at her apartment. "They can stay with me at Dad's."

Amanda hesitated only briefly. "You'll drive Jaycee to school?"

"Yeah."

Amanda relaxed. "Thanks. That's great. You'll love getting to know them," she gushed, as if she were doing Janine a favor rather than the other way around. She grabbed her purse, ready to go now that she'd secured a guardian for next week. "I gotta run. Jaycee won't be back until three thirty. I'll be home by six. Hailey won't bother you. She spends all her time staring in the mirror. That surgeon went too far. I barely recognize her." She waved and smiled. "Thanks! I owe you."

Janine watched the front door close. Then she walked into the first room off the kitchen. A long rectangular window faced the apartment next door. The room had twin beds and one desk. Not a poster on the wall. Not even a bulletin board. Hailey was dressed in sweats and a T-shirt, lying on one of the beds, but awake—not surprising, given that it was eleven in the morning. The other bed, presumably Jaycee's, looked as if it had never been slept in. Janine took a seat on it. Hailey smiled and sat up slowly, not taking her eyes off Janine. She'd clearly been eavesdropping on her conversation with Amanda. Her eyes were mischievous.

"Why didn't you get up and come out to say hello?" Janine asked. "I thought you were excited to see me."

"I wanted to give you and my mom alone time," Hailey said. "To make up."

"Ah, well. I suppose it was worth a shot." Janine laughed. "Look at you! You don't look like you need to be in bed at all." Hailey was barely bruised. The color and texture of her smooth skin reminded Janine of flan. The girl was a knockout.

"I'm still in a lot of pain. It was a four-hour surgery." Hailey turned to give Janine a better look at her profile.

"Well, you look great."

"Thanks. Do you really think so?"

Janine nodded. "I like the short hair. You look like a young Mia

Farrow." A lot of pretty young girls with short hair resembled Mia Farrow, but Hailey actually could have *been* her. It was spooky. Amanda
was right—her face was the work of an ambitious surgeon who had
started with a nicely prepared canvas and had created something
spectacular. Janine couldn't take her eyes off Hailey.

Hailey started to cry.

"What's the matter?" Janine asked. She moved to Hailey's bed.

"Sorry." She wiped her tears on the back of her sleeve. "That's the
best thing anybody's ever said to me."

"What is?"

"That I look like Mia Farrow. It's what my dad and, like, everyone
else told Jaycee after she got her hair cut short. Nobody ever says anything nice to me."

"I'm sure that's not true," Janine said, feeling uncomfortable and
wondering what they would do all day. Last time she'd been alone
with her nieces, she'd pushed them on a swing set at the park and
bought them ice cream cones.

"This is weird, right?" Hailey asked.

Janine smiled, relieved. "It's totally weird! I'm sorry. I'm not great
with kids or teenagers or whatever."

"That's okay. I'm just glad you came. I watched your show."

"Your mom mentioned that."

"Every single episode. You were really good. I mean, you were
amazing."

"Thanks, Hailey. It was a long time ago."

Hailey reached under her bed and pulled out a cardboard box. She
handed it to Janine.

"What's this?"

Hailey was grinning. "Open it."

Right on top was the *Seventeen* magazine with Janine on the cover.
She hadn't seen it in years. She didn't want to look at it, but she didn't
want to hurt Hailey's feelings either. Hailey seemed so pleased with
herself, staring at Janine with an expression she couldn't quite pin

down but that made her anxious nonetheless. She busied herself flip-
ping through the interior spread. It was like looking at a stranger.
Janine was surprised at how pretty she'd been, despite the atrocious
late-1980s styling. Under the magazine were years' worth of newspaper clippings and yellowed copies of *Sassy, Tiger Beat,* and *YM.* Most
of the covers she was on she shared with other teen idols of the day.
A lot of them, with the exception of Johnny Depp, James Spader, and
Michael J. Fox, were dead or forgotten. "Where did you get all this
stuff?" Janine asked.

"I found it when we moved. My mom had it in the garage."

"Your mom?" Janine couldn't imagine Amanda going to the trouble
of cutting all this stuff out, let alone keeping it for so long. "That's
weird."

"I think it was *your* mom's. My mom just didn't throw it out."

Janine smarted. Of course it would have been Pamela's. Amanda
would have been too young. Janine melted at the thought of her
flighty, inattentive mother scrapbooking, of her having had a special
place dedicated just to Janine. But she didn't have time to sort out her
feelings, not with Hailey staring at her like that.

Hailey's voice, when she finally spoke, was soft, as though she was
afraid that if she said the wrong thing, Janine would leave. "Being famous must have been the best thing ever."

"I don't know. It's not as good as it looks. Lots of expectations and
assumptions about who you are before you've figured it out yourself. I wouldn't recommend it."

"But all that attention. I mean, everybody asking you questions,
wanting to hear your opinion on designers and world disasters, wondering about your latest projects or whatever. Nobody cares what I
think. Nobody ever asks for my opinion."

Where was Hailey going with this?

"That episode where Jenny's brother broke his arm because Jenny
left her backpack at the top of the stairs—I mean, you were genius."

Janine was flattered. She'd completely forgotten that episode. It was a good one but Hailey was definitely overdoing it. She decided she needed to choose her next words carefully. That's probably what you had to do with teenagers.

"Thanks, Hailey. But I was just a kid reading a script. I was okay. Honestly, I'm not even totally sure I'd have been cast had my dad not been who he was."

"That's complete bullshit," Hailey said, shaking her head. "I don't believe that for a minute."

"Well, I appreciate the support." Janine put the lid on the box, hoping they could talk about something else now.

"Can I ask about your mental breakdown? Like, how did you go from all that to an insane asylum and then to living in a studio apartment?"

So much for a subject change. Janine tried not to laugh. Hailey had said *insane asylum* and *studio apartment* as if they were equally horrifying locations. She could only imagine the stories Amanda had spoon-fed her daughters. Or maybe Amanda hadn't told them anything much, simply glossed over the horrors Kessler-style, dropping the occasional morsel but leaving Hailey to cook up her own story, however subjective.

"It wasn't really a breakdown," Janine said, bridling at Hailey's word choice. "It wasn't like some dramatic after-school special."

In truth, it very much was. Janine had loved after-school specials when she was a girl. She often knew the kids in them. She'd wished she'd been old enough to audition for the daughter in the made-for-TV movie *Something About Amelia,* with Ted Danson playing the dad, the molester. Not that she would have been much good in the part. Shit, she couldn't even watch *Cheers* after that. Roxana Zal had played Amelia and won an Emmy for it, becoming the youngest Primetime Emmy Award winner in history. She'd been such a talent, Janine thought, wondering what had happened to Roxana. Maybe she'd bump into her at Directions.

"It was more like I needed time away," Janine explained. "Things were difficult after my mom died. I couldn't manage much. And I felt guilty."

"Guilty? Why?"

"I don't know. Your grandpa and I were so close. I felt like I let him down. I'd promised him I would be okay and I wasn't okay. It was hard for me." Then, looking at Hailey: "It was hard for your mom too, but in a different way. She was really close to your grandma," Janine said, tripping on the word *grandma* like it was a dust bunny on her tongue. It just didn't apply to Pamela. It never would have.

"What was my grandma like? Why did she do that?"

What was her mother like? Time had smudged the details. Janine knew they'd had good times but she clung to the bad ones, perhaps as a buffer against the pain of the loss. Whatever her memories, they weren't for sharing with Hailey, not now, anyway. And Janine couldn't explain to Hailey why her mother had checked herself into a room at the Beverly Hills Hotel and slit her wrists in a bathtub on a sunny afternoon. That kind of unhappiness couldn't be clarified. "I don't remember her that well." Janine hesitated, unsure how much honesty was appropriate. "I don't really know. She was obviously depressed. Probably she'd been depressed a long time."

"I see a therapist," Hailey said. "We've been talking a lot about why my mom and Jay handle things better than I do. I guess I wondered if maybe it was genetic. Being crazy. Sometimes I just feel like I want to evaporate or die. Like I'm a burden on everyone."

Janine's throat went dry. Hailey had pulled her knees up to her chest and was looking past Janine and out the window.

"Hey," Janine said. "You're not crazy and there's nothing wrong with seeing a therapist or taking medication if you need it. There's no shame in needing help." Janine was aware she sounded like she was trying to convince someone of something. She looked at Hailey, forcing her to make eye contact. "Antidepressants helped me a lot. Once I got the right ones. It takes a while. You're taking something now too?"

Silence.

"Hailey?"

"Hmm?"

"Will you call me if you feel that way again?"

Hailey reached up to touch her nose and exhaled, clearly reassured by the contours of her new face.

"I don't really feel that way anymore."

"Oh," Janine said, confused and a little embarrassed. "That's good."

"Yeah. I just feel like things are better now."

Janine paused before she asked her question. "Because of how you look?"

"Maybe. Or maybe it's the drugs. I don't know. How I look doesn't hurt."

"No. But it's not everything. You know that, right? It's not a competition. You'll never win if you look at life that way. There's always someone prettier, someone more talented."

"I don't compete with everyone," Hailey said. "Just Jaycee."

Janine was shocked by Hailey's honesty.

"I know it's weird, but I'm kind of glad Jaycee whacked me in the face. She did me a favor. I'm not the ugly twin anymore. I think I might be the prettier one now." Hailey gave Janine a cool stare. "What do you think?"

"I have a hard time believing people thought you were the ugly twin. Maybe you're a little paranoid. Not that I can't relate. I can."

"Relate?" she asked. "I don't think you can relate. I think you were to my mom what Jaycee is to me. I get that maybe you couldn't handle it, but at least nobody told you you weren't good enough or that you couldn't even try. Your mom helped you. The only person standing in your way was yourself. I have my mom always reminding me I'm not good enough."

"Mm." Janine was afraid to say anything. She knew her voice would break. Her version of the story had always been that Amanda had been Pam's favorite and that Janine had been the pariah. But Janine had gotten the TV role, something Amanda dearly wanted. And it was true that her inability to handle it after Pam died meant that Amanda would never have a chance at acting, not while Marty was in charge. It made sense that Amanda would have felt cheated out of something. The epiphany, if that's what it was, made Janine feel a little sick.

"I think that's what my mom resents," Hailey said. "You had something she wanted and you just let it go. So now she's taking it out on me."

Janine thought Hailey might be right.

Hailey took a deep breath. "I don't want to talk about this anymore, okay? I'm finally at a good place. I don't want to think about bad stuff. It hurts my face when I cry."

Janine smiled at her. She felt so sad and tired she could barely hold her head up.

"I'll get us some celery," Hailey said, as if Janine had asked for a snack. Janine watched Hailey walk quickly to the kitchen and return with a Tupperware bowl full of celery in one hand and a squeeze bottle of red sauce in the other. "It's really good with sriracha sauce."

"Are you on a diet or something?"

"I have to be."

"Why?"

"Do you promise not to tell my mom?"

"No."

"There's an audition next week. I'm going on it." Hailey squeezed a straight line of sriracha onto the stalk and took a noisy bite. "I'm perfect for it. It's an adaptation of this book I love."

"You're pursuing acting now? It's no way to grow up. Did you hear anything I just said?"

Hailey swallowed. "Now I stand a chance. You said so yourself."

"I did?"

"You said I looked like Mia Farrow."

"You do, but that doesn't mean you should be an actress. And what do you mean, you're going on the audition? Do you have an agent? Do you have headshots?" Is that what this was all about? Hailey wanted to be an actress? Janine felt an inexplicable urge to bash the movie business, to disillusion Hailey just like her father had tried to do to her and Amanda so many years ago. "Look at me. My life is pretty screwed up. I'm a little bit of a mess, more than a little unstable."

Hailey laughed as if Janine were being funny. "I'm going to a workshop at One on One to meet the casting director for a new movie."

"Jesus, Hailey. One on One has been around since I was a kid. You won't be meeting the casting agent, you'll be meeting some low-ranking assistant. And paying for it, right?"

"Just a hundred bucks," she said, chewing on a fresh piece of celery. "There's also an open audition. I'm going. Don't even bother trying to talk me out of it. The part is made for me."

Janine sighed. "What's the part?"

Hailey swallowed the last bit of stalk. "Undine Spragg. From Edith Wharton."

"From *Custom of the Country*?" Janine couldn't help but smile. It was one of her favorite books. It wasn't a well-known novel and Janine was impressed that Hailey had read it. It was true that Hailey would be perfect for it. It was about a beautiful Midwestern social climber trying to enter New York society. Hailey had the looks to play Undine. She also had the longing in her face that made her oddly more attractive, less ordinary. "I know the book," Janine said, and she registered Hailey's surprise.

"Then can't you see me as Undine?"

"What do you like about her?"

Hailey rolled her eyes. "I don't know how to *explain* it." She stared at the back of her hands for a few seconds. "I just want the chance. You had yours. I just want to try."

Janine helped herself to a piece of celery. Maybe Hailey was right. What harm could it do to help her? It's not as if Hailey would get the part. Maybe she just needed to feel supported. "Okay."

Hailey looked up, surprised. "Okay what?"

"Find out who's directing the movie. Send him or her a letter," Janine said, not knowing if this was a good idea but feeling inspired. The business might have changed, but anything seemed better than going to One on One or a cattle call. She dressed the celery with sriracha and took a bite, thinking as she chewed. "Overnight it, so it gets there before they hold auditions. Say why you want the part. Make it personal. But figure out why you love Undine and the book."

"A letter? To the director?"

"I think you'll have a better shot at standing out that way. You're smart. Show him *that*. Tell him why you think you're right for the role. Tell him you're sixteen, tell him who your grandpa is. Tell him you've been acting since you were a kid but that you haven't been allowed to audition for anything professional. It'll give you an air of mystery. Be original."

"Will you help me write the letter?"

"No way," Janine said, taking a prudent step back. "But I'll overnight it for you. And if they call you in, I'll take you to the audition." Janine really wasn't worried that Hailey would get called in, let alone get the part, but she thought her niece deserved to take her shot. And for whatever misguided reason, Hailey was asking Janine for help. Nobody had asked her for her help on anything real in a very long time. Amanda didn't need to know about any of it. She curled up on the bed, exhausted.

"Deal!" Hailey ran to her desk and opened up her laptop.

"Handwrite it," Janine said, closing her eyes. "Be original," she repeated.

"Right. Okay. You'll FedEx the letter for me, right? If it's good?"

"Mm. I'm just going to rest my eyes for a minute."

When Janine woke up three hours later, the letter was on the pillow.

Hailey

Mr. Ransom Garcia
Tiger's Foot Productions
2800 Sunset Blvd
Los Angeles, CA

Dear Mr. Garcia:

My name is Hailey Loehman-Kessler and I am a sixteen-year-old junior at Fair Hills Academy in Los Angeles. I am a great admirer of your work and would love the chance to audition for the role of Undine Spragg in your upcoming film, The Custom of the Country. *In the event nepotism carries any weight with you, I am the grand-daughter of Martin Kessler and the niece of Janine Kessler. If you hate nepotism, forget I mentioned it.*

My mother is a drama teacher at Fair Hills Academy (you might have seen her mentioned in the LA Times calendar section?). Like Undine, I am ambitious. I will stop at nothing to get what I want. What is it I want? A chance, Mr. Garcia!

Mr. Garcia, I am Undine Spragg. I am pushy. I know what it's like not to be liked. I know what it's like to want filet mignon and never get it. I also know what it's like to get on people's nerves. But I bet you've guessed that already!

I understand Undine is not a "nice" character and that my relating to her so strongly might reflect poorly on me. That said, there is nobody who can play this role like I can. I know that Wharton's masterpiece is as relevant today as it was in 1913. The world hasn't changed that much, Mr. Garcia.

What better way to introduce the world to The Custom of the Country than with an unknown actress who happens to have a Hollywood pedigree? It's just the kind of story the media likes! This is the moment. I am Undine Spragg.

I am available to meet with you at your convenience.

Hailey Loehman-Kessler
haileygirlmeme@gmail.com

Two days later, an e-mail arrived in Hailey's in-box.

To: haileygirlmeme@gmail.com
From: CClose@Tigersfootproductions.com
Subject: Audition

Dear Ms. Loehman-Kessler:

Ransom will see you Thursday at 11:00. Please be prepared with two monologues. Address TBA. Good luck and congratulations on your hilarious letter. It got you in the door!

Camille Close,
Assistant to Ransom Garcia, Tiger's Foot Productions

Henry

The ocean lay just beyond the bluffs under a blue, cloudless sky. Janine and Henry were walking slowly toward her car in the Directions parking lot, having agreed on the phone to meet in the lobby after seeing their respective parents. They would arrange the afternoon from there. The prospect of planning spontaneous fun had kept Henry up half the night.

"Do you want to go on a hike?" Henry asked. He was hoping that Janine would say no.

"Do *you* want to go on a hike?" she asked.

He thought she'd sounded distant on the phone and now she seemed nervous, biting her nails and stealing glances at him. "Not in the least."

"Then why'd you ask?"

"I thought women liked to go on hikes."

"Who told you that?"

"A friend."

"Huh. What else did he say?"

"He suggested a picnic, a bike ride, or some yoga." *Yoga!* What an ass he was making of himself. He saw a smile working the corners of her mouth as she reached into her purse for her keys.

"What friend?" she asked.

"Google."

Janine's face softened and she laughed. She pointed to Henry's vandalized car and looked at him with raised brows. "I know Google. He advised me to avoid men on the rebound."

"I'm not on the rebound. I'm on the run," he said jokingly.

She tossed her backpack into the rear of her car and looked at him, her face pinched with worry again.

There was a long silence as Henry mentally revisited their evening together last Tuesday. They'd spoken since and texted flirtatiously, but his teaching schedule had made seeing each other near impossible. Now she looked almost as embarrassed as he felt. There was nothing quite like daylight to expose the false intimacies of spontaneous sex between near strangers. And yet, he thought, it had been thrilling and oddly poignant. She was an unusual person, but after all, so was he. He felt companionship with her, as though they were together emotionally rather than just occupying the same physical space. Being with Janine was so comfortable and unexpectedly lovely.

She cleared her throat. "I've got to tell you something. And I don't know how."

"You've got syphilis."

"No!" Janine said. "God."

"Well?" he asked. "Whatever you have to say won't seem so dreadful now. Compared to syphilis."

Janine looked down at the asphalt and kicked away a pebble with the tip of her sneaker. "It's about your mom, actually."

"I take it back about the syphilis."

"She was married to my dad."

A short pause. "What's that?"

"Our parents were married. You know, before they were our parents."

Henry looked behind him for support and leaned back against the closest car.

"Your father is the—" Henry stopped himself. "You're Amanda?" he said, jaw dropping. "No," he said. "Of course you're not Amanda. You're Janine."

"That's very good," she said, obviously irritated and confused. "How do you know Amanda?"

"You're the plain one?" he said, regretting the words the minute they left his mouth.

"Apparently." She hardened, folding her arms over her chest. "Though I can't say I've ever been accused of it quite so directly. It's one of those things civilized people generally say behind my back."

"That's not what I meant," he said, flustered. "I mean, I don't think you're plain. Not at all. In fact, just the opposite. It's just that my mother saw a picture of the two of you and somehow thought that—"

"That you should meet my sister?" Janine said, finishing his sentence. "That's perfect. Why don't I give you her phone number? She's got great big boobs and a fantastic personality. I'm sure you'll really like her. And God knows both of you have equally arrested communication skills."

Henry stared at her, at a loss for words.

"Bye, Henry," Janine said, turning around. She tried to open the car door, fumbling with the handle.

"Whoa, Janine. Wait a minute." He pressed her arm so that she'd face him again. "Stop. Please. Give me a moment here, please? That was startling news. I had no idea *you* were Mum's first husband's daughter. And I don't know your sister. But I can tell you I'm not in the least bit interested in dating anyone my mother thinks is suitable. Forgive me?" he asked. "My social skills are . . . what was that word?"

"Arrested."

"Yes, that's it. Arrested. Please. I really enjoyed our evening, it was more fun than I've had since I can remember. I'd love to spend the day with you. I'd like it more than anything. My mother and your sister with her giant titties can hang it, for all I care."

Janine laughed. Henry suspected it was easier than crying.

"I didn't know my dad had been married before my mom," she said. "And he acted like not telling me was just an oversight. Like it wasn't a big deal."

"Mm. Perhaps marital obfuscation is a generational thing? My mum told me your father—um, her first husband—died, so consider yourself lucky things didn't work out between them. Anyway, you narrowly escaped a life of humiliation and parental neglect. You'd be named Georgia Garrick and you might be missing a limb," he continued, referring to one of his mother's characters who was all the more lovable because she was born without a left arm.

"But, Henry," she started, distracted by something pressing. "There's the possibility that we're, you know"—she winced—"related." She said this with such an agonized expression that Henry wanted to take her in his arms. Clearly she'd been very worried. He fished his cell phone out of his pocket, selected a photo, blew it up, and held it next to his face.

"My father," he said, smiling like Sam Holter.

Janine cried out with relief. "Wow, Henry, you look just like him."

"I do. Mum wouldn't have pushed your sister on me had there been any question about that. She's very proper. Very well versed in the comings and goings of her uterus. So we can definitely still do it. It's all perfectly incest-free, you see."

"If it's too weird now, please don't feel obligated."

"Obligated?" he said. "I don't feel in the least bit obligated. It is a bit weird," he admitted with a laugh. Henry extended his hand and Janine took it, almost bashfully. He smiled as her delicate fingers folded inside his palm. "Settled, then," he said. "What shall we do if not hiking or yoga?"

"I don't know. What would you do if you had the day to yourself?"

Henry guessed that searching online auction sites to find a replacement for his corn goddess wouldn't be a good answer.

"Henry?"

"There's the Marbury Hall Zeus, of course."

"Ah."

She didn't sound repulsed. In fact, she looked genuinely interested.

"And a beautiful marble Cycladic harp player. Very rare. It's right here at the Getty Villa. One of my colleagues was also raving about a fifth-century Roman Samson mosaic I've seen only in reproduction. It's on loan so I really wouldn't mind having a peek, since we're so close."

"We are close. I think you need a reservation, though."

"When you're with me, my dear, no reservations required. This privilege, sadly, applies exclusively to museums."

Janine looked pleased, perhaps a little impressed. Risa had never cared a lick about art or the meager perks of academia.

"There's a café too," he added. "And while I don't want to sound too arrogant, I believe I get quite the lavish discount. They may even have wine. You know, to kill the pain?"

"It doesn't sound painful."

"No?"

"No. It sounds fun."

"We could get very drunk," Henry said, nudging her gently against her car while lifting her chin with the back of his hand.

"Yes," she said, meeting his eyes.

"If we get too pissed we might miss the Hall of Colored Marbles and the—"

She kissed him then, maybe to stop his rambling or maybe because she wanted to. Either way, it was a superb kiss, just the sort to make him want to skip the museum altogether. Henry understood that Janine was circumspect, that she must fancy him to bravely take his hand and kiss him in a parking lot. He pulled her in close and she made a little whimpering sound so uncontrived, he went wobbly with desire.

She leaned back and smiled. "Let's go, then."

He walked round and slid into the passenger seat. Henry couldn't remember ever having felt so content as he did in that moment. It might have been the sun warming the buttery leather seat of her father's Range Rover, but he didn't think so.

Janine

Janine was as surprised as Hailey that Ransom Garcia had agreed to let Hailey audition and that his office had responded so quickly. Hailey's letter was cute but Janine suspected that dropping the Kessler name hadn't hurt. Hollywood was about whom you knew, and Marty Kessler, despite his age and current residency at Directions, still commanded respect.

She spent the drive over to her sister's second-guessing the wisdom of agreeing to help Hailey. When she realized the gorgeous girl with the long, auburn hair standing outside Amanda's apartment building *was* Hailey, she thought about not even stopping. Why was she wearing a fucking wig? Janine pulled up slowly, staring. Hailey waved and sashayed over to the car, allowing Janine ample time to absorb her niece's physical transformation. She slipped into the passenger seat and buckled her seat belt. Then she turned to Janine and laid a light hand on her shoulder. "Why, hello! I'm so glad you've come," she said in an artificial voice.

Janine stared at the wig.

"I borrowed it from the costume department at school," Hailey said. She twisted the long strands into a thick rope and knotted it into a low bun. "Wharton said Undine's hair was long and tawny.

I looked it up and *tawny* means 'reddish.' So this does the job, right?"

"I guess," Janine said. She was suddenly panicked that Hailey might get the fucking part and that her father and sister would string her up and then stone her to death. God knows Hailey was crazy, pretty, and narcissistic enough to be an actress. Janine could only hope she wasn't talented.

She entered the address of the studio into her phone, grateful that Amanda and Jaycee were both still at school. Come to think of it, why wasn't Hailey back in class? Wasn't it obvious the girl had made a full recovery, no matter how well she'd mastered the art of playing an invalid?

"I'm so nervous I could die," Hailey said in an affected tone. She pulled down the passenger sun visor and quietly admired herself in the mirror before snapping it shut.

"Hailey, I can't believe it's you."

"Do you like it? I think it's becoming."

"You're already in character?" Janine bit the inside of her cheek to keep from laughing. Still, Hailey's accent wasn't half bad. She pronounced her vowels just right, with her tongue slightly closer to the front of her mouth.

"But of course," Hailey said. She rolled down her window and looked into the side mirror to get another peek at her reflection. Hailey had managed to make the cheap wig look somewhat real and she'd been careful to apply only minimal makeup, just some rouge and lipstick. She wore a simple cotton dress that cinched tightly around her tiny waist.

There was no traffic, almost unheard of in LA. The drive to Robertson and Third took only twenty minutes. "Did you ever know such luck?" Hailey asked as they pulled into a parking spot right in front of Ransom Garcia's office building. Janine was eager to get Undine through the audition and back home before Amanda could find out about any of this.

The outside of the building was black and modern, a replica of so many uninspired edifices that had hijacked the Los Angeles skyline since Janine was a kid. Automatic glass doors opened onto a furniture-less lobby, forbidding in its lack of homeyness. Men and women in business suits, a woman with a little boy, even a doctor in scrubs spilled out of the elevators at regular intervals. The security guard directed Janine to Ransom's floor.

Hailey pretended not to notice people watching her make her way to the elevators. Her erect posture and challenging walk seemed to encourage the stares. She didn't make eye contact with anyone, but Janine could almost feel the girl's heart pounding with the victory of each appreciative glance. Pretty girls were like palm trees in LA—nice, but ubiquitous. Hailey was turning heads. Janine grew tense. She remembered watching people stare at her mother the same way. Of course, she'd been a kid back then and she'd been confused by the attention her beautiful mother attracted. Now she knew what it meant.

"Maybe you should take the wig off," Janine suggested in the elevator. "It might be too much. You don't want to annoy him."

"No fucking way," Hailey said. "I mean . . . I think it's fetching."

As they waited in a small lounge outside Mr. Garcia's office, Janine's thoughts drifted off to Henry. He'd handled the news about their parents really well, considering. Maybe being Bunny Small's son had forced him to deal with uncomfortable situations, not unlike what she'd been through growing up as a former child actress. She'd meant to ask him why he hadn't changed his last name, imagining it must be a nightmare going through life as a famous children's-book character. She'd wanted to change her own after the show ended but her father was emphatically opposed to the idea. "Your last name is Kessler!" he'd shouted. "I won't have the consequences of that goddamn show strip away one more ounce of your dignity." Even then, Janine had suspected Marty's outrage had more to do with his pride than her dignity, but it was easier to let it go. Maybe Henry had done the same. She'd ask him later.

Janine liked Henry. His occasional social awkwardness belied a deeper self-confidence. He was funny and self-effacing, and there was absolutely nothing awkward about how he'd expertly moved around his kitchen cooking for her or about the familiar way he always placed his hand at the base of her spine and pulled her in close. He was completely unapologetic about his opinions, almost gruff at times, but then there was this tenderness about him. She was touched by his careful consideration of everything she said, the way he seemed to really listen. And he was extremely smart. His animated tour of the Getty had been inspiring, particularly when he'd talked about a limestone funerary sculpture called *The Beauty of Palmyra*. A large group of visitors had latched onto them in the Hellenistic gallery, probably assuming he was a curator or docent.

She was a little embarrassed she'd slept with him so soon, but she hadn't had sex in a long time, and, God, it had been fun. Their second night together, after the museum, was even better than the first. He was amazing in bed. Crazy-amazing. She smiled to herself, not wanting to get too excited. She knew she liked him, though; how else to explain her offer to take him to the hospital for his ear surgery after their first night together?

"Aunt Janine!" Hailey said in a loud voice, elbowing her in the arm. Janine snapped to and saw a gaunt woman dressed in a brocade steampunk jacket and jeans approaching them.

"I'm Mandy," the woman said to Hailey, extending a businesslike hand, which Hailey shook heartily. Mandy had a complicated, funky look about her. Her hair was crisp with gel and her makeup was thick, as if she were hiding something. Chipped red nail polish flecked her fingernails. Janine noticed she had on a wedding ring and wondered that Mandy could be somebody's idea of a good time.

"Janine Kessler?" Mandy said with a curious grin. "Ransom mentioned your dad but we never thought *you'd* show up. Where've you been hiding? You just vanished."

Generally Janine just stared at the floor and denied who she was in these situations. That wasn't going to work today. Come to think of it, that had never worked. Hailey was staring at Janine now, waiting. "I've been around," Janine finally said, annoyed by Mandy's question but a little flattered that her presence was appreciated. She picked up her purse and followed them both down the hall.

Ransom Garcia was on the phone but he smiled and waved them in. They sat, and he carefully watched Hailey as he wrapped up his call. He was a small man in his mid-fifties, white as paper, with thin blond hair. Garcia? Really? He had red-rimmed blue eyes like a rabbit's and no discernible chin. The office space was big but in no way interesting other than the fact that it wasn't decorated with framed posters of movies he'd directed. Janine appreciated his lack of vanity—though for all she knew, such peacocking was no longer in vogue.

"Hi there," he said, reaching to shake both their hands after hanging up. "Your father and I go way back," he said to Janine with a genuine smile. "He green-lit my first film."

"I had no idea," Janine said, understanding now why Hailey had gotten through the door. She felt hugely relieved. This was a courtesy for her father, nothing more. They'd be done here in ten minutes, Janine would console Hailey on the drive home, and she'd have her back at the apartment before anybody knew a thing!

"How's he doing?"

"Great," Janine lied. "He's doing great."

Garcia clapped his little hands together and looked at Hailey. "Have you got something prepared?"

Hailey smiled and stood up to explain the context for her monologue. "So, this is the scene from the book where Undine tells her husband on their honeymoon how bummed she is that she's pregnant because now she won't be able to show off all her new dresses. It really shows how immature and selfish she is. She doesn't care about her husband or having a family. It's kind of the essence of Undine. That's why I picked it."

"Good." Ransom nodded. "Shall we, then?" He gestured for her to begin.

Hailey looked directly at Ransom. "'Sorry—you're sorry? *You're* sorry? Why, what earthly difference does it make to *you?*'" She took a few steps back and slouched, letting her thin arms dangle at her sides. "'Look at me. See how I look, how I'm going to look!'"

The girl didn't miss a beat, flub one line, or hit a single false note. She was dead-on. Hailey ended the scene by burying her face in her hands and sobbing convulsively. On one hand, Janine was so proud that her heart felt like it was going to blow clear through her chest. Hailey was terrific. Her accent was perfect. Her gestures were perfect—a little overdone, but that was the character. On the other hand, Janine was suddenly terrified that her niece was good enough to actually get the part.

"Hailey?" Ransom asked. He was leaning down and had put a hand on Hailey's shoulder. Hailey looked up, dry-eyed.

"Listen, can you do that again, with my wife, Mandy, in the room and without the wig?"

"Sure." She pulled off the wig, looking a bit embarrassed. Janine arched her eyebrows at Hailey, enjoying her I-told-you-so moment. "My aunt said it might be too much but I thought my real hair might seem, I don't know, confusing."

Ransom's eyes sparkled as he took in Hailey's cropped blond hair. As striking as she looked with the wig, she was like a Madame Alexander doll without it. Janine gazed at her as if for the first time, admiring her coloring. Hailey's body, which had seemed compact and athletic at the apartment, now looked delicate, as if a gust of wind might blow her away. Aside from her generous mouth, her features were small and perfectly symmetrical. Janine knew it was a face that would translate well to the screen. Based on Ransom's enchanted expression, he knew it too.

"Just so you know, we're not doing it as a period piece," Ransom explained. "We're modernizing it."

"Oh," Hailey said. "Should I do something differently?"

"No, no," he said quickly, as though he didn't want to mess her up with direction. "Do it just like that again."

Hailey did it again. She did it even better. She dropped the accent when he asked her to, seamlessly morphing from an early-twentieth-century Midwestern social climber to a twenty-first-century bitch. She was an actress. Janine was freaked. Janine was going to have a lot of explaining to do.

Bunny

"Let's take a trip," Martin said one night. He and Bunny were sitting in the outdoor lounge by a fireplace on opposite recliners. They'd gotten in the habit of talking together after dinner. After lunch too.

"Oh no," she said. "I'm staying put. I've had enough of your bad ideas. Mitchell was sniffing me for two days after your last boozy inspiration."

"Not now." He sat up. "Later. After we get out of here."

"Listen, Martin, I've really enjoyed spending time with you again. If I squint, I can *almost* remember why we got married in the first place. But I don't want to have sex with you. You'll have to make do with Dale."

"For the love of God, her name is Gail, and I don't want to have sex with you either. Why does everything have to be so loaded? I feel like shaking things up a little. You mentioned loving Italy. Why not go?"

"Did I tell you that?" she asked, smiling to herself. Bunny did love Italy—Bernini's library, Claudio Torcè's carrot gelato, the gardens of Villa Farnesina.

"I thought it would be nice to take a trip. You know, as friends. All of my other friends are dead, broke, or have told the same stories so many times I can no longer decide which is worse, the cheap Chinese food or the company."

"I don't really have any friends," Bunny said. "It's hard when you become—"

"Famous?" Martin said. "I know. You've told me."

"I've got Ian," she said, feeling defensive. "My agent. He's my friend."

"Christ. Is that a Muddy Waters hit waiting to be recorded."

"It is pathetic. But it's hard to trust anyone when—"

"You're so famous," Martin said again, finishing her sentence.

She frowned. "That's not what I was going to say."

"Pardon me. By all means, continue."

"Maybe it was," she said, more to herself than to Martin. "A trip, eh? To Rome?"

"If you like Rome, sure. It's a little loud but—"

"I never go anywhere for fun anymore. But you know something?" She paused. "If I tell you this, you mustn't tell anyone. Anyone."

He held up three fingers in a Scout's honor salute.

"I'm a bit blocked."

"Constipated?"

"No, Martin. Blocked as in I haven't been able to write in some time. A trip might be just the solution. And something to look forward to after all this." Bunny paused, thinking. "We can keep each other sober eating bread at Capo Boi! It's an addiction all its own," she said, her mouth suddenly watering. And then: "But what about your girlfriend? Did you forget about her?"

"No." He knit his brow.

"Well," she said, intrigued by the idea but compelled to state her terms straightaway. "You'll have to deal with her, obviously. And of course I'll have to pay for everything. I'm used to a certain standard, you understand."

"So am I," he said, offended. "I'm not a charity case. I can pay my own way."

She shook her head. Men were so tedious. "I don't think so, Martin. Don't get your knickers in a twist about it. It's just the way I prefer it."

"I fly first class," he said. "I can afford my own suite at the Parco dei Principi, thank you very much."

Parco dei Principi! Was that the best he could do? She tried to hide her derision. "There's a lovely boutique hotel where they know me. It's charming and exclusive. And they don't let just anyone in."

"Of course not. Wouldn't want to stay in a hotel where they allow anyone who can afford it to stay."

"So true. And I fly private. It's much easier. No press, no snooping photographers."

"Forget it," he said. "It sounded like a good idea."

"It is a good idea," she said, poking him in the arm. "Don't let your ego get in the way. We're too old. The expense is nothing to me."

Was he really going to let the *only* wife who hadn't taken a nickel from him drive him into bankruptcy so he could make a point? Certainly the irony couldn't be lost on him, Bunny thought. "So, then," she went on, "two old friends on a trip?"

Martin moved his jaw sideways, thinking. Bunny could see he was second-guessing himself now. "I don't know if Gail will go for it," he said.

"Do you need her approval? Is she your guardian?"

"No, but I hadn't really thought it through. It might be construed as a little disrespectful if I took a grand tour with an ex-wife, one who happens to be . . . what was the word?" he asked. "Ah, yes, famous. It's asking a lot."

"Pff," Bunny said. "If she's too insecure to let you have a bit of fun, she's obviously not worth the trouble. Are you a man or a mouse, Martin?"

He looked at her with disapproval. "They pay you for that level of originality? Surely you can do better."

Why had he gotten her excited about the idea just to put up roadblocks? How irritating! "Buy her a house or something. Isn't that the way you do things? My God, why shouldn't you take a trip with an old friend?"

"An old wife," he said. "It's reaching."

Bunny could feel him bending. He just needed a little push. She took out a cigarette and cleared her throat. "Forgive me if I'm over-stepping, but you talk about her as if she's put the fear of God in you. Like she's your disapproving mother. It's strange."

"Thank you."

"I'm just letting you know how it all comes off to a disinterested party." Bunny leaned forward and pointed the unlit cigarette between her fingers at Martin. "Throw Momma from the train, Martin!" She laughed, thrilled with her pop-culture reference. "Just for a couple of weeks. What's a bit of temporary insubordination? What are you so afraid of? I'm certain she'll be waiting for you when you get back. *Certain.* Is that your worry? Or does she have you believing you can't manage without her? That you can't hail a cab? That you'll lose your passport if she's not holding on to it for you?"

"Hey!" Martin grabbed both sides of the recliner and pushed himself up. "Do you have any idea how many premieres, how many fucking lo-cation sets I've had to travel to over the years? Ever try getting from LAX to Port Moresby in Papua New Guinea and back in two days?"

"I can't say that I have, Martin. No."

"Well, I think I can handle myself in Rome, for Christ's sake." He sat back down, grinding his teeth. Bunny felt sure she'd discov-ered the fertilizer from which his relationship with Dale bloomed. That girlfriend of his drew her power from making him feel helpless. Bunny wondered if maybe all his wives and girlfriends had done the same thing, at least as he'd gotten older and it had become a viable strategy. Bunny loathed women who preyed on good men. And Mar-tin, despite his many demons, was a good man.

"It's a bit ludicrous, isn't it?" she asked, opening her Cartier lighter. "Buying into the notion that you're too feeble to fend for yourself? The Martin Kessler I remember took risks. He built a career championing talent nobody else could see." Bunny lit her cigarette and smiled. "The same fellow who procured vodka at a drug-rehabilitation center."

"Of course it's ludicrous! Nobody tells me what I can and cannot do!"

"Well"—Bunny exhaled, smoothing her pants as she reclined—"for such a fierce dog, you've been put on a mighty tight leash by Dale."

"Gail!" he snapped. Then, in a voice that seemed to startle him with its conviction, he added, "Let's go to Rome!"

Bunny clapped her hands.

"But don't tell anyone about it yet. Nobody."

"Of course not," Bunny said, bubbling with joy. "Mum's the word."

Hailey

Hailey was confident walking into the callback with Ransom Garcia. With her mother out of town and Jaycee in school, she had her aunt's undivided attention for at least two hours every afternoon. She knew she had to make the most of their time together; she'd have to go back to school next week if she didn't get this part. They'd been running lines at Grandpa Marty's house. Other than the unexpected and slightly annoying presence of Janine's kind-of-cute English boyfriend (where he'd come from and what he was doing recovering from an operation in Grandpa Marty's bedroom, she had no idea), Hailey felt like everything was finally coming together for her.

She and Janine had made a pact after that first audition: they would work hard on the scene and never mention it to anyone unless she got the part. Obviously, if she got it, her mom wouldn't be mad at them for being secretive. How could Amanda be mad if Hailey took her to the Academy Awards?

The problem was that Janine hadn't told Hailey there would be a casting director, two producers, writers, and a camera guy at the callback! And she definitely hadn't been expecting to do a cold read before her scene.

"But I prepared the sides you gave me," Hailey told Ransom. "I worked on the lines a lot with my aunt. I thought this was a callback for that role."

"It is. Of course." Ransom looked at Davis, the casting director. Davis had a gray beard, a big stomach, and a bald head. Hailey saw Davis roll his eyes. "And we'll run through that," Ransom continued. "We just want to know if you can play a bit older. Undine grows older through the course of the story. The actress who plays her has to be womanly. Undine is a seducer. We need to see you do something...sexy."

Janine was looking nervous, chewing on her lip. Hailey didn't know what the hell Janine was worried about—*she* was the one being asked to pull some theatrical improvisation out of her ass.

"I'm not so great at improv," Hailey said. "It's not really my thing."

"It's not improv," Ransom said patiently. Janine was just visible behind Ransom, putting her finger to her lips, gesturing for Hailey to be quiet. "You'll have the script the whole time," he explained. "You're just going to read the lines. Stand over there by Guy, on the floor mark, so that you're facing the camera. When he gives you the thumbs-up, state your name and age and anything else you want us to know. If you don't want to do that, you can just start the reading. Right, then?"

"Right," Hailey said. She was trying not to cry, having trouble even focusing on the words on the page. She knew she was making a fool of herself, but she couldn't help it.

"Can we have just a second?" Janine asked. She ushered Hailey out of the big room without waiting for an answer.

"Sure," Ransom said as Janine was shutting the door behind them, "but we're on a schedule."

Janine walked Hailey to the end of the hall at a brisk clip. "Do not cry, Hailey!" Janine said, grabbing her by the shoulders. "Stop it! You need to pull yourself together. You are auditioning for the lead. This isn't just about how talented you are. It's about attitude and professionalism. They need to know that you're flexible and willing to take direction. Do you hear what I'm saying?"

Hailey nodded, not listening.

Janine snapped her fingers. "This is about your maturity as much as your ability, and you are crying. I don't think that's what they're looking for, do you?"

"It's a mean trick."

"Shit, Hailey. It's not a trick," she said, leading her back down the hallway. "Nobody's out to get you. They want you to be good. Ransom obviously likes you. Everybody who matters is in that room. You could get this part against well-known actors if you show them your commitment and the right attitude. So look over the pages." Janine's hand was on the doorknob. "I'll tell them you'll be ready in two minutes. Two."

Hailey nodded and took deep breaths. She looked down at the pages and saw the names Brick and Big Daddy. The words seemed to unlock a secret code, and she could finally make out what she was reading. It was a monologue by Maggie from *Cat on a Hot Tin Roof*. She knew this play! She had helped her mom stage this play!

She scanned the scene, centering herself, blocking the negative thoughts.

"I'm sorry," Hailey said, walking back into the room. "I just needed a minute."

"No problem," Ransom said, smiling encouragingly. "You ready?"

"Should I do it with you?" she asked Ransom.

"With Davis," he said, pointing to the old-man casting director. The sofa had been moved to the middle of the room, and the camera was set up behind it. Hailey noticed that Davis's body was kind of pear-shaped, like her old nanny's. He stretched his leg out, like Brick reclining on the bed with his drink. Hailey appreciated his following the stage directions, but his expression was impatient, as if he were doing this just to indulge Ransom.

She caught Davis's eye, and he yawned. He yawned! *Well, fuck you,* she thought. *I'm going to blow your fucking mind.* She pulled the neckline of her sweater dress so it was off her shoulders a little bit and cleared her throat. Davis was bored? Fine. She'd use it, as her mother would say, and turn it into hatred. She'd use it for the scene.

"Ready?" she asked the camera guy.

"We're rolling." He gave her a thumbs-up.

"'What makes you think Big Daddy has a lech for you, Maggie?'" Davis read, not even looking up.

"'Way he always drops his eyes down my body when I'm talkin' to him, drops his eyes to my boobs an' licks his old chops!'" Hailey put her hands on her hips. "'Ha ha!'"

"'That kind of talk is disgusting,'" Davis said, flatline.

"'Did anyone ever tell you that you're an ass-aching Puritan, Brick?'" She smiled playfully, letting on that she, Maggie, was only joking.

Hailey saw Ransom nod enthusiastically and whisper something to the writer. She straightened her dress around her hips the way Elizabeth Taylor had done it in the movie. The whole rest of the scene was hers. She looked at the script and knelt down so that she could be eye-level with Davis and his lady hips. When she leaned in like she was about to tell him a secret or kiss him, she felt his breath quicken. The closer she got to his halitosis, the heavier he breathed. Hailey continued her monologue, tracing her fingers in a small circle on Davis's forearm until the hairs stood at attention.

"*Cut,*" Ransom said. "That was great, Hailey. You okay there, Davis?" he asked with a laugh. The producers and writers were whispering among themselves.

"I will be," he said, lifting himself off the couch and giving Hailey a look. Maybe she'd surprised him by being good. Or maybe he had a boner.

"You ready for the scene you prepped?" Ransom asked.

"Yes." Hailey looked over at Janine, who winked and smiled, proud. Hailey knew she'd killed it!

Once again, Hailey would do the scene with Davis. He was reading the part of Undine's mother, who was waiting up for her daughter after she'd had a late night with her rich boyfriend, Ralph. The evening hadn't gone well.

Davis was sitting stiffly with the sides. Hailey wasn't nervous this time. She knew this scene.

"'Mom? Why are you still up?'" Hailey asked, walking toward Davis and showing just the right amount of annoyance.

"'What happened?'" Davis said apathetically. "'I want to hear everything.'"

He wasn't even looking at her! How was she supposed to stay in character when he wasn't giving her anything? He was delivering the lines like he was ordering at the Jack in the Box drive-through.

"I'm sorry," Hailey said, looking at Ransom. "I'm just...I guess I rehearsed the scene with my aunt and I got used to playing off her."

"But you'll be working with other actors," Ransom explained.

"I know but..." She looked at Janine, who had her eyes tightly shut. Shit. Now Hailey was screwing up the scene they'd prepared! It was Davis's fault. He was acting like it was so beneath him to waste his time with an amateur. He was throwing her off her game.

"Jesus, Ran." Davis stood up and tossed the pages to Janine, who startled.

"You want *me* to read with her?" Janine asked. Her aunt looked totally freaked out. *Well,* Hailey thought, *at least now you know how it feels!*

"Please," Ransom said and nodded at Janine. Then, to the camera guy: "Let's retake."

Janine sat in the chair, straight-backed, alert. She had the script in hand but Hailey knew she didn't need it. Janine had rehearsed the scene with Hailey for hours while Jaycee was at school. They'd even blocked it out in her grandpa's huge living room like they were on a stage. Hailey loved those afternoons. Hanging out with Janine and running lines in that cool house was about the best thing ever. Hailey badly wanted to impress her aunt today, the way she knew she'd done the past few days. She took a deep breath. She could do this.

"'Mom? Why are you still up?'" Hailey repeated.

"'What happened?'" Janine said. "'I want to hear everything.'"

There was a strain of panic under Janine's voice that sounded just perfect but that hadn't been there yesterday.

"'It's two a.m.!'" Hailey said. She turned a chair around and took a seat in front of a make-believe vanity, her back to Janine. "'You'll look terrible tomorrow.'"

"'*You* look terrible now, Undie! What's wrong? What happened tonight?'"

Hailey turned to face Janine, furious. "'Can't you leave me alone?'" She got up, walked briskly to Janine, and stood looming over her. "'You make me sick, staring at me like an animal in a zoo! I can't take it anymore.'"

Janine shrank back. "'I think it was just the lighting. You look better now. Beautiful.'"

"'Mm,'" Hailey said, softening. "'The track lighting is unflattering. Turn it off.'"

"'I'll get you some chamomile tea,'" Janine said after a perfectly timed pause. "'I bought some today.'"

Hailey turned away from Janine. "'I don't want tea. Go to sleep.'"

Janine sat quietly for a moment. She almost said something but then visibly swallowed her words lest they irritate Undie. Hailey could hear laughter from the far side of the room.

"'Okay. Good night, then.'" Janine stood and then wavered. She took a deep breath before speaking. "'Were they rude to you? Did something bad happen?'"

"'Don't be dumb! It was fine.'" Hailey pretended to undress, like they'd practiced, tossing her imaginary clothes onto the floor and walking away. Janine followed, bending down to collect the discarded clothing, carefully stroking the garments, avoiding meeting Hailey's gaze. "'Turn off the light, I said,'" Hailey ordered. "'I'm exhausted.'" She plopped onto the sofa and mashed her face into the cushions.

Janine, bracing herself, meandered back to Hailey and got on her knees. She leaned in so close that Hailey almost laughed. "'Undie— did something happen? You can tell me.'"

At the question, Hailey turned her head and glared at Janine. Then Hailey replied, "'There's nothing to tell. Go to bed!'"

Ransom shouted, *"Cut!"* and the room erupted in applause. Even Davis was clapping.

Hailey knew she was the prettier twin now. She was destined for greatness. She didn't need to hear anybody say so. She didn't need to ask. Some things a sensitive person just knew.

Henry

Only later would Henry understand that he'd violated what was assuredly a cardinal rule of all new relationships: Don't be a needy pillock right off the bat. Still, it had all seemed reasonable at the time. It began with his ear operation. What the surgeon had described as a straightforward procedure had turned into a complex four-hour affair. "We never really know until we're inside the ear," the doctor had explained to them post-surgery. "Mr. Holter will have to stay in the hospital if he's got nobody looking after him at home." Then he'd looked at Janine expectantly—as though she'd signed up for anything other than being Henry's designated driver. Janine didn't want to play nursemaid to Henry any more than he wanted to stay alone in that hospital. Henry sensed her reluctance, but she'd agreed to take him to her father's house, and Henry had allowed it.

Things had started out well enough. When Henry opened his eyes the next morning, he found himself in a strangely beautiful bedroom, an entire wall covered in Pima Indian baskets and another with a rare oil painting by Alexander Calder. A Nakashima headboard was flanked by two built-in bookshelves opposite a Mayan-inspired concrete fireplace, cleverly copied from Wright's Ennis House. Henry was dazed by the eccentricity of the space. The far wall was all glass, partially shuttered with wooden blinds.

Janine was perfectly charming, carrying in a variety of exotic soups on colorful wicker trays. Her hair was covered by some sort of bandanna. She looked very farm-to-table, Henry thought, like someone who'd know just what to do with dirty escarole.

Over the next two days he found himself increasingly delighted to see Janine and thrilled that he was no longer dizzy or in pain. Really, he was euphoric that the whole thing was over. He could have done without the Velcro headband that held the packing in place affixed diagonally over his right eyebrow and ear. And it was a little odd that he was in his mother's ex-husband's bed, but he was hardly going to carp about that. Gratitude overwhelmed him. He and Janine spent hours together, watching the telly, playing board games from her youth, recounting their histories.

He told her about the night he'd sneaked a girl into his room at Eton, so naive and ill prepared to lose his virginity that he'd tried to make a condom out of some cling wrap he found in the communal kitchen. God knows he'd never shared that story with anyone. And the time he'd lost his contact lenses before a swim meet and then chipped his tooth on the wall flubbing a flip turn. Janine admitted to crashing her father's car the first day she had her driver's license because she got spooked by a shadow on the windshield that she mistook for a giant spider crawling across the dashboard.

Henry divulged the origins of his ear troubles, the many frightened evenings he'd stood outside his mother's door. Janine seemed to intuitively understand Henry's dynamic with Bunny. She'd also had a tenuous relationship with her mother, always feeling like an outsider. The casual way she'd narrated the day her mother had killed herself, as if it had happened to somebody else, made Henry want to cry. When he reached for her hand, she'd pulled it away and laughed a little, as if he were making too much of the thing.

The twins Henry had heard so much about were loud and immature, but he found them entertaining (which he chalked up to the mellowing effects of painkillers). He enjoyed watching Hailey lord her new face and her new relationship with Janine over her sister. Hailey was like a puppy around her aunt, and, despite what Janine said, Henry could tell Janine liked the attention. When Janine wasn't with him, he could hear her in the living room with Hailey going over lines for a movie audition that Janine had told him he was not to mention in front of Jaycee or anyone. Who on earth would he tell? He was comforted by the sound of their voices from a distance, soothed by the tone of Janine's hushed laughter as it carried down the hall.

Less delightful was the obese cat, Roger, to whom Henry was severely allergic and the incessant barking of a nearby dog that nobody seemed to know anything about. And then there was Sandro, the gardener, glaring at Henry from the chaos of the yard, a travesty that reminded him of Barnes, a derelict cemetery in London. The garden had grown wild, weeds everywhere, ivy crawling up the trees, strangling the roots. A pair of life-size, art deco bronze geese sat on a yellowed lawn, one of them decapitated. Dried-up roses, overgrown shrubs, large cacti tipped over, soil spilling out of their terra-cotta pots. Even the outdoor furniture had been upended; one long green cushion floated ominously in a pool filled with eucalyptus leaves, pollen, and acorns.

The yard was unsettling but nothing was ever perfect. Henry knew that. All in all, his recuperation was going swimmingly well.

A few days after the surgery, he and Janine were on the bed playing a delightful game called Boggle. He was winning. Jaycee came into the bedroom without knocking and handed Janine an envelope full of cash.

"What's this?" Janine asked.

"I called Lynn like you asked about getting money for food and stuff. She told me Ed doesn't represent Grandpa anymore."

"Is your father buying *my* meals?" Henry asked, horrified. "Please, take my wallet—"

"Shh!" Janine silenced him with a curt wave of her hand. Then, to Jaycee: "What do you mean, Ed doesn't represent him anymore?"

Jaycee shrugged. "I don't know. Lynn gave me the name of his new money-management firm but I didn't know who to call there. So I called Gail."

"And?"

"Gail said she'd take care of it for me." Jaycee laughed. "The next Mrs. Marty Kessler dropped the envelope off at school this morning."

The ensuing silence filled the air like sarin gas, Henry thought as he held his breath. Jaycee looked at Henry apologetically. Slowly, she slipped out of the room. Henry's euphoria was deflating by the minute.

"Everything okay there?" he finally asked Janine.

Janine bit her lip. "No."

"I'm confused. What's happened?"

She squinted, deep in thought, as if piecing together the clues to an unsolved crime. "A while ago I had a very weird money conversation with my dad."

Henry nodded.

"But he never told me he'd fired Ed. Ed was his lawyer. But he was his friend too, like his, I don't know, his superego or something. At least Ed cared. Without Ed, it's carte blanche for Gail!" Janine said. "I mean, she's running interference on my per diem now? Is this a fucking joke?"

Henry was struggling to remember who Gail was. "She?" he asked, the word floating in the air like a grenade in slow motion.

"Gail, Henry! My father's girlfriend!"

He had to work hard not to lose the thread. Gail, Amanda, Marty, Hailey, Jaycee . . . the benefit of managing only one disappointed relative wasn't lost on him.

Then she turned to him. "I don't think your mom is helping. Gail is very threatened by Bunny's being at Directions."

Henry lay down and brought both his hands up to the wrapping on his head. He was shaken by the anger in Janine's voice and was hoping if he drew her attention to the bandages, she might remember that he'd recently been on an operating table. He swallowed before speaking. "Some men do better with controlling women."

"Yeah? Well, not him."

"How do you know?"

"Have you met my fifteen stepmothers?"

"But it's not really your business, is it?"

Judging by the look on Janine's face, this was, quite clearly, the wrong thing to say. "I mean," Henry said, not knowing at all what he meant anymore, "he's a grown man. If he's happy with her, it's his decision to make, isn't it?"

She shook her head. "You don't get it. You didn't know him before. He was this force. He was just so confident and kind. Do you know how rare that is?" she asked, not waiting for an answer. "There was nobody like him. He was like this mythic personality. Now he's a skeleton of who he used to be, being chauffeured around by Gail, playing the invalid, acting like he can't even take a piss without her permission. It's like she enables his feebleness, like she wants him to feel totally dependent on her. Is that healthy? Is that a healthy relationship?"

Henry didn't say anything.

"And if she makes him so happy, why is he taking drugs? Are drug addicts happy?"

Speaking of drugs, Henry thought, it was high time for another Percocet. He gestured to the bottle on the nightstand. Without pausing, Janine shook a pill out and gave it to him with the glass of water.

"I get that he's older now, but he can do better. There are loads of nice women who would love to be with him." Then, a hitch in her voice: "Why is he settling for her? It's like he's giving up."

Henry wrinkled his forehead. "But why get so involved? You'll drive yourself mad, getting caught up in his affairs."

She gave him a look. "Forget it. It's too complicated to explain."

"Is it the money?" Henry asked.

"No, Henry," she said, obviously offended. "I don't want to think about his money. He can do what he wants with it."

Henry pressed a folded tissue into his palm and waited. He sensed there was more she wanted to say.

"Though God knows," she said, trying to reassemble her anger, anything to fill the cavity of her sadness, "I'd have made very different choices had I known it would come to this. What am I doing with my life?"

Henry looked at her compassionately. "I'm not sure you can blame your father or Gail for your poor decision-making. Maybe your anger with her is really about your own insecurities."

Janine frowned. "Maybe. But rather than a psychotherapy session, I could really use a little sympathy right now," she said. "Can't we just agree that she's a grade-A gold-digging bitch?"

Henry had never heard this tone from her before. He forced himself to sit up and cleared his throat. "I'm not feeling my best. I so appreciate what you've done for me, but maybe I should return to my flat? You seem a bit overwhelmed. Not that I don't understand. I do."

Janine looked down at her hands and began fixedly picking a cuticle on her right thumb. She kept her eyes down when she finally spoke. "No. You're right. Being back here is just triggering my own stuff. I shouldn't be laying this on you." She looked up at him and smiled. "Will you stay? I really like having someone here to kick my butt at Boggle. I promise to be a less narcissistic nurse."

"It does pass the time, watching you lose," he said. She rolled her eyes. "And I do want to know what's going on in your life," he added, which was true. "I'm just sorry I can't really help." He paused. "Come, then." He tapped the bed, inviting Janine to curl up next to him. As she nestled into the crook of his arm, he closed his eyes and pulled her in tighter. "Tell me a story. Tell me a good memory you have of your father."

"Okay. But only if you tell me one about you and your mom."

"Mm. You go first. I'll need some time to think."

Janine laughed and burrowed in closer. He listened to her talk about a day she and her father had gone to catch frogs in a creek in Malibu. Back when Malibu had creeks. And frogs. Somewhere nearby, a dog was barking. The Percocet rounded off the edges of his nerves. Henry nodded and sighed knowingly at the appropriate moments. Janine seemed okay with his lack of conversational participation now. She had been so kind to take care of him. She just needed an ear, he thought, not without irony.

Janine

This takes the cake, Janine.
It takes the fucking cake!

> Huh? R u back? I'm driving.
> Going to get Hailey now.

I ask you for one favor in forty years and this is what you do?
Have you lost your mind? Again?

My God! Janine thought. Amanda was back in town. She wasn't supposed to be home until the weekend. Janine had taken Henry to his post-op appointment. By the time she dropped him back at her father's and gotten onto the 405, traffic was at a standstill. Now she was late to pick Hailey up from her latest audition with Ransom Garcia. How much did Amanda know?

Janine should have gone with her niece to this audition. Henry could have taken a car service, *especially* since he'd spent their travel time playing life coach. "Have you ever considered taking up some sort of vocation?" he'd asked, as if she hadn't been thinking about that for the past twenty years. When she tried to explain that she had no skills, that she couldn't even work a cash register, he'd *laughed* at her. "I wasn't suggesting you work at McDonald's," he said. "You learn. That's what people do. Do you honestly think everyone out there with a job is somehow more capable than you? Smarter than you?" Yes. Yes, that was exactly what she thought.

But there was no time to obsess about Henry now. She tried to call Amanda. That's when she saw the messages. Fuck. She'd turned her ringer off at Henry's doctor's office. She had five new voice-mail messages. Two were from Ransom, one from Hailey, one from Amanda, and one from her dad. She took a deep breath and pressed Play.

"Hi, Janine. It's Ransom. I wanted to call you myself, out of respect for you and your dad. I've got good and bad news. The bad news is that we're not going to go with Hailey. You know I love her to bits but she's just too raw and the producers are more than a little concerned about her lack of..." He paused, as if searching for a good word. "Professionalism. She's such a talent and we respect her ambition, and God knows she's lovely to look at, but even when she's on camera, you can see that she's not really listening to the other actors. She's just sort of waiting for her next line. I thought we could break through this— it's not uncommon with inexperienced actors—but she's just not taking direction, which is, you know, a problem. For me. The director." He laughed, sounding anxious. "I'm really sorry. I felt so good about her, but it's just not going to work.

"And she's very upset. I asked if we should call you but she said no. She said something about her mother and called a car. I'm sure she'll tell you all about it. I'm sorry about that part too." He laughed again. "Anyway, I—"

The message cut off. It didn't matter. What else was there to say? Janine's heart was pounding. She tried to imagine Hailey getting that news. She should have gone with her. She looked at her phone. The next message was from Hailey.

"I totally blew it. They all hate me. I ruined everything. I'm a loser!

I'm a tragedy. I'm Lindsay Lohan and Amanda Bynes all rolled into one, fat, uncastable shitcake! I'm Kathy fucking Griffin. *I want to die!*" she cried and hung up.

With her right hand, Janine fished through her bag for a Xanax. She played the next message, the second one from Ransom.

"So," he said with a sigh of what sounded like relief, "I know this is totally off the wall but we'd like you to play Undine's mother. I realize it's a small part, but what do you say?" His voice was excited. "Everyone was crazy about you on film. You've still got it. Let me know. Of course, I didn't mention this to Hailey. I'll leave that to you. Sorry."

Jesus. Janine tried hard to breathe. The next message was from Amanda.

"I cannot fucking believe you took Hailey on an audition for a fucking feature film—behind my back. Who are you, Mom? Do I have to remind you how totally fucked up you are as a result of your early career? Do you think that is what I want for my kids? I want to thank you for taking my emotionally fragile daughter right to the edge. What were you thinking? Next time I need a hand, I'll call Joan Crawford."

The last message was from her dad. "Hey, so what's the good news? Call me."

Henry

"Hello, Mother."

"Henry?"

"Of course it's Henry. Who else answers my phone 'Hello, Mother'?"

"Oh, I see. You're in one of your moods."

"I'm not in a mood. I'm fine."

"It's been ages. When are you coming to visit?"

"As soon as the last of the packing is removed from my head."

"And when's that happening?"

"Tomorrow."

"So you'll come tomorrow?" she asked. "It's beginning to look like you're the only person who visits me."

"I am the only person who visits you."

"Then you understand why it's important."

"I might need another day or two to get right. You know, before driving. In case there's bleeding or disorientation."

"Why don't you have the girl drive you? I see her here every day. She's very dutiful, I'll say that."

"I think I might have overstepped. She seemed cross when she left and I don't want to ask for more favors just now. And there's new drama brewing," he said, remembering that he'd heard Hailey come

276

in, sobbing. Janine had recently left the house to pick her up. Had she not gotten the big part after all? When he'd called out to Hailey, she'd told him to mind his own fucking business. Well, that was fine by him. Amanda would be back from San Francisco soon and he wouldn't be sorry to see the twins go. Maybe they'd take the cat.

"I see," Bunny said. "And I suppose it would be terribly inconvenient for her to drive with you from her house to a place she's going anyway. I don't understand, Henry."

"I don't want her to think I'm using her. She's sensitive. I don't want to hurt her feelings."

"Why on earth would it hurt her feelings?"

"The thing is, I think I should go. I've got to get out of this house."

"Tell me," Bunny said, nearly panting with anticipation, "is it awful? The house? Is Martin terribly poor?"

"The house is lovely, Mother. It's something of an architectural gem, really—"

"Well, why do you need to get out of the house?" she asked. "Is it the girl?"

"No. The girl, whose name is Janine, is lovely, but I have been living in *your* boyfriend's flat with a woman I'm just getting to know, a set of possibly psychotic teenage twins, and an obese cat named Roger who apparently has taken a real shine to me. I've tried explaining to him about allergies but he sleeps on my chest and won't be persuaded to move. He seems to find my wheezing soothing. And now Janine's cross with me for offering unsolicited advice. I wonder who I picked up that habit from?"

"Dear God, you're an adult. Man up and be honest with her. After she takes you to the doctor tomorrow, and after you visit me, explain that you'd like to return to your flat. She'll probably be relieved to be rid of you. Just don't pull one of your disappearing acts. *Nobody* likes those."

"I didn't disappear on you, Mother. I moved." Henry heard the front door open. "I have to go."

"And my birthday?" she asked, unable to let that one go. "You're too old to be so selfish, Henry. You disappoint people with your pathological passivity. I appreciate that you've been showing up for me here but I can't help but suspect that the minute I leave Los Angeles, you'll slip away again. Like a rat."

"How did you manage to make this about you? This is about Janine. I dread hurting her feelings. I have to go," he said again.

"Well, I can't say you've ever given me so much consideration."

Henry sighed. "I'm hanging up now."

Silence.

"Hello?"

His mother had beaten him to it. How very like her. He put the phone down and stiffened at the sound of a woman stomping around, calling Hailey. Her voice grew louder as she drew closer to the bedroom. He sat paralyzed in the bed, listening to the thud of doors opening and closing.

"Janine?" he'd called out. "Is that you?" Stupid, in retrospect, to draw attention to his whereabouts. He made a dash for the closet. Honestly, he didn't even know why he was hiding. He just wanted to avoid a scene.

The bedroom door swung open with such violent force Henry could hear it rebound off the wall. He was quite glad he'd opted to hide out now. "Hailey? Where are you?"

Henry watched the ferocious-looking blonde through the partly open closet door. The mysterious Amanda, no doubt. She walked to the unmade bed in her wrinkled linen pantsuit and picked up the Ron Childress novel that Henry had borrowed from her father's bookshelf. Then she laid her hand flat on the bed. "I can feel the heat, asshole," she said, calmer now, as she looked over her shoulder. Henry took a step back, deeper into the bowels of Martin Kessler's sports coats. He felt dizzy (whether from his hasty relocation to the closet or from fear, he couldn't say) and had to kneel down. That's when Roger gently, treacherously, weaved his downy, dander-coated body around Henry's bare ankles. "Bloody hell!" he whispered, tossing the cat out of the closet to the accompaniment of a loud, juicy sneeze. Amanda picked Roger up and opened the closet door. She looked down. Had ever a man found himself in such a compromising position?

"You must be Henry," Amanda said, smiling malevolently. "What the fuck are you doing?"

"I, uh," he stammered as he stood back up on shaky legs. He was dressed only in his boxer briefs.

"Where's my daughter?" she asked. Henry shook his head, too mortified to speak. "Where's Hailey?"

He shook his head some more, seemingly unable to form a sentence.

She looked him up and down with a curled lip. "Put some fucking clothes on. Is that how you dress with teenagers in the house?"

"No, ma'am," he said, pulling on the sleeve of a conveniently placed sports coat until it slid off the hanger. He slipped it on, the remaining scraps of his dignity in danger of utter extinction.

"Don't *ma'am* me! Jesus. Where's my fucking traitor sister? Where's Hailey?"

"I don't know." He held up his hands. "I don't know anything."

At that moment, Hailey—tearstained, snot-covered, red-faced—ran into the room, calling for her mother. "I'm soooooooorry," she cried, burying herself in her mother's embrace. "Oh, baby," Amanda cooed, holding on, resting her chin on Hailey's bowed head. They stood like that for what, to Henry, seemed an eternity. What was he doing playing witness to this scene? What did any of this have to do with him? "Let's go get your things," Amanda finally whispered to Hailey, nodding with encouragement as the girl sniffled and wiped her nose on the back of her arm. Then, looking over Hailey's shoulder at Henry, Amanda said, "Put some pants on, asshole. Preferably *not* my father's!"

The moment they left the room, Henry called a car, got dressed, and began throwing his belongings into his bag. He called Janine but she'd stayed on the phone only long enough to say she was in the ninth circle of hell with her family and would be home soon. Then she'd hung up. He knew he should wait for her but he couldn't. He tossed off a note instead. Assuredly she would understand his hasty departure. He scurried out the door. He wasn't about to wait for Amanda to come back.

part four

Torschlusspanik (noun): *The fear that time is running out in life; literally "gate-shutting panic"*

Marty

Marty was looking forward to brunch alone with Janine and Amanda. Thank God Gail was off riding. He'd tell her about going to Italy with Bunny later, when the time was right. Now that he had the trip to look forward to, he was excited about getting out of here. Whistling to himself en route to the dining hall, he caught sight of Bunny heading in the same direction. He'd hoped she'd already eaten, as she'd told him last night Henry wasn't coming to the family brunch today. He tried to duck into an alcove, not wanting to walk into the dining room with her, but she'd seen him.

"There you are," she said, waving him down. "I'm meeting Henry. I thought I saw you pass by in the lobby."

"But you said Henry wasn't coming."

"He changed his mind."

"Perfect."

"Do relax, Martin. I'll be sure Henry and I are sitting out of spitting distance."

"Be sure you're out of viewing distance."

"I've never known a man so terrified of his own family."

"I'm looking to avoid conflict. Whenever you show up, there's conflict."

"I think you had those wheels in motion long before I showed up."
She was walking alongside him now. "Is what's-her-name coming?"

"Her name is Gail. *Gail.* And no," he said, as much to himself as to
Bunny, "Gail is not coming. Just do me a favor and keep quiet about
the trip should there be any forced mingling. I need to keep things
under control until I'm back home."

"What's that supposed to mean? Keep quiet? Is it a secret? I already
left a message telling Henry."

He stopped short. "I told you not to say anything, for Christ's sake!"

Bunny waved him off. "I doubt he even listened to my message. He
couldn't care less either way. Then again, he's not as *invested* in my do-
ings as your clan is in yours."

The dining hall was packed. It was easy enough for Marty to spot
Amanda, who was staring at her phone. Even with that expression on
her face, she was by far the most attractive woman in the room. But
what the hell was Gail doing there? And why was Henry sitting with
them?

"What's all this about?" Marty mumbled under his breath. "What is
your son doing at my table?"

"You mean what is your family doing at mine?"

Gail stood up to greet them.

"I thought you were riding," Marty said. She was wearing her riding
habit, a look Marty found sexy in its orthodox simplicity. It was the
most flattering ensemble in her closet.

"I finished early," she explained in a delighted tone, as if it had all
been a great coincidence. Then, looking Bunny up and down: "We
saw Henry sitting there all alone and I asked him to join us. I assume
that's all right?"

Amanda had her arms folded across her chest and was turned
slightly away from Henry, as if he smelled badly.

"How thoughtful," Bunny said.

"Mm," Amanda said, her face pinched, like she'd bitten into a
lemon.

"Where's Janine?" Marty asked. He shook Henry's hand and pulled out a chair.

Henry shrugged as though he hadn't a clue who this mysterious Janine person was.

"Martin?" Bunny asked. She was seeking official permission before sitting down. He tensed his jaw and nodded.

Janine entered the room and walked over to the table, slowing considerably as she got closer. She looked confused as she took the empty seat next to Amanda at the end of the table. Odd, Marty thought. Why wasn't she sitting next to her boyfriend? Trouble in paradise already? Things had to be pretty bad for her to voluntarily sit next to her sister. Amanda inched her chair back, away from Janine.

"So," Gail said, narrowing her eyes at Marty and Bunny. "While Amanda and I were waiting, Henry was telling us that the two of you are heading off to Italy together? It was the first I'd heard of it. Fill us in, Marty. Please." Her voice was thick with artificial sweetness.

Bunny shifted in her seat and pursed her lips.

"Right. I tried to call you this morning," he lied. "It's not a big deal. Bunny and I decided to take a trip after we get out of here. As friends. Rehab friends." He laughed. "I know it's unusual but we thought it would be healthy after being in here."

Gail didn't say a word.

"I don't want to go to Europe and shop," Marty continued, rattled. "I want to see the architecture, go to the gardens. I'm not getting any younger."

Marty noticed Henry glance furtively at Janine, probably to gauge her response. Janine didn't look up. She was staring fixedly at the table setting, intent on not meeting anyone's eye. Amanda was looking at Bunny with a queer smile on her face, as if amused by the way brunch was unfurling. Maybe she enjoyed seeing Gail lose her grip on the reins for a minute. "Sounds fun," Amanda said.

"You and Bunny are taking a *vacation*?" Gail asked. "Alone?"

"It's not like that," Bunny said. "I can promise you."

"What is it like, then?"

"Don't start making it something it's not," Marty said. "Please. She's just a friend. A companion."

"A companion?" Bunny laughed, sitting up straighter. "You make me sound like a pathetic old lady from a Merchant Ivory film."

"I just mean that we've done the other thing. It obviously wasn't that compelling, right?" he said jokingly, a last grasp at levity. "That part of our story is over. I don't go in for intellectually curious women anymore. Nothing but trouble."

"Actually, Mum's not intellectually curious either," Henry said, speaking up for the first time. "That's a bit off base, really."

Everyone turned to Henry, and Marty exhaled, relieved to be out of the line of fire. Henry was a good-looking kid. A little uptight, but handsome. Janine glanced at Henry, a slight hint of a smile working the corners of her mouth. Marty's stomach tightened. He'd never seen that expression on his daughter's face before.

"I don't mean to suggest that you're not intelligent," Henry went on, looking at his mother. Bunny's expression was also amused, as if she were allowing Henry ample time to dig all six feet of his grave and wouldn't dream of stopping him. "It's just that everyone assumes that because you're a writer, you're some kind of intellectual, which is pretty silly because it's fiction, after all. Teen fiction."

An awkward silence ensued. Janine's face was bemused now; she was staring at Henry with all the affection one generally directed at a mime on a subway. "N-not that there's anything wrong with teen fic-tion," Henry stammered, pushing his hand through his hair. "I just mean to say that it's not as if she's a historian or a—"

"Quit while you're ahead," Bunny said drily. Henry looked down at his lap and began arranging his napkin.

"Can I say something, please?" Bunny asked.

"No!" Marty said.

"He's all yours," said Bunny, disregarding Marty and looking at Gail innocently. "If you can put up with him, God bless you. I just want to borrow him for a couple of weeks. Strictly platonic. I'm in an awkward position. It's not easy for me to travel because of my celebrity."

Marty cringed. Bunny as supplicant was about as convincing and authentic as Gail's lips. Henry squinted as if he were in pain and went back to his napkin.

"I know how that sounds," Bunny said. "But it's simply the truth. I could use a vacation. I don't have many friends. It would be a great gift to me if we could go with your blessing, Gail."

That was a nice touch! Marty thought. Asking for her blessing. He wouldn't have thought of that. Marty knew Gail would like it.

A waiter brought over menus and refilled their coffee cups. The interruption gave Marty enough time to organize his thoughts.

Then, to Gail: "You can meet me in Paris afterward. We'll have our own vacation. Just us. Okay?"

Amanda raised her water glass in a toast. "To a getaway after all this."

"Right," Henry said and lifted his glass. "It will do you both good to get away immediately after you leave this place."

Immediately. Marty laughed to himself. You couldn't blame the kid for not wanting his mother to linger in Los Angeles like a bad extra. She'd expect things from him, make demands on his time. Marty smiled as everyone reluctantly clinked glasses. He hadn't felt this good in he didn't know how long. He'd stood up for himself. He'd let everyone know he was boss.

"Oh, and a toast to Janine," Amanda added, turning to her silent sister with a nasty grin. "For coming into town to 'help,'" she said, making air quotes around the word, "and fucking up my daughter's life by trying to land her a role in the next Ransom Garcia film."

"What?" they all asked.

Marty put his glass down.

Henry

Henry had to call her name three times before she turned around. He was feeling better but he wasn't ready to sprint through rehab chasing an angry woman. He couldn't blame her for wanting to get out of Directions as quickly as possible, but her urgency clearly had more to do with him than with her family.

"Janine, wait! Can we talk, please?"

"About what, Henry?" she asked, stopping. "What do you want?"

"Uh, um," he stammered like a fool. "You haven't returned my calls or e-mails and you didn't look at me once through that, that..." He paused as he looked for a word that might describe the past hour. "Brunch."

"I'm busy," she said and started walking toward the exit again.

"Did you get the flowers I sent?"

"I got your flowers, Henry. Thanks. We're all squared up."

"I don't understand why you're being this way. Surely you understand—"

"No. I don't understand," she said, spinning on her heel to face him. He shrank back. How he loathed an altercation with a cross woman he'd slept with. "You couldn't have waited until I got home, Henry?" she asked. "You were so desperate to leave, you couldn't wait like a civilized human being to say good-bye? After *everything* I did for you? It was *so* bad you had to escape like a prisoner?"

"Yes," he said, incredulous. "It was that bad. It was terrifying, actually. Squaring off with your sister and Hailey and that cat!" He looked around to see if anyone was listening. "I was in my shreddies!" How could she not understand his position? Her family was a circus of dysfunction. It was all quite fascinating, but did she really expect him to jump right in and start spinning plates from a sickbed?

"You didn't even clean up. You left your clotted gauze strips all over the bathroom. What am I, your fucking maid with benefits? I took care of you. I took you into my family home. I ran myself ragged. And that day, the day you decided to make a break for it, I needed you."

"I—" he started, but Janine interrupted him.

"Surely you figured it out, Henry. You do have a PhD, right? That Hailey didn't get the part? That Amanda was on a tear? And what did I come home to? A completely empty house. Everyone just, poof, gone!"

"Yes, well, when you put it like that." Henry was at a loss. But he had tried to call her and explain. He had left her a message about Amanda. And he'd been calling and texting and e-mailing since. "I'm sorry. It just felt like you might also need some space. You seemed a bit annoyed with me and overwhelmed with the twins and your father."

"You mean *you* were overwhelmed," she said, pushing a rigid finger into his chest. The physicality of the gesture was shocking. "I trusted you. I never put myself out there, Henry. I just . . . don't. For exactly this reason," she said, looking past him, not able to meet his eyes. "So don't turn this around. Don't you dare manipulate me into thinking I did something wrong."

Henry was taken aback. "Okay. Maybe it was a bit much for me, but don't you think you're overreacting? It was a lot for both of us and I simply didn't want to overstay my welcome. It just seemed like an opportune moment to leave before another drama. I thought you might be pleased to have some time to yourself. Is that so terrible? My leaving doesn't change the way I feel about you."

"But it changes the way *I* feel about *you.*"

Janine was pale and Henry could see beads of perspiration forming along her hairline. He wanted her to sit down but he didn't dare imply she wasn't looking well. "What are you so gutted about? I don't understand."

"Did you even stop to consider that I . . . that I might have issues around people just vanishing?"

Henry was gobsmacked, starting to understand the implication. "That's not fair, Janine, I—"

"I told you what happened with my mom," she said, struggling to keep her voice steady. "Thirty years later and there I was again, like a dumb kid, looking around the house for someone just because they said they'd be there."

"Janine," he said, mortified. "It's hardly the same—"

"It felt the same. Maybe that sounds stupid to you, but it's how it felt." Tears were streaming down her face now. "It made me feel really bad, Henry. And I don't want to feel that way. I've spent a lifetime protecting myself from ever feeling that way again."

He was torn between indignation and grief. "Please. Tell me what I can do."

"Nothing. Do nothing."

Indignation got the better of him. "I don't think you're being at all fair here. I think you're choosing to be angry with me. I think that you're a hedgehog," he said, borrowing a bad metaphor from Risa.

"Excuse me?"

"The hedgehog's dilemma," he explained. "Your whole family. You want to be close, to stay warm, but you have to stay apart to keep from hurting one another."

Hedgehog's dilemma! What a stupid thing to have said. And couldn't the exact same comment be applied to him? Of course it could. That's why he'd bungled this whole thing up!

"Bye, Henry. I'm not interested in being psychoanalyzed by an art teacher."

"I'm not an art teacher," he said, feeling feeble. "And I'm just trying to help."

"Don't," she said. "You're not good at it."

She wobbled uncertainly, as if she might lose her balance. Henry reached out to steady her, but she pulled her hand away. Baffled, he watched her crouch down, balancing the weight of her bottom on her heels. "Shit," she said.

"Janine?" he asked, confused. Henry was in no way prepared for what she did next, which was to quickly stand up, pitch left, and vomit all over a marble Buddha.

He stared, appalled.

"Oh my God," she said, hands covering her mouth, looking nearly as stunned as Henry felt. Then, mortified: "How completely disgusting. I'm so sorry." She removed her cardigan, wiped her mouth with it, and tossed the sweater over the mess on the statue. "Sorry."

Henry hadn't a clue what to do, but as it turned out, that didn't matter. By the time he could think straight, she was already out the door, running away from him.

Bunny

Bunny was still reveling in what she felt was a victorious brunch with Martin's family. As far as she was concerned, it had been a smashing success. Gail had been put in her place, and whatever Henry was doing with Janine didn't seem to be going very well. That was fine. The girl struck Bunny as being too meek for Henry. He needed someone with more authority. Besides, she had behaved as if she didn't even know him. It verged on rudeness.

What an odd bunch of women. *The many moons of Martin Kessler,* she thought with a laugh. Anyway, it had been quite a show and she felt she'd come off rather well. She would treat herself to a smoothie. Yes, that was just the thing. A proper smoothie with bananas and strawberries, nothing green. She felt celebratory as she headed over to the nutrition bar. Where had Martin gone, anyway? They'd all dispersed like a gang of criminals at the sound of sirens.

She would have liked a post-party chat with Henry but he'd gone chasing after Janine like a lovestruck teenager the moment the girl had excused herself—which she'd done rather abruptly. It was clear as day the girl didn't fancy him. No need for him to make a fool of himself.

And what was wrong with the other sister? Bunny still wondered.

She was a stunner and she had a job. Leave it to Henry to pick the runt. He'd been a strange boy and he'd grown into a strange man.

She had Group in half an hour. Not that she needed it. If she was an alcoholic, then Gail was only fifty-five. *Please!* Gail was sixty-five if she was a day. All the chin-lifts in the world couldn't tighten that neck. Bunny stroked her own throat with satisfaction. She waited for her smoothie, trying to think of something to share in Group today. She hadn't been participating much.

She was walking toward the meeting rooms when she saw someone who looked like Henry slumped in a leather chair. She went closer.

"Henry?" she asked, walking around the chair. "What are you doing still here?" She took the seat opposite him and put her smoothie down on the side table.

"It's over. Janine's finished with me."

"Well," she said, reaching out to pat his knee, "there's a lid for every jar, as they say. Probably she was just a bad fit."

"She's not a bad fit!" he shouted, startling Bunny. "I'm the bad jar. She's a perfectly good lid."

As usual, Henry was taking her metaphors too literally, and it was clear they were on precarious footing. She wanted to tell Henry that it was for the best—that he could do better—but that would just lead to a row. She didn't say anything.

"Do you think I'm selfish?" he asked at last.

"We're all selfish, Henry."

"I mean, do you think I'm a narcissist? Am I thoughtless? A snob?"

"We're both thoughtless snobs. That's what makes us British."

"Perfect."

"You've known the girl only a few weeks. You can't possibly be that attached."

"But I am attached. I am."

"You only think so because she's off you. You're romanticizing her."

"I never intend to hurt anyone," he said, trying to explain, "but when I do, it usually seems like the right time to break things off anyway. This wasn't like that. I didn't want to break things off with her. I just wanted to go home."

Bunny leaned forward. "What happened? What did you do, Henry?"

"I'm not entirely sure," he said. "I'm so confused."

It was a terrible thing to realize your child was unhappy. Bunny knew there was a time when she could have made him feel better, though it had been many years ago.

"You must have some idea," she said.

"I left her house a couple days ago. Her sister had arrived in a rage. It was awful."

"So what is Janine angry about, Henry?" Bunny asked, irritated. "When exactly did you leave?"

"Friday."

"And when exactly did you tell her you were leaving?"

"I left a message."

"You told her you were leaving after you were gone?"

"I left a note! I called! Then I left voice mails. I wanted to spare her having to deal with me in the midst of what was clearly a very private and fraught family drama. I figured she'd be happy to have me out of her hair. You even said so!"

"Oh no," she said, wagging a finger at him. "That is *not* what I said, young man. I told you to be honest with her about wanting to go back to your flat. I didn't tell you to pack your bags and skip town. I specifically said not to do that."

"I called her that night but she didn't pick up. I sent flowers."

"Oh, Henry, that's awful. No wonder she was off you this morning."

"Why? Why is that awful?"

"Didn't I raise you better than that?"

"No, you did not, actually."

"Well, how you behaved is just terribly unkind. And embarrassing. Say what you will about her appearance or attitude, she's been nothing but gracious to you."

"What's wrong with her appearance and attitude?"

Bunny shrugged, reached for the smoothie, and took a noisy slurp.

"Damn it," Henry said. "Damn it."

"All you can do now is apologize."

"I did apologize! She wasn't having it. She wouldn't even look at me. I make her sick!" he shouted.

"Stop it, stop it," Bunny whispered. She poked his shoulder as she looked around the room. "Pull yourself together. It can't possibly be that bad."

"But it is," he said. "I think I might love her."

Bunny put the smoothie down. "Really? Why?"

"*Why?* I don't know *why.*" He paused. "We have a laugh together. I can be myself. I don't feel smothered. I never feel she's putting on a show or trying to be anyone other than who she is. She makes me feel worthwhile just because she likes me. She makes me feel like my life is bigger than just me."

Dear God. Bunny had to refrain from rolling her eyes. Henry sounded like a teenager from one of her books. "How can you be so invested in someone you've known for five minutes?" she asked.

"It's been four weeks."

"Well, then, go round and make it nice again, Henry. Women aren't *that* complicated, and God knows she'd be lucky to have you."

"I just told you she doesn't want to talk to me. She vomited, Mother. The sight of me makes her sick."

"What do you mean, she vomited?"

"She threw up on the Buddha by the valet and then ran away."

"Bloody hell, Henry, the girl's pregnant!"

A stunned pause. "Are...are you sure?"

"Of course I'm not sure, you idiot. I'm not a doctor. But she's obviously irrational and apparently nauseated."

"No," Henry said after a moment. He shook his head, revisiting the details of the evening and evidently arriving at the conclusion that having sex could never lead to an unwanted pregnancy. "It's impossible."

"Whatever you say."

"I hate when you do that."

"Do what?"

"Agree with me."

Bunny laughed, caught off guard by a wistful affection for her son. "I was a beast when I was pregnant with you."

"You were?"

"Ghastly. Everyone was sure I was having a girl. And I was so sick, I lost a stone the first month. At one point they had me hospitalized."

"You never told me that."

"It's not a very interesting story."

"It is to me."

"Well, there you have it."

"Hard to imagine you carried me around and got podgy on my account."

"I was keen on being a mother, believe it or not. I breastfed you too. For months. Nobody was doing it back then. I insisted."

Henry waved that away as if it were a bit too much information. "Well." He sighed. "That was nice of you."

"I thought so," Bunny said with a generous laugh. "I love you, Henry."

"Yes. Well, I love you too, Mother."

Janine

Janine was waiting for Gail and Amanda outside Directions. Her father was finally being discharged. Despite Gail's insistence that it would be less stressful if she picked Marty up alone, both Janine and Amanda insisted on being there. Gail didn't argue the point. She'd been surprisingly amenable the past few days, especially considering the humiliating scene she'd suffered at brunch last week. As it turned out, what they were experiencing was a virtual master class in the art of manipulation.

It began with Gail's outright enthusiasm about Janine's part in the Ransom Garcia film. No doubt Gail liked the idea of Janine's finally having a job, of *making* versus *taking* money, but still. It wasn't very much money (less than a topflight porn star commanded, Ransom had said, laughing apologetically, although slightly more than Esther the Wonder Pig made), but it was a start. And, as Gail had pointed out, what else was Janine going to do? She'd somehow managed to quell Marty's misgivings. "You can't possibly think her getting the offer has anything to do with *you* all these years later," she'd said. And then she'd added, "Won't you like having Janine in town, Marty? Isn't that what you wanted?"

Gail had even put the squeeze on Amanda. "Janine didn't take anything away from Hailey," Gail said. "She was trying to help her. And if it works out, when and if the twins are ready, maybe Janine would be in a position to help them." *Maybe,* Janine had thought, not quite as confident that this supporting role was the career kindling Gail insisted it was. She hadn't committed to Ransom but was already caught up in a myriad of concerns, questioning her talent, wondering whether she was actually good or just a carnival sideshow for the press to pick apart when the time came.

The root of Gail's sudden good-naturedness had revealed itself over their last family dinner at Directions two nights earlier in the form of a diamond-encrusted Cartier trinity ring. "What do you think?" she trilled, waggling her finger. "The news isn't for public consumption yet but . . . we're talking about getting married! I picked it out yesterday. It's just a placeholder, of course." She slipped the ring off her finger so the twins could try it on. "You'll want to pick out the real ring," she said to Marty, who didn't look up. He was busying himself with a scoop of salted-caramel ice cream as if he were an eight-year-old. Jaycee and Hailey passed the ring back and forth, pretending not to notice the sudden chill in the room. "Maybe we'll find something in Paris," Gail said with a wink. Her mascara was so thick that her top and bottom lids stuck together for a second.

Janine watched with detached amusement, glancing at Amanda, who looked back at her sister in disbelief. Had her father really held out the promise of marriage so that Gail would *allow* him to go away for *two weeks?*

The upside, of course, was that Amanda and Janine were united in their outrage. They'd smiled politely and congratulated the happy couple, but their indignation that Gail would manipulate their dad in such a way helped loosen some very old, very stubborn knots. They'd gone out for coffee after dinner and hurled such spectacular insults at Gail that the twins had begged to be dropped off at Menchie's for frozen yogurt so that mom and aunt could continue vituperating "the bitch" without an underage audience. At least she and Amanda were talking again. Their truce wasn't the stuff of Hallmark cards, but the Kesslers had always been more *Arrested Development* than *The Waltons*.

* * *

Janine ignored her ringing phone as first Gail and then Amanda pulled up to the valet. She knew it was Henry calling. She wanted to talk to him more than anything, but she was embarrassed at how she'd overreacted to his leaving, mortified that she'd nearly thrown up on him, and terrified that he'd feel some obligation to her if he found out about the baby. Mercifully, she'd managed to avoid him at Directions all week. She hated that she liked him so much when all she wanted was not to like him at all. She wished he'd stop texting because every time she heard those chimes, she imagined the baby kicking. That was crazy, of course. The baby wasn't even a baby yet. Just a bean. Not even a bean—just a few cells.

More to the point, if Henry couldn't even handle her family, how the hell would he take *that* news? And she still hadn't decided what she was going to do. She wasn't in any position to be anybody's mother. She couldn't shake the gnawing possibility that she was inherently defective. Viewed through the lens of Janine's impending motherhood, Pamela's suicide illuminated what she had always secretly suspected: that her own mom didn't think her daughter was worth hanging around for. Part of Janine wondered if she had been right.

Her phone rang again while she stood there, waiting for the valet to write out the tickets. Janine didn't even reach inside her bag for it.

"Are you going to get that?" Gail asked. "It might be your father."

"It's not." Her father's ringtone was set to Bessie Smith's "Tain't No-body's Biz-Ness If I Do," his favorite song. Gail was "The Imperial March" from *Star Wars*. Amanda was the theme song from *Jaws*.

"You went to the market, right?" Gail asked.

Janine shook her head. "I'll go after he's discharged. I'll meet you all at the house afterward."

"You didn't go to the market yesterday?" Gail asked again, as if she hadn't understood. "You said you were going yesterday!" Her voice was verging on shrill, as though not having snacks in the house was tantamount to not having electricity. This was a big day for her. She clearly needed Marty to know how well she'd handled things while he was away, what a good wife she was going to be. She sighed, exasperated. "Make sure you get gelato and yogurt. The Yoplait. Strawberry-kiwi. And the coconut one too," she added. "Why don't I call and send my assistant to get them now."

"I'll go," she said, wondering why Gail had an assistant and what on earth that person assisted Gail with. "He'll be knee-deep in strawberry-kiwi before his blood sugar dips."

Amanda laughed. Janine's phone rang, this time Bessie Smith crooning, "If I should take a notion, to jump into the ocean..." A welcome interruption.

"Where the fuck is everybody?" her father asked.

"We're coming in now."

"I'm sitting here with my bags like an asshole at a train depot."

"On our way, Dad. Okay? Hello?"

He'd hung up.

Bunny

Bunny wished Martin hadn't left. She had nobody else to
tell about her farewell Gather. Mitchell, the founder of Directions,
had made a florid speech and given her a diploma and a pair of
black abalone earrings. As if people walked around London with
endangered-sea-snail shells dangling from their ears! And yet Mitchell
had been very kind, stressing how proud they all were of her and of
the progress she'd made. She had done well and it felt nice to have
that acknowledged. She was sober. Her nose had healed. She had a
tan. And Henry was taking her to the airport tomorrow. Maybe Directions hadn't been a complete farce after all.

She was headed to the spa for a farewell massage when she saw
Janine curled up on one of the big leather chairs facing the ocean.
Martin was gone. What was Janine doing still there? She was staring
at her phone, which was ringing. Bunny thought this a perfect opportunity to talk to her. After all, the girl might be pregnant with
her grandson! Maybe she could help. She pulled her kimono snugly
around her waist.

"Janine?"

Janine started.

"I didn't mean to scare you," Bunny said with what she hoped was a friendly laugh. The girl was white as paper. "Do I look that grisly?"

"No. God, no. I just. I thought . . . I thought that you'd left already."

"I'm leaving for London tomorrow."

"Congratulations." Janine started to stand up.

"Sit, sit," Bunny said, taking the chair next to her so that they were positioned like two passengers on a bus. Bunny's tête-à-tête with Henry was still fresh in her mind and here was Janine, in practically the same position as Henry had been, clearly in need of her counsel as well. "Did you get your father all packed away?"

"Yeah. He went home with Gail and my sister. I should probably go." She didn't make an effort to get up. "He was in such a bad mood," Janine said after a minute. "He threw his certificate and flower in the trunk like a subpoena and a hot gun."

"Darling, can you blame him? A diploma and a rose?"

"I get that ceremony isn't his thing, but he wasn't even reflective. I mean, is he better? Is he clean? Who knows?" She seemed to be talking more to herself than to Bunny. Bunny understood Martin's misgivings. It wouldn't be easy going home. All the loved ones gathering around. Dreadful. London felt like a bad memory and she was trying not to think about going back.

"So . . ." Bunny began. "The carnival's left town but here you are?"

"I needed a minute. He'll be happier to see me later anyway. It's like he wants you around, but it's better if you have someplace else to be."

Bunny could see that Janine was clever. And pretty, despite her pallor. Her looks weren't an advertisement like her sister's, but there was something about her.

"I wouldn't be too disappointed that he didn't check out a changed man. There's only so much that therapy and organic green shakes can do."

"I guess I was just hoping for a little personal growth. Or maybe a thank-you."

"Some people don't go in for personal growth, or thanks, or apologies," Bunny said, wondering if the same thing could be said about her. "But he's an original. A deeply decent, funny man who tries to do the right thing by everyone. I think he's top-notch."

"Yes," Janine said, smiling. She visibly relaxed as she looked out at the ocean. Her phone rang again.

Bunny felt sure it was Henry calling. She cleared her throat. "May I ask why you stopped acting, Janine?"

Janine didn't say anything for a minute. Then: "I don't know."

"I'm sorry about your mother," Bunny said, because she was. She could see that Janine had glued herself back together, but there were fracture lines in every gesture she made.

"Don't be. You didn't even know her."

"My grandfather committed suicide," Bunny said. "Not that it's the same."

Janine looked at Bunny. "That's hard."

Bunny suspected Janine didn't think that counted. Losing a grandfather was not the same as losing a mother. Or maybe she just didn't want to talk about it with Bunny. *Fair enough,* Bunny thought, but she wasn't finished. "The suicidal are incapable of considering who they might be hurting other than themselves. There's no rational thinking. They just want the pain to stop."

"Like alcoholics?" Janine asked. "Or drug addicts?"

Bunny felt the reprimand like a slap. "It's different."

"How's that?"

"My mother was destroyed, obviously. She found him. He'd shot himself. He didn't leave a note. Then my father left her and she was forced to raise us alone. She was angry, bitter, miserable. My brother and I grew up hating her, hating each other. And we were living on the breadline on top of it all. We just wanted to get away from our childhoods as quickly as we could. Start over. And it wasn't her fault, really. I can see that now. But that's how it played out. His selfish act."

"Substance abuse is selfish too," Janine said, not letting it go. "If you have kids. Maybe suicide is more courageous than slowly dragging everyone along."

Bunny knew Janine was thinking of Henry and blaming her for her bad parenting. What had Henry told her? Had he no sense of propriety? For a moment, she wanted to choke Janine.

"I didn't drink when Henry was small," she said, her voice full of righteous indignation. "I turned my pain into my work."

"I wasn't talking about you and Henry."

"No?" Bunny didn't believe her.

"I was thinking of my dad. Nobody wants to think of their parents as being so unhappy they have to get high alone. At least a suicide is over quickly."

"You're a grim little creature, aren't you?"

"Sorry. I guess it all just seems sort of thankless."

"We all do the best we can," Bunny said. "The key is to stay busy."

Janine laughed in a way that left Bunny feeling exposed. "I have to go."

"I asked about the acting because your father told me about the film role," Bunny said, changing the subject, trying to get her to stay a minute longer.

"I'm not sure I'm doing it. I have a life in New York."

"Do you?" Bunny asked, sensitive to the personal ground she was traversing and aware of the fact that she barely knew this girl.

"It sounds like my dad or Henry or somebody has given you full disclosure on what a loser I am, so there's really no need for me to be part of this conversation."

"Wait." Bunny stretched her arm across Janine's chest just as she made a move to stand. Janine sat back and looked at Bunny. "Your father adores you. He's proud of you. You're all he talks about."

Janine rolled her eyes. "I've got to go to the market and buy strawberry-kiwi yogurt."

"Nothing happens in life if you don't do anything with it. You just get old. Inertia is a terrible thing, Janine."

"I'm not inert. I just know my limitations."

"I know that. But just look at what's happened since you've been here. You took your niece to an audition and you got a part. You came to Directions to see your father and you met Henry. It seems to me the world does want you."

Janine bit her lip. "Who said it didn't?"

"You did. You say it with every decision you choose not to make. Henry says you won't call him back."

"I don't mean to be rude, but this has nothing to do with you."

"I know. But I've never seen him so blue. Couldn't you forgive him for whatever he did?"

"He didn't do anything."

"For whatever he didn't do, then. It all amounts to the same thing, doesn't it? The expectations we have. The injustices we collect. It's just armor against being happy."

"I don't love him."

Bunny wasn't convinced. "You could still call him."

"And say what?"

"How about telling him you're pregnant?"

Janine's mouth arranged itself into a circle. "How did you know?"

"I didn't know. I guessed. Vomiting on a Buddha is often the first sign."

"Does he know?" Janine asked.

"I suggested it might be a possibility but he didn't believe me. He was quite ludicrous about the whole thing."

"Are you going to tell him?" Janine asked.

Bunny certainly thought Henry had a right to know but she wouldn't say anything to him. Not yet, anyway. "It's not my place to tell him."

"And my dad?"

Bunny shook her head. "No."

Janine grabbed her purse and stood. "I really have to go."

"Yes," Bunny said. She tried to smile. "They'll be wondering where you are."

Bunny watched Janine leave, knowing there was nothing more she could do. Henry would have to work things out for himself. The only thing she'd ever done well was make up stories. Disappointed children were so much easier to manage in fiction. Maybe Janine was right. Maybe it was better to know your limitations and accept them. All Bunny really wanted was a drink.

Henry

Henry was feeling emotional. He'd dropped his mum at the airport and had immediately driven over to see Janine. Now he wasn't sure if it was better to wait in his car or stand in the driveway. The car seemed the more natural choice, but it would involve an element of surprise that might not be welcome. He opted for the driveway. That way he wouldn't startle Janine. Still, there was something awkward about just standing around, staring at the gravel, whistling to himself like the village idiot.

It struck him that he'd never actively pursued anything in his life other than his career. Certainly not a woman. Overt acts of sentimentality embarrassed him. He suddenly felt preposterous, as if he were doing an impersonation of some floppy bloke in a romantic comedy. Why on earth was he standing like an ass in her father's driveway? It was no good. He started dashing back to his car just as Janine drove up.

"Henry," she said from the window. She pulled into the driveway. "What are you doing here?"

He couldn't help but notice that she looked a tiny bit pleased to see him. Her eyes were smiling even if her mouth wasn't.

"Oh. I was just, um—well. Hullo. Seeing as you're still not returning my calls I thought I'd pop round. I wanted to ask if you were feeling better. I just dropped my mum at the airport and, well," he said, his voice a bit too high-pitched, "I was hoping we could talk."

"It's not a great time." She got out of the car and began unloading shopping bags from the trunk. "I'm on standby market duty. I've been there three times since yesterday. Gail needed vegetables. My dad wanted more ice cream."

"Let me help you with that."

"I've got it. Please stop it, Henry."

"Stop what?"

"Smothering me."

"Smothering you?" He was aghast. If there was one thing Henry had never been accused of, it was smothering. Being cold? Yes. Emotionally cut off? Without a doubt. But smothering? It was a ridiculous accusation. "That's a ridiculous accusation!" he said.

"Is it?" She shut the trunk while balancing one bag on her knee and one in her hand. "You *have* to give me some space. You have to please stop calling and texting."

Henry didn't say anything for a moment. He needed to calm down. This was his mother's fault. She'd kissed him good-bye at the airport and whispered something to him about making very certain the girl knew how he felt about her. That's what he was doing! "I just want to talk to you, and given that you are playing some sort of game, you've really left me no choice but to show up unannounced."

"I'm not playing games. I'm not mad anymore. I'm sorry if I overreacted. I just need to sort my own stuff out."

"So sort. You don't have to ignore me while you're at it, do you? I'm trying to let you know how I feel here."

Her expression softened for a moment but then she arranged her face into a mask of resolution. "I can't do this now. Things are really complicated in my life and with my family. I just can't."

She slammed the driver's door with her hip and headed toward the house.

"Stop," he cried, trailing after her. He felt like a clown.

"Henry," she said, suddenly stopping and turning to face him. "What is it you want?"

"I don't want anything. I just don't want to not see you again."

"That's very sweet, but no, thank you."

"No, thank you?" he asked. "What does that mean?"

"It means go back to your job, go back to your life. That's what I'm doing."

"You don't have a job," he said, wishing he hadn't said the words the minute they left his mouth.

"I'll get one," she said.

"But what about the baby?" Henry asked. He'd come to think his mother might have been right about Janine's condition. It would explain a lot. Janine looked taken aback.

"I'm not pregnant." She shook her head. "There's no baby."

Henry didn't say anything. Leave it to his mother to get everything all wrong.

"Are you relieved?" she asked.

"No. I don't know what I am. Disappointed." In truth, he was crushed. He hadn't known until that moment how much he wanted her to be pregnant.

Janine looked at Henry and smiled, her face lovely, flush with color. "I think that's the nicest thing anyone's ever said to me." She put the grocery bags down and unexpectedly wrapped her skinny arms around him. He hugged her hard, willing himself not to cry. "Thank you, Henry."

"You're thanking me? I don't want you to thank me."

"But I'm not pregnant." She disentangled herself from their embrace. "And what would we do with a baby?" Her eyes filled up with tears as she looked at him.

"I don't know. I guess I liked the idea of being at the beginning of something. It's very depressing in the middle of it all with nothing to look forward to but the end."

She placed a chaste kiss on his cheek. He would have preferred a slap across the face. Any sign of passion would have been better than this apathy.

"I should go in," she said, picking up the grocery bags and adjusting her posture to accommodate them. "Before the ice cream melts."

"Right, then," he said with a shrug. He'd come to rely on shrugging as a means of expressing that the onus to do something was now on the other person. Still, the gesture was also meant to imply that he was open to further discussion.

He waved good-bye and thrust his hands into his pockets. This was one of those moments in life, he thought, that were so absurd one could hardly believe it. He felt entirely helpless watching her leave. And now he was standing there with nothing to do but attend Cody McDaniel's dissertation defense of "The Renaissance of the Hudson River School in Post-9/11 America."

Janine

Janine woke up early thinking maybe she'd cook breakfast for her dad. It was his second day back from Directions and she was hoping to spend some time alone with him before Gail showed up again with forty-dollar scones and artisanal fresh-drip coffee.

He didn't answer the intercom. She walked into his bedroom, expecting to find him asleep or reading. His bed was made. He'd showered. She spotted him through the glass doors. He was outside by the cottage, wearing socks and shorts, washing off his white sneakers with a garden hose.

"Morning," she said, walking toward him, trying not to step in the mounds of dog shit hidden in the overgrown grass.

"Do I have a fucking dog I don't know about?" he asked. He was cleaning his shoe with care, turning it over, scrubbing out the treads with a leaf. He was a meticulous man. The exactitude of his sock drawer had fascinated Janine when she was a little girl. Janine hadn't ever seen Sandro's dog, but she'd heard him. They all had. Another bit of unwelcome news she hadn't thought necessary to share with her dad.

"This," he said sarcastically, "is exactly what I wanted to do on one of my first days back."

Why had she thought he'd be in a good mood? That was dumb. "I bought eggs and matzo. Do you want breakfast? Or I can make oat-meal." She needed to eat. Eating had always been more an obligation than a pleasure for her, but since she'd gotten pregnant, her hunger was intense and immediate. The textures and flavors of food (what might satisfy her cravings, what might make her nauseated) had become a preoccupation.

"I'm not hungry," he snapped, looking at the withered roses. He put his shoe back on and turned the hose onto the dead bougainvillea. "What's happening today?"

"I don't know. Jaycee's spending the day with her boyfriend so I thought I might drive Hailey down to San Diego to see her dad."

"She's a good kid," Marty said, lightening up. "She reminds me of you a little bit." He screwed his face up like he was trying to solve a problem. He sprayed the surrounding weeds absently. "I barely recognized her the other night. Did she do something to her face?"

"It's probably the short hair," Janine said. How astonishing that her father knew nothing about what had happened. They were all united in an ongoing effort to protect Marty from any news that might upset him. His takeaway was that *Hairspray* had been a smashing success and that Amanda was currently casting for *Xanadu*. Hailey had suggested that musical. "Jaycee can't roller-skate," Hailey had told Janine with a fiendish smile. "But, you know, it's a comedy so she'll probably still get the lead. Not that I want the part."

What Hailey wanted was to help her mom produce the show. And Marty *liked* that Hailey wanted to be a producer. He took her budding career as a compliment, apparently no longer plagued by his past anxiety over family members entering the piranha pool.

"At least she doesn't want to be a fucking actress," he said now. Then, catching himself: "Not that there's anything wrong with being an actress." He held up his free hand, a guilty-as-charged expression on his face. "Listen. I hope you take that role in Ransom's movie. You were always good. Very good."

Janine was stunned. He'd never said anything like that before. "You think?"

"Sure. You know I always thought that."

"I didn't. I thought you were afraid I'd embarrass you or something."

"Embarrass me?" He turned around quickly to shut off the hose. Then, looking at her, he said, "Jesus Christ. You could never embarrass me."

"Okay."

"I didn't want you involved with those assholes," he said angrily, as if awakening to an emotion he thought had died. His face reddened. "I was trying to do the right thing. I just wanted you to have a normal life."

"And look how well that turned out," she said with a strangled laugh. Then she added quietly, "I guess after Mom, normalcy was pretty much off the table."

His jaw jutted out and started to tremble. "She'd tried once before," he said. "With pills. It didn't work. She wasn't going to make the same mistake. It's what she wanted."

Janine caught her breath. "When did she try?"

"A few months earlier. She promised up and down that she wouldn't do it again. The doctors believed her. I believed her." He shrugged. "I know I should have told you at some point but I was afraid you'd blame me for not doing more to stop her. But nobody could have. It's what she wanted," he said again.

How strange that they'd never really talked about what happened. Janine thought they could have helped each other. They'd each spent a lifetime carrying the weight of Pamela's suicide, but neither one of them was to blame.

He shook his head, reached over, pulled Janine in for a hug, and rested his chin on top of her head, like he used to. For the first time in what felt like years, she felt able to take a deep breath, to catch the air she needed. "Take the goddamn part and stay here while you're filming." He stepped back and looked at her. "Henry seems like a nice kid. See where it goes. You stay as long as you want, hear me? I'll be back in a couple of weeks. Gail won't mind."

Janine couldn't help but wonder how her father and Gail would feel once they knew she was pregnant with his ex-wife's son's baby. She'd finally ruled out an abortion, caving to the irrational conviction that it was some sort of a sign that she'd gotten pregnant at forty-one years old. Restlessness at how protective she already felt about the baby swallowed her up. Added to this was apprehension about raising a child alone, concern over what sort of part Henry might play. And then there was the movie. She was consumed by anxiety about the part—convinced that Ransom had made a mistake about her and worried that she'd be too nauseated to shoot or that she'd start to show before the movie began filming in six weeks.

The conversation with Bunny had gotten to her. Doing *nothing* wasn't an option anymore. And yet that's exactly what she wanted to do. She wanted to get on a plane and fly home to New York City, to her apartment, to her quiet life. Maybe she'd have enough money for New York if she ate only once a day, walked everywhere, froze her membership at the Y. Janine doubted supporting Bunny's illegitimate grandchild would be a priority on Gail's agenda when she was the next Mrs. Kessler.

"Are you really getting married again?" she asked her dad.

"I don't know," he said, turning the hose back on. "She's a nice lady. She looks after me. The security is important to her. I get that. And I like being married," he said. "I'm just not very good at it."

Janine looked at him. "You don't have to. You know that, right? We could all, like, I don't know, help out more or something."

He laughed, more to himself than to Janine. "What possible difference does it make at this point?"

A lot, Janine thought, but she didn't want to ruin his brightening mood. But Gail wouldn't be satisfied until she had the crown on her head. Better the legitimate queen to a crumbling empire than no title at all. Maybe Henry had been right. It was her father's life. Who was she to tell him how to live it?

"Well, you seem good, Dad. Are you happy to be home?"

His jaw began to tremble again but he turned away from her, ostensibly to water some more dead plants, before she could see his expression. "I'm happy *you're* home," he said. "Tell me you're sticking around, then I'll tell you if I'm happy."

Janine swallowed hard. "I don't know what I'm going to do yet."

"I get it," he said. He looked across the yard and sighed. "How about I drive you and Hailey down to San Diego later? We can grab doughnuts at that great dump in that Cardiff strip mall."

Janine couldn't believe how good that sounded. But wouldn't Gail be upset that he'd chosen to spend the day with his daughter instead of his fiancée? Then, as if reading her mind, he said, "Gail will understand."

Fat Roger walked out, sniffing the dog shit. "It's nice that you let Sandro stay here," she said, worried she might get weepy if she didn't change the subject. She was exhausted by emotions. Or hormones. Or both. "But maybe Gail's right about him."

"And so?" he said. "I wish everyone would stop telling me what a sucker I am. It's not like I can't see what's happening for myself."

"What are you going to do about the yard?"

"Clean it up."

"You are?"

Marty pointed to a rake and pooper scooper leaning on the wall. He handed the rake to Janine. "We are."

Janine glanced down at her pretty sandals and then gave her dad a look.

"Women and their shoes."

"They were expensive."

"Yes, I'm aware."

Janine laughed. "I'm glad you're home, Dad."

"So am I. Now go change your shoes."

"Right back," she said, turning toward the kitchen, feeling lighter than she had in years. "I just need to grab something to eat."

part five

Sehnsucht (noun): *A wistful longing or nostalgia for something indefinable*

Marty

Happy New Year, Marty thought as the new reader dropped a stack of scripts on his desk with the word *Rejected* scrawled on each one in bold red ink. It was his first day back in the office after a short Christmas vacation. Hello, 1971. The new reader turned around and left without a word. She didn't even introduce herself. Her hair was in a topknot secured with a pencil and she was wearing a buttoned-up man's shirt tucked into blue jeans. Marty watched her walk away. She was slight with long legs and a heart-shaped ass.

The next week she came in again with the same odd outfit and an even larger rejection pile. He was on the phone. He tried to hang up before she left but Jed Buckwalter was complaining about an actor on one of Marty's films. (Back then, Marty couldn't just hang up on a director when he was done with a conversation. He was still hustling. He had a small office at Aces Up Productions on the third floor at Twentieth Century. He wouldn't be there long, but only he knew that.)

Marty watched for the girl in the following weeks but she never returned. When he asked the receptionist what had happened to the new reader, she gave him a keep-your-pecker-in-your-pants look. So he'd put her out of his mind and more or less forgotten about her.

A few months later he saw her again at Howard Blum's cocktail party in Benedict Canyon, apparently as Blum's date. Howard was a very successful literary agent. Had she abandoned film for books or did she simply like old men with money?

Marty watched her mingling for the next half an hour, easily tracking her among the sea of long crocheted dresses and hip-hugging bell-bottoms. He'd taught himself early to smother his self-doubt with confidence. Timidity made you useless in Hollywood. When he saw her head to the bar, he excused himself from his party.

"So?" he said, standing behind her at the drinks counter. "You and Howard?"

"Howard and I what?" she asked sharply.

She was British. He'd had no idea. Her round vowels struck him as aristocratic, a welcome respite from the Valley drawl. She had straight, almost waist-length blond hair and a curtain of bangs that came just below her eyebrows. Her dark eyelashes looked like expensive paintbrushes. It wasn't easy to see what was going on underneath that kimono or caftan or whatever she was wearing, but Marty's imagination was as good as his memory.

"Are you two dating?" he asked. "How old are you?" He reached across the bar for a lime to squeeze into his vodka tonic. Marty wasn't a drinker. Everyone got loaded regularly, but he'd order one drink and nurse it with soda water and lime all night. He was never drunk but he did a good enough impression. It was a useful trick in a room full of inebriated, coked-up, or stoned colleagues. He was always discreet but he made a note of the seams that unstitched after hours.

"What if we are?" she asked. "Dating?" She was waiting for the bartender to pour out wine to a group of identical-looking actresses dressed in pastel minidresses. (Nobody in California cared about grapes back then. There was white wine, there was red wine, and there was liquor.) The actresses looked at Marty and smiled invitingly before they walked away, clutching their glasses and giggling.

"You've got quite the little fan club," she said and ordered a Negra Modelo. That was surprising. Not many women drank beer. Dark beer, no less.

"You smoke?" he asked, though he wasn't sure why. He didn't. Something about her accent made him wish he carried a cigarette case.

"Yes," she said. "And twenty-three."

"Huh?"

"I'm twenty-three. You asked how old I was. Anything else? My weight? My food preferences? Vaccine history, address?"

"Yes, please," he said. "All of it."

She laughed. It was a warm laugh, from the gut, almost man-like. But there was nothing masculine about her other than a sort of boyish bravado. She blew her bangs out of her eyes.

"You don't remember me?" he finally asked, incredulous.

She stared at him blankly.

"You worked for me," he said after an uncomfortable silence. "You were a reader at Aces Up."

"Was I?" She looked honestly puzzled. "When was that?"

"A few months ago! You don't remember?" he asked with a chuckle meant to cover his embarrassment. True, they'd never had a conversation, but he thought he was more memorable than that. Women liked him. He was good-looking. A man on the rise.

"I'm Marty Kessler," he said and extended his hand.

"Bunny Small," she said, shaking it vigorously. "Now that you mention it, I do remember you. You were the one staring at my ass when I dropped off the shitty scripts in your office."

Marty blushed. Did she have fucking eyeballs in the back of her head? "Well, I don't know about that, but I do remember you. You never liked anything from the slush."

"It was all rubbish," she said, drinking her beer straight from the bottle. "Pure, utter rubbish. There ought to be some sort of an exam before one can call oneself a screenwriter. From what I gather, the only requirements are a knowledge of the proper screenplay format and a propensity to overuse capital letters."

"So you're working for Howard because he reps real authors, not screenwriters, that right?"

"It's a living I can tolerate." She took a sip from her beer. "Until I write my own."

"Your own book?" Marty asked, riveted by a tiny birthmark in the bow of her upper lip. She wasn't wearing lipstick. Marty liked that too.

"Screenplay," she said. "Which will be based on my book."

"Ah."

"What does that mean?"

"Nothing. It's just, well, look around. Everybody in this room wants to be a screenwriter. Or an actress."

"That may be," she said. "But most of them will fail."

"And you're the exception?"

"Everyone will know soon enough."

Marty was charmed. Maybe it was her accent, maybe it was her arrogance, or maybe it was the goddamn birthmark. "Fair enough, Bunny Small. Why don't you send me what you're working on?" He leaned forward and lowered his voice. "I'm forming my own production company. You never know, right?" He held his glass up for a toast.

She walked away without clinking her bottle against his glass.

"Hey!" he said, chasing after her through the crowd. "What's the rush?"

"I don't like your condescending tone. You're wasting your time. And mine."

"Don't get touchy," he said. "I was being serious. Anyway, Howard knows how to reach me if you change your mind. I've got two of his authors in deals for adaptations."

She stopped short and squinted. "Which two?"

Marty looked at her in disbelief. "What difference does *that* make?"

"It makes all the difference. I'm curious if you've got any taste."

He laughed hard as Howard walked over and slung an arm around

Bunny's little shoulders. "I spy two future luminaries here," Howard said good-humoredly. He raised his Scotch glass. "Watch out for this one, Kessler," he bellowed. "She's all fire."

"I'll do that," Marty said and turned to go. "Enjoy the party."

Bunny and Marty were married in June. Marty was nominated for his first Academy Award that February. Bunny missed London and didn't really enjoy living in Hollywood. She went back to working on a novel that, as far as he remembered, wasn't very good. However much they might have liked each other, they were both too young and driven. They had different things to accomplish and they weren't ready to sacrifice their dreams. They had amicably divorced a year later.

* * *

Directions had cost a fortune, but since Marty had put the whole thing on his credit card, there was an upside: he had racked up enough miles to fly first class without spending even more money. Bunny insisted on paying for the hotels, cars, and incidentals, but Gail had drawn the line at him flying around in her private plane. That was fine by him. Gail was, after all, very likely going to be his wife. Not that her steely-eyed realism was lost on him. Even with the promise of marriage, she hadn't let up about "feeling very vulnerable" until she saw the e-mail from Jim Keating last week confirming that Marty was bequeathing the bulk of his assets to her, tax-free. She hadn't seen Jim's e-mail asking if Marty had lost his mind (this despite the fact that Jim represented Gail too). What did he care what Keating thought? He just wanted a little peace for now. Was it so much to ask?

Besides, he'd change things around later. Finessing his will had become something of a sport. In addition to the house, he'd have to leave at least one painting each to the girls and set up some sort of a fund for them, especially if he got remarried. He wasn't sure he could count on Gail to do the right thing, and he was pretty sure his daughters couldn't survive without his largesse, no matter Gail's opinions on the perils of enablement. It wasn't that his feelings about anything had really changed, but he was seeing his family (his daughters, Gail, even himself) a little more clearly now. Being sober, however briefly, had changed his perspective. The clarity wasn't necessarily welcome, but now that he was looking at it, he had to own his part. He'd have to make some adjustments. Not right away, but eventually. The goal, as he'd learned at Directions, was to take things one day at a time.

So, yes, he nodded to the stewardess, he would have another glass of the Laurent-Perrier Grand Siècle. It wasn't Krug, but not bad for airline champagne. Marty sank back into his leather seat. He was looking forward to Italy. He hadn't been to Rome in years, and not once, he thought, had he ever gone there on vacation. There had always been a premiere or a meeting or some other bullshit event he'd had to attend.

He chuckled to himself at the peculiarity of his having made a new friend at his age. How ironic that that friend happened to be his first wife, a woman he'd all but forgotten until running into her at rehab. Her sudden appearance, both then and now, punctuated the speed with which those fifty years had passed. So much had happened but he hadn't really changed. Inside, he still felt the same as he had at Howard Blum's cocktail party, just a kid doing an impression of an adult in charge. The only real difference was that now he knew that he'd never been in charge, and that he never would be. There were too many variables. The best he could do was to try to relax a little, maybe enjoy the good things in life more. Marty took a sip of his bubbly and closed his eyes.

Janine

Janine had been to Rome exactly once before. She'd gone with her father and Amanda for a movie premiere. She was eight, maybe nine years old. The trip was an unusual treat. They'd stayed at the Parco dei Principi grand hotel. She remembered how the bellboys and concierge had fawned over her father like he was Caesar himself. At the height of his career, her dad was a king everywhere he went. And they were Renaissance princesses. On that trip, at the gift shop he'd bought her a notebook with the name of the hotel embossed on it. She kept it for years. Even then, she thought, she was hoarding good memories, worried there might not be enough.

She remembered thinking the hotel was an actual castle. There were tapestried beds with canopies, Carrara marble bathrooms and thick, heavy curtains that framed the gorgeous views of the Villa Borghese. Janine had walked awestruck beneath the baroque chandeliers in the halls. She sidled up to the fully dressed breakfast tables, careful not to knock over a glass or upset the lavish place settings. But it wasn't the luxury she loved so much as the rigid order cushioned in excess. The seamless rotation of uniformed maids, the room-service trays that were cleared away when nobody was looking, the way the staff spoke in tones of competence and ease. All that regularity, that tidiness and propriety, illuminated everything she didn't have at home with her mother.

When they arrived back in LA, Janine had been horrified to find Pam at the airport, sitting *on the floor,* dressed in tight jeans and a blouse unbuttoned down to her belly button, smoking a cigarette. Amanda ran to her, covered her in kisses, thrilled to fill her in on the highlights of their trip. Marty kissed them good-bye and said he'd see them the following weekend. Janine hated leaving Italy as much as she'd hated leaving her father that day. She saw her mother as a human needle bent on popping the bubble of her happiness.

She'd always assumed she'd go back to Rome someday, maybe with her dad, or maybe she'd study there on her junior year abroad. Or maybe she'd go there on her honeymoon. But she never did go to college and she never got married. What had she been doing all this time in New York? Who had she been hiding from? Why hadn't she ever gone back to Italy? Why hadn't she spent more time with her dad? It was too late now. Her father was gone.

That surreal phone call from Jim Keating—she'd almost ignored it because she hadn't recognized the number. It must have taken her two or three minutes to grasp what he was saying. How did *he* know Marty was dead? She didn't believe him at first. She'd just spoken to her father the day before. Where was Jim getting his information and who had decided that some lawyer or money manager she'd never met should be the one to give her this news?

The calls started coming in quick succession shortly afterward. First Amanda, inconsolable, followed by a solicitous Henry. Janine very much wanted to talk to Bunny, but Henry just apologized for his mother, explaining that she was still too upset to talk. *She* was too upset? Janine asked, incredulous. Henry stayed calm and told her that he'd booked Janine and Amanda on a flight to Rome and arranged for a car to take them to the airport that afternoon. He'd also set up a car to take Hailey and Jaycee to San Diego.

Where the hell was Gail? Janine wondered, managing to throw some clothes in her suitcase between trips to the bathroom. Wasn't she the one they'd have expected to arrange everything? She liked being useful. That was her thing. Both Janine and Amanda had called Gail but her phone had gone straight to voice mail. Gail was nowhere to be found and Janine was both surprised and grateful that Henry was picking up the slack.

Seeing Amanda in the back of that black town car made it real for Janine. They held on to each other for what might have been the first time in thirty years. The twelve-hour flight passed in a haze. If youth is wasted on the young, first class is wasted on the bereaved. Neither of them ate, drank, or even reclined on the sheepskin-covered seats. Nothing had prepared them for the death of their father. He'd *always* been there. Having their North Star blown out like a candle was like having the ground give way beneath them. They were wobbly and shaken with nothing to rely on but the surprisingly reassuring sight of each other.

The Jumeirah Grand Hotel on Via Veneto, where Bunny and Marty had been staying in separate rooms, was close to the Parco dei Principi. Amanda pointed to the Parco as they passed it in the car Bunny had ordered to collect them from Fiumicino Airport. Janine nodded. Amanda grabbed her hand. Bleary-eyed and exhausted, Janine wanted only to go to sleep and wake up to find this was all just a nightmare.

The check-in process at the hotel was a sit-down affair filled with espressos and condolences from the Italian staff. But the sisters were no longer princesses. They were orphans.

The Jumeirah was a restored nineteenth-century villa made modern. Janine disliked it immediately, with its art deco furniture and nearly bare walls peppered with contemporary installations and paintings by Dalí, Picasso, Guttuso, and Miró. Her father must have hated it. Why hadn't he told her how disgustingly hip it all was when they'd spoken on the phone two days earlier? He'd been happy, telling her a funny story about Roman fish and chips and the orange trees in Savello Park. That sounded good but, my God, did anyone want to sleep (let alone die) in the vicinity of a Cattelan installation? She thought of Henry, knowing he would agree with her about the art.

"And Gail Engler?" Amanda asked the hotel clerk. "Does she have a reservation?"

"Ms. Engler is already here," the clerk said.

"Oh, Gail is *already* here," Amanda repeated loudly, as if Janine hadn't heard for herself. Amanda had quickly decided directing her rage at Gail was easier than dealing with the reality of their father's death. "So that explains why we couldn't reach her. She was already in the air, burying her grief by flying private. She must have flown private, right? We were on the first commercial flight. So who paid for *that* and why didn't she invite us?" Amanda, unhinged, hands in the air, asked Janine. "She didn't even have the courtesy to call us! Dad dies and we don't hear from his fucking fiancée? Who does that, Janine? Who?"

As it turned out, Gail's head start was for naught. Bunny had refused to see her without Janine and Amanda. She had left them a message at the desk explaining that she would see "the family" together in her suite.

Once Amanda and Janine were in their room, Amanda reluctantly called Gail to announce their arrival. Gail was at the door within minutes, the image of the perfect widow, heavily perfumed and dressed in black. She sobbed extravagantly upon seeing them, smothering them both in a long hug. "I knew this trip was a bad idea," she said. "I had a terrible feeling all along." She apologized for leaving so abruptly, for not calling. Her assistant had gotten her on an empty-leg charter flight, she explained, and she'd had to run to the airport with just minutes to pack. There was only one free seat anyway, she said. The ticket was cheap but she'd been forced to endure the long flight with a group of Chinese businessmen. Janine could barely look at Gail, let alone listen to her. She believed the woman was genuinely upset, but her hysteria felt calculated, her inexcusable behavior too well reasoned. And she couldn't help wondering if Gail's grief was fueled by the fact that she was *never* going to be their father's wife.

They took the elevator to Bunny's suite together in silence. A Do Not Disturb sign—NON DISTURBARE—hung on the door handle. Gail knocked. Bunny answered the door and just stood there silently before asking them in. She was disheveled and puffy-eyed and seemed surprised to see them, though she obviously knew they were coming. After giving each of them a hug and mumbling something unintelligible about how sorry she was, she directed them all to the seating area. She looked ten years older than she had when Janine last saw her at Directions.

Tissues and papers were scattered all over the spacious room decorated in gold and black. Bunny apologized for the mess and started off immediately explaining that she'd arranged everything so that there would be no complications with the remains at the airport or the embassy. "Just try getting a Jew cremated in Rome," Bunny said with a nervous laugh as she fumbled to light a cigarette with her shaking hand. "You'd think they were hoping for a last-minute conversion. I had to pull every string in town, including calling Matteo."

"Matteo?" Gail asked.

"She means Matteo Renzi," a stocky older man with a British accent said as he came out of the bedroom. He smiled sympathetically, shook their hands, and introduced himself as Bunny's agent, Ian. He had on an expensive-looking suit, and his dyed dark hair was slicked back with pomade, as if he'd spent some time getting ready for them. He pulled a platinum lighter out of his pocket and held it up to Bunny's cigarette. "Matteo is the former prime minister."

"Of Italy?" Gail asked.

Bunny nodded and pushed her hair off her forehead. "Ian's been helping me." She exhaled as two tears ran down her face. She wiped them away quickly. Ian touched Bunny's shoulder.

"Matteo came right away," Bunny went on. "He's been so dear. My

God, that was a shocking thing. Really," she said, dissolving into tears. "I feel somehow responsible."

Ian shook his head.

"You're not," Amanda said. "Obviously. But if you don't mind, I'd like to know what happened," she said, her voice breaking on the last word.

Bunny looked at Ian. He sat on the armrest of the sofa and started talking, directing his words to Amanda. "Bunny and your father had planned to meet in the lobby at nine a.m. yesterday. A car was taking them to Pompeii for the day."

Amanda nodded.

"Pompeii?" Gail asked. "Isn't that a long way?"

"He wanted to go," Bunny said, defensive. "Said he'd never been. So I had someone arrange it. But he wasn't downstairs, so I finally had the concierge call his room. No answer. I thought maybe he'd gone out for a walk but he didn't answer his mobile either. They finally sent someone up," she said, taking a deep breath. "A bellboy, I believe."

Janine couldn't think straight. Her father was dead and she was pregnant! Gail was crying now. Amanda was crying too.

"He was just lying there in the bed," Bunny finally said with a haunted expression. "His heart must have just given out. It was an awful, awful thing."

She straightened up and reached for Ian's hand. "Ian's really been a godsend. He dealt with the death certificate and the cremation authorization at the embassy. It might have taken weeks without Martin's next of kin here. Even if you'd been here, well, you've no idea how impossible the Italians are."

"We were on the first commercial flight," Amanda said, glaring at Gail.

"Oh, I'm not blaming you," Bunny said. "Of course not. There's nothing you could have done anyway. I'm having a bloody religious debate about your father's wishes for cremation and they're arguing with me, despite the fact that it has to be done immediately, before the authorities get involved and insist on an autopsy, which, according to your father's attorneys, he absolutely did not want."

"No, he didn't," Gail said, shaking her head. "Absolutely not."

Ian looked askance at Gail and poured himself a glass of water. Janine could see that he was protective of Bunny and that he expected the worst from the three of them. What did he think they were going to do, blame Bunny? Janine was thirsty and sick to her stomach. She watched Ian take a sip of water and put his glass down on a long table.

"It's nearly impossible to avoid an autopsy when an American dies in a foreign country," Ian continued. "Officials have to rule out foul play and such. So this had to be done quickly, before the authorities got involved."

"Perhaps a little too quickly," Gail said. "Not that we don't appreciate all you've done, but I can't help but—"

Ian narrowed his eyes at Gail. "The possibility of foul play was quickly dismissed. Nobody in Italy had anything to gain by Martin Kessler's death." He left the question as to who *might* benefit from it floating in the air.

Bunny grabbed another tissue. "Thank God Ian came. The paperwork alone. There was so much back-and-forth with Martin's attorneys in Los Angeles. As if the shock of the thing weren't bad enough."

"I don't understand why you didn't call me first thing," Gail said. She moved over to Bunny as if to impart how useful she might have been, how useful she still might be. "I'm very close with Jim Keating."

"Naturally his daughters were called first," Ian said, his mouth tight. "And of course we called you as well. But you're not his wife, and you've got to understand, once the body was removed, there was no time to waste if we wanted to respect his wishes. Which I assume we all did?"

"Yes." Amanda nodded.

"Of course," Gail said stiffly.

Janine turned the word *body* over in her head. Was the body so divorced from the person already? Her father? The knowledge that his body was already ash, that it was a fait accompli, sent a fierce chill up her spine. She felt as though someone was pulling her organs out of her via her throat. She would never hear her father's voice or follow him, limping slightly, as he worked his way through the yard. She would never see his balding head, hold his freckled hand, or curl up in his arms for one of his hugs. A world in which he wasn't present didn't feel like a world Janine could fully occupy. There would be more space but so much less room. Unlike with the death of her mother, Janine didn't feel at all liberated. She felt like part of her had been amputated. What if she hadn't gone to LA, if she hadn't had those last few weeks with him? She tried desperately to reassemble that last day together in San Diego with Hailey. That was a great fucking day. But what had they talked about? She couldn't remember anything.

"I'm just so sorry," Bunny said. "Poor Martin. Poor girls."

"Anyway," Ian said as he rubbed Bunny's shoulders, "I think everything's been done as your father would have liked. I hope so, anyway. We did our best."

"Yes," Amanda said, her voice unsteady. "Thank you."

Bunny began babbling on again about all the difficulties: the certificates of exportation, his passport, the paparazzi outside the hotel. Janine wondered if Bunny was drunk. Not that Janine would blame her, but still. She scanned the room for another glass but didn't see one. That her father didn't want an autopsy confirmed Janine's suspicions that he was still taking drugs, a fact he never would have wanted in his obituary. Bunny's super-celebrity powers had spared him that humiliation.

"Thank you," Janine said. "For your help."

Bunny looked at Janine and smiled a little, as if saying she was sorry she hadn't been able to do something more. Janine could feel the sharpness of Bunny's pain. It was important to Janine that Bunny understand the depth of her gratitude.

"You're welcome, Janine." Bunny leaned forward and fished a small piece of folded paper out of a bowl on the coffee table. "This is for you."

"What is it?" Gail asked, looking at Bunny and then Amanda.

"It seems Martin carried it with him in his wallet. I didn't want it to get lost." Bunny looked at Janine, her expression unreadable.

Janine unfolded the paper and stared. It was a typed poem and a little drawing she'd sent to her father when she was a teenager staying at McLean. Janine was struck dumb. She felt tossed back in time. It showed a cartoon of her with four figures, some of them wearing glasses, one with a guitar hanging from a strap around his neck, one with a medal in his hand. The ink on the poem was faded, the letters pecked out on an old-fashioned typewriter.

```
I'm okay, Dad, things aren't so bad, McLean is a
    pretty sweet place!
I don't feel confined, the doctors are kind and
    agree I'm a very mild case.
From this cuckoo's nest, I can say you're the
    best, to visit each week like you do.
Don't worry at all, I promise I'll call if I crack
    up and land at Bellevue.
```

The figures were meant to represent the luminaries who'd frequented McLean, perhaps a stab at normalizing her stint: Ray Charles, James Taylor, John Nash, Robert Lowell. She remembered wanting desperately to draw Sylvia Plath and Anne Sexton but feeling she had to be careful not to include anyone who'd committed suicide. Her job, she'd felt even then, was to amuse her father, to cheer him up and assure him that she was okay. It was a terrible poem, an even worse drawing, but that he still had it broke her fucking heart. And he *had* visited her in Massachusetts, every single weekend, from Los Angeles. She'd forgotten that or hadn't realized how hard it must have been for him. Despite all the time that had passed, he'd kept that stupid poem and drawing in his wallet. Her father had loved her and he'd known how much she loved him—and he'd carried a reminder of both facts around with him, folded and safe, for all these years.

"God," she mewled, losing the battle with her emotions, "I was a better artist as a teenager than I am now."

A strangled sob distorted Bunny's attempt at laughter.

Janine held the drawing to her stomach, close to the baby her dad would never meet. She felt inexplicably allied with Bunny. She wanted to comfort her however she could. "He was excited about this trip," she said. "And he sounded happy on the phone. He would have said that there were worse ways to go than having a heart attack in bed in a five-star hotel room in Rome."

Amanda let out a queer little chirp and smiled at Bunny, acknowledging the truth of what Janine had said. Bunny nodded, wiping away her tears. She laughed, uncomfortable in the joint stifled sobbing that followed. "Thank you, Janine. That's true. Yes. He would have."

"Well," Gail said, contributing nothing. Her lips were a thin line. She really had no place here.

"Can I ask what you guys did on Monday?" Janine asked, eager for anything solid to lean on. She knew this might be her last chance to talk about him at length, to learn how he'd spent his final days. Bunny might forget the details or not want to talk about it later.

"Not very much," Bunny said, almost apologetically. "I wish I could say we danced on Caesar's grave or at the very least met the pope, but we just went to the Borghese museum and gardens. He wanted to see the Berninis."

"That sounds like a perfect Dad day," Amanda said. Janine nodded.

Ian cleared his throat and began picking up the tissues. He was obviously done with this morbid, if mandatory, little meeting. "Anything else?" Janine asked, trying to prolong the conversation. She wondered where the ashes were, knowing it was time to go now. She tried to get herself together as she folded the drawing into her purse.

"But what did he have for dinner?" Gail asked, as if the explanation for his death lay in the rich Italian cuisine Bunny had force-fed him.

"Fish," Bunny said, blowing her nose. "And gelato. He had another gelato after dinner."

"Another?" Gail asked. "Two gelatos?"

"He had one after lunch. He was mad for it."

"He was," Janine said. She remembered eating lots of gelato when they'd visited Rome together. The craze hadn't hit the States yet. His freezer in LA was still filled with half-eaten cartons of gelato. She felt some small consolation that at least he'd had two gelatos that day.

Despite Ian's impatience, Bunny settled into her seat and lit another cigarette, seemingly not wanting them to leave just yet. She told Janine all about the gelato process in Italy, how it was made fresh, in small batches, with butterfat and less air churned in than ice cream. That's why it tasted so good. Amanda asked about the Borghese gardens and Bunny laughed and told them how Marty had compared it to Central Park with its carousel for the kids, the artificial lake, the replica of the Globe theater. She was telling them about a miniature monkey they'd both liked in the Bioparco whom Martin had quickly named Luigi Baby Shanks when Gail stood up and interrupted Bunny to ask for the ashes.

Ian hustled to the other room, eager, Janine suspected, to move them all along. He returned with a cardboard box and handed it to Bunny. Janine felt a swell of queasiness; she was unsure if it was morning sickness or seeing her dad's remains in what looked like a to-go box from a restaurant. Bunny apologized for the container and explained that stone and metal weren't allowed through X-ray at the airport. She held on to it for a moment before standing up and offering the box to Janine. That Bunny seemed to feel Janine was the rightful carrier, and that Amanda nodded as if she agreed, was more than Janine could handle. She didn't move.

"Do you want me to take him?" Amanda asked, putting her arm around Janine's shoulder.

Gail stepped forward and reached for the box. Bunny straightened up and pulled it back. Then she gave it to Amanda, who gently placed it in Janine's hands. Janine shook her head and held tight. Even though it was too late, she wasn't letting go.

Bunny

Ian was looking out the window of Bunny's bedroom, past the courtyard, at the distant Trellick Tower. His hands were pushed into his pockets. His slacks were wildly unflattering; they made his bottom look enormous. She thought of telling him that but decided not to. For better or worse, having a joke at his expense had lost its luster. The cigarette smoke burned her eyes as she watched him from her bed.

She'd considered telling Bettina not to let Ian up, but what would be the point? He'd just come back later. That's what agents did. As grateful as she was for his help in Italy, she didn't want to see him. The idea of everything just returning to normal was unbearable. She didn't give a fig about her book or getting back to it. She was preoccupied with what had happened in Italy, revisiting her many conversations with Martin and, finally, that last day with his family.

If only she'd had a chance to talk to Janine privately, to tell her how sorry she was about the baby. "She isn't pregnant, Mother," Henry had told her over the phone before she'd left for Italy. Bunny could only assume the poor girl had miscarried sometime after their conversation. Perhaps it was for the best, but how awful to suffer two losses in such short order. She'd even thought of calling Janine, but what on earth would she say?

"You look like hell, Bun," Ian said. "You need a vacation."

"I've just had one." She stubbed out her cigarette and lit a new one. Bettina had lingered for a moment after showing Ian in, scanning the room and then making a somewhat frantic dash to empty ashtrays and collect old cups of coffee. She pulled a spray bottle out of her apron pocket and spritzed at a water ring on Bunny's side table.

"That's enough," Bunny said, not unkindly. "Thank you, Bettina."

A little smile worked the corners of Bettina's mouth as she disappeared from the room.

Ian waited until Bettina shut the door to turn around. He leaned back against the windowsill with his arms folded across his chest. "It's been two weeks. You've got to snap out of it. And the smoking. Since when do you smoke so much?"

"Since I quit drinking."

"Can I open the window? It smells like Keith Richards died in here."

Bunny shrugged, a gesture she'd picked up from Henry in Los Angeles. She hoped it conveyed indifference but suspected it suggested despair. She'd been surprised she hadn't wanted a drink. In fact, the very thought was repellent, as if drinking would nullify the time she'd spent at Directions with Martin, with Henry. She also knew being drunk wouldn't make her feel any better, only worse.

"Are you all right?" he asked.

Bunny had been crying for days. She couldn't stop. It was a mammoth effort to pull herself together for Ian. Even the sight of Bettina depressed her, which was why she'd given her so little access to her bedroom. The poor woman was desperate to tidy up. Bunny was lonely, but not for Ian or Sam or Bettina's company. She didn't want to see anyone in London. She missed the past few weeks of her life. She'd felt like a different person in California, felt like she'd been inserted into an interesting play and had grown fond of her fellow actors, and she'd been happy enough to step out of the spotlight (for a change) and watch their narrative unfold. But she hated the ending. How very unjust to drop the curtain like that.

"*That* obviously didn't turn out to be a vacation," Ian said. He made an unsuccessful attempt to furrow his brow and sat down on the edge of her bed. "Why don't you go to Fiji or Tahiti? Somewhere you can just, you know, relax."

"Relax? That's the last thing I want to do." She looked at Ian as if he were a stranger. "Did you have Botox put in?" she asked.

Ian's hands flew to his forehead. "No," he said. "No!"

Bunny shrugged again. "Anyway, what on earth would I do in Fiji?"

"Swim, lie on the beach, read. Smoke."

"Don't be absurd."

"There's a wonderful place in Spain," he said. "Ian McEwan goes."

"Is that supposed to be a selling point?"

"There are no paparazzi. You'd be left all alone."

"I don't want to be left all alone," she cried, upset that her voice exposed her sadness.

"Right. Sorry." He fiddled with his cuff link.

Bunny took a deep breath and tried to collect herself. "Why can't you just let me be? I'm not causing any trouble. I'm not drinking, if that's your concern."

"You're not writing either."

Her anger, something she'd hoped she'd let go of, came back like a fire cloud. "Are you really so worried about your paycheck, Ian? I've just had a man I was very fond of die on my watch. Can you please just give me a minute? I'm blue. I keep thinking there's something I could have done to prevent it."

"Don't be so hard on yourself. There's nothing you could have done, Bun. He was a seventy-five-year-old man with a drug problem. And look what he did to his girls."

"Don't," Bunny said, shooting him a warning glare. "Don't talk about him. You didn't know him." Her eyes were full of tears again. The well was infinite. Henry had told her about the will. She couldn't believe that Martin had left his daughters high and dry—that he'd given it all to that harpy of a woman—but she wouldn't have his name disparaged either. She believed, in her heart, that Martin hadn't really understood the consequences of what he'd done. He was like a child, Bunny thought, a very foolish child. His vulnerability both touched and disgusted her. It was so important to do the right thing. Why didn't Martin know that at his age? That was all anyone could do.

"I'm feeling very mortal. It's terrifying. Just like that," she said, snapping her fingers, "and it's over."

"But *you* are immortal," Ian said. "Don't you see? That's the beauty of your work. It lives on even after you die."

"Is that supposed to be helpful? What good does that do *me?*" she asked. "I know it does *you* good. But it doesn't do much for me, Ian. Life doesn't add up to much. One day you're eating a pistachio gelato, the next you're a pile of ashes in a takeaway box. I see no logic."

"You're stewing. How long have we known each other?"

"Please," Bunny said. She was opening another box of Parliaments.

"You keep smoking like that, you'll be dead soon enough."

She lit a cigarette.

"This ruminating is beastly," he said. "You ought to distract yourself. Why not start working? Carry on with your old routine?"

"Brilliant. Why don't you drizzle some gin on the laptop keyboard and see if I mate with it?" Couldn't he see the old routine was the very last thing she was interested in? She felt different. She knew it was absurd, but nothing that mattered was in the room anymore.

Just then the phone rang. Bunny didn't move to answer it. A minute later Bettina knocked on the door and poked her neatly coiffed head into the room. "Mrs. Bunny?"

"What?" Bunny asked, irritated at the way Bettina always said her name as if it were a question.

"Mr. Henry's on the phone."

"Ah. Thank you, Bettina."

"I suppose that's my cue," Ian said, collecting his coat.

"If you don't mind? I'll call you tomorrow."

"I won't hold my breath," he said.

Bunny wasn't listening. "Hello, darling," she said, finding a false cheer as she waved Ian off.

"Hi, Mum. How are you holding up?"

"You know. Same as yesterday. And the day before. Sad, really. I don't know why I'm so sad but..." She stopped herself, feeling her throat tighten. "I miss him," she said, laughing. "Did you see the obituary in the *New York Times*?"

"Mm," Henry said. "He was a very impressive man."

"You know, Henry, part of me wishes I hadn't run into him again. I'd forgotten how wonderfully demented he was. Time has a way of collapsing in on itself. I felt less blurry with him. Now I feel so old all of a sudden."

"But you're not turning up your toes just yet, are you?"

"No," she said. "I suppose not just yet." For some inexplicable reason this thought cheered her up. "How are the girls?" Bunny asked. "How's Janine?"

"Not too well but it's hard to say. She won't stay at her father's now and the house is being prepped for the sale anyway. She still sleeps in my extra bedroom some nights." He laughed self-consciously. "I suspect it's only because it's more comfortable than her sister's sofa."

"So he really left them *nothing*?" Bunny asked for what must have been the sixth time in the past seven days. When she wasn't talking to Ian, she found focusing on Martin's stupidity rather than his finer qualities comforting.

"Not much other than the house, which is valuable, but they'll have to sell that in order to pay the estate taxes, including the taxes on Gail's bequests."

"Beastly."

"Oh," he added, almost an afterthought. "They also have to pay a neat sum to the gardener, and there seems to be an elephant in Georgia expecting something."

Bunny felt the talons of a headache taking hold.

"It's certainly a blow," Henry went on. "But nothing very unusual about these stories. My sense is Janine's okay, just sad, a bit adrift." He paused. "Can't say the same about Amanda. She's furious. Wanted to fight it."

"As she should!"

"A no-contest clause was written in." He lowered his voice. "Just before Italy."

"How disgusting!"

"Apparently it's all Amanda talks about. She's gone a bit off the rails from the sound of it."

"I don't blame her," Bunny said. "What a first-rate ass Martin was."

"I thought you missed him."

"That's beside the point. What will Janine do now, Henry?" Bunny asked.

"She's talking about going back to New York after she helps Amanda sort his affairs out."

"New York?" Bunny was stunned. "What tosh! There's nothing in New York for her! What about the movie? That's an opportunity. It's a job."

"She's concerned about putting herself out in the public eye again. And it pays surprisingly little. Either way, I suspect she'll go back," he said, sounding sadder than Bunny had ever heard him. "It is her home. She has a flat there. A cat."

"A cat?" Bunny asked, as if that were the most appalling thing about all of this. "Who's had the cat all this time?"

"Her ex-boyfriend and his wife."

"Try with her again, Henry," Bunny said, suddenly exhausted. She could practically taste her frustration that life was so altogether disappointing. "Try."

"Mm," he said noncommittally. "Are you taking care of yourself, Mother?"

"I'm not drinking, if that's what you mean," she said. "But I'm not writing either. They may go together. I haven't figured it out yet."

Neither of them spoke for a minute, withdrawn into their private sorrows. Bunny chewed the inside of her cheek, not wanting to ask her next question but not really caring about anything other than the answer. "Will you come for the holidays?" she asked, hating herself for sounding needy.

"Yes," he said. "Of course I'll come."

There was a long silence.

"Are you there?" Henry asked. "Mum?"

"Thank you," she managed to say in a strange, creaky voice. "Bye," she said and hung up quickly. She hoped he hadn't heard that she was about to cry again.

Janine

Janine was sitting in the car outside her father's house talking to Jürgen. She'd called to thank him for the flowers he'd sent. He'd apparently seen the obituary in the paper. His wife, Birgit, had left it on the coffee table. Jürgen laughed a little, explaining that Birgit was concerned that now Janine was going to come and take back her cat. Birgit had grown attached to the cat, Jürgen said. Janine's chest had compressed at the sound of Jürgen's voice, at his use of his old pet name for her, Chippen.

When she'd told him about the will, queerly relishing dropping the news of the injustice so plainly, he'd told her, in typical Jürgen fashion, that she'd been naive not to have seen it coming. "You know there's a word for that," he'd gone on. "*Drachenfutter*. It's what a man gives his wife to appease her when he feels guilty about something. It means 'dragon food.'"

Janine thought *Drachenfutter* would be a good title for a biography of her father.

She wondered why Jürgen's excitement about the movie and the pregnancy had annoyed her so much. "Are you looking forward to the film?" he'd asked. She was struck dumb by the simplicity of his statement, divorced as it was from the burden of her family's expectations and disappointments. She didn't know how she felt. She still hadn't decided what she was going to do about the part, despite the impending start date and Ransom's need for an answer. Going back home to New York seemed like the simplest solution. But she was going to have a baby. That much she'd decided. The pregnancy and her father's death, both so unexpected, felt inexplicably connected. She had to tell Henry, but the logistics of her future were a complete fog.

"You want to rent out your apartment here for a while?" Jürgen asked. "Birgit could do it." Janine was surprised that she hadn't even considered it. She'd forgotten Birgit was a real estate agent. "You could get a lot of money for it. Let it out furnished, even better," he added. "It will give you extra cash and time to sort things out." Janine liked the idea of making a decision she could undo, although she knew that if she rented out her place, she'd most likely sell it eventually. "Birgit would take a cut," Jürgen said. "You know, because she doesn't hate you or anything—but she doesn't like you *that* much. Not enough to forgo her commission."

Janine could get something nice in LA if she found a tenant for her apartment in New York. LA was less expensive than Manhattan. And maybe the part *would* lead to something. "Can I have some time to think about it?" she asked Jürgen. "I have to talk to Amanda. And Henry. But it might be good."

Jürgen cleared his throat. "I think it would be," he said. "Good."

"For you or for me?" She was suddenly unsure whether he was genuinely helping her or pushing her out of town.

"For you."

She wanted to know how he felt about her leaving New York permanently but decided there was no reason to ask. "That's a really nice offer, Jürgen. Thank you. And please thank Birgit."

"I will," he said.

"Do you still have the key?" she asked. "What about all my books and stuff?"

"I'll box it all up and put it in the Queens workshop. Not a problem."

"Wow. You seriously don't miss me at all, do you?"

"I do miss you," he said, emotion cutting his deep voice. "Very much."

"But you really want the cat?"

"Yeah," he said, clutching at the humor. "We really want the cat."

Janine put her phone in her bag and walked into her father's house for what she knew might be the last time. She hadn't liked going into the house since Italy, preferring to stay away while the appraisers and agents came and went. She'd been sleeping in Henry's guest room, which he'd kindly offered, and sometimes on Amanda's sofa. The house had sold in a swift transaction, the details of which none of the beneficiaries (Janine, Amanda, Gail, Sandro) were privy to. Once Gail and Sandro received their bequests, Amanda and Janine would pay the taxes and split what little was left.

Amanda was sitting on top of the island in the kitchen, legs crossed, flats tossed onto the floor. They had a long day ahead, packing up photographs and whatever sentimental objects they might want. Her sister looked at home there, Janine thought, more at ease than usual. Amanda had always been so frantic when she came to the house—cleaning, cooking, wrangling the girls, or otherwise engaged in the business of avoiding a conversation with their dad. It struck Janine that there might be a small part of Amanda that felt the same way Janine had felt when her mother died—relieved that the person who judged her was no longer standing there, frowning.

"Hi," Janine said. She walked through the living room and put her bag on the island. "What is all this?" she asked. There were pink Post-its with the letter *G* written on them on most of the art and furniture.

"Gail made her sweep last night."

Janine sat down on a stool. "Already?"

"Yep."

"God. Did she come in with her assistant and a black Sharpie?

They're fucking everywhere." The house looked like a deconstructed stage set over which someone had tossed pink Post-it confetti.

The appraiser had calculated the worth of every last tapestry, painting, poster, lamp, and basket. Janine hated having a monetary value placed on the landscape of her childhood. And according to the will, Gail had been given the opportunity to take anything she desired first. No surprise that Gail had claimed everything valuable. More disturbing were the Post-its duct-taped to the rolled-up rugs, the flatware and dishes, the books, the coffee table, and the outdoor furniture. That Gail felt entitled to their family heirlooms was impossible for Janine to wrap her head around. But nonetheless, they were hers for the taking. That's how her father had left it. Janine wondered what on earth her father had felt so guilty about that he had to feed the dragon *everything*.

"She doesn't even have a backyard," Amanda said with disgust, pointing at the lawn tables and chairs that Gail had pulled inside the living room, apparently so that they wouldn't be overlooked when the movers came. She smacked her lips together. "She's just going to sell it all! I stupidly left her a message about maybe setting up something for the girls' college. Even twenty thousand dollars. She never called me back."

"I hate her," Janine said.

Amanda lit a cigarette, clearly relishing the impropriety of smoking in their father's house. She lay down on the butcher-block island, stretched out, and stared at the ceiling. "It's so quiet here," Amanda said and inhaled deeply.

"Too quiet." Janine looked around for anything without a Post-it. "You want the dining table?"

Amanda rolled her head to the left and looked at it. "God, no."

They silently considered the Equipale Mexican table and six matching chairs. It was the kind of table used in cheap Mexican restaurants. Their dad thought it was amusing, a nod to the house's hacienda-style roots. Above the table hung a stunning Tiffany Dogwood chandelier, estimated at $120,000, with a bright pink Post-it on it.

Janine and Amanda walked through the house together, taking in the Post-its, both realizing how meaningless all the stuff was without their father breathing life into it. "I don't want anything," Janine said. "Just photos and maybe his passports and whatever art books she didn't take."

Amanda plopped down hard on the bed in the guest room. She expelled a melancholy sigh. "Dad always liked you so much more than me. I spent my entire adult life tap-dancing for him and he wasn't even looking. I was so desperate for his approval. I passed up career opportunities to stay close to him. I thought that's what he wanted. But I just annoyed him. You, a million miles away in New York picking your nose, he couldn't get enough of."

Janine sucked in her cheeks. She knew what Amanda said was true and that Janine had always taken it for granted, as if it were fair. "I'm really sorry that it felt that way."

Amanda pulled one of the decorative bed pillows behind her onto her lap. She leaned forward on it and looked fixedly at Janine. "So when are you leaving?"

Janine took a deep breath and screwed up her courage. "I was thinking I could sell my apartment," she said, deciding at that very moment that this was what she needed and wanted to do. She suddenly had no idea why she'd been in New York, from whom or what she'd been hiding. "I could afford to rent or even buy something nice here if I sell my place."

"You're not going back?"

"I think I want to be here. With you. And the girls. Is that lame? Am I too late?"

Amanda didn't say anything right away but Janine could see the disbelief, the tightening of her face. Was she mad? Maybe Amanda didn't want her to stay.

"I think that part could be good for you," Amanda finally said, her voice level. "And obviously Hailey likes having you around. It's been nice watching you together. You could get to know Jaycee better too."

Neither one of them spoke for a minute, both unsure how to navigate this new terrain.

"LA might be a healthy change of pace for you," Amanda continued. She was trying to sound unemotional but Janine could see that her hand was shaking. Amanda looked down and started thumbing the inside of her palm. Then, in a desultory fashion, she added: "Maybe it would be good for me too."

Janine started to say something but Amanda interrupted her. "What about a mattress?" She fished another cigarette out of her pocket and slowly placed it between her lips. "You'll need stuff to furnish your place here."

"Maybe."

"No pressure. You can keep staying with us until you start getting paid or sell your place. Or I guess go back and forth between our apartment and Henry's."

Janine didn't know what was going on with Henry. He'd been nothing but helpful and accommodating since Italy, but, except for a few brief moments, she felt as though they were just friends now. Grief, or maybe too many practicalities, seemed to have smothered the passion. He wasn't pushing things either. If anything, he was too polite, too respectful of her space. She missed the way they'd been together before, but she hadn't a clue how to get back there again. Maybe being friends was better. She didn't want him to feel obligated to be with her, but she figured that's how he'd feel once she told him about the baby. In any case, she didn't want to think about Henry right now. She was thinking about the effects of secondhand smoke on a fetus. "You probably shouldn't smoke in here. It stinks."

"That's true," Amanda said, puffing away. She stood up and opened the door to the yard, her back to Janine, and exhaled bit by bit as she spoke. "I always loved this house. Once it's gone, it'll be like none of it, none of us, was ever here. Jaycee and Hailey deserve better than that shit-box apartment. College loans and a shitty rental. I hate that I can't give them more than that."

"Jim Keating made it clear we can't afford the house," Janine said. She was tired from standing. She leaned on the dresser and looked at the familiar Miró lithograph hanging over the bed. It had a pink Post-it stuck to the glass. *Drachenfutter,* she thought again, hoping her dad would have been disgusted by Gail's behavior. She felt an irrational urge to take a picture of that lithograph and send it to him, wherever he was, to prove to him the kind of person Gail was.

"That Keating guy is the worst," Amanda said, turning around. She sat back on the bed, cigarette still dangling from her lips as loose ash dropped onto the white duvet. Absently, she rubbed the ash until it almost disappeared. "He always sounds so annoyed on the phone. It's like he can't wait to wash his hands of us, like he can't get the money to Gail fast enough, right? There's something deeply, *deeply* fucked up about us having to sell the only thing Dad left us in order to pay Gail's gift taxes!"

Janine nodded, exhausted by Amanda's rage, and narrowed her eyes at her sister's cigarette. "But either way, the new owners won't appreciate it reeking of smoke."

"You're so calm about this whole thing! Since when did you get so Zen? It's infuriating."

Janine flicked a rubber band off the dresser onto Amanda's bare foot. "Maybe it's the baby. Can you stop with the cigarettes? It's seriously making me sick."

"Baby?" Amanda sat up and stubbed out her cigarette in a candle on the bedside table. "Holy shit."

"I know."

"You can still get pregnant?"

"Thanks."

"I didn't mean it like that, it's just—shit. Is it Henry's?"

Janine nodded.

"Are you getting *married?*" Amanda asked. She threw out the last word like gristle in a piece of chicken. "Did he ask you? Does he know? About the baby? Are you keeping it? How long have you known? Why didn't you tell me before?"

Janine couldn't help but be charmed by the muddle of her sister's questions. "Yes, I'm keeping it, and no, he doesn't know. Not yet. We're just...I don't even know what we are. I haven't known about the baby that long. I've been trying to figure out what I'm going to do."

"Oh my God," Amanda said, putting her head in her hands. "My life sucks! You're going to be a movie star and have Bunny Small's grandchild, and my kids' new stepmother is named Gilbert! Why is it the universe just shines on you and shits on me?"

Janine laughed at the absurdity of Amanda's observation. "I'm about to be a single mother with no place to live and exactly one, finite, job opportunity. You have two great, albeit slightly weird, children, a career you like, and you're still beautiful. I don't pity you."

"You should."

"I don't."

"You should," Amanda said, trying not to smile. Then, clapping her hands, she said, "A baby. I get to be an aunt. Dad would have been excited." She knit her eyebrows. "I think?"

Janine smiled. "I don't know how he would have felt either."

"Screw this. We have to do *something*."

"What do you mean?" Janine asked.

"I need revenge. When does Gail take his car for good?"

"I think as soon as she gets the title transfer or whatever it's called. Probably this week." Janine hesitated a minute before pulling a small envelope out of her back pocket. She handed it to Amanda. It said *Marty* on it. The handwriting was square.

"What's this?" Amanda asked. She wrinkled up her forehead and opened the letter. Janine watched the smile spread slowly across her sister's face. She read aloud:

Dear Marty,

You've become so important to me this past year. You're generosity and kindness have meant more to me than I can say. I've never felt so truely treasured as I did on my thirty-fifth birthday. What a night. That necklace! I know your going through a hard time but I just want you to know I am always here for you. You have touched me in a whole new way.

With so much love and a million little kisses,
Nicki

"Where did you find this?" Amanda asked.

"I wrote it," Janine said. She touched her stomach, as if maybe doing such a petty thing might hurt the baby.

"Fuck." Amanda popped off the bed and squinted at Janine. She pointed to the letter again. "This isn't your handwriting."

"It's Henry's," she explained, remembering how willingly Henry had jumped in last night to help her execute her childish prank. He hadn't been judgmental. If anything, he had seemed to like being included in the duplicity; it was as if Gail had wronged him too. And they'd kissed afterward. A not so nothing of a kiss either. It was a great kiss, actually, much as Janine was trying not to think about it. She was committed to keeping things clean with Henry. Until she figured out what the hell the rest of her life was going to look like.

Amanda read the letter to herself again. "You used *your* and *you're* wrong. And you misspelled *truly*."

"On purpose."

"Won't it just make Gail think she's dumb?"

"It'll make her think she's uneducated, maybe a little helpless. A perfect side dish. Henry said it was a nice touch." She thought she felt the baby kick her, though of course it was too early for that. "Jesus. Is it too mean?"

"JJ," Amanda said, using her old nickname, "I didn't think you had it in you."

Janine felt inordinately pleased with herself as Amanda purposefully started for the kitchen. Janine trailed after her and nodded obediently when Amanda handed her the letter and walked into the pantry. She came out with a can of tuna fish.

"It's not lunchtime." Janine felt a wave of nausea pass over her. "And I hate tuna."

Amanda peeled the lid off and tossed it into the trash. "Come on. Bring the letter. Come."

Janine followed Amanda back through the house and out into the driveway. Amanda dangled the car keys from her index finger as she carried the can of tuna ceremoniously, in the flat of her palm. She opened the car, took the letter from Janine, and carefully slipped it between the pages of the owner's manual in the glove compartment. She proceeded to pour tuna juice under all the floor mats, between the seats, and finally into the trunk. Then she cranked the heat up to high and sat down in the passenger seat. She looked at Janine, beaming. *"What?"* Amanda asked, taking in Janine's stunned expression. "Hailey showed me a bunch of revenge videos on YouTube. This is a lot more benign than some of them."

"We're really pathetic," Janine said, unsure whether to be amused or appalled by their petty acts of revenge. "You know that, right?"

"I could always kill her," Amanda said, wiping her hands on her pants. "But jail seems like a drag and I'm curious about what's going to happen now. This orphan thing is oddly liberating."

Janine made a face. "What if she doesn't find the letter? Maybe it should go somewhere more accessible."

"Mm. Like your little poem in his wallet?" Amanda asked with a tilt of her head. But rather than dwell on it, as Janine might have anticipated, Amanda removed the wrinkled letter from the owner's manual and slipped it inside the pocket on the driver's-side sun visor. Janine could easily imagine Gail spending loads of time looking in that mirror—assuming she could stand the smell. She'd find the note.

Amanda got out and shut the car door. They stood outside together next to the hot, still-running Mercedes. Amanda looked at Janine and smiled. A tear ran down the side of her face. Janine hoped that getting each other back would be a consolation prize for both of them, considering all they'd lost.

Hailey

Hailey and Jaycee were sitting in the backseat of their mom's car. The car thermometer said it was forty-four degrees outside. Their mom and Aunt Janine were down on the beach, huddled together under a big Pendleton blanket, pointing up at the occasional small plane overhead.

"This is weird," Hailey said. She pulled her sweater up over her chin. "Grandpa *never* woke up this early when he was alive. What kind of funeral is this anyway?"

"It's not a funeral, you idiot. His ashes are being scattered over the ocean. That's what he wanted. That's all he wanted."

"It's too foggy to see anything. How do they know what plane it even is?" Hailey looked out the window. "I don't get it. Who wouldn't want a real funeral or at least a nice memorial?" she asked. "Especially Grandpa. It would have been a big deal. I bet Steven Spielberg would have had it at his house. I bet a lot of famous people would have been there. Do you think he was just afraid nobody good would come?"

Jaycee rolled her eyes. Hailey looked away indifferently, still surprised that she was no longer preoccupied with her sister's every move. She was equally stunned at how well she'd handled the transition from being almost famous to being just a regular high-school student. She did get checked out a lot more than Jaycee now. That was a positive. But the best part was that she knew that she most definitely did not want to be an actress. Jaycee could have that heartache. Hailey was thinking she'd be a producer now. She liked working with her mom. And Janine promised to ask Ransom Garcia if she could intern on set once filming started. Now that Janine was going to stay around, Hailey felt like things would be okay.

"When I die, I'm going to have a *huge* funeral," Hailey said. "I want everyone who's anyone to be there. You'll be stoked about being my sister one day."

"Yes," Jaycee said, putting her earbuds in. "When you're dead, I'll be stoked about being your sister."

"Hey, I think that's the plane." Hailey nudged Jaycee.

Down on the beach, Janine and their mom were pointing up at a small plane with one red blinking light. She could faintly hear them shouting for the girls to look up. The car was nice and warm now. Hailey could hear the song "I'm Alive" from *Xanadu* screaming out of Jaycee's iPhone.

"That's kind of an inappropriate song, considering," Hailey said. She yanked the buds out of Jaycee's ears. "Besides, it totally sucks. Those lyrics totally suck."

"Give it to me," Jaycee snapped. "You chose it. You're the one helping Mom with your big ideas!"

"Jealous much?" Hailey asked. She snatched her sister's phone and threw it over the backseat.

"Hey!" Amanda opened the car door. "Are you two fighting?"

"No," they both said, resuming their funereal positions.

Amanda slipped into the driver's seat, her eyes glassy. "Did you guys see the plane?"

They nodded. Janine got into the passenger seat, her face chapped and red. She looked miserable, and she silently rolled down the window as soon as Amanda turned onto the Pacific Coast Highway. Hailey didn't dare complain about the cold air.

The phone rang about ten minutes into the drive back to the apartment.

Janine answered. "It's the Neptune Society." She put the call on speaker.

"Hello?" a man's voice said. "Hello?" He sounded like he was standing in front of a fan. "Ms. Kessler?"

"Yes," she said, yelling to be heard. "This is Janine Kessler."

"Ms. Kessler?"

"Yes, I can hear you."

"This is Jeremy Lappin from the Neptune Society. I wanted to let you know we're having delays due to the fog. Visibility is bad. We should be taking off in about an hour. I'll call you when we're over Pier Eighteen."

"You haven't left yet?" she asked. She sounded like she was about to cry. "We thought we just saw the plane."

"Nope. I'll call you back with an ETA," he said.

"What a joke," she said and hung up. A long silence.

"Do you want to go back?" Amanda asked Janine. Her cheeks were pink and still dry with tears and cold.

"I don't want to go back," Janine said, shaking her head. "Let's get breakfast."

Henry

Henry had driven by Carneys Express Limited hundreds of times. The thought of dining there had never occurred to him. Why would it? It was just another absurd tourist attraction on the Sunset Strip, a place one sped past en route to a more logical destination. What kind of person over the age of eight would choose to eat dinner inside a yellow Union Pacific passenger car? Not exactly what he had in mind, but he was too excited about the evening to object to Janine's restaurant choice.

"Tell me again why we're eating here?" he asked, walking up behind her in line after parking the car. She was wearing a black cotton dress that showed off her delicate pale legs.

She turned to look at him with a queer little smile. "Their chili fries are amazing."

"Chili fries?"

She nodded. She looked very tired. She had dark circles beneath her eyes and she was too thin. If she wanted chili fries, so be it.

"Hey," said a man behind them. Henry turned. The man was bearded, paunchy, and wearing a Cleveland Indians jersey.

"You can't cut the line like that," the man said.

Henry was unclear on queue etiquette in a train car where one orders food from a man in a paper hat who jots down what you want on a cardboard box. "I'm sorry. I was just parking the car."

"I don't care if you were fucking your sister, buddy. No cutting."

"Pardon?"

"Pardon?" he repeated, mocking Henry's accent and elbowing his slovenly little friend, an equally unsavory-looking fellow with a limp mustache and a tattoo of a deer's head on his arm.

"Never mind," Janine said. She took Henry's hand. "We'll go to the back. We're not in a rush."

"There you go," the man said, looking Janine over. "Why don't you behave and go to the back of the line with Olive Oyl."

Henry cleared his throat and pointed at the man's belly. "Looks as if skipping a meal might be just the ticket for you. Or might I suggest you rot in your Studebaker until the next time your *team* wins the World Series."

The guy looked down at the Indians jersey he was wearing. "Is this prick fucking kidding?" he asked his friend as Henry watched his face turn the color of a beefsteak tomato. "Might I suggest," he said, holding up his pinkie and imitating Henry again.

"Forget it, Henry," Janine said. She pulled hard at his arm. "I'm not even hungry, okay?"

"Yes, you are hungry, and no, it's not okay," Henry said. Janine would have her chili fries. This was not a night on which he would be humiliated.

"Didn't you hear her, *Henry?*" the man said, managing to make his name sound ridiculously effete. "She's not hungry. So why don't you and the skinny bitch get the fuck out of here before I turn your face into a—"

Henry was not a fighting man. He'd never hit anyone or anything in his life. So it was curious the way his hand balled up into a fist and flew, as if in a practiced motion, directly at the enormous face of this stranger. Contact was made! The sound of Henry's fist clubbing the man's jaw was loud and enormously satisfying. It was less curious (in retrospect) that Henry missed him entirely on the second round, nearly dislocating his own shoulder, while the man retaliated with a series of hard punches to Henry's stomach, ribs, chest, and face.

The pain was gutting. When the police arrived, Henry was curled up in a ball on the ground, condiments all around him. Not the evening he'd imagined at all. A crowd had gathered. He was covered in relish. He had a bloody nose. Janine was in tears. The police had gotten there fast, so they must have been nearby. Perhaps they had even been in a booth eating chili fries, watching the whole thing transpire.

If he'd expected compassion from Janine, he was sorely disappointed. She was furious with him. What was he trying to prove? she'd asked. *Prove?* He'd thought he was protecting her honor. Wasn't that the protocol at a place like Carneys? And the police—had they even attempted to chase down his attackers? No. They were taking him in. Taking *him* in? For disturbing the peace and disorderly conduct, they explained. Apparently he who throws the first punch is guilty. No wonder the justice system in America was in tatters, he thought.

Janine and Henry sat in a loaded silence in the backseat of the police car listening to the officer who was driving the car recount to his partner, scene by scene and in painstaking detail, the plot of a film he'd seen involving a narcoleptic nanny.

"I'm bleeding on your seat," Henry said, knocking hard on the bulletproof divider to get the cop's attention.

"Hey!" the officer shouted, not turning around. He was too engrossed in his film synopsis to be bothered. Janine pulled a wet wipe out of her bag and gave it to him. She always had the right things in her pocketbook: hand sanitizer, wet wipes, mints.

"What a stupid thing to do, Henry," she said. She dabbed at his bloody face with a tissue. He winced. "Is your ear okay?"

"Yes," he said. "He missed that side."

"Missed?" she asked. "And what do you know about baseball, anyway? What the hell was that?"

"It was that jersey. A few years back, we had a fanatical professor on the faculty who'd come from Case Western. The man couldn't grasp the fact that his team hadn't won a World Series since before Warhol was a novelty. Every year leading up to the season, he'd walk into faculty meetings wearing a cap and that ridiculous jersey chanting, 'This is the year! This is the year!'"

Janine laughed. Maybe her anger was thawing.

"And at the end of every season, he'd fly into a rage looking for someone to blame for his team's ineptitude. He was very emotional for a John Copley scholar. Finally got fired for sleeping with an undergraduate. From Dayton."

Henry noticed that the officer who was driving was looking at them in his rearview mirror. He'd stopped talking, and now he slid open the plastic screen. "Hey, you look familiar," he said to Janine. "I know you?"

She shook her head.

"Do you have any water?" Henry asked Janine.

She went back to her bag to forage for liquids.

"Really," the man said. "I've met you before."

"I'm sure that's not true. I don't even live in LA." As she handed Henry a bottle of water, she accidentally upended her purse, sending its contents across the floor of the car. "Shit."

"Janine Kessler?" the officer asked. She looked up, startled, before she could collect her things. Henry gathered what he could into his lap. "It's me, Teddy Volk."

Janine shook her head. The name clearly didn't mean anything to her.

"I was on *Family Happens*!" He turned all the way around so she could take in the beauty of his middle-aged face.

"Hey!" Henry shouted. "Watch the road." The driver turned back and adjusted the rearview mirror so he was looking directly at Janine. "I played your cousin Archie. From Michigan?"

"Oh my God," Janine said. "Archie! I mean, Teddy!"

"What happened to you, Janine? You were the bomb!"

"The usual. I wanted to get out of Hollywood. Live a regular life. You know how it is. What about you?" she asked. Henry could tell she was pretending more interest than she felt. She was focused on the articles from her purse collected neatly on Henry's lap.

"Life," he said. "Now I'm a cop."

"I can see that," she said, staring at the pack of prenatal vitamins Henry was turning over. "Listen, Teddy," she said. "Can you drop the charges? As a favor? Henry didn't do anything wrong. That guy was a total jerk."

Teddy looked briefly at his partner, who nodded. "For you, Jenny B., why the hell not?" He made a U-turn and headed back to Carneys. "Who's this guy, though? Your husband?"

"No." She pulled her phone and the prenatal vitamins out of Henry's paralyzed hands and looked at him. "He's just my baby daddy."

A yeti stepped on Henry's chest.

"Whoa," Teddy said, laughing. "How old are your kids?"

"Really, really young."

"Those years are brutal. Mine are grown. Out of the house."

"Wow," Janine said. "Congratulations!" She was still looking at Henry.

"You call me if you need anything while you're in town, all right?" he said, slipping his card through the partition with a hint of flirtation despite Henry's presence. "Janine fucking Kessler. Small fucking world." Teddy turned back around and started saying something to his partner.

"You *are* pregnant?" Henry asked quietly, pointing at the vitamins.

"Shh!" Janine nodded. "No. Yes. I don't know. I wasn't sure I was going to keep it," she said. "But then, after my dad—"

"Oh God," he said, licking a trickle of blood that was dripping into his mouth. "You can't do that."

"I didn't." She handed him another wipe. "Are you mad?" she asked.

The car stopped in the parking lot at Carneys. Teddy got out and opened the door for Janine. He took a selfie with her as Henry crawled out awkwardly, clutching his aching torso. Teddy gave Janine such a hard, loving hug that she made a little squeaking noise. "You take care, now," he said, giving Henry a look before getting back into his car. *Two former child stars,* Henry thought. *Dimmed but still shining.*

"Thanks, Teddy. I will. You too."

The patrol car pulled away.

"You have any idea who he is?" Henry asked her.

"Not really."

"Brilliant."

"He seems happy," she said, waving.

"Why are we talking about Teddy?"

"I don't know. I don't know what to talk about."

"How about our wedding?"

"Wedding?"

"Let's get married."

"That's funny. Are you concussed?"

"Perhaps," he said, touching his head. "But I'm quite certain I want to marry you. I love you."

"Jesus, Henry."

"I don't believe you would have kissed me like you did the other night if you didn't feel the same way."

"*You* kissed *me,*" she said and took a small step toward him.

"No. *You* kissed *me,*" he said sternly.

"Okay." She blushed. "I kissed you."

"And I don't believe you would have done that or let me help you write that letter . . . I just don't think you're the sort of person who would have let me help you at all after I hurt you if you didn't love me."

"But I don't want to get married."

"Why not?" he asked, his voice strident. "I thought all women wanted to get married."

"How very sexist of you. What gave you that impression?"

"All the women I've dated," he said, realizing how offensive the words sounded. He was an idiot. He had no polish. Of course Janine didn't want to marry him. "I don't mean that they all wanted to marry me. It's just that people want to couple up, don't they? Being alone is, well, it's lonely. I never realized how very much I didn't want to be alone until you left." He'd never sounded so daft, even to his own ears. He was more nervous than he'd ever been in his life. "But it's more than that," he went on before Janine could interrupt him, before the phantom lump in his throat clogged his airway. "I adore you, Janine. I love the way you smile when you're actually sad, I love your white skin all mottled up with freckles, and I love the way your hair sticks up in the morning or when you get upset. It just pops up, like antennas."

"You don't have to marry me because I'm pregnant. You can help, you know, if you want. But you don't have to do that either, if you don't want. I'll have enough money to buy an apartment. Amanda can help. You and I really barely know each other."

"Don't talk rubbish. I'm not finished," he said. "Mostly I think, and don't correct me if I'm wrong, that we sort of complement each other." He took a deep breath. "I love you. I want to marry you. It has nothing to do with whether or not you're pregnant."

"But I am pregnant."

"All the better." He got down on one knee and fished the black ring box out of his pocket. He was grateful it hadn't gotten lost in the fight. The inanity of proposing in the parking lot of Carneys wasn't lost on him.

"I don't understand," she said. She took the box and looked around. "Get up, would you?"

"You see? I was going to ask you to marry me anyway," he said, embarrassed, standing up and wiping off his pants. "I was thinking a posh café with a good Cabernet but this is fine too. Life is short! One day you're eating a gelato and the next day—" He stopped himself, realizing his mother's epiphany might come off as tactless.

She opened the box. "Jesus! It's the size of Texas. I can't wear this."

"It was my mother's."

"Your mother's?" she asked, staring at the large cushion-cut diamond ring with emerald side stones. "Well, that explains the size."

"She bought it for herself for my father to give her. I would have preferred to buy you something on my own but she wouldn't let it go. She insisted."

"She did?"

"She did. You know how she is."

"I don't, actually."

"She's difficult and pushy but quite decent once you get around all that. I've grown fond of her lately. All her criticizing has its upside, it turns out. She's helped me sort things out a bit."

"So she approves of me?"

"Oh, she's an enormous fan."

"Of mine?"

"Mm."

"When did you decide you were going to propose?"

"Somewhere between being hopped up on Percocet at your father's and your vomiting episode. I knew that if, after that display, I still wanted to see you naked, then there must be something to my feelings for you."

She wrinkled her nose.

"I hoped you'd come around eventually. Underneath all my churlishness lies the heart of an optimist." Henry cleared his throat and pointed to the ring. "And Mother thought that might help smooth out the kinks."

She laughed. "But I'm not mad anymore. You don't have to marry me."

"I know I don't have to marry you, you fool. I want to. Why is that so hard for you to understand? I'm not exactly an impulsive fellow. I've just been waiting for the right time. Then your dad passed and I figured you needed space, so . . ."

Janine looked confused. "Did my dad know you were going to propose?"

"Mother has a tendency to overshare."

Janine bit her lip hard. "When? When did she tell him?"

"I don't know exactly. Before Italy. She told me he'd tried to convince you to stay in LA. I think he was hoping. I can't say for sure…"

Her face was red and blotchy now. Henry wasn't sure if she was crying about her father or his proposal but realized it didn't matter. Marty's gravitational force had expired, leaving all his moons and planets spiraling in senseless orbits.

Janine looked down at the ring. "It's ridiculously huge."

"You don't have to wear it."

"Can we slow things down a little? It's just a lot all at once."

"Mm. Bit of a damp squib, but all right. Can I at least put it on you? No pressure. I trust you'll give it back if you decide to run off with your old friend Teddy." She nodded and Henry slipped the ring on her finger. "How does it feel?"

"Heavy." She reached for him and held him tightly. "You smell like a snack bar, Henry."

"Yes. Pickled cucumbers. Mustard."

"Henry?" she asked, looking up at him.

"Mm?"

"If it's a boy, I want to call him Marty. Marty Kessler."

Henry nodded. "That's a good name."

"It is a good name."

"So none of this 'going back to New York' nonsense. We'll see what happens, but in the meantime you'll come live with me. Yes?"

She took his hand impulsively, as though she couldn't believe she was agreeing to his mad plan.

"Can I call you Mrs. Holter? Just one time?" Henry asked. Then he frowned, questioning the wisdom of saddling someone he loved with a name he had such mixed feelings about. "Sorry," he said. "Never mind."

"I always wondered what it would be like to have a different name. I wanted to be Amy Tanner once."

"Who's Amy Tanner?"

"Nobody. It was a long time ago. Let's hear it," she said. "As an experiment."

Henry's heart was beating so quickly he could hear it rapping to a steady rhythm in his ear. "Do you want to get some chili fries, Mrs. Holter?"

"Yes," she said, tightening her grip on his hand as she looked down at the ring. "But I won't be changing my last name and you can't say things that sound like the last line of a bad romantic comedy."

His relief was visceral, almost painful. "I've never been accused of that before," he said and emptied some chopped onions out of his shirt pocket with his free hand.

She looked him up and down with a laugh. "No, I bet you haven't."

Janine

"Janine, it's Jim Keating."

She was driving from the pool to meet Amanda at Henry's for dinner. Amanda had agreed to go over lines with her for the movie. Filming started the following week. Janine was nervous, nauseated, and, because of the pregnancy, completely unmedicated for the first time in twenty-six years. The last person she wanted to talk to was her father's attorney. Janine couldn't imagine how her dad, a man who wanted *only* the good news, had put up with Jim Keating and his bleak biweekly forecasts.

"I have news," Jim said quickly. His Irish brogue still unsettled Janine, always reminding her of their first conversation, when he'd called to tell her that her dad was dead. Nothing Jim Keating had said subsequently had been anything Janine wanted to hear. She gripped the steering wheel tightly.

"You've settled on a firing-squad execution for me and Amanda?"

Jim laughed enthusiastically. Janine had never heard him laugh. "Delivering good news this time," he announced.

She took a deep breath. "Okay, Jim," she said, channeling her father, "tell me the good news."

"As you know, your father's house was bought quickly."

"I know that. That's not good news."

"But the buyer is interesting. Very interesting. The whole thing is as mad as a box of frogs, really."

"Please, Jim," she said, braking softly as the traffic slowed. She glanced down at the ring on her finger. She had things to do and she was tired of Jim Keating, tired of his formalities and instructions, tired of the indignities he'd made her and Amanda suffer without a thought to their emotional well-being. She wanted to focus on Henry and the baby now, on Amanda and the girls, and especially on getting through her part in the film before her stomach popped. Ransom had been so nice about the whole thing. He'd even offered to shoot all of her scenes first, as if she were somebody who mattered.

"The buyer is Bunny Small. The author!"

Janine felt her heart slide into her stomach and slosh around. Her eyes went blurry. She put the blinker on and started to pull the car over to the right shoulder. This was easier said than done on the 10 Freeway at five thirty in the evening. Cars started honking. "Watch it, dumb ass," a guy with a beard and a baseball hat yelled while giving her the finger. Janine tried to block him out as she jerked the car in and out of traffic. Someone threw an empty coffee cup at her car just as she eased onto the shoulder.

"Janine?" Jim asked. "You there? Are you driving?"

"Just give me a minute." She was struggling to catch her breath as she put the car into park. She'd have given a kidney for a Klonopin. She sat in silence, trying to focus. She forgot Jim was on the line until she heard him breathing. "Jim?"

"I didn't have permission to tell you until the sale officially closed, which it did, this morning. It never went on the market. Ms. Small paid cash. Twice the estimated value! Twice!" he said, repeating the word as if it were a poem or a song.

"Why would she do that?"

"She wanted you and your sister to have the house and then some." He laughed out loud, as if this were the strangest thing he'd ever come across in his many years of dealing with very strange people. "She didn't think your dad would like the idea of its being sold out from under you to pay the estate taxes." He cleared his throat. "My guess is she was afraid you might say no to an outright gift."

Janine was quiet.

"She said she wants you both to have the option to keep it. She thought that's what your father would have wanted. I can't disagree. Not in the least, Janine."

She was aggravated at Jim's sudden solicitousness after weeks of his detached condescension. "I thought we couldn't afford to keep the house up even if we'd had the money to buy it. You made that clear enough."

"That's the kicker," he said with enthusiasm. "Ms. Small's supplied a provision to pay for the entire maintenance of the house—insurance, yard, pool, pest control."

"For how long?" Janine asked, incredulous.

"In perpetuity."

"Are you kidding?"

Jim chuckled, his tone much more ingratiating now that Janine was a person of substance, or at least a person who knew people of substance who could potentially become new clients. "I can't say for certain, but it seems she was very fond of your father. Apparently they'd known each other a long time?" He was fishing for information.

"I couldn't imagine living in his house without him. That's weird."

"That's entirely up to you and Amanda."

"Does Henry know?" Janine asked. She was sure Henry didn't know. He'd be embarrassed, probably. Janine didn't get the sense that he appreciated grand gestures, especially from his mother. She was completely, as Henry would say, gobsmacked.

"Who's Henry?" Jim asked, doing very little to maintain his professional distance now. Janine could practically feel the pull of his curiosity through the phone. She wasn't about to give him the satisfaction of responding.

"Does Amanda know?" she asked Jim.

"I just phoned her. Yes. Who's Henry?"

"Okay," she said, ignoring the question. "Thanks."

"Of course, you can sell it and take the money," Jim continued. "The estate taxes have been covered. The house is in both your names. All proceeds from the sale would be yours to split free and clear. And the market's strong. If you want my advice—"

"I don't. But thanks."

"Oh."

"I gotta go," she said and hung up the phone.

She sat there another few minutes thinking things over. Then she called Amanda.

"Oh my God," Amanda said. "Did you talk to Jim?"

"I just did. I'm in shock. I'm thinking."

"About the house?"

"Mm."

"Your boyfriend's mom is a peach, Janine. I mean, who does that?" Amanda sounded elated but hesitant. "It's crazy!" Amanda went on. "Can we even accept it?"

Janine knew Amanda was afraid that Janine wouldn't accept it, and in truth, she wasn't sure how she felt. "I think it's done."

"What do you want to do with the house?" Amanda asked.

"Sell it, I guess. I mean, what do you want to do?"

"It's not really up to me," Amanda answered. "She obviously did this because of Henry. Because of you and Henry."

"I don't think so. I think she did it because of Dad."

"Really?"

Janine bit the inside of her cheek and nodded. "Henry would never take money from her and it's not like we need a place to live. I bet he doesn't even know."

"Maybe she wants you to have the kid there or something?"

"No." Janine turned the key in the ignition. "Jim said she put it in both our names. It doesn't have anything to do with Henry."

"Both our names," Amanda said in a far-off voice. "Wow. It's just...I don't know. I can't believe she'd do that." Janine could feel Amanda weighing her right to such kindness, probably feeling that somehow she didn't deserve it. There was a long pause as the full significance of the gesture settled. Neither one of them had ever been on the receiving end of such a gift.

Despite how their father had left things, Janine was sure he would have wanted them to have the house. He would have wanted his family to have the option to be together. How he would have reacted to his ex-wife saving the day was unclear, but Janine had no doubt that he would have been pleased at the outcome.

"Do *you* want to live there?" Janine asked Amanda. "With Hailey and Jaycee?"

Amanda made a strange, high-pitched noise and then burst into tears.

"Do you?" Janine asked again, finally understanding that having her own home in which to raise her daughters without having to worry about money was the thing Amanda wanted most.

"I do," Amanda said, her voice almost inaudible. "Can you imagine what it would mean to me, to them? To have that beautiful home? Dad's beautiful house. They'd have their own rooms," Amanda went on, trying to calm down. "You should have heard Hailey talk about the place while I was gone. She loved being there."

"It wouldn't creep you out? You wouldn't feel like it was, I don't know, haunted by Dad or something?"

"No way. I don't want somebody *else* living there, decorating it with their bullshit midcentury-modern furniture. And I can probably pay for college if I don't have to worry about housing."

"Then do it."

"It would be half yours, of course," Amanda said, rambling on, "if you ever needed the money or wanted to sell it or whatever. But at least we could keep it for a while. It would mean a lot to the girls. And I don't know. We'd have our family home."

"You can have it for more than a while."

Amanda started crying again, the little squeaks punctuated by loud, wet sobs. Janine didn't say anything. She didn't want her sister to hear her own voice break. She was undone at the prospect of being able to help Amanda and her girls in a real way.

Amanda exhaled in a long, low whistle. "I miss Dad."

"Me too."

"Too bad he won't meet baby Marty," Amanda said.

"Let's just hope it's a boy," Janine replied, happy to change the subject. "Actually, let's just hope it doesn't have flippers or webbed toes. You know this is considered a geriatric pregnancy? That's what my chart said. Who thought of that term?"

"A man," Amanda said.

"I'll pick up food," Janine said. "Henry's joining us after work. But you have to help me with these lines. You promised. It's such a long scene."

"Stop obsessing. I'll make sure you don't blow it," Amanda said with affection. "See you soon."

Without thinking, Janine turned the key in the ignition again and the car made a loud grinding noise in protest. The engine was already running. Henry would be teaching but she would leave him a message telling him what an amazingly kind thing his mom had done. She dialed his number but then quickly hung up. It would be better in person.

She checked the rearview mirror. Behind her, the sun was setting over the Pacific Ocean, illuminating the endless lanes of crawling cars. The drive to Henry's would take her over an hour, she thought, checking her impatience with the realization that she had somewhere to be. Somewhere she wanted to be. She turned on her blinker and merged her car into the slow flow of traffic.

Acknowledgments

Special thanks to my agent, Sarah Burnes, for all she's done for me and this book, to Colin Dickerman for his loyalty and friendship, and to Lee Boudreaux for seeing the promise in an early draft and giving the manuscript a home. Enormous gratitude to Judy Clain, Reagan Arthur, Jayne Yaffe Kemp, and everyone at Little, Brown, especially super-editor Asya Muchnick, who is the kindest, sharpest, coolest editor around. I really couldn't have asked for more. I am very grateful to those who read the book along the way: Coralie Hunter, Carina Guiterman, Amy Scheibe, and Tracy Roe; your suggestions and input were invaluable. Thank you to my friends who put up with me through this process, notably Brooke Dunn Parker, for always answering the phone to listen; Colleen Wellman, for screening my calls only once in a while; and Ruth Woodruff, for whisking me away when I needed a break. And, finally, a giant hug to my family: Ned Tanen, my incredible father; Kitty Hawks and Larry Lederman, for their unconditional love and for always keeping the faith; my sister, Tracy James, for being my companion on the journey; Gary Taubes, my amazingly supportive husband, for reading the manuscript sixteen times and crying and laughing every time; and my boys, Harry and Nick, for reminding me always what's truly important.

About the Author

Sloane Tanen is the author of nine illustrated and YA books, including the bestseller *Bitter with Baggage Seeks Same: The Life and Times of Some Chickens* and *Hatched! The Big Push from Pregnancy to Motherhood*. This is her first adult novel. Tanen graduated from Sarah Lawrence College and holds master's degrees from both NYU and Columbia University. She lives in the Bay Area with her husband, the writer Gary Taubes, and their two sons.